# Cold Revenge

## by

## Jo A. Hiestand

*The McLaren Mysteries*

**Cold Revenge**

Cover Art by *Angela Anderson*

The Wild Rose Press, Inc.
PO Box 708
Adams Basin, NY 14410-0708
Visit us at www.thewildrosepress.com

Publishing History
previously published as Siren Song
by L&L Dreamspell, 2010
First Mainstream Mystery Edition, 2015
Print ISBN 978-1-62830-890-7
Digital ISBN 978-1-62830-891-4
*The McLaren Mysteries*
Published in the United States of America

## He brought the photo closer

so he could stare at the woman. She appeared to be in her mid-forties, a brunette with hazel eyes that looked amusingly at the photographer. She came up to her husband's chin. The husband was a graying brunet and while her son had inherited her eye color, he was blond. McLaren had no time to comment on this.

Linnet said, "The others..." She leaned forward, her left arm bent and supporting her, and tapped each photo as she mentioned their names. "The group shot is Marta, her boss, and the vet for the shelter. This..." She skipped over the others in the photograph and pointed to the woman to the extreme left. "That's Verity Dwyer."

"The wrongly suspected coworker." The woman in the photo had auburn hair that shone in the sunlight; her blue eyes smiled at him.

Linnet nodded. "Yes. Suspected of killing Marta, though that wasn't proved. But she was convicted of stealing money from the shelter. She's three months into her sentence. She was... Oh, it's extremely involved."

"I've got more time than money. Tell me."

# Characters

Michael McLaren, former police detective, Staffordshire Constabulary

Jamie Kydd: friend and detective, Derbyshire Constabulary

Dena Ellison: McLaren's former girlfriend

Gwen Hulme: McLaren's sister

~*~

Marta Hughes: murder victim

Alan Hughes: Marta's husband

Chad Hughes: Marta's and Alan's teenaged son

Neal Clark: Marta's brother-in-law, boss and owner of Noah's Ark

Verity Dwyer: coworker with Marta at Noah's Ark animal shelter

~*~

Karin Pedersen: hiker

Linnet Isherwood: Marta's friend

Sean FitzSimmons: Linnet's friend

Herb Millington: the Hughes' neighbor

Danny Mercer: Herb's friend

~*~

Lloyd Farmer: police sergeant, Derbyshire Constabulary - retired

Ian Shard: police constable, Derbyshire Constabulary

Charlie Harvester: former colleague of McLaren's in the Staffordshire Constabulary

Tyrone Wade Antony: convicted burglar

## Dedication

For David.
There are not enough superlatives in the English language with which to laud you. I can never thank you enough for your untiring help in setting up McLaren and the core of this story. Or for your repeat reading while the postmistress got acquainted with the nick.
*Diolch!*

## Acknowledgments

Sincere thanks to my friend Paul Hornung, St. Louis-area police detective, who rewrote fight scenes and gave me good and bad news about the manuscript. A handshake also to Detective-Sergeant Robert Church and Detective-Superintendent David Doxey (ret.), Derbyshire Constabulary, for answering questions while preparing to attend the Cheltenham jumps. Heartfelt thanks are also due to Richard Brook, for his suggestion about the classic car, and to Dr. Ruth Anker for the medical information.

My deep gratitude goes to all my friends and readers of my Taylor & Graham mystery series for giving me the support and confidence to continue writing. I hope the McLaren series retains your readership and that you'll love him as much as I do.

Jo Hiestand
St. Louis, February 2015

Chapter One

"I'd like you to solve a murder."

McLaren straightened up from the pile of rocks, cocked his right eyebrow, and eyed the woman standing before him with the accumulated years' experience of a police detective sizing up a reliable witness. He tightened his fingers around the stone, torn between getting back to work and satisfying his curiosity. His cop's inquisitiveness won. He said rather reluctantly, "Whose murder?"

"Marta Hughes."

"Who's Marta Hughes—personally, professionally and otherwise, Miss…"

"Oh, sorry." She extended her hand and spoke in a remarkably steady voice for having legged it up the steep hill. "Bad habit of mine. I get tunnel vision at times." She paused, as though debating how to proceed. "I'm Linnet Isherwood. Marta is—was a friend of mine. She's married. Sorry. *Was* married." She flushed slightly and McLaren thought how attractive the pink of her cheeks accented her green eyes.

"Fascinating, I'm sure, but what about the murder?"

Linnet took a breath, the pitch of her voice settling to a near monotone. "She'd gone missing several days before the police found her body outside Elton. She—She'd been dumped alongside the road. Like a sack of

1

rubbish." Linnet fumbled for a facial tissue in her skirt pocket.

"What's the matter with the police?" The right corner of his mouth tightened as he exhaled heavily, and for a moment his eye held the pain of separation from a loved one. He thought he had distanced himself from the hurt of leaving the job. Or at least numbed himself to the ache constantly. Would it always be with him, or would it lessen? Did he even care any more? A kestrel called as it circled overhead, drawing McLaren's attention and shoving his anger aside for the moment.

Linnet blotted her eyes, then stared at him, the tissue crushed in her fingers. "Pardon?"

"The police. The coppers, the PCs, the local constabulary. The bill. They investigated the case, I assume." The words held an underlying tone of fatigue—with the police, with people, with life.

"Well, yes."

"So?" He said it with a hint of sarcasm, as though his suggestion was laughable, or he already knew the outcome of similar investigations. He exhaled heavily, slowly, waiting for her answer his arms crossed on his chest, and wondered how she had found him. Not 'why,' particularly. His home village was rife with the knowledge of his previous career. And the circumstances that had led to his return there.

"They never found who killed her."

The information had no more effect on him than a fly settling on a stone wall. He sighed, unfolded his arms, and said as though he'd recited it a thousand times, "I'm sorry, Miss Isherwood. I'm not in the job anymore. And I'm too damned hot." An understatement, he thought, as he tried to swallow; it was the hottest June he could remember. He removed a glove and wiped the sweat from his forehead. "Talk to a solicitor." He turned from her and laid down the stone, silently dismissing her.

"But the killer's got away with murder!"

"Tell me about it. We live in a world of injustice."

"And the person they suspected now has a blot on her name that will stay with her the rest of her life."

"Relative of yours, I take it."

"No. A coworker of Marta's, actually. I don't really know her."

"So why—"

"Because she's innocent. Because I heard that you fought against injustice."

Chapter Two

"Abhorred injustice, actually," she said as McLaren slowly turned to face her.

He tilted his head, aware of her physical assessment of his height and the way her gaze moved from his muscular shoulders to the weighty stones at his feet. Connecting the dots, he thought, suddenly finding it humorous. Yet, he didn't smile. The irritation at being disturbed in his work made him impatient...for her information and for her to be gone.

Holding his gaze, she said, "Abhorred it as only personal experience could produce." He opened his mouth to reply, but Linnet rushed on. "Which is why I took the trouble to find you. I thought if you heard about Verity's situation, you'd want to take on the case." She paused, and dabbed her eyes again with the tissue. She added unnecessarily, "The case has gone cold."

McLaren snorted again. "It's usual for a case to go cold, Miss Isherwood, if the police either can't identify the victim or are unable to learn where the victim or a suspect went. If there's no trail to follow, no locality or time in which to place the suspect, the case grows cold, as you said. They come to a stone wall." He stopped, aware of the simile, feeling momentarily uncomfortable at having spoken harshly. He waited for her to continue, shifting his stance, and a shaft of sunlight fell across his

4

face. His skin had tanned to the golden hue of a fox or newborn fawn, accenting the brightness of his hazel eyes.

Linnet thrust out her chin, looking resolute and hurt simultaneously. "Sorry. I didn't mean to insult your intelligence. Perhaps I'm intruding on your time after all." She started to turn when McLaren said, "Verity...who?"

She smiled tentatively and pulled up the sides of her skirt. It was damp from wading through a pasture of dew-drenched grass to get to him. She shook the garment so it would catch the breeze and dry more quickly. "Verity Dwyer. Marta's coworker at the shelter. They were friends besides being coworkers. Verity gave Marta money for her trip to the casino, money that Verity stole from the shelter, unfortunately." Linnet's face flushed with embarrassment. "It was quite a large sum. Since Marta didn't live to replace the money from the cash till, the police thought it motive for Marta's death."

"Marta leaving Verity holding the empty bag, as it were."

"Yes...and when the money from Marta's casino win wasn't found...well, that's when Verity was suspected of theft and Marta's murder. She lives in Youlgreave, but—"

"When was this?"

The question caught her off guard. She grasped a ring strung on a silver chain around her neck, her fingers sliding over the polished metal as though she was saying the rosary. Or feeling it as worry beads. Her eyelashes caught the sunlight, and she asked what he meant.

"I mean when did it all happen? When was the murder, when was the body found, how was the body found, by whom? You mentioned she was found near Elton…" His voice had turned from the earlier hint of sarcasm to take on a hard edge. As hard as the stones of his wall. He coughed, embarrassed he'd let his emotions intrude.

Despite having left the job a year ago, he was still intrigued with a good story, still a cop at heart. He crossed his arms again, as though challenging her to persuade him. "Let's have the story first. You want to sit down?" He grabbed the bucket that had held his jacket, trowel, string, chisel and work gloves, and turned it upside down. "Or if you'd rather sit in my car…" His voice trailed off as he glanced downhill. His car was presentable, the rear hatchback section holding a few of his stone wall tools, the passenger seat free of work clothes or CDs or his guitar.

"No. This is fine." She said it quickly, and his right eyebrow shot up again as he wondered if she was hesitant about being in close quarters with him. Despite his irritation at the interruption, he admired her hair, which was the color of new corn silk.

"I'm all right standing." She gestured around her. "Actually, I love the outdoors. I sit inside too much. I'm a secretary in Chesterfield."

McLaren nodded as he asked again for the facts of the case. But he concentrated on Linnet's face, on her emerald-green eyes that seemed bottomless and filled with pain.

"Last June, Marta and I had a girls' night out. Oh, nothing wild," she added as McLaren frowned. "Just a few hours away from the dullness of our lives."

"Away from the husband and kids?" McLaren supplied. "I assume she was married?"

"Yes, with a teenaged son."

"You?" He eyed her, trying to put her into a convenient slot. Her left ring finger was bare, but that didn't put her into the unmarried category.

"A boyfriend. Sean FitzSimmons. He's a writer."

"He was okay with your girls' night out thing?"

"Of course. I'm not chained to him."

"And Marta wasn't to her husband or son either, I assume. So you and Marta spent a few carefree hours doing…what?"

Linnet took a breath, as though steeling herself for a tale told one too many times. "We went to a casino. We don't make a habit of playing—"

"Which one?"

"What? Oh. Brennan's."

McLaren nodded at the name of the Nottingham room. "When was this?"

"Last year. Eleventh of June. We'd been playing the slot machines for an hour or so. Won enough to make a small profit, but really no great luck. Nothing like we hoped. So we switched to roulette. We'd been playing for twenty minutes or so when Marta screamed. I had just ordered a drink, so my back had been turned. I thought maybe some berk had grabbed her handbag or spilled his drink on her. But when I saw her yelling and waving her fists…I remember the croupier pushing the stacks of chips toward her. I thought the table would tip over." She paused, as though reliving the scene. "I'd never seen so much money. It was like a miniature skyline of skyscrapers, or the Pennine Mountain chain. The croupier kept corralling the stacks and scooting them toward her. People were clapping and slapping her on the back. A man in a dark suit near the entrance glanced in our direction at first. I thought he was going to come over and say we'd done something wrong, but he stayed at his post. I helped Marta gather the chips and we left the table."

"How much did she get? Do you know?"

"Of course! We took it into the Ladies' and counted it…over and over. Then carried it to the cashier to trade it for the notes. We returned to the Ladies' and recounted it! I'll never forget the sum. It was huge. £253,500. A *fortune*. I—Neither of us had seen so much money at once. It was like a fairy tale."

Or a folk song, McLaren thought, the words and tune of "The Female Highwayman" running through his mind. "So, was Marta killed outside the casino?" He eyed Linnet, wondering how she had escaped injury if this were true.

"No. We weren't so elated that we forgot to be vigilant. I know that's a common happening, some bloke following the winner and then robbing her. So we looked around as we went into the Ladies' and the cashier's window and again as we left the casino. No one was overtly following us. I would stake my life on that."

McLaren didn't comment on the inappropriateness of the phrase. Or that Marta had been the one to forfeit her life. "So you made it outside without being mugged. What happened after that? How and when was Marta killed?" He hadn't been taking notes—he had nothing to use for that—but he was taking it all in with a cop's mind for facts. He would remember everything.

"I don't know."

"*What?*"

"I mean, I know how she was killed but not when. She was shot. In..." Again she paused, looking ill-at-ease. "She was shot in the head. Nearly point blank range, the pathologist said." She watched McLaren's reaction.

"Where on the head? Back, front, left side..."

Linnet screwed up her face and mumbled, "Back."

"What about the ballistic findings?" He added, "Caliber?" when she looked puzzled.

"Oh. A thirty-eight."

"Was it traced to a specific revolver or pistol? Did the police seize all .38 caliber weapons around Elton and other relevant areas, and test fire them?" God, what a job of work that would have been. He envisioned the house-to-house requests, the confiscating and testing of weapons, the cartridge cases compared via ballistics...

She shook her head, glancing at her feet. "I don't know."

The answer surprised him. "Why not? You were at the inquest, weren't you?"

"Yes, but I stepped out of the room around that time. I-I felt like I was going to faint. All that talk about Marta's body and the bullet wound."

McLaren recalled cases he had worked—testimonies at inquests, stuffy oak-paneled rooms, the warmth of too many people, the rumors and speculations and whispered fanciful accusations, the tiresome drone of legal and medical jargon...

"I heard something later that the bullet couldn't be tested, but I don't know why."

"Was she in her car—either when her body was found or when she was shot?"

"They found her car at her house, in Chesterfield, and—"

"At her *house*! How'd it get there if her body was discovered outside Elton?"

"The police surmise that either she drove home and met someone, then got in that person's car where she was killed…" Linnet swallowed. "Or they drove to Elton, to the place where her body was found, and they got out and she was killed there."

"What's the significance of Elton?"

"Pardon?"

"Elton. The village is very small. Did Marta know anyone there? There's some reason why she went or was taken to Elton."

Linnet shrugged, her eyes downcast. "I'm sorry. I don't know of anyone."

"So she ends up in Elton and her car is at her home in Chesterfield. Her car was examined thoroughly, I assume. What was the result?"

"There was no blood in the car, nor any hair or fingerprints that weren't hers, her husband's or her son's."

"Which eliminates her being shot in her car, then. Evidently her casino money wasn't in the car, either." He sighed as Linnet shook her head. "Was her handbag with her body?"

"Yes. It held the usual things: latch key, car key, wallet, lipstick—"

"But not the £253,500."

"It disappeared."

McLaren refrained from saying "How surprising," and instead asked, "So what about Marta's body? Any defense wounds? Bruising on her hands or forearms, skin under her fingernails…" Probably not, he answered himself. Shot in the back of the head signified she never saw it coming, never had a chance to fight for her life.

"No."

"And she was found…"

"Ten days later. Twenty-first of June. She had been dumped along the B5057. Just off the road, actually, which was why no one found her body immediately."

"It's a rather uninhabited place." McLaren didn't notice her discomfort. "It'd take a while to find her, or anyone, in that area. A lot of moorland to contend with."

"Yes."

"So the police had no idea where to search for her the night of your big adventure. And Elton's a bit of a distance from the casino in Nottingham."

Located in Derbyshire, he would have added if the region's geography weren't so obvious. Nottingham was located in Nottinghamshire, the county east of Derbyshire. Another police force, another mode of life.

As though privy to McLaren's thoughts, Linnet said, "I know it's odd, being so far from where we were that night. And from our homes."

"And yours is…where?"

"We both live in Chesterfield."

McLaren did a quick mental calculation. Nottingham was perhaps twenty or thirty miles from Chesterfield, nearly on the Derbyshire-Nottinghamshire border. And about the same distance from Elton, which put the village on the western side of this triangle. Why go to Elton to dispose of a body, he wondered again.

"Who found her?"

"Some rambler. I can't recall his name."

"Someone above suspicion, evidently."

Linnet reddened but ignored the remark otherwise. "Neither Marta nor I know anyone who lives in Elton. She has a brother-in-law who lives in Matlock, but no one in that part of Derbyshire."

"When did you two separate? You didn't drive down to Nottingham together?"

"No, we were coming from different directions that evening. It was a Friday, which is Marta's half-day at the shelter. She gets off at noon. And since it was her half-day, she drove to Matlock to have lunch with Neal. He takes Fridays off." She paused, then explained. "His name is Neal Clark. Besides being her brother-in-law, he's also her boss."

"Her boss!" The suspicion that it might've been a complicated relationship crept into McLaren's voice. He rubbed his forehead, hoping to hide the astonishment in his eyes.

"It was dreadful. It led to some strained working conditions at the animal shelter."

"Strained between them, you mean?"

"No. They were completely professional. She called him Mr. Clark and he treated her as any other employee. But you know how some people get when they learn that one of their own is related to the boss."

"Makes for a tense atmosphere."

"That's putting it mildly, Mr. McLaren. Rumors circulated, gossip spread. It was ridiculous."

"What type of thing?"

"Oh, things like Marta getting a raise when everyone else didn't, Marta getting a larger Christmas bonus, Marta getting her choice of the working schedule—"

"Were the rumors true?"

"No."

"Did these rumors and gossip bother her?"

Linnet murmured that they had never discussed the problem that deeply, but Marta didn't quit her job, so things couldn't have upset her too greatly. "She and Neal didn't really see that much of each other at the shelter. He spent most of his time in his office, seeing to the running of the establishment. When he did venture outside, he'd chat up everyone and look to see that the place was clean and that the animals were well cared for. That was it." Linnet sighed, shaking her head. "I suppose even if he merely said hello to Marta, moved on and talked for a half hour with everyone else, there'd still be some who would see that as favoritism."

"So, if Marta saw her brother-in-law every work day, why might she stop to see him after your trip? She couldn't talk to him at the shelter, or ring him up at home?"

"Maybe it was something that couldn't wait until Monday, or maybe it was just her being cautious about adding to the office gossip if she went into his office. I didn't ask because it was none of my business."

"Understandable."

"Anyway, we had arranged to meet at the blackjack tables at six. I get off work at five, so I easily got there on time. Marta was several minutes late. We played a few hands, then had dinner and tried the slot machines and the roulette table."

"And then you both separately drove to your homes. Did you follow her?"

"What, like making certain she wasn't followed?"

"Not necessarily, though that would have been a laudable precaution. I just want to know if you drove home together, or where you separated. Helps me make sense of when her car appeared at her house."

"She *had* to have driven home. Otherwise the police—"

"Would've found a third party's DNA in the car."

Linnet bit the end of her fingernail. The sound of sheep bleating carried downwind, reminding McLaren of the unfinished stone wall that stretched over the hill. But he made no move to resume his work; Linnet Isherwood's narrative held his interest. The pause continued for another minute before she continued. "I *think* we split up on the other side of Ripley."

"Ripley?" Clearly, McLaren hadn't expected the parting to be so near to Nottingham. Ripley lay approximately equidistance between the casino and Matlock, farther northwest.

"I believe so. We'd driven up the A610 and then I turned north onto the A38. I've tried to recall exactly when we split up. The trouble is, one set of headlights in a rearview mirror looks remarkably like another."

"You weren't following her, then."

"No. I had started out that way, riding shotgun, as you said." She gave a slight smile, as though envisioning an old American western film. "But we'd changed places quite soon after leaving Nottingham. I passed a lorry a bit farther on, and when a car passed and fell in behind me, I assumed it was Marta. The car stayed with me all the way to Ripley, as I said."

"And outside Ripley you turned right onto the A38, heading for Chesterfield."

"Yes. I don't know when I realized that the car

following me hadn't turned where I had."

"You didn't turn into a lay-by and ring her mobile? Weren't you concerned with her driving home alone with that amount of money?"

"She told me before we left the casino that she was thinking about going back to her brother-in-law's. So when the car behind me disappeared, I figured she decided to do that and I continued on toward Matlock. I didn't think much about it until her husband rang to say that Marta wasn't home, and she wasn't at Neal's."

A lamb called to its mother somewhere higher up the hill. McLaren said, "Matlock isn't really that far from Elton where her body was discovered. Certainly, it's not next door and there are closer places, but it's not ridiculously far away like Manchester, for instance."

"No, I suppose not."

"But Elton could be significant because it's out of the way. Don't forget, Elton is close to Matlock."

"You can't think her brother-in-law—"

"I don't think anything one way or the other right now, Miss Isherwood. Except that this friendly coworker of Marta's, this Verity Dwyer, lives in Youlgreave. And Youlgreave is about three miles from Elton. As I said, suggest anything to you?"

Chapter Three

They had ended the talk unsatisfactorily—Linnet walking back down the hill, disappointed and angry, and McLaren having heard enough to convince him that the woman was on a fool's errand. If the Derbyshire Constabulary hadn't been able to find a murderer by now, who was he to open a can of worms one year later?

But the case nagged him, whispered to him the rest of the afternoon as he worked on another section of the wall, murmured questions as he sat at his kitchen table over tea, rumbled over the dialogue of the television program he tried to watch. Finally giving up, he switched off the telly, grabbed a beer from the refrigerator, and sat at the dining room table, a map of Derbyshire, a pen and a sheet of paper in front of him.

Ten days Marta's body had lain in the heather and grass alongside the road. Ten days for the insects and animals to work on her. He'd seen enough corpses to know what time, exposure and carrion produced. Sometimes you ended up with a body barely recognizable. Sometimes it was recognizable enough to be unbearably heartbreaking. And in the warm summer months, when a body goes off much more quickly, that ignoble end comes faster. He shook his head, wondered briefly how her husband and son had handled it, then forced himself once more to think as a detective.

How long he worked, he didn't know. Time ceased to flow as he jotted down questions and bits of information from the case. He stared at the map, trying to make sense of the site where Marta Hughes' body had been found. Other than Elton being a fairly isolated village, did it offer another significant reason for its choice?

Since the casino money wasn't found on Marta's person, it gave weight to the police theory of a robbery gone wrong. But if no one from the casino had trailed her, how did Verity Dwyer find out about the casino win? Had Marta rung up Verity on her way home to tell her the good news? Was their friendship that close?

Without mobile phone records, McLaren had no answer to his first question. And without knowing Marta or Verity, he couldn't answer the second. Her car had been parked at her house, locked, the car key in her bag. The car bore no damage, so Marta hadn't been forced off the road. It appeared as if she'd merely left it in the driveway, and had been accosted as she walked into her house. No one heard her scream or fight off an abductor; nothing like broken twigs on bushes or shoe scuffs on pavement marked a kidnapping.

The more he had thought of the case, the more he realized he had no resources to help with an investigation. He was no longer a cop. Wasn't even a private detective. He was a laborer. A builder and repairer of dry stone walls. Even if he wanted to help, he was hesitant to do so. Even if his professional police life had been in Staffordshire and the Marta Hughes case was here in Derbyshire, news traveled. Traveled about cases and coppers who had been disciplined or who had mucked up. Traveled with the excited whispers of back-stairs gossip. Especially in police departments. Was there a cop in England who hadn't heard what had happened to force him from the constabulary?

He took a long drink of beer, trying to push the horror from his mind, trying to ignore the words that echoed in his head. But the map danced before his eyes, the face—imagined though it was—shimmered beneath his handwriting on the page. If Verity Dwyer hadn't killed Marta but lost her job and friends due to it, and living with that residue, as Linnet had said…

The glass slammed onto the beer mat as the familiar feeling of rage washed over him. Injustice. As Linnet had pointed out in the first minute of their meeting. She had known how it would affect him. She had learned, somehow, of his past. The word rattled in his brain, taunted him, dared him to uphold his values.

He stood, shoved his chair into the table, and got out his guitar. A large, Martin Dreadnought model that laid a rich, full foundation for his voice and the voices of the members of his folk singing group. He launched into 'Travel the Country Round,' not bothering to tune the instrument, not thinking of the song's lyrics.

> *When up to London I wandered*
> *A deal of money I squandered,*
> *I masters tried a hundred,*
> *No work was to be found.*
> *And as I wandered up and down,*
> *Some called me "a fool,"*
> *some "country clown,"*
> *And bade me get out of their fine town*
> *To travel the country round!*

The third verse and chorus slid by before the

significance hit him. He'd sung about squandering money. Was his subconscious whispering about Verity Dwyer? Cursing the song choice, he began the introduction to 'Cold, Haily, Rainy Night,' a favorite of his and one of his group's most requested songs. But the words died on his lips before he finished the second verse. For the first time, music could not penetrate his black mood, could not lift his spirits. Perhaps Marta and Verity preyed too heavily on his mind. And heart.

He returned the guitar to its case and got another beer from the fridge. There was more than one way to quell the maddening rush of words that persisted in his mind even beyond his singing. He wandered into the back room, sank onto the sofa, propped his feet on the coffee table, and downed half the bottle. He leaned back, feeling dazed and unsettled—the framed citation on the wall seemed to mock him. He didn't bother reading the words he'd memorized years ago, yet knowing what it said.

*Chief Constable's Commendation*
*Detective Sergeant Michael Duncan McLaren*
*Commended for the professionalism, commitment and determination you showed whilst carrying out your role of Family Liaison Officer during the investigation into the death of Hadley Davis. The sympathy and consideration you showed to the family undoubtedly helped them cope with not only the death of Hadley, but also with the distresses of the police investigations. Your effort helped secure the successful conviction of Larry Tomkins at Nottingham Crown Court on 3 December 2004.*

And here he was, a year after Marta Hughes had died, refusing sympathy and consideration to another murder victim's friend. Was the Chief Constable's commendation merely words? Had his role then been a sham? Maybe it was a sham now. Had he abandoned every principle he had ever believed in merely because he had suffered an injustice?

The questions mocked him, echoed in his mind, as he sank against the back of the sofa and shut his eyes.

He woke the next morning, the situation still needling him. The night on the sofa had been comfortable enough, he supposed, for he hadn't remembered falling asleep. Frowning, he turned off the table lamp. The commendation still glared at him from behind its glass cover; the photos of familiar faces smiled at him from their wooden frames. One in particular silently chided him. Dena Ellison, his former fiancée. She had constantly commended him for his sense of right and integrity. Had he changed so much in the year since he left her?

To block the memories, his gaze shifted to a photo of himself and another cop, his mate through police training. They'd had the good fortune to be appointed by the same Constabulary after leaving university, and had worked together for ten years. But he'd lost track of the man when they eventually drifted to different departments. Now McLaren stared at his one-time friend before looking at his younger self. They were incredibly happy back then, ignorant of what could happen to a career, unaware of backstabbing and lies. McLaren's hazel eyes seemed alive with hope for the future, his smile bright and unforced. Sun lit his blond hair, giving him a healthy glow that hinted at a long, robust life.

He snorted. What the hell was he doing—playing at fortune telling?

He grabbed the bottle from the coffee table and downed the remaining beer in one long gulp. It was flat and tasteless. Seeing Dena's photo smiling at him from over the top of the bottle, he set it back on the table. Nothing marred its smooth surface but the brown glass bottle and the television remote. In fact, nothing much occupied the room—or his house. Like the kitchen, the rooms were sparse in furniture and personal items. He had disposed of a quantity of things when his life turned upside down last June, ridding himself of painful memories by boxing up or throwing out his epaulette number pins, tie tacks and other uniform items. So why were these few photos and this particular commendation still on the wall—to taunt him?

Dena's mocking gaze pulled his eyes back to her but he quickly glanced at the adjoining wall, feeling strangely uncomfortable. Several nails protruded from the apple-green painted surface, mute reminders of the sequestered photos and certificates that had decorated the space. Why haven't I removed those nails? Because I'm lazy? Because I never saw them? Because I haven't had a chance to hang the new family photos? He shook his head, opening up to the truth that he had barricaded from his mind and heart. The admission hit him as hard as a stone. Because deep down in his soul he still loved the job; wanted to be part of it. The reason, once acknowledged, left him shaky yet feeling empty, as though his heart or brain was missing. He leaned forward but stopped as he reached for the bottle. What would his life be like now if it hadn't been shot to hell last June? What would this room be like now—full of Dena's laughter and scent and the myriad things that make a house feminine, lived in, and loved?

The doorbell's sharp ring burrowed into his thoughts. It was just on to half past five. Hell of an early hour to be calling. Exhaling loudly, he struggled up from sofa, pushing his fist into the scatter pillow for leverage. The bell rang again, longer, as if the caller were eager to be let in. Or it was an emergency. Shouting that he was coming, McLaren stumbled into the front room, grabbing chair backs or sides of bookcases as he walked. He misjudged the corner of the display cabinet and slammed his thigh into the edge. Grimacing and grabbing his leg, he hobbled to the door and yanked it open. "Yes?"

No one was there.

McLaren limped outside. The sun was peeking over the eastern horizon, tinting the gray pre-dawn landscape with splashes of rose-hued light. Ashen shadows still claimed the western sides of the trees and shorter vegetation, wallowing nearly black in the thickets of roses and in the deeper wood. But the air at his front door was releasing the darkness, and McLaren could just make out images, rather like the slow evaporation of fog along a seacoast. He ignored the dew-laden grass that shed its moisture on his shoes and stepped onto the patch of lawn. A breath of wind carried the scent of evening primrose, and he thought for a moment a woman stood beside him. He moved on. The willow near the far side of the house waved its leafy boughs, startling him with the impression someone stood there. But the breeze parted the dense, hanging branches to reveal nothing unusual at its base.

Neither did the ancestral oak harbor anyone. Nor the clump of daylilies outside his bedroom window. The birdbath, too, stood alone, offering no sanctuary but for the birds frequenting it for water. He peered at the hedgerow lining his side of the road, but could discern no one crouching there. Besides, a person would have to be daft to hide in those brambles. Dafter yet to ring his bell at this hour.

Why? He stood on his front step, taking one last glance around. No, no one was in the garden, drive, or road. No vehicle other than his own was in sight. Muttering, he marched inside and slammed the door.

An emphatic pounding on the kitchen door halted his return to the back room. He yelled again that he was coming before giving his thigh a quick massage. When he opened the door, no one was there. He cursed the impatient visitor in a rush of anger as he dashed down the steps.

Again, only the gray light half-hinted at shapes of trees, rock wall and bushes. Nothing moved to suggest human flight.

This time McLaren walked around the house, calling to the visitor. He tripped over a tree root, and fell heavily, knocking the breath from his lungs. He lay there, cursing in pain, getting his wind back, then rolled onto his side and eased up from the damp earth. A check of the front and back gardens, his car and the blind side of the stone wall revealed nothing. Anger and frustration prodded him into the road, and he walked several hundred yards in both directions before admitting defeat. Minutes later he reentered the kitchen without having heard from or seen anyone.

He paused at the electric kettle, thinking he would

have a cup of tea. But the effort seemed too great at the moment, so he returned to the back room. A minute later, he fell asleep.

He woke thirty minutes later, grabbed the empty beer bottle, and slowly stood up. The room was cold and dim in the early morning light. He stretched, feeling in his back and neck the effects of his rock lifting and night on the sofa. He stumbled to the window, shoved the curtains open and daylight flooded the room, making him squint and lower his head. Without looking up, he left the room.

He rinsed out the bottle at the kitchen sink, put it in the glass recycling bin by the back door, then wandered into his bedroom. Removing yesterday's shirt from the linen bin, he grabbed the scrap of paper from the front pocket. Unfolding it, he returned to the kitchen. He paused in the doorway and stared undecidedly at the phone. It was one way to dam the whispers in his head. But was it the best way?

He filled the electric kettle with water, flipped on the switch, put a tea bag into a ceramic mug, and dialed Linnet's number.

As the phone rang, he looked around his kitchen, perhaps truly seeing it for the first time. Though why, he couldn't later remember. It was an ordinary room, perhaps smaller than many: white appliances standing stark against royal blue painted walls—police lantern blue. His mates in the job had joked when they had descended on him for poker or to watch the game on the telly. Nothing adorned the walls except a battery-operated clock. Navy blue and white cotton curtains bracketed the windows, and the electric kettle and a toaster were the only smaller appliances he owned.

Essentials for his life in an equally elementally furnished room. Now, as Linnet's phone rang, he gazed at the walls. He had vowed to repaint them last autumn, needing to cover the reminder of his days with the police.

He had nearly talked himself into abandoning the call when she answered. He could have hung up or apologized that he had a wrong number, but something made him answer her expectant "Hello?"

"Good morning, Miss Isherwood. Michael McLaren. I've thought it over and I'll investigate the murder case."

Chapter Four

He was thirty-seven, about to plunge into detective work again, he told himself as he listened to Linnet's excitement. Was he kidding himself that he could investigate a case alone? What would happen when the Derbyshire Constabulary got wind of his nosing about? Surely, there would be repercussions.

But the questions faded to trivialities as Linnet asked if he wanted to meet somewhere to get more information.

"Might be best," he said, ever cautious of overheard phone conversations. "When?" He tried to ignore his mounting heart rate but if he were honest with himself, he'd admit he wanted to be back in the job. However distant it would prove. And, he thought as he looked around his kitchen, if he were excruciatingly honest, he would own up that he was also doing it for the money. Stone wall repair work may be easy to come by, but it didn't pay as much as police work. So he fought back the rush of adrenalin and jotted down meeting time and place on the pad of paper. "Bring along photos of anyone Marta knew, if you have them." He tapped the tip of the pencil on the paper. "It'll help."

He rang off, excitement and dread and a tinge of fear surging through his body. Had he lost his mind? Was he about to step back into the fire?

He shuddered, and his eyes caught sight of the

smooth rock he used as a paperweight. It normally brought remembrances of the hike last April with Dena. Yet, now it whispered to him, mocked him. Was he about to trade the stones that formed his career for the stony silence of annoyed acquaintances? The paperweight stone was as different from the sharp-edged rocks comprising his stone walls as his life had become after abandoning his police career.

He had an hour to kill before he left to meet Linnet. He wandered to the dining room table to study the map of Derbyshire again. It was purely a time waster; he knew Derbyshire as well as any constable or Royal mail postman. True, Elton was farther south than his home village of Somerley, but he had roamed the county in his youth and probationary days, been on holidays to the Manifold, Matlock Bath, Ashbourne and Hathersage. So why was he consulting the map? To take him back emotionally to a less troubled time?

His phone rang and he grabbed it, not looking at the caller I.D., his mind still on Elton, the village where Marta Hughes' body had been found. So the feminine voice that wished him good morning more than destroyed his contemplation; it dragged him out of the room and plunged him into cold water.

"Dena?" He managed to squeak out her name before his throat constricted.

"It's good to hear your voice, too, Michael."

He wiped his hand across his forehead, suddenly damp with sweat. A glance at the calendar confirmed the suspicion burgeoning in the back of his mind: 12 June. One year to the day that he had unceremoniously shoved her from his life. Was she trying to nestle back in?

"You're not outdoors, working on a wall? I didn't know where you'd be, but I thought I'd try your house before your mobile." She hesitated. McLaren thought she might be unsure what to say or how to say it once the words did come to mind.

In the brief silence Dena's mental image faded, to be replaced by Linnet Isherwood. She still unsettled him. Was it her green eyes or the nearly imperceptible pleading in her voice? Or the way she had discovered his whereabouts? He had thought himself fairly isolated from the world, from the source of his wounds, but she had tracked him down not only to his village but, more importantly, to the wind-swept hill where he worked. No matter how, she disturbed him.

McLaren picked up the rock on the table, cradling it in his palm and hefting it several times, judging its weight. A good weapon if hurled hard and accurately enough. Enough to kill a man…He set it back on the table, shaking off the images of death he'd seen during his police career. But the stone wall on which he'd been working stood rock solid in his mind's eye. As did his meeting with Linnet.

McLaren shook the impression of that morning's thirst-defying heat from his mind, and swallowed slowly. "No. I'm not out. I'm still at home."

"A bit unusual, isn't it, being Friday…"

"Good to know your calendar's not slow." He tried to think of something to say. He knew it was inane, that he should have been friendly, but a kernel of fear took a toehold in his heart.

"God, you haven't lost your manners. You always did know how to sweet talk me."

The silence grew between them and McLaren

could hear her faint breathing in his ear. "You didn't ring me up just to remind me of the date, Dena. What do you want?"

"I would've thought that was obvious, Michael. If the date isn't significant—"

"It's not exactly the occasion for flowers and chocolate. I repeat: what do you want?"

"You."

A dog yapped somewhere on the road outside his house bringing a bit of normalcy to the surreal conversation. McLaren closed his eyes, mentally counting to ten. "It's over, Dena. One year ago it was over. Or don't you remember standing outside my door, crying—"

"You don't need to remind me, Michael. It's all too well engraved on my mind, thank you."

"Then what?"

"As you said, it's been a year. I thought…I hoped enough time had passed that you missed me, that you wanted to get back together. I know how much you've been hurt, Michael. You *know* I do. I was with you through the entire ordeal. I understand. But you can't be bitter all your life, darling. You've got to pick up your life and move on. Just because someone did an unspeakable…"

"Look." McLaren's voice cut through her sympathy like a magistrate's gavel pounding for silence. "I appreciate you must still be hurting, too, or you wouldn't have rung me up. I'm sorry for that. Sorry you're in pain and sorry I ended our engagement. *However…*" He heard her intake of breath as he swallowed. "I've no desire to renew our relationship or engagement. Don't take it personally. I'd feel like this about any woman in my life. I'm just not ready to relive that segment or open myself to those memories."

He paused, aware of his racing heart, aware that it was a lie. He *had* opened his heart to memories simply by staring at her photo and the Chief Constable's commendation. And now he was going to be a cop in all but name when he looked into Marta Hughes' death. He pulled in his bottom lip, his upper teeth pressing into its flesh, as he considered what to say. He didn't want to hurt her; there was enough pain in both of them to last the rest of their lives. But he didn't want to feed her false hope.

"You needn't change your phone number, Michael. Don't worry that I'll be retaliating by ringing you at two a.m. Have a nice life." She rang off before McLaren could apologize.

He stood there, staring at the receiver, picturing Dena tearing up his photo—if she hadn't done so a year ago. She was entitled to her anger; he'd been a jerk. But his anger, his sense of justice…

The mantel clock struck the hour and McLaren realized the irritating beeping sound was coming from the phone. He hung up, torn between ringing her back and letting go. His fear won. He showered, shaved and dressed, grabbed a quick cup of tea and downed a slice of toast before heading out the door. He cleared his car of work tools and consulted the note once more before treading down on the car's accelerator. The Peugeot's tires squealed as they bit into the roadway and the speedometer kept pace with McLaren's racing mind.

The village fell behind him in a blur of gray and green, giving way to the gray and green of the surrounding countryside. Stone walls, rock cliffs, hedgerows, and trees melted into an indistinguishable mass as he concentrated on the ribbon of black asphalt and Marta Hughes. He was barely aware of the roadside sign declaring Castleton as he turned left onto the A625, so many times he had driven the route. But as he parked opposite the hotel and got out of the car, he was more than aware of the umbrella tables in the outdoor dining section, the person chalking the day's lunch special on the two-sided blackboard by the wrought iron gate. He felt alive for the first time in a year.

Linnet saluted him with a glass of tomato juice and waited until McLaren had joined her at one of the tables before she spoke. She was dressed similarly to the previous day, but had changed to a short, floral-printed silk skirt instead of the ankle-length cotton piece. Her tee-shirt was of the same green hue as yesterday's. A silk scarf of the same print was tied loosely around her neck, obscuring most of the silver chain and the ring dangling from it. "What would you like?" she asked as McLaren took the opposite chair. The chair leg scraped across the pebbled concrete, startling the sparrows attacking a bread crust on the pavement.

"I assume you mean from the menu, which rather limits the options."

"Cuts out world peace, wisdom, and happiness, then. Pity." She returned his smile and pushed aside her handbag.

McLaren sighed deeply and gazed at the hotel's façade. Flower boxes and planters overflowed with red geraniums, a brilliant splash of color against the ash-gray stone of the building. The front door, hung on massive brass hinges, was propped open with a brass kettle filled with books. "Looks like someone's going to be doing some major reading." He nodded toward the volumes. "Not worried about theft, I take it."

"I believe they're free. There's a sign, though you probably can't see it..." She craned her neck. "Yes. They're donated by various libraries as well as some locals. It's a nice thought, isn't it, finding a book you might like. Now, what would you like, other than the aforementioned non-menu items? I'm buying. Part of the investigator's fee. Plus expenses, I think you said. You might as well begin the expense bill right now."

He half-turned in his chair to read the chalked menu on the side of the building.

"I can recommend the juice, if that has any weight with you." She rocked the glass slightly. The juice caught the sunlight and momentarily looked like a pool of blood.

McLaren shook his head, and the image, if not his headache, vanished. Craning his head to his right, he called to the waiter. "I'll have some coffee, please. Black." The man nodded, left his chalk and sign, and wandered into the hotel.

"Bare coffee, as my sister calls it? No latte? No cappuccino? Nothing like mocha hazelnut?"

"No. Plain and simple, like me."

"Just the essentials. I see." She smiled, holding the glass as though waiting to toast their collaboration.

The wind whipped a stray strand of her long hair around her head, and for a moment he thought how it mimicked a stalk of greater tussock sedge dancing under the light, breezy buffeting. Why can't we be like that—free, deep rooted to the land, harming no others...

McLaren sat back in the chair; the cold metal dug into the soreness of his back. It jolted him awake more than the beer and tea earlier this morning. More like the water up at the wall repair yesterday. The afternoon had been blisteringly hot, the heat coming off the pasture and rock face like someone opened an oven door. He had tilted back his head, taking gulp after thirsty gulp of the cool water before tipping some on top of his head. Its coldness had hit his scalp with the sharpness of a rock edge. He had shaken off the excess water, gasping as he ran his fingers through his hair, combing the hair back into its crewcut style. That was how the metal chair back bit into him today—sharp, frigid and jerking him awake. He waited until the waiter brought his coffee before continuing with his questions.

"Are you always so cautious, Mr. McLaren?" Linnet nodded toward his left hand.

He glanced down at his hand that covered the small notebook. His fingers curled to lightly run across the open spine. "I've never been accused of writing legibly, but there's always a first time that someone else can read my scrawl." Pausing with the pen tip on the paper, he reread the notes he had jotted down, then asked for Marta Hughes' home phone number and address.

"I haven't said a thing of her husband, Alan," Linnet said as McLaren notated the information. "I didn't feel it was my place. Also…" She watched a tourist take a photo of Peveril Castle before continuing. "I thought you had decided against taking the case."

"A little voice convinced me this morning to change my mind."

"Then I salute the little voice." She raised her glass toward McLaren, finished the last of the juice, then set the glass on the tabletop. He thought how well it complemented her lipstick—dark crimson and catching the light. She brought a folded sheet of paper from her handbag and handed it to him. Several photos were paper-clipped to it

"Key players, I take it." He slipped off the clip and opened the paper.

"In happier times, too." Her voice held a suggestion of regret and sadness. "But most of our youthful days were happier, weren't they?"

He examined the faces and the typed information.

"Alan and Chad…you can figure out. They're the man and teenager. That's Marta with them."

He brought the photo closer so he could stare at the woman. She appeared to be in her mid-forties, a brunette with hazel eyes that looked amusingly at the photographer. She came up to her husband's chin. The husband was a graying brunet and while her son had inherited her eye color, he was blond. McLaren had no time to comment on this.

Linnet said, "The others…" She leaned forward, her left arm bent and supporting her, and tapped each photo as she mentioned their names. "The group shot is Marta, her boss, and the shelter's vet. This"—she skipped over the others in the photograph and pointed to the woman to the extreme left—"is Verity Dwyer."

"The wrongly suspected coworker." The woman in the photo had auburn hair that shone in the sunlight; her blue eyes smiled at him.

Linnet nodded. "Yes. Suspected of killing Marta, though that wasn't proved. But she was convicted of stealing money from the shelter. She's three months into her sentence. She was…Oh, it's extremely involved."

"I've got more time than money. Tell me."

Chapter Five

McLaren settled back into the chair. The wrought iron had lost its coldness and now just held the unyielding support he needed. He moved the notebook to his lap.

Linnet pushed the empty glass to her right, as though considering how best to tell the story. "As I explained yesterday, Verity and Marta worked at the same place."

"An animal shelter. On Blackbeech Road. Noah's Ark, I recall."

Linnet blinked in surprise, then said with a somewhat tremulous voice, "Uh, yes. Quite right. I'm impressed with your research."

"It's included in the price." He allowed himself a quick flash of a smile, took a sip of coffee.

"Well, Verity and Marta became friends. At some point, Marta asked Verity for the loan of £200."

It was McLaren's turn to blink. "What did she need it for, did she say?"

"Same thing she always needed money for. Same thing she did on our girls' night out."

"Gambling. She couldn't take money out of her bank account or ask her husband?"

"It's rather involved. Just accept the fact that they're very well off, but not dripping rich."

"If that's true, her husband must get a nice pay

35

packet. Marta couldn't make much, working in a charity shelter."

"She didn't. But Alan is in senior management…at National Westminster Bank."

"So they live on his money, for the most part."

"Yes. And because he works at National Westminster…"

"Their accounts are with that bank. She couldn't withdraw cash on her own and spare involving Verity in this?"

"Marta could do, certainly. And she often did. But Alan didn't know about her gambling. Well, that's not exactly true. He knew she went to the casino—that we both went—but he thought it was just for fun, a few times a year. She didn't tell him every time she went or how much she lost. Gradually she became addicted to it. She tried to keep it from Alan, so of course she couldn't withdraw the money. He would have seen the reference to it on their monthly statement."

"And Christmas or a birthday, presumably, was too far away to furnish her with that story."

"I'd loaned her all the money I could, so she turned to Verity."

"Was she in the hole to you or anyone else? If she asked people for money—"

"She *always* paid it back, Mr. McLaren. That was the weird thing about it. Marta loved to gamble, but somehow she usually won. Even on the nights she lost heavily, she'd win huge on her return trip."

"So she always had money to repay her debts." He tapped his pen against the notepad as he considered his next question.

Linnet threw the last of her Danish to the sparrows

hopping over the flagstones, watching them flock to the offering.

Over the noisy chirping, McLaren said, "You said yesterday that Verity stole some money. I assume this comes into play in the broad picture of what happened to Marta."

"It was last year. Third of May. Verity took some money from the cash drawer at the shelter. Yes, I know," she added as McLaren swore, "it was stupid, dishonest, and unethical." She shrugged. "Sometimes you do stupid, dangerous, and dishonest things for a friend."

"And Verity got caught in a trap of her own making, I assume."

"Marta swore Verity to secrecy and said she'd pay it back the next day. Marta went to the casino that night and promptly lost everything. She didn't know how to tell Verity."

McLaren knew the feeling, phrases of his conversation with Dena welling in his mind. Breaking bad news, especially news that reflects badly on the teller, is always hard. Even as a cop, he'd never found an easy way to tell anyone that their world was about to be knocked out of orbit. He rubbed his forehead as one of the sparrows grabbed a large crumb and flew away to eat in peace. Dena had taken their engagement breakup rather peacefully. At least there had been no screaming. Just tears as she quietly asked questions.

McLaren gave his forehead one last vigorous rub and leaned forward, resting his forearms on the edge of the table. "Had this ever happened before? Not Marta losing; her taking the shelter's money or getting a personal loan from Verity, and then having to explain why she couldn't repay the money promptly?"

"No. Those who loaned her money considered her a safe risk."

"But you said Marta didn't frequent the casino that regularly."

"She did when she owed someone money. She'd go back the following day or two in order to win it back. It preyed on her mind if she couldn't reimburse the person. She felt strongly about her debts."

"So she returned to the casino the next day or so."

Linnet grimaced, shaking her head. "Unfortunately, two days later she became ill. She was out of work for a week."

McLaren paused, as though mulling over the consequences. "Did she get back to the casino then?"

"No. More back luck. The company treasurer dropped in for an audit on the 10th while Marta will still at home, and—"

"Don't tell me... The treasurer discovers the shortage. Ouch." Was that why Verity was suspected of Marta's murder? "Something obviously happened in conjunction with this gambling episode and the theft. What?"

"In a roundabout way, yes. When Verity couldn't explain the discrepancy she was arrested."

"Why?"

"Because she ran the gift shop. It's in a room off the main reception area. She was the only person with access to the cash."

He opened his mouth to say something but Linnet continued.

"The register is locked overnight, you see."

"And Verity has the only key."

"Yes. Well, Neal, her boss, and the treasurer have keys. But Neal wasn't even under suspicion of the theft."

"He have an alibi for the time in question?"

"I believe so. Anyway, he wasn't ever seriously considered as a suspect."

McLaren snorted and shook his head.

"Verity works ten to four, Tuesday to Saturday. The rest of the time the shop section is closed. Verity took the money from *that* cash drawer, thinking it wouldn't be missed so readily. Sales for the dogs and cats and other animals up for adoption are transacted at the main register in the reception area. That's always busy. Marta knew the money was counted each morning, at the beginning of shift, so the employees know how much change they have for the day's business."

McLaren nodded, his eyes fixed on Linnet's face. "Good news, bad news."

"I suppose so. Anyway, the discrepancy was discovered and Verity was blamed."

"Hell of a finger-pointer, that." He picked up his coffee. The cup was cold to the touch. He started to angle in his chair, searching for the waiter. Last time McLaren had seen him, the man was chalking items on the menu near the street. As McLaren grabbed the chair arms, Linnet said, "Maybe it's nothing, but I think someone's fooling about near your car." She nodded toward McLaren's Peugeot. He stood up.

"I could be wrong, but I thought…"

Her voice trailed off as McLaren said, "I'll be right back," and darted across the road.

Of course no one was loitering at the off side of the

car. The far side, along the pavement, harbored no one other than the usual tourists consulting guide books or taking photographs, and villagers hurrying to shops for the day's marketing. McLaren paused at the passenger door and squatted to peer at the door lock and window. No telltale pry marks marred the pristine paint job. He tried the latch. The door remained closed.

But if anyone had been tampering with the car, was he farther down the block, waiting until McLaren returned to the café? Unnerving thought.

McLaren jogged to the corner, eyeing everyone, glancing into alleys and store windows. No one seemed to be watching him. When he got to the end of the block, he jogged back, again passing the same people and stores, again looking for suspicious activity. At the end of the row of shops, he paused, unsure if he should try the opposite side of the street. What good would that do? If someone had been trying to break into his car, he wouldn't be leaning against a lamppost, advertising. McLaren turned and walked back to the hotel.

"Anything?" Linnet asked as he reclaimed his seat.

"Not even a sparrow," he said as one lone bird landed on the back of a vacant chair.

"Sorry. Guess I was wrong."

"That's all right. I didn't get in my morning jog before I came."

"Then it wasn't in vain." She smiled, her voice taking on a lighter tone.

Jotting something in his notebook, he said, "Always best to be sure. Someone could have been trying for a quick grab, though there's nothing in my car that's visible. Or valuable."

"I would have felt terrible if something had been

stolen and I never said."

"I applaud your call to good citizenship, then." He settled back into the chair. The morning sun had warmed the wrought iron and the heat felt good on his stiff muscles. "So, Verity was blamed for the missing money from the cash drawer."

"Yes. It was awful. A farce, in my opinion. The trial was held several months later and she began serving her sentence last year in June."

"So they didn't pin the murder on her, then. Just the theft."

"Yes. They knew it wasn't embezzlement because the money had gone missing in one lump. The prosecution tried to link this to Marta's murder, but they couldn't make a case of it."

"It would've been hell to go through the process of overturning a false conviction of murder. She was lucky in that aspect."

"And her defense council couldn't come up with anything the jury believed, I take it."

McLaren rubbed his eyes. He could almost hear the prosecution ranting that Verity had hired a hit man to rob Marta after she won big at the casino. He tossed the pen and notebook onto the table. The whole story stank, as far as he was concerned. And as for circumstantial evidence... He'd seen many cases 'solved' with just this type of reasoning and evidence no more concrete than theories, bad personal histories, and gossip.

"Marta never returned the loaned money, then, or testified on Verity's behalf at the trial. You know." He stared at Linnet, his look cold and uncomforting. "Never explained she was behind the shortage from the cash till."

"No. She didn't want to embarrass Marta." Her voice softened as she searched McLaren's face for his reaction. "Please don't judge her too harshly, Mr. McLaren. She was actually a good person. She was a loyal friend and would do anything for anyone."

"A prison sentence is a stiff thank you for helping a friend."

"You'll still take the case?" She leaned forward slightly as she opened her handbag. "I know it's probably a bit more than you expected, but none of us believe Verity's involved any way in Marta's death. She's not that sort of person. She just had the misfortune that the treasurer showed up when he did. If Marta had lived—" She broke off and avoided McLaren's eyes. Running her tongue over her lips, she looked at him. "Marta would have paid back the money. She wasn't a thief. You'll help her, won't you? You'll take the case?"

McLaren nodded and watched Linnet's pen make out a check for a down payment. When she signed it and handed it to him, she said, "Her husband, Alan, would certainly be glad to talk to you. He doesn't say so, but I know he's dying inside."

"I better see him immediately, then."

Linnet seemed to search McLaren's eyes for a sign of understanding or sympathy. He merely stared at her, as though he hadn't yet decided on something. She said, "The police couldn't find the killer. Maybe it was because too much time had elapsed before they found her body. But I don't believe everyone could have proved their alibis, could they? You'll be able to find her killer?"

He stood up, folded the check, slipped it into his

pocket, and thanked her. "Slugs aren't always under the first rock you turn over."

Chapter Six

Linnet Isherwood had satisfied his curiosity as to why she knew so much about the financial problems of the confession. As she put it, when your best friend's been murdered, each fact is branded upon your heart, never mind that she had been in court each day of the trial.

McLaren sat in his car, coaxed the check from his pocket, and stuffed it more securely into his wallet. He'd have to wait until Monday to deposit it, but it comforted him knowing a transfusion for his bank account was less than two days away.

His mobile phone rang. The caller I.D. display said it wasn't Dena calling. She wasn't going to catch him again. Though it was nearly as bad, he conceded, answering the ring. It was his sister. He took a deep breath, silently cursed, then forced an artificial cheerfulness into his voice. Perhaps his sister wouldn't notice the strain. "Hi, Gwen. Up awfully early, aren't you?"

"You forget about the early bird, Mike." Her voice was strong and laced with the Derbyshire accent of their upbringing.

"And which are you—the bird or the worm?"

"Better not ask. I'm still deciding. You at work?" She didn't have to specify his job; she'd emotionally held his hand through his decision to leave the police and had encouraged him to take up the stone wall repairing, believing he needed time away from people in order to heal.

"Yes, but not what you think." He told her about his decision to look into the cold case.

The silence on the other end of the phone told him she either was surprised or disapproved of his decision.

He said, "You're always encouraging me to get back with people."

"I was thinking more about you and Dena, not a murder victim, however metaphorically you take that."

"Is that why you rang me up?" He had a suspicion she knew the significance of the day's date. "Why aren't you painting something? You run out of canvas or is your easel broken?"

"I'm serious, Mike. You've been alone too long. You need to make an effort to get back with her, with your friends. With Jerry and me. We miss being with you."

"Let me heal in my own way, in my own time, Gwen," he snapped, the calculated cheeriness forgotten, the bitterness creeping back into his voice. "You don't know what I went through or how I feel. You have no right to judge me."

"I'm not judging you. I just want to see you happy again and spending some time with us."

"It'll happen, Gwen. Just don't push me."

"No one is pushing, Mike. We're just concerned for your health. You've shut us out of your life. We can't get near you. You won't share anything with us. Not your thoughts, your work, your feelings…"

So that was it, his emotions again. "I'll call when I'm ready, Gwen, and not before. I know you mean well, I appreciate your concern, but don't hound me about this. I still need to sort this through." He flipped the phone closed and tossed it onto the passenger seat. She would never understand his hurt and anger. She hadn't the years and the history that made it so crushing.

Suddenly hungry, he searched through the car's glove compartment. Sometimes a chocolate bar or package of trail mix or packet of biscuits lurked between the maps and petrol receipts and tire pressure gauge. He slammed the compartment door. Nothing.

Glancing at the outdoor dining area, he considered going back and ordering something. Linnet had remained at the table and was now making a call on her mobile phone. He watched her animated hands as she talked, silently emphasizing her conversation. He was still there when she paused several feet from his car, pursing her lips against the phone's mouthpiece. Cooing to her boyfriend, he thought, as he heard the name Sean. Dena and he had been like that, but now…

A flash of bright red caught his eye and he half-turned in his car seat to look. The rear half of a car's back wing shone in the sun for a second, then disappeared behind the edge of a shop. He half leaned out the window, trying to see around the building. But the row of shops presented a seamless façade, at least as far as he could see from this viewpoint. He was about to start his car and zip up the side street, when Linnet waved her free hand and mouthed something to him. Exhaling heavily, he removed his hand from the ignition key, promising himself that he'd somehow find out if that had been Dena's red MG, as he suspected. And if she were following him.

Smiling, Linnet stopped opposite his window. She held out the phone to McLaren. "My boyfriend. Sean. He'd like to ask you something, if you have a minute."

McLaren shrugged and grabbed the mobile. "This is McLaren." He glanced at Linnet for a hint of why Sean wanted to speak to him.

"Hello, Mr. McLaren. This is Sean FitzSimmons, a friend of Linnet's. Has she mentioned me to you?"

What was McLaren supposed to know, the man's life story? McLaren replied that Miss Isherwood had spoken of him.

"I know this will sound positively bonkers, but I'd like to ask if you would answer some police questions for me."

Whatever McLaren had been expecting, it hadn't been this. "Police…"

The voice went on. "Nothing confidential. God, no! Just some procedural things."

McLaren glanced at the photos on the car seat next to him. How'd he get into this? What was Sean FitzSimmons on about?

"I'm a writer," Sean explained. "I write thrillers."

McLaren's breathing returned to normal. "Oh, yes. Miss Isherwood had mentioned that when we first met. I'm sorry I'd forgotten."

"No harm. I've got a plot I'm working on now for my current book, and I have this situation I'm not sure about. I was hoping that you, being a police detective, could—"

McLaren stopped Sean right there. "No, I'm not a police officer any more, Mr. FitzSimmons. Besides, I doubt if I'll have time to confer with you. I'm taking on this job just to help out Miss Isherwood. After it's finished I'll return to my current line of work. Sorry I can't help. Ask at any of the larger police stations. They've got officers who do that sort of thing. Best of luck." He handed the phone back to Linnet and shrugged again, as though to say that was all he could do.

"Don't loose any sleep over it." She pocketed the phone. "I love him to death but he's basically lazy. He thought you could sort out his plot problem for him. It'll be fine. And, uh, thank you again for taking all this on." She flashed him a smile before continuing down the street.

He wanted to say, "Thank me when you see how this turns out." He turned the key in the ignition, hesitated as though weighing the odds of finding Dena on the road from Castleton, then eased away from the curb. He'd do a bit of research in the public library before talking to Marta's near and dear.

The reference librarian furnished McLaren with what press cuttings and reports she had from the murder investigation. The coroner's hearing had been big news in the local newspaper, which gave McLaren a break. He sat at a table, making notes of the medical information, the police findings, and statements from those who knew Marta. The bullet that killed Marta was, as Linnet said, a .38 caliber, but no extensive ballistic tests had been conducted with the few guns that could be found around Elton. Besides, the bullet had been too badly smashed up inside Marta's skull for a match.

He considered phoning his friend Jamie, a serving police officer in Derbyshire, to get the more detailed police files and statements. But he didn't want to explain that he was taking on an investigation. Jamie would think him daft. Anyway, Jamie's career could be at risk if he should get caught giving out confidential police information.

When McLaren finished with the last account he sat back in his chair and rubbed his eyes. The reading per se hadn't brought on his headache; his brain thudded from the amount of information he absorbed in so short a time. Like being back in university, cramming for a test.

The librarian accepted the returned files with the same wary monotone when first handing them over. She glared at McLaren, muttering something about the average citizen playing at Inspector Morse. McLaren felt the familiar race of his heart, the tightening of his throat. Had she heard about McLaren and his departure from the Force? Or was it just that someone postponed her tea break? He had no way of knowing. And it really didn't matter. He slammed the door as he left to talk to Alan and Chad Hughes.

He'd just emerged from the Winnat's Pass, on the eastern side of Castleton, when he noticed a hiker limping toward him along the side of the road. He slowed to glance at the woman—a habit from his cop days. She leaned heavily on the walking stick, took a step, then stopped to rub her ankle. But the thing that held McLaren's attention was the hiker's bloody knee. He stopped on the grassy verge and called to her.

She looked up, perhaps not certain where the voice had come from, then noticed McLaren waving to her.

He let two cars pass before he called again. "You're hurt. Do you need any help? I can phone someone or give you a lift someplace." He eyed her knee, assessing if it were a hospital job.

She got to her feet. "I think I'll live. Thanks for stopping. Everyone else…" An articulated lorry and motorcycle whizzed past, kicking up a plume of dust.

"Yes, I see. Too busy."

"Or too afraid of a hitchhiker."

"You wouldn't be afraid of them, if it came to accepting a lift?" He took in her small, thin frame. Even though she had the well-developed calf muscles of a walker, her biceps didn't impress him. Besides, the area was desolate, more renowned for its heather, lonely moors, and rock outcroppings than for help should anyone try to assault her.

Perhaps sensing his concern, she pulled something from her pocket. She held it up so McLaren could see it—a pocketknife. "I can hold my own."

"Glad to hear it." Two motorcycles bulleted past, filling the air with exhaust fumes and noise. McLaren sat back in his seat and waited until the sound and stench dissipated before turning again to the hiker. "Since we don't have to worry about you holding your own, how's your trust level? Want a lift somewhere? Or does that take the glory out of your adventure?"

"I've had enough of that for today, thanks. And I'd like a lift, if it wouldn't take you out of your way."

"As long as it's in Derbyshire, I think I can manage it." He leaned across the front seat to unlock the passenger-side door. The woman discarded the impromptu walking stick. Ordinarily, he would have got out and opened the door for her. But he thought that might be considered a threatening movement, knife or no knife; her ankle would have prevented her escape. "I won't be offended if you want to keep your knife at the ready…if it'll ease your mind about accepting the ride."

"I already decided on that." She settled into the seat, fastened the seat belt and closed the door before he asked where they were headed. "The Hanoverian, in Hathersage, if that's not too much bother. I've got a room booked for tonight."

"No bother at all. Right on my way, in fact. You…" He paused as he checked his rearview mirror, then accelerated quickly as the car claimed the road. "You will be all right there? You don't want me to find you a doctor in Hathersage?"

She had bent forward to examine her knee. McLaren glanced at the red patch of skin as she gingerly touched it. "Looks nasty. Is it still bleeding?"

"Not much. Just occasional ooze when I bend it. Ouch." She straightened up. "Mum always says I never leave well enough alone."

"Here." He yanked a cotton handkerchief from his shirt pocket and held it out. "Not exactly a sterile gauze pad, but it might help."

She murmured her thanks as she wrapped it around her knee. "The only good thing about this is that I didn't rip a pair of jeans." She tugged at the hem of her walking shorts. "Skin heals. A ruined pair of jeans would cost twenty or thirty quid."

"Then again, wearing a pair of jeans might have protected your knee and prevented your cut."

"I guess we'll never know, will we?" She gave the handkerchief one last knot and leaned back.

"I still think you need someone to look at that. You couldn't have washed the wound properly."

"I poured some of my drinking water on it. It'll be

51

fine."

McLaren made a sound like a disgruntled cough. Her sock was damp. "Water won't help your ankle."

"It's not sprained. Just a little sore from my fall. I'll be fine in the morning." She settled her rucksack against her feet before transferring the open knife to her left hand. Holding out her right hand, she said, "I'm Karin Pedersen, by the way. Thanks for stopping."

McLaren glanced at the extended hand, grasped her fingers in what he hoped would pass for a handshake, then concentrated on the road. "Mike McLaren. My pleasure. You on a walking holiday, then?"

Karin returned the knife to her right hand and settled back into the seat. "Yes. I started this past Sunday. I have until this Friday to tramp about."

"Do you walk a lot?"

"You mean, hiking like this? Over the moors?"

"Yes. Or just stroll after tea, down your street."

"I like to walk. It's a great stress reliever. Plus I meet interesting people and get some smashing photos of the land."

"So you're a photographer."

"Not really. Just amateur stuff. But it's fun."

"You're not scared walking about like this on your own. Your boyfriend doesn't mind, doesn't worry about you." He'd estimated her age to be in the early twenties, but without a wedding or engagement ring on her finger, he could only guess at the boyfriend.

"Not at all. You forget I have great peace of mind." She waved the knife as he said, "I didn't forget."

They lapsed into a brief silence, McLaren occupied with unwanted mental images of Marta Hughes' body sprawled in roadside weeds. Of course he knew hardly anything of Karin Pedersen, but her life was just beginning and he didn't want to read about her premature death.

He slowed the car at the village limit. Traffic funneled between the buildings standing shoulder-to-shoulder along the B625, nearly forming a solid line that obliterated the tarmac. He exhaled loudly, disliking the stop-and-go of Hathersage's market day, and cranked up the window against the noise of car engines, radio, and talk. This was not his idea of peaceful living.

They inched past a handful of shops before McLaren turned into the Hanoverian's car park. Gravel crunched under the car's tires and sent up small puffs of dust that quickly vanished into the air. The gray stones of the tall inn were blackened with the soot of decades of coal fires and the exhaust of countless passing cars. But the sign, depicting a somber king, showed the effect of its recent cleaning, for the sunlight glanced off the painted surface. "This all right, then?" He scrutinized the side entrance, as though inspecting it for safety and cleanliness. "You want my phone number in case you aren't well enough to walk tomorrow morning?"

"You seem to be a rare type." She swung open the car door.

"I'd ask what type, but I'm afraid of the answer."

"White knight. Gallant. Helpful. Awfully kind of you but I repeat, I'll be fine once I rest up a bit. Besides, I have my mobile. I'm just as capable of calling my boyfriend as you. Or picking up the bedside phone to summon the hotel proprietor. Thanks for the lift."

She got out of the car, then grabbed her rucksack

with her free hand. Her weak ankle buckled and, in trying to regain her balance, the rucksack tipped, spilling much of its contents onto the ground.

"Let me help." McLaren said before Karin held up her hand.

"No big deal. *Mea culpa.* I didn't latch the flap when I pulled out the bandana to wipe off my knee. It'll only take me a second." She bent over and moments later had the contents back inside the pack. "There. Sorry about holding you up." Her hand rested on the edge of the upholstered seat as she leaned inside. She extended her hand. "Thank you again, Mr. McLaren. I don't know when I would've hobbled in here if you hadn't come along."

"Glad I could help. I hope the rest of your ramble is uneventful."

"You and me both." She dragged her rucksack out of the way and slammed the door. As McLaren shifted into first gear, she crossed her fingers and waved them at him. She was still waving when his car regained the main road, rounded the bend, and lost her from sight.

McLaren could never recall later exactly what time it happened, but he did recall it was outside the Longshaw Estate. Blue, flashing lights of a police motorcycle loomed in his rearview mirror and a yellow-jacketed police officer waved him over. McLaren sighed, confused and curious at once. He hadn't been speeding. He was always conscious of the posted limit signs. Besides, that had been one of his crusades when he was a constable.

He turned off the engine, placed his hands on the steering wheel, and watched the officer approach. McLaren turned slightly toward the officer, his raised eyebrow mirroring his bewilderment.

"Yes, Officer?" McLaren said, aware of the remembered identical question echoing in his mind. "Did I do something wrong?"

"Name please, sir." Without replying to the question, the constable flipped open his leather-bound booklet.

"McLaren. Michael. If I did something—"

"Is this your vehicle, sir?"

McLaren glanced around the car's interior, as though expecting it to have changed. He moved his hand to the top of the center console to help shift his body so he could glance into the open hatchback section.

A warning—a clearing of a throat and the words, "Hands on the steering wheel, sir, where I can see them"—stopped McLaren's inspection. He murmured, "Certainly. Sorry," and settled back into the seat.

The constable stepped slightly away from the car door yet kept his eyes on McLaren. He spoke briefly into his shoulder microphone and seemed to be talking to someone for an eternity. McLaren heard snatches of the conversation, but didn't need the entire dialogue to know that his car was being run through the PNC listings, that it was insured, that it had a current m.o.t. certificate. He also knew it would be verified as not stolen, but that didn't help his anxiety or confusion as to why this was even happening. The officer finally jotted something down in his notebook and returned to his original position at the car door. He stared down at McLaren. "You admit this Peugeot 207 is registered in your name, correct?"

The second misgiving that something was wrong

kicked him alongside the head. Was his number plate light burnt out? "If you would tell me what is wrong, officer—"

"Have you been in continuous possession of this car today, sir?"

"Continuous?"

"From the time you started your journey to this moment?"

McLaren's throat tightened. He fought to keep his breathing even as he replied, "Yes. I've been in the car continuously since I started, haven't left this seat. What—"

"Where did you begin your trip, sir?"

"Castleton. Mid-morning. I don't know the exact time. Close to eleven o'clock, I should think. If you would tell me—"

"And what is your destination?"

"Chesterfield." He hoped that was enough. If he had to give Alan Hughes' home address and explain why he was going there, this would turn into a can of worms.

"Thank you, sir. You have a driving license, I assume." The officer looked at McLaren as though someone in his late thirties should know the law.

"Certainly. I can produce it if it's required. Would you please tell me what this is all about?"

"Yes, sir. Our station received a phone call about a red, 3-door Peugeot 207, with number plate numbers that match yours."

"*Match* mine! My car?"

"The driver's description also matches you, sir. White male, late thirties, dark blond hair in a crew cut, hazel eyes." The officer paused, perhaps assuming

McLaren would deny something. When McLaren merely stared at him, the officer said, "Now, sir, if you would kindly exit the car for a moment." His hand was on the door latch and opening the door before McLaren could blink.

As McLaren stepped onto the packed, bare soil of the verge, he stumbled slightly as the toe of his shoe became tangled in a tuft of grass. Steadying himself against the side of the car, he stuttered, "Wh-what's this all about? I-I don't understand."

"Perhaps not, sir. The driver of this car, your car, was just reported as driving erratically, as though he'd been drinking. Have you had anything to drink today, sir?"

McLaren blinked, not believing this was happening. "Nothing alcoholic, which is what you mean, I assume. Just tea and coffee."

"Would you consent to taking a breath analyzer test, sir?"

"*Breath analyzer* test!" My God, I'm about to be given the entire treatment: warning, statement of prescribed limits, declaration of moving traffic offence... McLaren moved sideways and tripped over a rock protruding from the soil.

"Yes, sir." He eyed McLaren as if sizing up how much the man had already consumed. "Hands on the car bonnet, if you please, sir. For your safety as well as mine."

McLaren shook his head in disbelief and placed his hands on the front of the car. "But there's no need for a breath analyzer test. I've not had a thing to drink, other than this morning's tea and coffee. This is all..."

"Ridiculous?" the constable supplied, walking

around to the passenger side of the car. He opened the car door and looked inside.

"Yes. I've been—" He stopped abruptly, aware that he had been about to say he'd been a cop. Besides holding no weight, he didn't want his name or history made public.

"You've been...what, sir?"

McLaren tried to think of an answer. What could he say? He'd been framed? Converted through religion? Dry for a decade? A model member of R.A.C.? Ashamed of his relapse? He stared stupidly at the officer, trying to make sense of the situation.

The officer bent forward and searched the interior. When he straightened up again, he was holding a beer bottle in his gloved hand. A quarter inch or so of liquid sloshed around inside as the officer gently shook it. "How do you explain this, sir?"

## Chapter Seven

Of course there had never been a question in McLaren's mind that he would fail the breath test. The two swallows of beer he'd finished off before breakfast would not be enough to register on the breath analyzer. He was completely under the prescribed limit of 35 microgrammes. Still, the realization that someone somewhere knew him, knew his car and registration plate number, and had reported him to the police was sobering. Frightening.

The constable left him with a "Thank you, sir, and drive safely," his motorcycle roaring into the distance. McLaren sat in his car, staring at the man until traffic and the bend in the road obscured him from sight, trying to make sense of what had just happened. The breath analyzer test had registered nothing; there was nothing wrong with his car registration, license, or insurance. A waste of time for the officer; an inkling of some blunder for McLaren. He turned his car and headed back to Hathersage. That hiker, Karin Pedersen, had been in the passenger seat. Perhaps the bottle was hers.

Despite his urge to hurry, McLaren kept the car's speed under or at the limit. A handful of minutes slipped by as he lumbered behind an articulated lorry near Surprise View, unexpected scenery of the Derwent's thickly-wooded valley and the boulder-studded slopes of the hills. His fingers drummed on the steering wheel, increasing his agitation. The lorry's motor growled, as the driver shifted gear to slow the vehicle's downward pace. As an outcropping of boulders crawled past his window, McLaren shoved a cassette tape into the tape player, and after several seconds of silence, the background sounds of pub patrons filled the car's interior and his strong, baritone voice sailed over the noise of the crowd, followed by three other men's harmonies and the supportive sounds of guitars, viola, and soprano recorder. *My father's walking on the street; my mother the chamber keys do keep; the doors and windows they do creak; I dare not let you in O*, the lovesick lass told her soldier lover. "You're not the only one who's been betrayed," McLaren muttered to the tape player. He let himself finish the verse of 'Cold Haily Rainy Night' before he jabbed the player's Stop button. He was in no mood for the song, no matter how much he liked listening to his folk singing group. Keen to get to the hotel and sort out this event, he swung his car around the lorry at the first opportunity, and a minute later parked in the Hanoverian Inn car park.

His footsteps crunched on the gravel, making indentations as he walked hurriedly to the front of the building. A strip of grass, nearly a foot wide, kept the gravel from spreading onto the main road and immediately deadened the thump of his boots. He stepped onto the pavement curling around to the front door, stopped to let a lady pass, then sprinted up the four steps. His hand gripped the brass door handle and he yanked impatiently at it.

The hotel's front door eased closed behind

McLaren as he stepped into the hallway. A runner carpet of an intertwined floral design done in tans, oranges, and greens softened the sound of his steps. He ignored his reflection in the gilt-framed Georgian style mirror and strode down the hall.

The name suited the inn-turned-hotel; it seemed to have been pulled from an upper class house of the 18th century, with its dark wood paneling and silver wall sconces. A large reception desk lifted from an ancient pub stood guard in front of a row of wooden cubbyholes for guests' mail. McLaren marched to the desk and slammed his fist on the chrome reception bell.

Faint though it was, the bell's ping evidently sounded loudly enough. The tone had barely died when a tall, thin man materialized at the far end of the cubbyholes. He seemed to be part of the ancient building, clothes, hair, and eyes the same dark hue as the wood, his skin the tone of the polished brasses over the fireplace. A fireplace large enough to roast oxen, McLaren judged, then turned to the gaunt man as his 'May I be of service?' broke the stillness.

"Please." McLaren braced his left palm on the edge of the desk and leaned forward. "I believe you have a Karin Pedersen registered here."

"The name does not sound familiar, sir."

"Perhaps not, but she arrived here about an hour ago. I wonder if you could ring her room and let her know I'd like to talk to her."

"We've had no one arrive in the last hour, sir."

"Well, maybe it's three-quarters of an hour. I'm not sure of the time. But I know she's here. She had a reservation for the night."

"I can assure you, sir. Three-quarters of an hour or

one complete hour, we've had no one arrive yet today. There are a number of guests scheduled to arrive later, nearer tea time, but no one has registered any time today."

McLaren stared at the clerk as if the man had lost his mind—or was trying to convince McLaren that he'd lost his. He leaned against the counter's edge. "But she *has* to be here! She has a reservation! I dropped her off *myself*, just an hour ago, at your car park."

"I assure you, sir, no one has—"

"She entered your side door. I watched her. She walked inside. Maybe she has a different name." He tried to make sense of the clerk's information. "Maybe she's married and registered under her married name. Could that be it?" His fingers gripped the edge of the counter as the room began to tilt.

"Perhaps. What name did you say, sir? I'll look it up."

"Pedersen. Karin Pedersen. I know that's her name. At least, that's what she told me." Why would she lie? She didn't seem to be on the run from something. And if she were, people hiding from the law or from angry boyfriends don't take a leisurely hike through the Derbyshire Dales; they take the fastest exit they can and bury themselves in the anonymity of a city.

The clerk flipped slowly through the small stack of registration cards, silently reading them as he said, "These are all from this week. There is no Karin Pedersen registered."

"A small, thinly built woman. In her early twenties. Vivid red, curly hair."

"I'm sorry."

"Her knee was cut pretty bad. It had been bleeding

and she had tied a handkerchief around it."

"As I said, sir, no one of that description has registered here."

McLaren threw his head back and exhaled slowly. The plaster grape clusters and cupids on the ceiling shifted into and out of focus. He closed his eyes, trying to think. This was beyond a joke. Then he lowered his head, stared at the clerk and said slowly, "All right. Could she have registered while you were on break? Do you have another employee who was on duty an hour ago?"

"I am the only front desk staff during the day. Another clerk takes over at 4:00, and someone else is on call during the night. But I am the only person here right now. This is my normal working time."

"No one relieves you if you...you know...there's a call of nature?"

The clerk drew himself up to his full height and his voice turned cooler. "There are arrangements, certainly, but that has not happened during the time you say this person supposedly came into the hotel."

The front door opened, causing the long fabric panels at the opening of the reception area to move. An older couple sauntered down the hall, talking about their dinner reservations, then disappeared from McLaren's view. He turned back to the clerk. "Would you at least check your registration book to see if she has a room for tonight? Maybe I've got the time wrong..." That wasn't possible, but anything to appease the clerk into looking.

Sighing, he opened a large monthly planner. He flipped several pages consulting dates prior to and after the day's date, then set the open book in front of

McLaren. He pointed to the day's column. "This is highly irregular, allowing you to view this book. But I assume you won't believe me if you do not see it for yourself. As you can see, sir, there is no reservation for Karin Pedersen. Now, if there is nothing more—"

"But she *has* to be staying here. She couldn't walk anyway. She fell and bloodied her knee. Perhaps she went to a clinic or saw a doctor before registering here. Is there one in town?"

The clerk eyed McLaren as though he had just walked into the room nude. "Hathersage is a village, sir. The nearest medical facility…"

"Okay. Fine." He ran his fingers through his hair, trying to stimulate his brain. Needing to concentrate, he closed his eyes for a moment and vocalized his thoughts slowly. "Maybe she found a local doctor. Is there one in town? Surely someone's name must be on file for a guest who might become ill during the night."

"We keep a supply of medical supplies here, sir. If a guest is truly in need of professional care, we dial 999 or drive them to the Devonshire Royal Hospital in Buxton. I have seen no one of her description, nor have I seen this knee you keep referring to. Now, if you don't mind."

"But she came in here, dammit!" he exploded. "I dropped her off. She entered the hotel by the side door. She told me her name. I talked to her for quarter of an hour."

"No one has registered—"

"She has a reservation for *tonight!* She's *got* to be here!" He leaned over the counter and grabbed for the cards. The frantic glance of dates and names still failed to reveal Karin Pedersen's name. Silently admitting defeat, he dropped the stack onto the counter and leaned against it. "Why would she lie? There's no point in it. Why would she come in here if she has no room?"

The clerk gingerly stepped forward and said in a strained voice, "I'm afraid I can't help you. If you don't leave the premise immediately, I shall have to phone for the police."

"No need to trouble yourself, mate. We already know each other."

Murmuring something unintelligible, the clerk picked up the stack of cards and disappeared into the small inner room behind the cubbyholes.

McLaren nodded and walked into the hall, pausing in front of a painting of King George III. "Got the name of a good psychiatrist, Georgie? I'm going to need one very soon." The door eased shut on his retreating figure.

Sitting in his car in the hotel car park, McLaren thought over the sequence of events. Nothing made sense other than Karin Pedersen had changed her mind about the overnight stay and had moved on. But her cut knee would necessitate someone driving her. He eyed the hotel sign, a stylized portrait of George III, and wondered briefly how long the paint lasted in these harsh Derbyshire winters before he walked to the payphone on the side of the hotel. The yellow pages had one listing for a doctor in the village and the next nearest one was in Bakewell, which was more than ten miles distant. Buxton and Chesterfield were heavily represented and seemed the most logical choice for care if her knee was cut deeply. Still, McLaren wanted to be certain.

The call was answered almost immediately, and

nearly as immediately McLaren was back to no solution. The doctor had not treated a Karin Pedersen, the receptionist informed him. He had treated no one that day with a cut knee, but did he try the hospital in Buxton?

McLaren sat heavily in his car seat, confused and frustrated. His fingers reached for the tape, yet rested on the cassette's edge. Was this a 'message' from Dena? A flex of her muscles to show she could upset his life? But he hadn't seen her today, hadn't told her that he'd be in Castleton. She couldn't have done anything.

His gaze drifted over to the passenger seat, then out the car window toward the direction of Castleton. He imagined the small lanes of the village, the stone shops, and the castle ruin perched on the hill overlooking the comings and goings of the residents. He had parked across from the hotel, sitting in the outdoor dining area with his back toward his car. Could Dena have planted the beer bottle while he was speaking with Linnet? Was she the person Linnet believed she had seen at his car? If Dena had done it so quickly and casually that she hadn't drawn attention to herself, she could have bent over, cracked open the door, and jammed the bottle in the floor well between the passenger seat and the door. Maybe he hadn't locked the door after all; maybe she had pushed down the door lock.

He rubbed his forehead, trying to envision the scenario. Could it have happened? Was he imagining enemies at every corner? He shoved the cassette tape back into the dashboard tape player, adjusted the volume to the next song, 'The Blacksmith,' and leaned his head against the headrest. Castleton's main street shimmered in his mind's eye, Linnet's face and the waiter at the chalkboard sign and the road lined with cars had seemed normal. And a hiker in the Peak District wasn't unusual. But somewhere, some time, something odd had happened and he needed to figure it out.

He sat up, leaving the blacksmith's fair lady to ponder her own doubts, and turned the key in the ignition switch. The car engine roared into life but he let it idle. Yes, he thought as he slowly nodded. Dena's red MG. He'd swear in court the car he'd seen had been hers. A burst of applause from the recording drowned his muttered "Damn." Swinging the car onto the main road, he grumbled, "I hope the cheers are prophetic," and headed to Chesterfield.

Marta Hughes' husband, Alan, poured McLaren a second cup of tea before explaining his last statement. They were seated in the kitchen of Alan's house, warm from the mid-afternoon sun and the chicken casserole baking in the oven. Alan, a graying brunet in his late forties, leaned forward, his forearms on the chrome edge of the tabletop, and nodded toward the front room. "Most of the damage was in there." His voice sounded weary with having to relive the event.

McLaren settled the cup back onto the saucer, eyeing the room through the kitchen doorway. Nothing was out of place, but he could imagine the wreckage. He'd seen dozens of such rooms during his police career. "So the coppers never discovered who ransacked your home, then."

"No. But we had our suspicions."

"'We' meaning…"

"The police, my family, and the neighbors."

"And did you all come to the same conclusion as to the suspect?"

"Yes. Without even having to discuss it. Herb Millington. Or at least his mate, Danny Mercer."

"Who's Herb Millington? Have you, your family, neighbors, or police had run-ins with him before?"

"A neighbor. And no, not run-ins. Not exactly. But he's brushed up against the law before."

"So he has a reputation, then."

"Unfortunately. No strong-arm stuff, however. Nothing like intimidation, which this rifling suggests."

"What, exactly?"

"Drugs."

"He's a dealer?"

Alan picked up his cup and held it as he considered his answer. "The aforementioned We believe so, but no one's ever caught him red-handed. At least, I don't think so. We would've heard, or realized his house was vacant for—" He broke off, looking thoughtful. "What's the prison term for dealing drugs?"

"Long enough for you to know he wasn't occupying his residence."

"We thought so." Alan sounded disappointed.

"If he's never done time, why do you believe Herb Millington or…"

"Danny Mercer."

"Herb Millington or Danny Mercer is your culprit?"

Alan took a sip of tea, his fingertips drumming on the side of the cup. "Many of us have smelled marijuana on him. At times he acts strung-out, like he's on something. Bursts of violence, occasionally. He doesn't drink, so he couldn't have had one too many to cause his bizarre behavior. In fact, that's how this whole mess started."

"Your home being ransacked."

"Yes. Marta used to see them quite often, sitting in front of Herb's house. Danny didn't look too bad, but Herb began looking like hell. Weight loss, his face all scarred. Marta was concerned, because basically Herb's a nice guy. Well, when he doesn't get violent."

"Which amounts to…what?"

"Tearing down part of his picket fence because he thought the paint job was bad, taking a rock to the handle of his car door when he'd locked the key inside, throwing a portable telly out the living room window."

"Anything directed physically at anyone? His wife, for instance? Marta?"

Alan snorted. "His wife left him several years ago. A nasty divorce."

"What's he do for a living, or is he just a drug dealer?"

"He's got money. Separate from selling drugs, if he does do that. His parents left him a bundle. They owned a website building and hosting business before selling it for several million quid."

"So he lives off his inheritance."

"The income, I believe."

"He does nothing but collect his annuity and drug money, I take it."

"That's all we know."

"In addition to occasionally throwing temper tantrums and assaulting the furniture."

"Joke if you want to, Mr. McLaren, but it's not pleasant living next door to such radical behavior. At least he's smart enough to know any assault would land him in jail. No, his violence is confined to his own property. We were concerned about that and about the obvious decline of his health, so Marta talked to them several times, in a friendly way. She didn't come right out and accuse him of taking drugs, but she made it sound like he may've been overdosing on aspirin or caffeine. Not that exactly." He eyed McLaren before adding, "She just told them that they should be more careful about their physical wellbeing, but they ignored her."

"How old are Herb and Danny?"

"Old enough to have more sense, but that doesn't seem much of a deterrent any more. I don't know for certain, but Herb has to be nearly fifty. And Danny is probably thirty. Or close enough to call it that. The whole lot of them act much younger, however."

"But they didn't take to your wife's friendly advice."

Alan snorted and screwed up the corner of his mouth. "It was like they never heard her. We suspect Herb, at least, continued with the drugs."

"Deaf ears."

"Or nothing between them."

"Or too greedy for the drug trade money, we assumed."

"So, if the suspected drug use or dealing continued…"

"Marta talked to the police. I don't think that got us anywhere either. Herb was never jailed."

McLaren was going to say there was such a thing as evidence and catching the suspect in the act, but instead replied, "How did this lead to the ransacking of your house?"

"As I said, we don't know whether Herb and Danny did it or not. The police couldn't prove a thing." He pressed his lips together, looking thoughtful. In the moments of silence, McLaren heard a lawn mower engine start up with a long series of coughs. As the motor caught, it settled into a lower pitch.

It was a nice street. McLaren recalled each home's neat front garden, trimmed grass and swept front steps. Well looked after and quiet, like this kitchen, crisp in its white, green, and blue color scheme. The street held no derelict buildings or litter that silently spoke of urban crime. Perhaps that's why urban crime in such peaceful neighborhoods was so startling. Even behind the most expensive façade, people were criminals. Drug use was just one example.

Alan nodded, relaxing somewhat. "Now I remember. PC Shard. Ian Shard. He talked informally to Herb, made it look like he was asking if Herb knew some bloke, like he wanted information about this other guy. *That's* how it started."

"From the talk?"

"Yes. Herb must've suspected the officer's chat was a ruse." Alan poured out some more tea and added a lump of sugar. His teaspoon clanked against the sides of the cup as he thought aloud. "You'd think Danny, at least, would try to be a more upstanding citizen, from all the stories I hear about his grandfather's glorious WWII record, the relics Danny grew up around. You'd think some of that would have…"

"But right after that your house was broken into and ransacked."

"Like I said, Mr. McLaren, we all have our suspicions it was Herb, either alone or with Danny."

71

"For revenge."

"Or as a mute warning to keep away from him."

McLaren considered the scenario for several moments. "Was anything damaged?"

"Not really. Just things pulled from drawers, the linen stripped from the bed, lamps knocked over, food from the fridge and cupboards dumped on the floor. That sort of thing."

"How did they gain entrance to your house?"

"By the bedroom window. The police told us it was forced open, probably with a crowbar."

"Would you mind showing me?"

"Not at all." Alan sounded surprised and walked toward the bedroom when McLaren said, "I'm sorry. I meant outside. Would you show me the window from the exterior?"

"Oh. Yes. It's this way."

The two men went out the back door to the north side of the house. Holly bushes, cut low to form a three-foot-tall hedge, bordered the property line several feet from Herb Millington's residence. A patch of lily of the valley claimed the area beneath the window, while bluebells, columbine and other woodland flowers fanned out toward the back garden.

"Of course," Alan said as McLaren inspected the windowsill, "we've had it repaired. It happened last June, you recall."

"Of course. I just wanted to see how far from the ground the window is, its proximity to plants or a storage shed."

"We have one." Alan pointed to the six-foot square metal outbuilding in the northwest corner at the back of the garden.

"But not near to the window to afford the vandals a privacy screen. I believe the holly hedge did that."

"Yes. They probably squatted behind it to wait until no one saw them."

"And you've no security light, I see." McLaren scrutinized both corners of the roof.

"No. We've never felt we needed them. It's been such a quiet neighborhood."

"No alarm system either, then. Or family dog."

Alan shook his head, looking rather embarrassed.

"Well, at least they didn't break into your shed to grab a ladder."

"No. We were spared that further bit of vandalism. The window provides easy entry to the house, the police reckoned."

"Yes. What is it…four feet off the ground? As you say, easy access. All the person had to do was hop inside once they forced open the window." McLaren bent slightly, looking at the brickwork. Nothing marred its surface. "Did the police find any signs of shoe scuff marks?"

"A white smear or two, yes."

"Trainers." He straightened up. "Was there any suspicion that they chose this room on purpose?"

"What do you mean?"

"Do you or the police believe the vandals were after something in the bedroom and, perhaps not being able to locate it and therefore being angry, vented their anger on the house in general? It would fit with Herb's violent outbursts."

"Oh, yes, I see. No, we thought at first that they might have been after money or credit cards or my wife's jewelry, but none were taken. Just the general vandalism."

"So no one room was targeted more than another. It's not common knowledge in the neighborhood that you have a priceless collection of stamps, let's say, and they couldn't find it."

"Good lord, no! Nothing like that. I admit I earn a nice salary, but I've never collected anything as an adult. Nothing expensive, I mean. I do have a rather extensive collection of beer memorabilia. Old tin trays, beer mats, advertising posters, pitchers and the like, in addition to several dozen bottles of different brands from around the world. But nothing in the class of rare stamps or coins. We use our money mainly on plants for the garden, and for holidays."

"Then they entered your home because this window is lower off the ground than any other, or the holly hedges afforded sufficient cover for their entry."

"I believe so. Would you like to see?" Alan led McLaren through the back garden to the south side of the house. There was no hedge, nor were there any large bushes or garden furniture. The land held only flowers and a pedestal birdbath.

"Hardly enough to hide behind," McLaren said. "The other side does offer the best entry in terms of seclusion."

"Yes," Alan said as they reentered the house. "That's what the police said, too."

Back in the kitchen, McLaren looked at the door, trying to understand why it hadn't been used as an entry point. Surely the rear of the house afforded more privacy than a side window. But the small light fixture above the door's exterior and the double locks answered his question. No one would be foolish enough to stand under a floodlight while fighting with two locks. Number twenty Dunstan Terrace had probably seemed invincible to Alan and Marta.

"The police tried to make the connection between the bedroom entry and Herb Millington."

"May I impose on your kindness for one more favor, Mr. Hughes?"

Alan's head jerked slightly. He opened his mouth, then merely nodded.

"I'm sorry if it will be painful, but I'd like to see the bedroom."

"Uh, certainly. It's just here." Alan again led the way. He opened the door and stood aside to let McLaren enter first, then slowly followed.

McLaren went to the window, raised the lower half of the casement, and leaned out. He looked at the ground near the foundation, at the near side of the hedge, and at the windowsill. Satisfied, he straightened up, turned, and asked Alan what items had been disturbed in the room.

Alan frowned for a moment. He tugged at the collar of his cotton shirt as though he had difficulty breathing, then crossed his arms on his chest. "Why, uh, I believe they yanked the clothes from the dresser drawers."

"All of them?" McLaren asked, his gaze on the large, wooden bureau. It occupied most of the wall at right angle to the bed.

"Yes. They were pulled out randomly, not lined up...you know. Only the bottom drawer contents were dumped on the floor. The other drawers had been opened and rifled, the clothes disarranged." He glanced at the window as though seeing the intruders entering the room.

"And the sheets were off the bed, I believe you said."

"Yes. Everything on the floor. Even the mattress. I guess they'd been looking beneath it for something."

"Not necessarily. Could be just plain cussedness." McLaren glanced around the room. The queen-sized bed was on the wall opposite the window, a good location to catch the breezes. An upholstered chair angled out from the corner, near the closet. The small bedside cabinet was close to the door and matched the wood of the bed. "That was disturbed too, I assume."

"Yes. They'd gone through the airing cupboard, too. Taken things off the linen shelf, shoved aside our hanging clothes. Nothing broken, though."

"Just disarray. Thanks. I've seen enough." McLaren was glad to leave the room, with its mementos of Marta's life: her photograph still propped on top of the dresser, smiling at Alan; her jewel box and perfume bottle of cut glass; a favorite straw hat, no doubt, topping one of the bed posts; a watercolor of some Mediterranean vista, done by Marta, he noticed, seeing her penciled signature.

Alan cut McLaren's burgeoning sadness short as he stopped at the baby grand piano in the front room. Its sleek, ebony side shone in the sunlight. "They did the same sort of thing in here. Cushions from the sofa, some of the pictures off the wall, a lamp knocked over." He gestured toward a tall, wrought iron lamp with an open filigree pedestal. "That Windsor chair overturned, but not broken, thank God. The ends of the curtains either were stuffed behind the sofa or laid across the back."

"Sounds like they were looking for something. The piano was undamaged?"

"Yes. On first seeing the mess I feared they might have cut the wires or poured water or something onto the soundboard, but it was fine. Easy enough to clean up." His gaze shifted to the piano as he swallowed slowly.

McLaren trailed his fingers along the instrument's top before he jammed his hand into his pocket. He nodded, glancing around the room once more. "Well, at least it wasn't too bad."

"No." Alan wiped his eyes with the back of his hand. "We got off lucky." He pressed his lips together, and McLaren wondered what constituted 'unlucky.' Alan picked up the sheet music on the piano top and pinned it against his chest as he crossed his arms. "We phoned the police, of course, and even though they couldn't prove Herb or Danny was responsible, privately we believe they did it so Marta would keep quiet in the future. A little harassment sometimes works wonders."

It was McLaren's turn to press his lips together. Obviously, he wasn't the only one with a helpful acquaintance. Someone else was being taught a lesson.

Chapter Eight

McLaren sat in his car in front of the Hughes home, fighting the all too familiar anger and sadness that filled his heart and soul. Marta Hughes had been loved; some piece of trash had taken her life, taken her from her husband and son, disposed of her in an obscene way. No one deserved to be tossed away like a sack of rubbish. His fist slammed into the upholstery of the passenger seat in his frustration. Had she died over her casino winning or was it something else, something connected to her work or her family or friends? And did the stone barn where her body was recovered have any significance? She didn't live in Elton. And according to Alan, she didn't know anyone there. Nor had she been born there.

McLaren breathed deeply while he took in the neighboring residences, his mind trying to make sense of Alan's account of their house break-in. The man had seemed surprised to find McLaren on his doorstep. But Alan was helpful, eager to relay anything that might discover Marta's murderer and bring his nightmare to a close.

Leaning his head against the car seat, McLaren rubbed his temples. The simple quest for Marta Hughes' killer was fast turning into a branched road, with nagging questions down each path. Had the ransacking of the Hughes home anything to do with

Marta's death? Was something else behind the vandalism, something Alan Hughes wasn't telling? And why had Marta stopped at her brother-in-law's house after winning at the casino? Did that hold the key to the mess?

McLaren gazed down the road. Other questions needled him. Hathersage lay the way he had come. Beyond that was Castleton. Were either or both of those places linked to Karin Pedersen's disappearance? Had she secreted the beer bottle in his car and then rung up the police? Why? She and he were strangers. But if she wasn't responsible, was it Dena?

Scratching his head, McLaren leaned forward. The houses beyond Six Mills Road petered out swiftly, giving way to the green and gray countryside of dales, mountains, streams, stone house villages, and stone walls. Why had he abandoned, even briefly, his wall work? Was it ego that whispered he could solve a cold case where equally competent police detectives had failed? Or was it something else—something deeper than ego, a need to be accepted again, to vindicate himself, to yield to the siren song of police work? To remove the blot from his name? He jammed the key into the ignition slot, started the engine, and shot away from the curb in a roar of racing motor, screeching tires, and muttered self-contempt.

Verity Dwyer, Marta Hughes' one-time coworker, was unlocking the front door of her home when McLaren parked his car opposite her house. He called to her, wanting to relieve any concern she might have. She remained by the door and waited for him to speak, her handbag securely wedged under her arm. When he had introduced himself and explained the reason for his visit, she nodded, opened the door, and led him into the house.

"So, you're investigating Marta's murder." Verity seated herself on the sofa across from him, the late afternoon sunlight on her face, and stared at him.

She's had time to master the meaning behind uttered words, McLaren thought, watching her gaze. Had time to interpret the subtle shifts in facial expressions or moods that flitted across the eyes. No doubt her time working through her community service sentence told her the truth behind the eye movements and voice inflection even when the words were lies. No wonder she's scrutinizing me, in no rush to tell me anything, not anxious to relive the horror of the past year.

McLaren shifted in the chair, content to proceed slowly, to take in her blue eyes and the freckles that splashed across her nose and cheeks, her hands that looked older than her thirty-five years, dry and calloused from rough work. Sometimes printed information was better, he thought, watching Verity's frank gaze. It doesn't lie to your face.

He inclined his head toward the wall calendar in the next room. "Your time is almost finished, I see."

Verity nodded, sighing. "I've been Xing off each day, counting down this sentence. It'll be wonderful to resume my life, as I call it. Though I don't know how many friends I'll have left. But I'll see, won't I?" She tried to smile, but only managed to look pathetic. She resettled herself in her chair. "What happened to rekindle interest in Marta's case? I thought it had gone cold."

"It has. I've been asked to do some investigation

on the side. Entirely as a private concern."

"Meaning you're not a copper."

"No, I'm not."

"But you were."

"You think so?"

"Of course! I can spot one a mile off. Even an ex-cop has an air about him. When you've been around them as much and as long as I have…" She shrugged and fluffed her shoulder-length auburn hair.

He relented, his eyes locked into her gaze. "You're right, Ms. Dwyer. I was a cop. But now I'm trying to get to the bottom of Marta Hughes' death."

"I see. A highly trained citizen." She tilted her head slightly, as though thinking through something. The refrigerator clicked on in the kitchen, filling the awkward silence. She pursed her lips before she went on. "So you have no authority, then. You can't haul me into the nick for refusing to talk to you."

"I can't. But I'm hoping you'll agree to help me."

"For the sake of justice or to help out a mate of yours who botched the case in the first place?"

"Justice is always a concern, Ms. Dwyer. It shouldn't make any difference if the injustice was directed toward a cop or a person connected to the case."

"Justice is blind, in other words, like the statue." She eyed him, perhaps trying to discern the cause behind this new probe, the motivation for his involvement. "You weren't connected with the original case, were you? I'd have remembered you."

"Oh yes?"

"Don't flatter yourself that it's because you're nice to look at. Though I *am* partial to blonds."

He laughed and leaned back in his chair. "Because you've had every one of those marked off calendar days to recall who worked on your case and who testified in court?"

It was her turn to laugh. "Something like that, yes."

"Just so I'm not one of your nightmares, that's all right."

She picked up the packet of cigarettes on the side table but made no move to slip one from the pack. Instead, she said, "Who hired you? You can't tell me you're doing this because you miss being a copper."

He hesitated, wondering himself if that were true, the questions he asked himself minutes ago resonating in his mind.

Verity supplied an answer. "Just want to be back with the boys, then. You need the adrenalin rush, the after-work beer with your mates." Her voice had hardened, as though she had lumped him with the stereotypical copper who let off steam with one-too-many beers and affairs.

Feeling the need to defend himself, McLaren said, "This isn't about me. It's about your friend. Should it make a difference who hired me? Isn't my pursuit of Marta Hughes' killer grounds enough for you?"

"Certainly it matters! If you're working for someone I think is guilty of the crime, or who Marta hated."

"You'll refuse to say anything."

"Are you working for someone like that?"

"Who would that be, Ms. Dwyer? I've just met you. I have no way of knowing whom you suspect."

"True. I forgot." She tapped the pack against her index finger and pulled out the cigarette. "I also forgot you're not a cop and might not know all the personnel or pertinent information."

"I do know you and Marta were friends as well as coworkers."

"And, being friends, I should rush to help you."

"I don't know why you shouldn't. And if there is a reason," he said as she lit the cigarette and took a puff, "that's as important as anything else you might tell me." He waited in the quiet room, looking at the framed certificates of appreciation and merit that claimed the wall in the adjoining room, studying her face as she had done his, judging her character and her hurt over her treatment at the hands of the English legal system.

A group of young children ran down the street, laughing and calling to an adult to hurry. The cigarette dangled from her fingers as she once again looked at McLaren. "You're right. Justice shouldn't be dependent on anyone. I was Marta's friend. I'll help you just as I tried to help her. Which, if you haven't heard, is how I ended up convicted of theft."

"What is the length of your sentence? I see it's up in two weeks." His eyes strayed again to the calendar and the large red, circled date a few days away.

"I received a community order for eleven months. It's been the longest months of my life, Mr. McLaren."

"I believe you." He refrained from saying it was a better sentence than serving time in jail. Verity knew that.

"I'm assigned to a homeless shelter. I do some cooking and cleaning there. Kind of fitting, don't you think?"

"In what way?"

"Marta and I worked in an animal shelter, taking in

strays and unwanted pets. I've just moved up a notch in the chain, looking after stray and unwanted people. Though some might call it a step down, I suppose."

"Tough work, that. And your sentence was due to your conviction of theft from the animal shelter."

"Yes. A stupid mistake, that, stealing the money for Marta."

"Money she didn't pay back."

"She told me she would return the money the following day." Her words came louder and faster now that the painful subject had been opened. Her hand holding the cigarette fell onto the chair's arm and she leaned forward. She practically shook as the pitch of her voice rose. "But she *didn't!* That's how the discrepancy was discovered. The organization's financial officer came by and checked the books."

"You didn't know he was coming?"

"No. It's always unannounced."

"To keep everyone on their toes."

"Or keep us honest." She colored and paused, and McLaren realized her verbal slip referred to her. "Anyway," Verity continued, "I was caught with my cash drawer short, the money missing and unexplained."

"What are we talking about? How much?" He knew from the case report, but he wanted to hear it from her, to see if she'd try to sugarcoat her guilt.

"£1,000."

"Damn."

Verity nodded and took a drag on her cigarette. "My sentiments exactly, Mr. McLaren. And I was damned. In the eyes of the financial examiner, the animal shelter higher-ups, the police, and the court."

"You said you took it."

"*Stole* it." Verity corrected his word choice and sat up straighter. It looked like she defied McLaren to challenge the truth. "Marta took it. Supposedly for twenty-four hours so she could go to the casino. Roulette was her weakness. She played fairly frequently but she usually won. She'd make incredible winnings. So when she asked for the money, I really didn't think we'd get into trouble. If she didn't win, she'd go back the following day or so and play again. She'd wind up with enough money to repay everyone's loans."

"*Everyone?* She'd done this before, this taking cash from friends or from the animal shelter's till?"

"From friends, yes. There were three or four she usually touched. But from the shelter? No. That's why I hesitated to give her the money at first. Yet, she had such a good record of winning and prompt repayment, so I finally gave it to her."

Again he asked a question he could have answered, but he wanted Verity to tell him. "Gave it to her. What does that mean? Did you have access to the office safe?"

"No. Just my own cash register. I work one specific register. The one in the gift shop. That money is my responsibility. I have the key to unlock it in the morning and then, when the day is over, I relock it. I also count up the day's transactions and balance the drawer at the end of the day."

"So, because you had this particular cash register under your jurisdiction, you could get her the money."

"It *never* dawned on me that we'd be caught!"

"That seems like a huge amount of money to have in a charity agency, if you don't mind me saying so. Is

£1,000 normal, or were you about to deposit it in the company's bank account?"

"It was a lot, which is why Marta knew to ask me. Usually all our tills carry £300. That's to make change in the store and for customers who might adopt the animals."

"Where does the other £700 come from?" He looked at Verity as though he expected her to say she always carried that amount in her handbag.

"From the back room. We hide that amount back there in case there's some emergency. It's come in handy more than once." Her voice drifted off, as though recalling her court testimony.

"How many people know about that £700? All of the staff, or just a few? Did that reserve amount ever vary?"

"I think we all knew about it. Well, all the clerks, I should say. And our boss."

"Marta's brother-in-law."

"Yes. The directive came from him. He trusted the employees and didn't want financial problems to arise. Well, you know what I mean." She colored as she looked at him.

"Did Mr. Clark mention why he set it up this way?"

"Just that he'd been in a similar situation when he first started work as a teenager and he didn't want his employees to panic as he had."

"Thoughtful chap."

"I doubt if the vet knew about the stashed money, though. He really has no need to know. He's just concerned with the health of the animals. He doesn't come out into the main area unless he takes in a sick animal."

"How many clerks are there? Exactly how many people would know about the cache?"

Verity screwed up her lips, mentally ticking off the staff. The ash from her cigarette dangled precariously over the arm of the chair. "Six, I think."

"Including Marta and you?"

"Yes. We didn't talk about it during our breaks, of course, but I think we all did. Mr. Clark made sure we all knew. For an emergency." She repeated the phrase again, as though to convince herself she hadn't actually stolen the money.

"It is always kept in the same place, I take it. Well, it would be. How else would you know where to find it if you needed it?"

"Yes. Mr. Clark had debated about the whole thing for rather a long time. He felt uneasy keeping £700 in the shelter, but he's a person who likes to be prepared."

McLaren refrained from calling him a Boy Scout and instead asked where the hiding spot was. Verity paused, mouth open, and looked at him.

"I'm not going to burgle the place, Ms. Dwyer." McLaren smiled at her apparent judgment of his honesty and need to know. "If there's any hesitation on your part, you needn't tell me."

"Don't take it personally, Mr. McLaren, but I'd rather not."

"That's fine. The place was easy to get to, though."

"Yes, but not obvious."

He thought about people hiding money beneath their bed mattresses or inside biscuit jars, and wondered briefly if the back room had an unused teapot.

"So, you see, Mr. McLaren, it all pointed to me.

Oh, the backroom money could have been stolen by any of the other clerks, but the cash from the till…"

"Pointed directly to you, yes. When was all this? I know you said you're serving an eleven month sentence, but when did you give Marta the money?"

"Third of May last year. The examiner came the 10th of May, as it turned out, and found the discrepancy in the drawer."

"But a week!" McLaren couldn't keep the surprise from his voice. "If Marta had a week to replace the money—"

"She got ill two days after she took the money, on fifth May. She had said on the third when she took the money that she'd go back to the casino in two days to play the wheel again if she didn't win that night. I remember we laughed about that because she hardly ever loses."

"And she became ill before she could return to the casino."

"Yes."

McLaren grimaced, mentally picturing the women's panic. "So Marta finally returns to the casino in June and makes her big win. And you were arrested…when?"

She smoothed the wrinkle from the sleeve of her blouse. "Fifteen June. The company's director had given me four weeks to come up with an explanation and to return the money. Of course I couldn't come up with £1,000. Not in four weeks. I barely have anything in the bank, and I'd just spent a large sum on a new roof." She flicked the ash into the ashtray on the coffee table. Some of the ash fell onto the ashtray's lip and over the edge, onto the tabletop. Verity didn't seem to notice. "I could ask anyone for the money. It was tempting, and I toyed with the idea for a while, but it was too embarrassing. What was I to say to them? I couldn't say a friend of mine had taken the money from our work place and I was covering for her."

"So you took the blame," McLaren suggested. If it were true, Verity was an exceptional friend.

"I did all the usual stuff people do when they need money. I tried to sell some things, such as my good silverware and a rare book, but it wouldn't have been enough. I suppose I should have sold my car, but…"

"They're hard to part with once you've become used to independent travel."

"Not that so much, but yes, they are nearly essential. I had a friend who was interested in it, and he came one evening to look at it. But he took nearly two weeks to give me a definite answer. By the time he refused, it was too late to advertise or find another interested party."

"You didn't tell your boss about all this? If he had known your efforts, wouldn't he have extended the payback period, especially if his sister-in-law was involved? Surely he'd know her character, which might help your defense."

She took another puff on the cigarette. "I honestly don't think it would have made any difference. Mr. Clark was bound by the board's decision. Besides, it might have added fuel to the office gossip that Marta got special treatment from him. I do admit I was fairly frantic by then. It felt as though the walls were closing in on me and I would never survive a prison term. I was more scared of the prisoners than of standing trial and the remainder of my life, being branded a criminal and not knowing how friends and acquaintances would greet me once I finished my time. Part of it's the fear of the unknown, I realize. And seeing what hard prison time has done to people. Many come out bitter and angry, having no faith in anyone or anything, finding no joy in the simple things they once did. But part of it was the complete feeling of being alone that never left me, day or night. I'm a rather timid woman, as you might guess, Mr. McLaren, and I've never been particularly outgoing or joined many groups. As a consequence, my friends number a mere dozen or so. And of those, I have only one or two really close friends."

"And they couldn't help you raise the money."

"I didn't ask. They didn't know about any of this until the trial began. You think it's funny, I know. Strange that I wouldn't talk to a friend. I learned early, Mr. McLaren, to keep my hurts and disappointments to myself. No one likes a whiner."

"Hardly whining, Ms. Dwyer. This was your reputation, the rest of your life."

"Even so, I told no one other than my brother."

"And he didn't help." He said it more harshly than he intended, his voice cracking from the stupidity of the entire episode.

"No, he didn't." She raised her hand, the cigarette smoke curling above her head. It drifted on the faint breeze coming through the open window, catching the sunlight before fading against the blue-gray backdrop of the room's walls. "I know you're already judging him, Mr. McLaren, but please don't. You're wrong."

"I'm sorry. I didn't mean to pronounce a verdict against your family, especially when I don't know him."

"It's natural, I know. As I said, you're wrong. My brother couldn't help simply because he's in prison."

The surprise registered on McLaren's face. He blinked and opened his mouth slightly.

"Wealstun."

He cleared his throat. "West Yorkshire."

"Yes. I won't bore you with his crime, sentencing, or history. They're public record and can be looked up. But now perhaps you'll understand why I couldn't ask him."

Or your friends. The newspapers would have had a feeding frenzy if word leaked out that a convicted criminal's sister was charged with theft. And from a charity!

"In spite of how this all turned out, the company's director is a kind person. I think he didn't want to go through the arrest and trial rigmarole, but he was being pressured by the board."

"But of course, £1,000 is a lot of money to come up with. Not just for you, Ms. Dwyer, most people."

She nodded and exhaled slowly. "It was a nightmare. I was guilty of theft, I assumed the rights as owner of the money when I gave it to Marta, but I couldn't tell my boss or the director about it." She rotated her cigarette, as though looking for something. "I just remember vividly when the police came and handcuffed me. God!" She avoided his eyes, even now humiliated by the event.

"And the date of your trial and sentencing?"

"In July. I am grateful for the community order instead of jail time, of course, but..."

"Of which you got eleven months. Yes, it's better than breaking rocks." He realized rather belatedly that he broke rocks nearly every day. The difference was that he was a free person and chose to break rocks to repair stone walls, whereas Verity…He coughed, trying to gloss over the verbal *faux pas*. "Where was Marta through all this? I assume she knew about your arrest and the trial. It must have gone on for a bit. Why didn't she speak up?"

"That was one of the things I had to work through emotionally. I *still* have to work through. I felt betrayed at first. Marta was my friend. She should have spoken up, but she didn't."

"Because…"

"Marta's husband is a big man in the community. He holds some senior management position at National Westminster Bank. She didn't say anything because she didn't want the story to get out."

"Wife of bank vice president, or whatever, involved in stealing money."

"Exactly. It would have ruined his reputation."

McLaren blinked. "Never mind yours, right?"

"I guess husbands are more important than friends."

"Or at least the truth." He shifted his position in the chair, feeling uneasy with the bent of the conversation. It echoed the tragic event that forced him from the police force. "So where in this timeline is Marta killed…or, at least, disappear?"

"I'll never forget. A Friday night, 11 June."

"And you were arrested on 15 June."

"Yes."

"Damn."

"Exactly. I had four days to get even with Marta for her silence, to kill her and hide her body."

## Chapter Nine

"Why weren't you arrested for murder, then?" McLaren let the tension relax between them before he spoke. "Seems like you had motive. Look what she did to your life." He paused, his eyes again on the calendar in the kitchen. Of all the tales of injustice he'd heard, this was close to the top. His gaze sought her face again and he asked rather hesitantly, "Or did something happen later?"

"No. Besides, I had an unbreakable alibi the night of Marta's death."

"Glad to hear it. What was it, if I may ask?"

"I was in church. Mending hymnals. There were about a dozen of us, I guess. Anyway, the vicar was there, too. They all swore in court that I was there."

"But if Marta wasn't found until ten days later, how did your one evening's alibi serve you?"

"Linnet had gone with her to the casino in Nottingham. Oh, do you know Linnet?"

"Yes. I've spoken with her."

Verity nodded and took another drag on her cigarette. She exhaled into the air above McLaren's head. "It took Marta a while to get over her illness in May. I never did know exactly what she had. But she didn't just bounce back like you do with a sore throat. So it wasn't until 11 June that Linnet and Marta found the time to go back to the casino. Of course the police were interested in when they both left. They were trying to set up some sort of time schedule for that night. Anyway, Linnet told the police the night's events. The time was confirmed by the CCTV tape in the car park. It shows Marta's and Linnet's cars leaving."

"That establishes she was alive then. But what about the time of her death? If her body wasn't found for ten days…"

"She never made it inside her home that night. Alan rang up the police after he had found the car in their drive. He then rang up Marta's brother-in-law to see if Marta had stopped overnight there, for some reason."

"But the car."

"I know. But Alan didn't know if Marta went off with someone, or someone followed her and kidnapped her. So Alan called Neal. At least he could start eliminating possible places to check for her."

"Neal lives in Matlock and is her brother-in law," McLaren said his thoughts aloud, getting the timetable and people straight in his head.

"Yes. Of course, Marta wasn't there. That's when Alan got very worried and phoned the police."

"And since the pathologist cannot possibly establish time of death from her body condition, being outside for ten days or so…"

"That's all the police could really go on, having no witnesses. At least none who came forward. We just had that rough timetable of when she was last seen. You see." She leaned forward slightly, tinting her conversation more as a confession than as information. "They couldn't prove I killed her because they couldn't establish when she died. It could have been 11 June, the night she disappeared, or 16 June, or any date in between. And by then I'd been arrested."

"15 June."

She leaned back, looking sad. "Exactly."

"Five days is more than enough time to murder someone." He said it rather apologetically, as though he wished he could alter the facts.

"The police tried to say I could have met up with Marta somewhere later that night and killed her, but they had no evidence. It was all just speculation."

"Where was her body found?" McLaren had the information from the inquest report, but he wanted to see if Verity's account was the same.

Her voice timber changed and the words came slower and softer, as though she were again feeling the pain of her friend's death. "Near Elton. In a ditch near the road. It was awful. She was pretty badly decomposed by then. The weather and animals…" She broke off, her face devoid of color.

"Do you know if Marta had friends in Elton?"

"Why was she found there, in other words?"

"It would give me a lead if she knew someone in the village."

"Sorry. Haven't a clue. But, then, I didn't know a lot of her friends. I didn't mingle with them. She and I were merely friendly at the shelter. I hardly ever go anywhere, in fact, so I'm not the best person to ask about her friends, either living in or out of Elton."

"Where were you after the hymnal session was finished? Where were you the rest of the night?"

"We finished up around half past ten, I believe. Close to it, anyway."

"Marta and Linnet left the casino…at what time?"

"Just about eleven on the dot."

"Thirty minutes difference. Have you an alibi for eleven?"

"Just that I was home."

"Anyone see you?"

"No."

"Probably didn't matter to your case."

"But I reported my neighbor's dog. He was barking loudly, incessantly, and had broken out of their back garden. He was running around in my flowers, chasing a rabbit or something. I tried to catch him but I couldn't. My neighbors weren't home, so I couldn't get their help. Some few minutes later, at half past eleven, I think, I heard the dog somewhere down the street, in a fight with some other dog. That's when I called the police."

"And they would have a log of your call. Right. Well, the time constraint and distance work in your favor. You couldn't have driven down to Nottingham at half past ten, found Marta, killed her, and been back by half past eleven to complain about the dog." Even if someone else phoned from your house, he thought, there'd still be a record of it. It would have been played at the inquest and the case would have taken a different turn.

"Do you have any ideas yet, Mr. McLaren? Do you think you know who might have killed Marta?"

He smiled at her enthusiasm. "I've just taken on the case, Ms. Dwyer. I need more than a few hours."

She nodded, suddenly sober.

"Perhaps *you* have an idea. Do you know of anyone who might have held a grudge against her or wished her dead?"

"Oh, yes!"

She said it so quickly, so forcibly, that McLaren blinked. "Really?"

"Yes. The neighbor of hers. Herb Millington. She told me about talking to the constable about the suspected drug dealing."

"And you think Herb killed her? If he did ransack her house, it's a long way from mere vandalism to murder." His voice held both skepticism and astonishment. "Why do you believe it was Herb?"

"Because he kept coming on to Marta and she wouldn't have anything to do with him. She loved Alan deeply, so she wouldn't risk her marriage by having an affair with Herb Millington."

"Perhaps not intentionally, but a lot of people believe they'll be faithful for their entire marriage and then suddenly they're involved with someone."

Verity shook her head. Her fingers fumbled with her cigarette, as though she were deciding whether to put it down. "You didn't know Marta. She had an iron will. She wouldn't have done such a thing. Especially not with someone like Herb Millington."

"Aside from the suspected drug dealing, which in itself may set many people against him, what was wrong with Herb Millington?"

"Have you seen him, talked to him?"

"Not yet."

She shuddered and scrunched her lips. "When you do, you'll know what I mean." She hunched her shoulders and took a drag on the cigarette.

"So, what you're saying, then, is that Herb Millington killed Marta because she refused his sexual overtures, correct?"

"Could have done. He gets mad, shoots her..."

Which, if true, would confirm Alan's assessment of Herb's violent outbursts.

"I realize it's not as good as a written threat or a string of police complaints," Verity continued, "but stranger things have happened."

McLaren nodded, picturing the fight. If it had taken place in Marta's home, there would have been blood from the head wound. Had Alan found it, cleaned it up, kept it quiet for some reason? Or had the fight taken place in Herb Millington's home, or outside somewhere? It could have happened. "And you know about Millington's sexual advances because you were over at her house once and witnessed it?"

"Not at all. But we were coworkers. We talked a lot."

"About that?"

"Yes. And about other things. You know. Girl talk."

McLaren knew what she meant. He'd grown up in a family of women and he'd been engaged. He'd heard enough discussions—serious and comedic—about husbands, boyfriends, girlfriends, jobs, diets, bad haircuts, actors, kids, school grades, health food, and love to last him until he turned one hundred. He could imagine very well Verity and Marta talking about Herb Millington—pro and con.

"I always wondered if she was killed for her money." Verity's voice had taken on the heavy, slow manner of someone waking from a deep dream and still held in its spell. She rose from her chair, went to the bookcase, and grabbed a photograph. Three women grinned from the confines of a gold-toned metal frame:

Marta, Verity, and another woman stood side by side, cheek to cheek, their arms around each other's shoulders. Best friends, enjoying a joke. The photo had been sharing part of the shelf with a half dozen small, ceramic animals. They were lifelike, painstakingly detailed. Several books on raptors, European badgers, and wildflowers filled the rest of the shelf. She angled the photo toward McLaren. "Funny, isn't it? I feel closer to Marta now than when we worked together. Why is that? Does it have something to do with guilt?"

"Why should you feel guilty? You've taken the blame for the missing money. Surely you don't wish you had been the murder victim instead of Marta."

"No." She said it slowly, almost begrudgingly, as she stared at the picture. "At least…No, I don't know. At times I'm all right. I go about my day, resigned to my lot and making plans for when this all ends. But there are other times when I think about Marta and how her husband and son must ache from her death. She had a good many friends, you know. More than I'll ever have. They must miss her dreadfully."

"So to ease or erase their suffering, you think you should have been killed."

Verity swept dust from the shelf before gently returned the photo to its spot. "Sounds absurd when you talk about it. But no, I wouldn't go that far. I've no death wish."

"What is it, then?"

"I don't know. Maybe it's that she was so young and warm, and funny and full of life. Forty-five is awfully young to die, isn't it?"

"Most people leave unfinished dreams, Ms. Dwyer, if that's what you're thinking. Even if you live to be a hundred, there will probably be something you've not done that you wish to. Don't let Marta's brief life and her incomplete works haunt you. You had nothing to do with any of this other than be a pawn. It seems to me that you've been more than giving." Who else would make your sacrifices, he thought. Taking the blame, keeping silent.

"I told Alan just before the trial began that I wasn't going to jail for Marta," Verity said finally. "I had taken that money, I admit, but I wasn't going to be saddled with suspicions of her death, no matter how good my motive was. Those suspicions would cling to me the rest of my life. I said I wasn't taking the blame for any of it."

"What did Alan say?"

"Nothing much. He just looked at me with those big brown eyes of his, threw his arm around his son's shoulders like some talisman or bulwark or challenge, and said he was sorry but he couldn't believe Marta had anything to do with the stolen money. What a laugh. Like he couldn't believe Marta was capable of anything like that."

"He didn't know about her gambling, then."

"Sure, he knew, but not about its frequency. It was like she was some perfect little saintly statue, perched atop a pedestal. Only her plaster façade had developed cracks that he couldn't see. Or he chose to overlook." She took another drag on her cigarette. The cloud of smoke hung in front of her but she ignored it. "I liked Marta. We'd been close friends. Or so I thought until this happened. Until her silence."

"But she didn't explain why you'd given her the money," McLaren suggested.

"No. Other than that little squeak, she didn't defend me in any way."

"From what you just told me about Alan's response, Marta didn't say a thing to him about the money, either."

"If she did, Alan wasn't admitting in public that his wife was involved in a theft."

"Nice couple."

Verity snorted. "Not as bad as Bonnie and Clyde or Rosemary and Fred West," she said, recalling the serial killers. "But bad enough for me."

"Especially when you considered her a friend."

"And then she repays my friendship that way."

"Hard to take."

"Harder than Alan being momentarily embarrassed at his precious bank, yes, or having to find another job if his boss looks at him funny."

"A slight inconvenience when measured against your situation."

"I guess it just showed their true colors, which hurt me deeply." She crushed out the cigarette. "I suppose the suspicion of revenge could've landed me in prison, for her murder, I mean. Lord knows I had motive enough for revenge, but I didn't kill her. I wish I knew who did."

McLaren let the silence well up between them. Revenge was a powerful motive for many crimes. He struggled with it himself.

"I've had a lot of time to think about all this, Mr. McLaren. Well, you do, don't you, when you're serving a sentence?" The street had grown quiet. No traffic drove down the road, no dogs barked, no birds twittered at the windowsill or in the trees. The world seemed to be listening for Verity's thoughts. "It's kind of hard to forget. If there hadn't been all that money, well, maybe none of this would have happened. What do you think?"

"Do you mean the money from the animal shelter?"

"No. The money she won that night at the casino."

"I thought she lost. I thought that was the reason she couldn't put the money back in your cash register, the reason that led to—" He nodded toward the kitchen and the calendar.

"My year of new experiences. Sorry. I didn't make it clear. No, I was talking about the night in June when she won, the night she was murdered."

"Eleven June."

"She'd won a huge amount of money. I know about it because it was brought up at the trial. The croupier testified as to her winning, a player at the table also testified, the cashier testified, and Linnet testified. They all remarked as to the amount. It was the same in each person's telling: £253,560."

"A lot," McLaren agreed, exhaling loudly.

"More than several year's salaries, and earned in a moment with a flick of the croupier's wrist and Marta's positioning of her chips. Must be nice."

"I've heard of big wins before, but rarely of a win that large. She must have been over the moon."

"I suppose so. I never got to ask her." She let the implication hang in the air between them.

"If she was killed that night, what happened to the money she won?"

"Presumably stolen. It wasn't found on her body."

Chapter Ten

McLaren was nearly home, approaching Somerley from the copse of birch and willow that sheltered the remains of an old stone barn. It'd been a full day and he had a lot to consider—not only with the case but also with Dena and Karin. Was it coincidence that these two personal segments had cropped up the moment he'd taken on this cold case? He'd left his mobile phone number with Verity, getting her solemn assurance she'd ring in case she thought of anything else. Which he hoped she would—she seemed a reliable witness besides being a person who had a stake in what had happened. That she appeared to hold no grudge against Marta, despite her eleven months community service order and lost job at the animal shelter, told a lot about her character. So yes, he was hoping she would come up with something he could use when she'd had a chance to think.

He was considering the disappearance of the casino money when he turned down Somerley's main street. Dena's red MG was parked opposite the pub. He stopped behind hers, locked his car doors, and strode into the courtyard. She was sitting at a wrought iron table, writing a letter, but stopped and looked up at him.

"Thirsty? Or just thought of a good retort from last night's conversation?" She shoved a strand of her hair behind her ear. It caught the golden rays of the early evening sun, bringing out the hints of chestnut coloring in its brunette hue. It was also fragrant with the scent of her shampoo: honeysuckle. Like the soap and perfume she used.

McLaren stared at its beauty, nearly drowning in her scent.

"Well? Am I supposed to be intimidated by your strong, silent stance, or is this a game of charades and I'm to guess what you're portraying? Rock of Gibraltar, right? Or a statue of Adonis. It can't be that you're tongue-tied, Michael. I've heard you rabbit on about cases."

"For God's sake, Dena."

"Well, that's a start. Maybe not as nice as 'Hi, how are you?' but it's something. You're probably rusty. No one to talk to but your pile of rocks. Not that you ever were a smashing conversationalist, but you could always talk about police work. It was just the personal topics, the unleashing of your emotions that you couldn't handle. Are you any better at that now? Had any practice standing in front of the bathroom mirror?"

He stared down at her, feeling pain and anger. "Why do I, or any copper, get crucified and criticized for the very traits that make us good cops? We're taught from Day One that we must show no emotion on duty, that we must wear a public face in order to be seen to be in control of any situation."

"I've heard your recital, Michael. Your safety and your career are on the line if you lose control. *Any* control. And the damned list is endless! Control of your emotions, the victim's emotions. Control of the traffic, people, the crime scene. Calm down, submit to orders, submit to authority, don't let the suspect know you're scared or repulsed or angry or sad or humiliated. You'll lose your power."

"Those aren't just words, Dena. They're what we have to remember if we're to keep the floodgates closed on emotions that could harm us. We've seen it all so we've experienced it all: anger, pity, pride, excitement, revulsion, fear, cowardice, envy, hate. But we keep it beneath our public face so we can do our job because the victim is counting on us to handle the situation. We can't cry and effectively do our job, for Christ's sake! We can't turn our feelings off and on like a water spigot."

"I know, Michael. I've experienced it."

He paused, aware that he had been implying he was still part of the 'we' and 'our' he had just mentioned, aware again of the honeysuckle scent of her, the dark eyelashes that cast shadows on her eyes. "We...we live in a world of orders, Dena. If we're not giving an order to someone, we're receiving orders from the top brass."

A phrase of a song slipped outside as a waiter entered the pub. When it had grown quiet again, Dena said rather reluctantly, "I understand that. But it's more than that. I can't get close to you! You've put up a wall around yourself."

"If I have, it's nothing personal. It's left over from my old job."

"So you want me to smile and just take your orders and love your silent, stand-offish attitude."

"Of course not. But you should know that I'm trying to learn how to do it." He looked at her, wanting her to say she realized his dilemma, that she had been too demanding in wanting him to pour out his feelings to her. But she merely stared at the table, her eyes lowered, her fingers tracing the rim of her glass, as though she were considering something.

A lifetime passed before she spoke. Her voice hadn't softened in those few moments; the edge was still there, a sign of her frustration and pain. She shifted in her chair so she squarely faced him. "Fine. Smashing. Whatever you say, Michael. I'm tired of it all." She laid down her pen but kept her fingers on top of it. "I repeat, are you thirsty? You want a beer?" She eyed him when he grabbed the back of a chair. "You're awfully dressed up. Trousers, cambric shirt, tie. You quit early from work? Must have done. No stone dust in your hair, no work boots. What's the matter?" She eyed him, concern evident in her brown eyes.

"Mind if I sit down?" He remained standing until she nodded, then he pulled out the chair. The wrought iron legs screeched against the flagstone paving. He lifted the chair for the remainder of the way and then set it down, angling it toward her. "No, I won't have anything. You're drinking wine."

The mundane observation startled her. "Uh, yes. I always do."

"You drank a beer once, I recall."

"Did I?" She screwed up her mouth, clearly puzzled at the subject. "Yes, I did. At your birthday party. But it was a shandy."

"Still, you did have a beer once. The night of my folk group's first appearance. A Bass."

"What a memory! Fine, I had a beer. That once. And I disliked it. Is this why you're here? To see if I've developed a taste for beer?"

"Actually," he said, his voice softer, "I just spotted

your MG and thought I'd talk to you."

"Was it something I said last night? I haven't seen you for a year, Michael. Not since you left your job."

"I know. I'm sorry."

"About what? Not seeing me, or leaving your job?" The sheet of stationery rustled in a breath of wind. Dena set her mobile phone on it.

"Both. It's just that—"

"You've been hurt. I *know* that! So does everyone near to you: your parents, your sister, your brother-in-law, your friend Jamie. We know what you went through and we feel for you. We always will. You got a rotten deal. But there has to be an end to your wound-licking. You have to shake it off and get on with your life. I've waited for a year, hoping for an overture of love."

He pulled in the corner of his mouth and looked past her shoulder, staring at the church tower at the end of the street. The sunlight glanced off the brass cross topping the steeple and tinted the gray stones gold. A magpie floated down from the half-closed bell louvers and settled on a bough of a stately oak.

"If that's too strong a word, an overture of friendship, then. You can't keep your feelings and yourself walled up forever. You can't live like that. You are a warm, caring person. At least, you used to be. And I believe you still are, deep inside. That warmth and caring drove you into police work in the first place, Michael. But you can't become stony and unfeeling like those damned stone walls of yours."

"Were you in Castleton this morning?" He had shifted his gaze so that he now looked at her face, judging the truth in her eyes.

107

"Pardon?" Her eyebrow arched. "What's Castleton got to do with—"

"A lot. At least, it could. I need to know. Were you in Castleton?"

"Are you serious?"

"Very."

"We were talking about you and your feelings and your life from here on out."

"And my feelings and my life, and our relationship, if it's to continue or improve or get back to where it was…"

"Depends on Castleton this morning. Honestly, Michael!" She picked up the wine and took a sip before replying. "I don't know what you want. Will you believe my answer?" Her gaze shifted to his eyes. They were dark and unreadable except for the suggestion of desperation. She set down the glass, rather frustrated. "This really means a lot, doesn't it?"

He nodded, not trusting his voice.

"Well, I don't know what you want."

"I want the truth, Dena. Just that."

"That's all I've ever given you, Michael. From the first day we met. And when I fell in love with you, I told you so we wouldn't be playing games. It's not fair to play games with someone's emotions."

"About this morning…"

She took a deep breath and leaned forward so that she was closer to him. "No. I wasn't in Castleton." She watched as he slowly let out his breath. "I don't know whether I've helped or hindered my cause with you, but I wasn't in Castleton. Will you tell me why you wanted to know? You weren't involved in a hit and run, were you?" She angled her head, trying to see his car.

"It *was* a hit and run, Dena, but not that sort." He stood up and looked down at her.

"You're going? Just like that, without telling me anything? Have I said something to anger you?"

He stared at her, expressionless.

"What happened in Castleton that matters so much? Won't you tell me?" She held out her hand. "Please. Tell me. I can't help you if I don't know what's troubling you."

"You want to help me?"

"Of course!"

"Even after all this time, after how you felt last night?"

"That was anger talking last night. I wouldn't have called if I didn't feel something toward you."

"But love turns into hate sometimes. Just pick up a newspaper or listen to a television news program. There are dozens of stories about spousal abuse and murder."

"And what happened in Castleton... Should that lead me to murder you? Or you murder me?" She added the statement quickly as he took a deep breath.

"No. That's extreme."

"Then what?"

"Just a little mystery I have to solve, that's all. Good night, Dena."

"This isn't the end, is it?" There was urgency in her question as she called after his retreating figure. "You're not running out on me again."

"I'll be around." He turned toward her, his hands in his trousers pockets.

"So will I, Michael. At the same phone number and the same street address."

"Just so I don't hit and run again in *your* life,

right?" He wished her good night again and left.

He got into his car. Why would she put the beer bottle in my car when I made it plain last night that I didn't want her around? The last rays of sun hit the west-facing roof tiles, ignited a house's brass weather vane in brilliant ochre and red, and shimmered through the tops of the trees. There was at least another hour of sunlight on the hills, but here in the valley the shadows were already forming and it would be dark soon. He turned his car onto the road to his house, just beyond the village proper, the questions and suspicions crowding his mind. Why would she get tangled up with someone who doesn't want her? It made no sense.

McLaren passed the last house in the string of wall-to-wall residences along the road's northern side. A light burned in the front room, ready for the twilight. He entered the smaller lane that led to his house, a narrow strip of black among the greens and browns and grays of the landscape. As he emerged into the clearing, the limestone rock face on his left reflected the sun's light with a near-blinding intensity. It was a relief when his car gained the gloom of the wood again.

He was rounding the bend where the wood was its densest. A sliver of light glanced off the water that fell from the rocky crevice dozens of stories above. The pool where the water collected was deep and cold, inviting to animals and small boys. He glanced at it, the memories of summer swims sharp in his mind, then quickly jerked the wheel. A car raced from the leafy darkness, its nearness frightening. McLaren jammed on the brakes, steering the car as far to the left as possible. As the sickening sound of metal scraped against stone, a flash came toward him. A horn blared. A moment later a beer bottle slammed into his door and crashed onto the road. He jerked his head to his right. The other car disappeared in a cloud of dust.

He took a deep breath, then slowly got out of his car. Dust hung in the air like the questions crowding his mind. He covered his mouth, trying not to breathe, but the dust seeped into this nose and mouth. Coughing, he pulled open the door and sat inside with the windows rolled up until the dust dissipated. When he finally looked at the front of his car, he shook his head. He'd braked within centimetres of a massive oak tree. But the car's passenger side hadn't escaped so luckily. It was nestled against the cliff face.

He slowly walked to the far side of his car, his head lowered, searching the ground. Near the rear of his car, several yards back, he found what he wanted. He picked up a rock and judged its weight, much as he did when working on stone walls. The rock eclipsed his hand. Curling his fingers around the rock, he walked several dozen yards farther up the road in the direction from which the other driver had come. Tire tracks showed plainly on the damp patch of earth near the bend. They were the only marks on its otherwise clean surface. The driver hadn't even tried to stop or swerve.

McLaren strode back to the center of the road opposite his car. He didn't attempt to cap his anger. He ran several feet, his right hand slightly behind him, his left shoulder leading, as a thrower revving up for the launch of a javelin. He threw the rock after the long-departed car. The rock arched into the air, clipped a few leaves from low-hanging branches, then dropped onto the tarmac several hundred yards down the road.

He drove slowly home, anger at odds with the

confusion that tried to make sense of the incident. The accident, he could understand. The road was narrow and curved at that point. It was fairly dark and hard to see. But why throw a beer bottle? Was it related to the bottle incident earlier today?

He parked his car in the wide space off-center of his driveway, put some leftover fish and chips in the microwave to heat, and rang up his mate, police detective Jamie Kydd.

Chapter Eleven

"The damn thing about this," McLaren said when Jamie answered his phone, "is that I didn't get the registration number on the damned car." Having given his friend the details of the incident he was now releasing his anger and frustration between his gulps of beer.

"I would've thought your car's condition would've been the worst part." Jamie ran his fingers through his short-cropped light brown hair and settled back into the upholstered chair..

"It *is* scratched." McLaren reluctantly admitted the car's condition as he set the bottle down with a thud. "A minor dent to the left front wing, but nothing serious."

"And it's drivable."

"If it weren't, I'd still be running after the berk."

"And you'd smash his face in when you catch up with him, I know."

McLaren's grunt acknowledged his agreement.

"Did you get a look at the car or see any occupants?"

He hesitated, aware he would sound like the majority of victims and witnesses he'd interviewed during his police career. At Jamie's urging, he finally said, "It was a Mercedes coupe. A dark color. Green, I think. Yeah, a hunter green. I don't think it was navy blue or black. Registration number begins YV. That's all I could get. I think there was someone in the backseat. I think *he* threw the bottle."

"The backseat? Implying there were three or more people in the car?"

"Because he was in the back and not in the front passenger seat?"

"You don't think he was deliberately sitting in the back just so he could toss the bottle at you?"

"Well…"

"That implies it was premeditated, Mike!, what've you been doing?"

"What do you mean?"

"To warrant this? Have you made an enemy of someone?"

"I've been out of the job for a year now, Jamie."

"You think those thugs you sent away will forget you just because you're no longer a cop?"

"A year's awfully long to hold a grudge and do something about it. Besides, if you don't remember, I was stationed in Staffordshire. I now reside in Derbyshire. That's a hell of a big distance between the station and my house."

"And you moved back to Derbyshire on purpose, I know."

"Yeah. For just this sort of thing. So none of those toe rags could find me."

"Well, unless some farmer is upset at the way you mended his stone wall, *someone's* mad and looking for revenge. What's with this beer bottle episode, anyway? You still think it's related to that walker this morning?"

McLaren grabbed the beer, looked at it, screwed up his mouth, and set it down again. He needed a clear head to sort out everything. "I don't know. That's why I phoned."

"The impartial outsider looking at this unemotionally."

"I thought perhaps something would stand out."

"Like, you forgot that the hiker was drinking a Duvel when you stopped to assist her."

"Nothing that expensive." McLaren recalled the price of the Belgian ale. "But something like that, yes. I've got a lot on my mind right now."

"Well, unless you haven't told me something, I can't see how this is connected with your cold case. Probably just coincidence."

"Don't give me that, Jamie. You know my opinion of coincidence."

"But things do happen. And the beer bottle's not part of your cold case."

"Which is another reason I needed to talk." He speared a chip, now barely more than lukewarm, with his fork. He didn't care particularly what he ate, as long as he could fill his stomach. Breakfast was a long time ago.

"I'm all ears."

"I had hoped you'd be part brain, but I'll let that pass."

"Fine. Shoot."

"Good word choice."

"What, shoot? You weren't shot at too, were you?"

McLaren shook his head. There was no mistaking the anxiety in his friend's voice. "No. I'm referring to the cold case. Marta Hughes murdered and dumped along the roadside."

"Sure. So what do you want? Yes, I know Elton's in B Division and I'm in B Division, but I didn't work

115

on that case, Mike. There were other things that kept me busy last June."

"I know. I just thought you could get your hands on some information for me."

The silence at the other end of the phone grew uncomfortable and McLaren was about to apologize when Jamie said, "What kind of information? If it's something about running a car through the police national computer…"

"No. Nothing so risky." He pushed the bottle away from him and forked another chip. PNC checks were strictly controlled, monitored internally by the Force. PNC use for anything other than official use resulted in officers being sacked. It was a chance and ramification he would never ask Jamie to take. He laid the fork back on the plate. "You've got access to the police reports."

"Yes…" His answer sounded wary.

"I'd like to know about the place her body was found, the exact location."

"Are you daft?"

McLaren seemed not to hear Jamie. He continued. "How far out from Elton, on the left or the right side of the road? Where was she found precisely? If you can't get me a copy of the photos—" He held the phone away from his ear as Jamie's yelp boomed over the receiver. "Let me know exactly. And I'd like the pathology report. *And* the biologist's, if you can wrangle that, too." He paused as Jamie snorted, "You'll give me a few minutes to rustle this up, I hope."

"Whenever you get it is fine."

"Thanks." Jamie exhaled loudly, as if he already imagined the swift boot out the door if he were caught looking up the information.

"Just don't lose your job over it."

"I don't intend to. Uh, Mike?"

"Yeah?"

"Be careful, will you?"

"I always am."

What Jamie didn't say was that McLaren had not been careful the night of his altercation with Charlie Harvester. McLaren was more than aware of that.

Jamie looked up from his notepad. "The lads did a thorough search of the area. I don't know what you'll find there now, but I'll ring you back when I've got the info for you."

"I just hope our boys in blue overlooked something."

McLaren was running, his legs painful to move, his strides agonizingly slow as he struggled his way through the mass of beer bottles that had somehow filled The Hanoverian Hotel lobby. He had just reached for the hit-and-run driver when his bedside phone jerked him awake.

He groped for the phone in the darkness, knocking over the bottle of aspirin and sending a book thudding to the floor. The ringing guided his search and after several seconds his fingers closed around the receiver. He leaned toward the bedside table, throwing off the bed sheet, and answered even before the mouthpiece was against his lips.

There was no answer. The line was dead.

Grumbling that some people should learn to dial more carefully, he hung up the phone and lay down. The sounds of the night seeped into his room—bleats of sheep, the bark of a fox, the faint purr of a car motor, the yowl of a cat. He turned over on his side and went back to sleep.

The moon hadn't wandered much in its westward path when the jangling phone wakened him again. This time he sat up and grabbed the receiver on the third ring. His terse "Yeah?" was answered by silence.

He barked his response again, and again there was no reply.

Slamming the receiver back onto the phone, McLaren cursed the unknown caller and looked around the darkened room for something to throw. The book was on the floor, out of reach. He needed the two pillows, so they weren't considered. Then he glanced at the alarm clock. Its luminous dial stated it was 2:45. Hell of a time for someone to be making calls, he thought as he fell back onto the mattress. His head hit the pillows, sending a soft 'whoosh' into the room.

Was someone deliberately harassing him? He was ex-directory, so either someone had randomly dialed his number or the person knew him. He would have named Dena, but in light of today's talk he was certain she wouldn't do that. So who was calling? And why?

He rolled onto his side again, punching the pillow so he could see out the window. The land lay quiet and dark, devoid of the earlier night noises. Everything beneath heaven was still and slumbering, it seemed, and McLaren shut his eyes, trying to do the same.

Minutes later he gave it up as a bad job and leaned against the headboard. The caller had to be connected to something currently happening in his life; no one would wait a year for revenge. Unless he'd just been released from prison…

McLaren stared into the blackness outside his window, more dense and real than the gloom inside his house. He had enemies in prison—what copper didn't? But for someone to find out where he lived, what car he drove, that suggested tenacity and intelligence. Or a connection inside the police department.

But what copper would turn on another copper like this? Who would betray him to a con?

The answer screamed at him with all the certainty of a slamming cell door. Charlie Harvester.

McLaren sat up, his body rigid, his heart pounding. He pulled a pillow to his chest and wrapped his arms around it, squeezed it, wishing for the first time in a year that it were Dena. The room seemed to pulse in rhythm to the blood pounding in his temples. He fumbled for the glass of water beside the clock, then drank it quickly. Wiping the back of his hand against his mouth, he tried to think. Even Harvester wouldn't do that. They may have hated each other's guts, but to set up something like this, something that smacked of revenge, after more than a year…

He set the glass back on the nightstand and got up. Tossing the pillow onto the bed, he glanced at the clock. 3:03. Perhaps he could sleep late. If he ever got back to sleep. Funny thing was, he never had trouble sleeping when he worked on stone walls.

Perhaps because there was nothing threatening about them or because he knew what to expect. Like the wall he had been working on when Linnet had interrupted. He had sighted down the wall's length, making certain the addition was in keeping with the wall's cant. Not an edge had ruptured the overall symmetry. Except for the absence of lichen wallpapering the stone face or moss wedging into minute recesses between stones, his work was

119

indistinguishable from the original wall, blending into its ancient age. Was that part of the attraction he found with the work, cherishing the link to the original waller? Perhaps he, too, had been an outsider as McLaren was. Perhaps the original craftsman had found his comfort in sun, wind, and kestrels soaring overhead, had shunned other men's company, wanting only to get on with his life and job. Which was what McLaren wanted right now. Not dredging up recollections of injustices until your emotional wounds lay raw once more.

He had thought them buried in the year he'd been here, this desperate attempt to keep his soul and body together when he left Staffordshire to return to his home village in Derbyshire and to the work of a stone wall builder. He would never want for jobs, he had told himself. Not with the thousands of miles of walls crisscrossing the county. And even if the work was back breaking, it suited his mood. More than suited his personality. A loner, a maverick cop didn't chase after the camaraderie of the workplace office.

The mantel clock struck the quarter hour and McLaren stretched, the faceless builder fading from his gaze, Harvester's face grinning from the darkness.

He walked to the window and stood there, the cool breeze chilling his feverish body. Charlie Harvester. He hadn't thought of the man in ages; he didn't even know where he was. The first few months after McLaren left the job, he heard snippets of office gossip—humorous cases or who was engaged or the current idiotic police regulation. But that had diminished as the weeks of his absence increased, until he rarely heard from anyone in the department any more.

Taking a deep breath, McLaren leaned against the edge of the windowsill, his eyes on the sliver of moon nestled in the branches of a birch. Was it only a year ago that he'd left? Dena had reminded him of the dubious anniversary date when she called last night. He rubbed his eyes, suddenly exhausted. One year. Twelve short months ago he'd left in response to an injustice dealt him.

But it had started years before, he reminded himself. When he and Harvester had been in police training school. He, the serious student who always made top marks in class; Harvester, the son of the Chief Constable, sneaky, getting by on instructor favoritism. On completion of their initial training course, their animosity had increased. Working in the same department, they both attained detective status, though McLaren had one solid year's experience before Harvester finally wormed his way in. It was constant comparisons after that: McLaren, popular, hardworking and intelligent; Harvester, shunned, doubted, sliding by on his daddy's name—a brilliant example of the Peter Principle. He was also jealous of McLaren.

And then one spring night, the years of ill feelings and envy exploded in one fateful event.

McLaren had just finished with a case and was at his desk, attacking the stack of papers menacing the entire office. He'd reached for his coffee when a colleague sauntered into the room and sat in a chair. McLaren looked up, both grateful for and irritated by the interruption.

"No action tonight?" McLaren eyed the detective from over the rim of his coffee mug. "Or maybe you've cleared up your backlog." He smiled at the shared joke.

There were always cases to work. They flooded the department daily, the new file folders placed on top of yesterday's, creating the stacks of miniature towers that threatened to consume their desks, their office and their lives.

"Just taking a breather. Thought I'd bother you for a bit. What are you working on?"

McLaren shoved the open folder and his notepad away and leaned back in his chair. "A pub fight."

"Sounds fun, that."

"Six people involved."

"Bloody hell. Something else besides property damage?"

"One chap's in hospital. He's bad off."

"Damn. Anyone talking?"

"We'll know soon." McLaren stretched, suddenly exhausted. "We've started interviewing those involved."

"Sounds like a mess."

"Even more of a mess. As our luck would have it, the assault happened just out of the range of the CCTV. We've no more idea right now of who beat up this poor bloke than my dog knows."

"Bloody hell."

"It's more serious than a black eye. The chap's in the IC unit. Stabbing to the abdomen, arm, and neck. Just missed the jugular vein, but…"

"Damn."

McLaren nodded. "Hopefully it won't turn into a murder charge."

"The chap's that bad off, then."

"Unfortunately, yes. He keeps wavering. At first, he showed signs of improvement. Then his blood pressure fell and it was looking bad. Last time I checked on him, he was improving. The hospital staff is cautiously optimistic."

"Well, they would say that, wouldn't they? Well, I wish him luck."

McLaren pointed with his cup to the electric kettle on top of the metal file cabinet. An assortment of ceramic mugs, a box of tea bags, a canister of coffee, packets of sugar and a pint bottle of milk crowded the kettle. A beer mug held several metal spoons.

The detective sighed. "No, thanks. I've got to get back."

"Tough case?"

"Not really. Just tedious." The man yawned, throwing back his head. "Isn't it the end of our shift yet? Sunrise ought to happen just about now, shouldn't it?"

"Sorry, mate. It's only three."

"Damn. Well…" He made no move to leave, sitting there and glancing at McLaren's desk. "Here's luck to that chap in hospital. I know Charlie Harvester's not your favorite subject…"

McLaren's snort cemented the unspoken, shared opinion of the other man.

"…but at least his case of assault sounds easily sorted out."

"Not that I want to hear, particularly, but I suppose you're about to tell—"

"An old man. Oh, must be 70 if he's a day. He coshed a burglar on the head."

"A round of applause for the old man. Where was this…a home invasion?"

"No, oddly enough. A pub. The old man lives

upstairs. Why? What's the matter?"

McLaren's fingers blanched as he gripped the edge of his desk. "Who? When? What's the address?"

"Bloody hell, man, what's the matter?"

"What pub?" McLaren shouted, halfway getting to his feet. "Who is it?"

"I don't know the bloke's name. I just heard this roundabout."

"When?"

"When did I hear—"

"When did this happen?"

"Now. Quarter of an hour ago. Harvester's still at the scene. Why?"

"Where? What pub?" McLaren was standing now, leaning over his desk, a menacing tower of anger.

"I don't know. Yeah, I do. It's in Tutbury. The Broken Wheel. Hey!" he yelled after McLaren's darting figure. "Where you off to?"

His reply was the slamming of the office door and the stirring of loose papers in the breeze.

The drive into Tutbury—beyond the castle and to the pub—slid by in a dark blur. Road, trees, and buildings slipped behind his car window as he thought of Charlie Harvester and what had probably happened at The Broken Wheel. McLaren leaned forward, peering into the blackness ahead of the car's headlights, and pressed down on the accelerator. The car shot ahead, took the turn into the village on two wheels, and gained speed on the straight lane. He flashed past a row of houses, barely missed a fox as it crossed the road, then braked in front of the pub and dashed up the front walk. He left his car, headlights on and the door open, sitting squarely in the middle of the road.

Inside he found the usual bustle of police constables and detectives, fingerprint technician and photographer, and the myriad others needed at a scene. But the unusual find alarmed even him, a ten-year veteran of the job. An angry Charlie Harvester was reading Nigel Forester, the pub owner, his rights.

"What the hell's going on?" McLaren yelled, his gaze darting between Nigel and Harvester. "Nigel, are you all right? Where's Maureen?" He glanced around the room, expecting to see her sitting at one of the pub tables.

"Maureen's in hospital, Mike." Nigel's voice shook and he blinked repeatedly, trying to hold back the tears. He sat in a chair, his face bruised and cut from some physical altercation.

"*Hospital!* Why? What's happened? Are you all right? You need medical attention?" He glanced at Nigel, then at the constables huddled in the background. When no one spoke, he yelled the question again.

"Mrs. Forester has been taken in an ambulance." Charlie Harvester spoke quite calmly in the sea of agitation.

McLaren turned, focusing his eyes, anger and energy on the police detective. The man approached McLaren, tapping a pad of paper against his left hand. "Why?" McLaren shifted his gaze back to Nigel. "What happened? Did—" He seemed to see Nigel's wounds for the first time. He turned back to Harvester. "Was Maureen injured in the break-in?"

"You seem to know a lot about this case, McLaren. How'd you hear about it?"

"I want to know about Maureen. Why did you call an—"

"She suffered a heart attack."

"God!" He turned his attention back to Nigel, who was silently crying. "How bad is it?"

"I don't know." When Nigel raised his head, McLaren could see the man's cheeks were wet from his tears. "I don't know, Mike. She just kind of moaned, clutched her chest, and collapsed."

"You rang 999?"

"Not I. Your mate, here, did it. Maureen just collapsed as he came in. I was going to ring 999 anyway, for the burglar, but..."

McLaren glanced at Harvester, as though silently confirming what had happened.

"When was that?" McLaren returned to Nigel. "The *burglar* needed an ambulance? Why? What went on?"

Nigel pulled in his lips, reluctant to speak. After McLaren repeated his question, Nigel said, "He needed medical attention."

"Euphemistic way of putting it." Harvester grunted, obviously fed up with the entire incident. "But it's adequate. If you need convincing, McLaren..." He indicated the fireplace poker that a Crime Scene Investigator technician was examining. The wrought iron tool had a definite curve to its otherwise straight length. "What's that tell you?"

"Not bloody much," McLaren snorted.

"Look, McLaren." Harvester grabbed McLaren's shoulder and turned him around.

Shaking off the detective's hand, McLaren scowled. "Let go of me, Harvester." The words were low, barely audible, but remarkably calm.

Harvester shrugged and crossed his arms across his

chest. "This is my case, if it's not perfectly clear to you. *My* case. *I* got the call. *I've* interviewed the victim and the assailant. *I've* arrested the guilty party, which is your friend, Nigel Forester, as it turns out. So what you're doing here, sticking your nose into something that doesn't concern you."

"Doesn't concern me!" His bark was a mixture of amusement, disbelief and anger. "I thought the welfare of any honest citizen was my concern. Every copper's concern. Just because you got the call doesn't preclude me from being concerned."

"Could it be something more than that?" Harvester's eyes narrowed, mirroring his anger and contempt for the man before him.

"What the hell's that supposed to mean?"

"Seems to me you're a bit over the top with your 'concern' bit."

"When I come to find the pub owner apparently arrested merely for protecting his property against a...a..." He barely glanced at the bent poker. "Against a burglar engaged in questionable activities...yes, I am concerned."

"As I said, your concern seems more than a cop would express. Could you be guilty of something else?"

"Harvester, you're full of crap."

"And you're overreacting. You're upset because I've just arrested a friend of yours." He smiled as McLaren reddened. "Score one for me, I think."

Trying to keep his voice in check, McLaren said, "What's Nigel Forester done to warrant this outrage?"

"Assaulted Mr. Tyrone Wade Antony. To be specific, assault with intent to kill."

"Assault! The hell he did. He was defending his

property and life. And protecting Maureen, too, if I know Nigel."

"That's where you're wrong, McLaren." Harvester nearly laughed, then recovered himself as the police photographer walked into the room. "Galls, doesn't it? The ace detective, the top cop of the team, and you're wrong. Well, it may surprise you to know that we have proof."

"Like what?" McLaren bit the words off in his growing anger.

"Mr. Forester attacked Mr. Antony with that fireplace poker."

McLaren looked at the pub owner. "Is this true, Nigel?"

The older man nodded. He looked older than his seventy years at the moment, his white hair vivid in the light of the police work lamps, his face pale from shock. "But I was defending myself. He'd broken into the pub by the back door. I heard the door bang open as it hit the cases of empty bottles I'd put inside there. I rushed downstairs. Maureen and I were getting ready for bed." He paused, his eyes overflowing with fear at his arrest and his questionable future.

McLaren envisioned the upstairs living quarters. He'd been up there many times, ever since he'd been a teenager. Nigel Forester had saved him from drowning in a nearby lake, strolling past by chance and hearing McLaren's friend screaming for help. Nigel had swum out to McLaren, got him into a lifesaving hold, and brought him back to shore. Since that day, twenty-one years ago, McLaren had practically cemented himself to the older man's side, mowing his grass, washing his car, painting the walls of their living quarters. Anything and everything to repay for his saved life, especially so because a third boy in their group had drowned before Nigel could get to them. McLaren knew he could never fully repay the man, but he appeared monthly to do some chore or just sit and chat over a pint or cup of coffee.

McLaren's sense of Right, his need to help others, blossomed. Two years later he had joined the police service. When he had completed his initial training, at the top of his class, he had honed his determination to serve where and how he could.

"I could hear him." Nigel took a deep breath to steady his voice. "I knew where he was, even in the dark. There's a floorboard that creaks. I snapped on the overhead light and surprised him with the cash register till in his hand. He was emptying it into a sack he had with him. He'd also put some bottles of liquor or beer into it. I heard the coins hit the bottles as they fell into the sack. I saw a crowbar on the countertop. The tool wasn't mine. I don't own one. He smirked at me and called me a name. I guess the crowbar was too far away from him 'cause he reached into the sack and brought out a bottle. He had hold of it by its neck. He hit it against the edge of the serving counter so the bottom of the bottle broke off. Then he rushed at me holding the edge toward me like he was going to dig it into me. I was scared, for me and for Maureen. As he ran up to me, I picked up the fireplace poker and hit him."

Chapter Twelve

"Hear that, McLaren? It's a confession. Mr. Forester struck Mr. Antony." Harvester smiled slowly, the smirk broadening into a grin as though it were a personal triumph.

McLaren glanced around the bar area, perhaps expecting to see great pools of blood. The oak-paneled walls, stone floor and fireplace were as he remembered them. The massive beams, nearly black against the white plaster ceiling, had not changed. Yet the room's warmth and intimacy had become cold and menacing from the night's event and Harvester's presence. McLaren doubled up his fingers, ready to slam his fist into Harvester's leer, then shoved his hand behind his back. "Since when are the police so protective of a burglar? You make me sick, Harvester."

Harvester grinned, unconcerned with McLaren's opinion. "I've cautioned Mr. Forester and he acknowledged that he understands it. There's nothing you can do. We've got the evidence of the assault—"

"What evidence? If you're talking about fingerprints on the poker, that's no evidence. It's *his* poker! I'm taking this up with the Superintendent."

"What's the matter with you, McLaren? You hard of hearing? Or just so thick skulled that you don't understand? I said, it's not your case. Mr. Forester attacked Mr. Antony so severely that the wrought iron poker bent over his head, for God's sake! That's proof of an assault. That and Mr. Antony's blood on it. It's a clear case of Section 18, causing grievous bodily harm. And, if Mr. Antony dies, it'll become a case of murder."

The years of antagonism seemed to solidify into this exact moment. And now, in his friend's pub, McLaren felt the determination to help others, the need that had sent him into the Force in the first place, growing within him. The anger and frustration at seeing Nigel Forester so wrongly arrested spilled out. He strode to the CSI officer, grabbed the poker, and marched into the men's loo. Turning on the cold-water tap, he thrust the poker under the running water. As he moved the poker back and forth, he wiped the blood and hair from the tool. When he had removed all the physical traces, he straightened the poker over his knee. Satisfied, he strode back into the main room and threw the poker onto a table. The poker bounced once as it thudded against the table's wooden surface.

"*Now* where's your evidence?" McLaren barked, hatred in his eyes as he glared at Harvester.

Every eye in the room was fixed to the poker, now clean of recognizable prints, blood, and hair.

Harvester shifted his gaze from the table to McLaren's face. He stared at McLaren, matching his anger as he yelled into the silence. "I'll have you up before the Chief Constable, McLaren! You've just destroyed vital evidence in a case."

"Nigel Forester stays right here." He took a step toward Harvester and slammed his fist into his cupped hand.

The two constables in attendance exchanged

nervous glances, but remained where they were.

"I'll have your job, McLaren." Harvester's hiss slid beneath the constables' ragged breathing. "Yours and anyone who assists you. You're interfering with a police case." He didn't have to look at the constables to make his meaning clear.

"Hell." McLaren strode to Nigel, who was leaning his head against the wall. As this angle, with the light falling full on the older man's face, the bruises and the cut beneath his eye showed up markedly against his pale skin. Turning a chair to face his friend, McLaren sat and leaned forward, as though having dropped in for a chat. His words came quietly but firmly, "You'll be fine. You're not going anywhere with Detective Harvester. You've done nothing wrong. You defended your and your wife's lives against an armed intruder. Please don't worry. We'll go see Maureen when they've got you patched up, shall we?"

During this conversation, Harvester had stepped out of the room, but he now returned, his face red and a smile playing about the corners of his lips. He walked up to McLaren but stopped several feet from him. "I've just radioed for a Superintendent to be turned out, McLaren." He paused, watching McLaren's face for the full effect of his words.

McLaren rose to his feet, the knuckles of his right hand pressing against the tabletop.

Harvester continued, smiling more broadly now that he had McLaren's attention. "I'm making an allegation against you. Perverting the course of justice. We'll see what the Super has to say about that."

McLaren grabbed a handful of Harvester's jacket with his right hand and seized his right upper arm with his left hand. Turning Harvester around, McLaren stepped behind him. As he dragged Harvester outside, the constables rushed to the doorway, wanting to witness history. McLaren dragged Harvester across the flagstone patio, kicking aside chairs and tables as he made for the edge of the garden. The few constables outside stopped their activities and parted like the Red Sea for Moses as McLaren flung Harvester around to face him. Taking a deep breath, McLaren slammed his right fist into Harvester's jaw, sending him reeling backwards into the rose bushes.

"You should thank me, Harvester. I've just instigated a family reunion for you." He snapped off a broken rose stem, sniffed it, and threw it at the man. "Harvester's your name. Now you're with the rest of your kind, the arachnid harvesters, the spindly-legged predators who infest bramble patches. How's it feel to be home?"

Harvester yelled in pain and tried to stand up; McLaren remained rooted to the spot, his chest rapidly rising and falling, his face flushed. Towering over the sprawled-out man, McLaren growled his order. "And about Nigel Forester…he's going nowhere. Understand?" He waited for a moment, sizing up the man at his feet.

Harvester lay where he was, staring up at McLaren.

McLaren turned abruptly, pushed his way through the coppers who were hesitantly moving toward Harvester, and thundered back into the pub.

The scene faded from McLaren's eyes as he stood by his bedroom window. The night had darkened while he had relived that terrible event more than a year ago.

The moon had disappeared behind a bank of clouds while he lost himself in the memory, and a cool wind had sprung up from the west. In spite of the warmth of the June night, McLaren shivered. He rubbed his forehead, telling himself it had all been for the best, that he was glad to be shut of a department whose Chief Constable eventually had sided with the extremist councilors and a ranting media out for blood. But he was lying to himself. He had loved the job, still loved the job. Regardless of the constables' testimony that the poker had never been bent or bloody, that it was Nigel Forester's word against a known career burglar—all of which left Harvester out on the proverbial limb and madder than ever with McLaren—McLaren had been suspended from duty.

He slammed his fist into the wall. When the Chief Constable had offered him the option of resigning from the Force instead of being prosecuted for assaulting a police officer and perverting the course of justice, McLaren knew a brick wall when he saw one. Knew the handwriting on that wall, too. Knew he'd forever be a marked man, and back in uniform in days.

He had resigned in an overwhelming rush of sadness and anger, the hurt of being torn from the CID branch, which he loved, as painful as a loved one's death. Now, he was reliving that fiasco of justice, that moment of Harvester's triumph. It was something he had no desire to unearth.

A fox barked in the darkness and the moon emerged from its nest of clouds before McLaren wandered to his bed. He sat on the edge of the mattress, his toes burrowing into the deep pile of the lambskin throw rug, his heels resting on the cool wooden floor.

It's been a year, he reminded himself. Surely it's time to get on with my life, to mend the pain. If not for my own good, then for Dena's.

He opened the bottom drawer of his bedside cabinet and rummaged within its depths. His fingers felt the cold, metal photo frame and wrapped around one of its corners as he pulled it from the drawer. He opened the easel stand on the frame's back and set the photo on top of the cabinet, next to the alarm clock. Sitting in the darkness, he stared at the photo. He needed no light to see Dena's brown eyes, or envision her smile. Hadn't he conjured up her face countless nights this past year when the nightmares had awakened him, when he had downed too many beers?

Telling her picture that he'd think about the two of them, he lay down. The night closed around him, obscure and soothing. The wind caressed his bare chest, cooling his anger. A flash of lightning crackled beyond the oak. In that second of near-blinding brightness, Dena's face jumped out from the darkness, seemingly alive and blessing him with her smile. Then, as the blackness reclaimed the land and his room, he turned onto his side, facing her portrait. He lay again in the darkness, aware of the storm, the smell of rain approaching downwind. And as he drifted off to sleep, he thought that the storm mimicked exactly his life at the moment.

The ringing that awakened McLaren later that morning at half past seven was not from his alarm clock. He hadn't set it the previous night. The obnoxious noise came from his phone on the bedside stand. Forcing his eyelids open, he cautiously sat up, testing his stiff back and his aching head. The phone rang again as he rubbed his hand across the back of his neck and he muttered "Yeah? What?" to the unknown caller. His tone and temperament changed when Jamie Kydd's cheerful voice sang into his ear.

"Late night, Mike?" Jamie's humor was evident in his voice even if McLaren couldn't see him.

"More like an early morning."

"Storm keep you up?"

"That and…" He glanced at Dena's photo and laid it face down on top of the bedside table. I must've been drunk last night to get that out, he thought, then ran his left hand through his tousled hair.

"The case bothering you, won't let you sleep?"

"Yeah. I've a lot to think about." He pushed the photo frame slightly farther away from him.

"Well, here's another little something to think about." Jamie paused, as though bracing for his friend's explosion of gratitude. "In regards to getting that information you wanted…"

McLaren sighed heavily. "Don't tell me."

"I thought you wanted to know. You rang me up."

"I meant don't tell me you got caught lifting a file or something."

"What kind of detective do you think I am? No, don't answer that."

"Did you get anything, then?" He ran his fingers through his hair, once more astonished at the depth of Jamie's friendship.

"If you haven't looked at your email yet this morning…"

"Bloody hell."

Jamie grinned. "I'll take that as a 'not yet,' shall I?"

"Get on with it. Did you get anything or not?"

"I emailed those reports to you."

"I must be still half asleep. You emailed the reports? How?"

"Simple. I scanned them on the computer, saved them as .pdf files, and emailed them as attachments."

"Must've taken hours."

"Well, it did take a while." Jamie exhaled heavily, but McLaren wasn't fooled.

"Acting's not your strong suit, Jamie. Cut to the chase."

Jamie muttered something about a genius never being appreciated in his home town. "I stayed late, after my shift ended. Not too many lads around the station in the wee small hours so I had a better chance of getting the files and scanning them. I, uh…" He hesitated momentarily, as though wondering how to phrase this bit of news. "You didn't get the entire report. I sent you the pages I thought were most pertinent."

"Smashing!"

"I also emailed you a few photos of her body…*in situ* and of the area itself. I just chose a few to send."

"Sure. I didn't expect the whole bloody file. That would've taken hours to scan and send. As it is, I hope my damned computer doesn't crash. Thanks."

"Uh, Mike…I can tell you now, if you'd like, where her body was found."

McLaren withdrew a pad of paper and pen from the drawer in the nightstand. "Yeah?" He wrote swiftly, making no comment as his friend related the details. When Jamie finished, McLaren sank back against the bed's headboard and stared at his notes. Half mile out…right side of road…in a depression two yards from the road's edge...stone barn searched...victim's right shoe missing..."This is first rate, Jamie. Ta. I'll get to those emails right away and let you know what I find at the barn."

"I just hope it's more than straw and stones."

The ballistics report stated that the bullet that killed Marta was a .38 caliber fired from a revolver. Most likely a Webley. The pathologist reported that although casino personnel stated Marta had been drinking that evening, the alcohol was no longer in her blood. Marta had been shot at close proximity, perhaps six to ten inches. Gunpowder markings were consistent with that distance, the particles embedded into the skin. Death was instantaneous, or close to it. Fixed lividity and other usual indicators that help pinpoint a time of death could not be used due to the advanced decomposition of the body. The entomologist established the presence of ticks, spiders and several species of flies, as well as maggots, on the remains...

McLaren looked up from the computer monitor. Insects, especially flies, went through life cycles that could be clocked, from laying eggs, to developing larvae, to adulthood. Knowing the type of insects on and under the body, the quantity of a specific insect, and the stage of the life cycle pointed the finger at the time of death. Insects were a witness more reliable and unvarying than the human kind. Especially in this case, with Marta's body lying for over a week in the open, in the summer heat.

He went back to the report. 'Although not conclusive, death probably occurred the night of her last casino outing. The insects' activities are consistent with the time...'

He next looked at the photos of the stone barn, the immediate vicinity, and Marta's body *in situ*, and printed them out. After logging off, he laid the photos on the kitchen worktop, next to his keys. Then, whistling, he went to take his shower.

The storm of early morning left a blanket of mist that still hugged the valley and wallowed in depressions in fields and gardens when McLaren left his house at nine o'clock. A chill laced the air and condensation coated the cooler surfaces such as outdoor water pump handles, farm machinery, and ungaraged cars. The small willow at the edge of his garden took on a phantom-like quality, its leaves a green smear beneath a wash of gray. There was a stealthy movement as a bough waved faintly at McLaren and a tendril of mist swirled past the dark lump of the cypress. A bird chirped somewhere in the obscurity, then everything was still.

Except for McLaren's whispered "Damn."

As he approached his car, he saw it. Eleven empty beer bottles set up like a frame for tenpin bowling. The extra bottle was placed in front of the bottle at the triangle's apex, which pointed toward the car's windscreen. A twelfth bottle lay on its side, pinned beneath one of the windscreen wipers. Deliberate. A mute message.

He returned to his kitchen, dug around in the closet and located a pair of rubber washing-up gloves and a large paper sack. Back outside, he pulled on the gloves and placed the bottles inside the sack. Perhaps Jamie could work on them off duty, he thought, then folded the top of the sack closed. He stood there for several seconds, staring at his car, aware of the weight of the bottles. Again he asked himself the unanswerable question: what was going on and who was doing this?

The gravel area where the car was parked held no hints. No footprints, no castoff shirt button, no blood spatter. Still, the detective in him was too strong to ignore, and he carefully stepped away from his car and walked around it in a wide circle. Nothing.

He set the bag on the car's passenger seat, intending to drop it by Jamie's house later in the day, then got into his car, and drove to Noah's Ark. But the bottles haunted him all the way to Chesterfield. Was he the trapped, fallen beer bottle?

The animal shelter was a modern one-story building of steel and white-painted cement blocks. A row of windows near the roofline encircled the structure as a strand of pearls claimed a woman's neck. McLaren parked beside a panel van that declared 'Noah's Ark' in brilliant green paint along its side. He swallowed another sip of coffee before settling the travel mug into the cup holder, and opened the door.

The mist had burned off in the thirty-minute drive to Chesterfield, leaving the air warmer and hinting at a still-warmer day. Blackbeech Drive, on which the animal shelter was located, hummed with traffic this Saturday morning, and McLaren wondered if the neighboring businesses saw enough custom to keep them going. He locked his car and wandered up to the shelter's front door. An electronic tone, like a doorbell, sounded toward the back of the reception area as he entered.

A young woman barely out of her teens straightened up from her bent-over position behind the front desk. Giving McLaren a smile, she asked if she could help him.

The sunlight slanted through the glass insets bookending the front door and the row of windows near the ceiling. Nice, he thought, noticing the pale blue walls and white ceramic floor tile. Bright, airy, cheery. Nice for the animals, too, if the upper windows circle around toward the pen area.

Then, he suddenly knew they did. Any place touting itself an ark and shelter would see to the comfort of its animal residents. And that included a light, airy spot for the cages. He took in the pamphlet stands and signage for dog training classes before grabbing a blue poker chip from the supply in the plastic cube on the countertop.

A clever bit of marketing, he thought, reading the advertising printed on the chip. 'Don't gamble with your pet's health. Noah's Ark.' The other side gave the shelter's name, address and phone numbers. Other colors of chips mixed with the blues in the cube. He pulled out a red chip. 'When the chips are down, call Noah's Ark.' The emergency phone number ran in bold print beneath the slogan.

The black chip announced 'Stack the odds in your pet's favor. Noah's Ark health care.' All three chips gave the same shelter information on the back. He smiled again at the slogans, stuck the chips in his trousers pocket, and leaned against the edge of the counter, focusing on the woman's face.

"We're offering a discount," she said, seeing what had held his interest. "It's good until Saturday week on spaying and neutering of your animal if you adopt one through us and have our veterinary staff perform the procedure." There was an accent to her voice that

McLaren couldn't pinpoint. "Plus," she added, getting no response, "we're giving coupons for £25 worth of pet food, which is good for cat, dog, or rabbit. The coupons become active upon animal adoption. They're redeemable at most supermarkets, pet supply stores, or here at the shelter. Does that interest you?" She smiled again, this time showing perfect, white teeth.

"Ordinarily, yes." McLaren smiled back. "But I'm never home to let a dog out, I'm allergic to cats, and I have still nightmares about Harvey."

She looked blank.

"The six foot tall invisible rabbit. James Stewart starred in the film."

She shook her head. Too young, McLaren thought. Still, there are the classic flicks on the telly.

"We have several nice birds," she continued, unruffled. "An African gray parrot, several budgies, a cockatiel…"

"I appreciate your assistance with the pets, but I'd like to talk to you about another matter, if you can spare me a few moments."

"If it's a matter of your pet's health," she began before McLaren interrupted her.

"I'd just like to ask you a few questions."

The girl glanced around the area. Seeing no one who wanted her, she nodded hesitantly. "What's this in regard to?"

McLaren had begun walking slowly to a corner of the reception area and she followed. They stopped beside a shoulder-high cardboard display stand offering sample packets of various dry pet foods. McLaren turned so his back was toward the corner and he faced the front door. Old habits die hard, he thought before returning his attention to the girl.

After introducing himself, he explained why he needed to talk to her. She frowned and pressed her lips together, and for a moment McLaren feared she would refuse to help. A dog barked from the kennel area behind them, enticing several more dogs to answer before she shook her head.

"Bad business, that." She plunged her hands into her skirt pockets and shifted her body slightly so that a shaft of sunlight illuminated the top of her head and brought out the red streaks among the brunette strands.

"Were you here when the money was stolen? That was last—"

"A year ago this past May." She shook his head again. "It was so terrible."

"So you were working then. Did you know Verity Dwyer?"

"Yes to both questions. I've been here for three years."

"This seems a nice place to work, taking care of animals."

"I love it. The only downside is becoming attached to our residents. The animals." She smiled and glanced toward the room where the animals for adoption were held.

"Did Verity like it here?"

"Yes, as far as I knew."

"You weren't particularly friends, then."

"Not real close, no, but I knew her. I liked her, too. She was a splendid worker and an equally splendid person. That's why this was all such a shock, you know. I would have sworn she was honest. But stealing like that..." She pulled in her lips and sighed heavily.

"Well, you never know, do you? No such thing as a criminal face, is there?"

"You didn't hear her explanation about the missing money, then?"

"Yes. Both from her when the financial officer discovered the discrepancy and during the court trial. I wanted to believe her, but…"

"Why didn't you? If you believed initially that she was an honest person…"

"The story was absurd! I also knew Marta. She hadn't any more of a gambling problem than I'm the Lost Dauphin."

"She evidently kept her gambling secret from many people, Miss."

"That may be, but it still doesn't replace the money that Verity took from the cash register. Since it was her register, she was responsible for it."

"So her sentence doesn't bother you in the least, then."

"Of course it does! But if she was guilty of theft…"

"It's hard to believe, I know."

The girl's face flooded with color. "I like Verity. I stop by her house every month or so to see how she's faring. I take her a little something to cheer her up. That's a rough sentence, doing community work."

"Isn't this rather a contradiction? First you state that she's responsible for the money in her till and therefore, since it's missing, it's her fault. Then you tell me you ease her hardship by bringing her gifts. Which is it? How do you feel?"

"I hate to see anyone doing time if she's wrongly convicted, but Verity's the only one who had access to that money. I know, I know." She rushed on as McLaren opened his mouth. "The Great Explanation. Marta was going to repay the money but she fell ill. But that still doesn't excuse the fact that Verity stole the money from the shelter in the first place. It's too bad she did it and too bad she got caught, but facts are facts. We can't change the past."

"I agree." McLaren exhaled slowly, as if considering another idea. "All that brought a bit of a scandal to the shelter, didn't it?"

The girl nodded. "Unfortunately, yes. We were in the newspapers and on television for weeks. People were reluctant to patronize us."

"How long did that last? Did the shelter suffer, either financially or with fewer animal adoptions?"

"It was difficult for a few months, yes. Not only weren't the animals adopted out, but also donations slacked off. We depend on monetary donations for about one third of our operating costs." Her voice grew calmer now that her frustration was spent. "With no animals going to people's homes, we had more animals to provide for and less money coming in to buy food."

"Plus, the shelter was minus the missing £1,000. That must have hurt."

She frowned and stared at McLaren, as if amazed he knew about the missing reserve cash. "That wasn't the half of it. The board and a few of our staff were furious at the position Verity and Marta had put us in. The fact that Marta was related to her boss, and the workplace rumors that she and Verity got their jobs here due to that kinship didn't help smooth any stormy waters."

"Was that true? Was Mr. Clark guilty of

nepotism?"

"I wouldn't know. I don't delve into office gossip. But they were both hard-working employees, from what I saw."

McLaren wondered just how much the receptionist did see or know about personal goings-on at the shelter, but didn't ask.

She shrugged and moved slightly, leaving the patch of sunlight. "If things hadn't ended as they did, they both would've been asked for resignations. Or fired." The words sounded harsh against the chirping of a bird somewhere in the building.

"Sounds like a bad time for everyone."

"As they say, if looks could kill."

"Including yours?"

She hesitated before replying. "Yes. I admit it. I was furious. The missing money tainted all of us here. I figured they'd be scrutinizing me next, make me sign some kind of daily tally sheet or install CCTV aimed at my register. I could've been involved, but I wasn't. I could've been fired, too."

"But you weren't. Know anyone who was mad enough to kill Marta, then?"

She blinked, unsure if he were joking.

He glanced around the area. The dogs had quieted down. "Is there anyone else here at the moment? I thought I could talk to everyone I could. Would the vet know anything about the trouble with Verity?"

"He's in surgery, but I doubt if he'd know anything other than what the Board decided. He doesn't come out in front, here, and he really doesn't go into the gift shop."

"So he wouldn't know Verity." McLaren sighed

heavily, thanked her for her help, and left. It wasn't until he unlocked his car and got inside that he noticed the bag of beer bottles was gone.

## Chapter Thirteen

McLaren stood in the car's open doorway, his hands propped against the doorframe, his arms stiff and holding him upright. He leaned slightly into the interior, as though a closer proximity to the seat would clear his vision. And mounting confusion. The extra millimetres didn't help; the seat was still empty.

His hands slid off the car body, making small squeals as they rubbed against the metal, and he slowly sank onto the driver's seat. He stared, disbelieving, at the closed passenger door. It was shut. And locked. And he had unlocked his door to get inside. He exhaled slowly as his head hit the headrest. He wallowed against the upholstery, thinking, replaying the scenario in his mind. It didn't make sense. How could his car have been burgled?

He closed his eyes, going through every minute of his morning. There'd been Jamie's phone call, the details of the area where Marta's body had been found, then McLaren's hasty shower and dressing prior to his grabbed breakfast and leaving his house. Twelve beer bottles had been placed on his car sometime during the night. He had bagged those bottles carefully to take to Jamie later today.

Rubbing his forehead, he turned his head and looked once more at the seat, now convinced he was losing his mind. He ran the tip of his tongue across his lower lip. The skin was dry and cracked, from too many hours mending stone walls in the sun and wind. His tongue had no moisture, either, to remedy the roughness.

Sitting up, McLaren glanced at his watch, then at the clock on the dashboard. Both registered the same time. Good, he thought. At least I'm not in some strange time warp. Unless the aliens have fiddled with the watch and clock.

He glanced across the street. A road sweeper was brushing up a bit of litter with his broom; a police officer was directing traffic around two cars that were involved in an accident. He got out of his car and crossed the road.

As he stopped on the curb, the road sweeper looked up. When McLaren made no attempt to move on, the man leaned against his broom. "Lose something, mate?"

McLaren fought back the urge to say, "My mind," but merely replied, "No. I was just wondering if you saw anyone in the car park across the road."

The man squinted into the sun, shielding his eyes with his hand. The parking area was barely visible beyond the constant stream of vehicles crowding the road. "What? At the animal place?"

"Yes."

"When?"

"Just now. Well, a few minutes ago."

"What's your game, mate?" The man eyed McLaren with suspicion, as if expecting a man-on-the-street interview complete with video camera and microphone.

"I just need to know if you saw anybody over

there, possibly near that red Peugeot."

The man sniffed without giving the shelter another glance and went back to sweeping. "Not likely to, am I? I've got me work to do. I don't have time to gawk at the landscape." He made a vigorous jab with his broom at a piece of paper stuck to the tarmac.

"This was just a few minutes ago," McLaren insisted, following the man's progress down the street. "Not more than ten, probably."

"Here, now." The man turned to face McLaren, his broom held upright like a rifle at attention. "I don't know why you're so interested in that car. If you want to know something, go ask that copper." He pointed the end of the broom handle at the officer standing in the center of the road. "I've just got here, myself. So you ask him. I don't know nothin' about no car. And I don't like your nosiness. Now, bugger off!" His turned back dismissed McLaren as clearly as if he had waved goodbye.

The police officer directing traffic had no time to talk to McLaren. Or inclination. He viewed McLaren's question with the same suspicion as the road sweeper, except that the officer stared at McLaren—probably getting a lasting mental image of his face—before telling him to file a police report if his car had been damaged.

Sighing heavily, McLaren returned to his car and drove to the house of Marta Hughes' neighbor.

Herb Millington was outside, washing his car, when McLaren walked up to him. The Millington house was much like its neighbors—a detached dwelling of brick and wood, built years ago as Chesterfield grew beyond its status as a 13th century market town and 19th century industrial center. Suburbs had stretched the town's boundaries, yet unspoiled countryside still flourished just outside its thoroughfares. The town's residents had the best of both worlds, McLaren thought, stepping over the water running down the Millington driveway. A town with modern conveniences, yet the Derbyshire countryside minutes outside its confines.

Herb turned off the water at the outside tap, lay down the hose, and watched McLaren strode up the driveway. "Anything I can do for you?"

"I hope so." McLaren stopped several feet from the man before introducing himself and stating that he was investigating Marta Hughes' death.

"Marta! Aren't you a bit late with all that? That happened a year ago." Herb cautiously eyed McLaren and jammed his right hand into his front jeans pocket. "Who'd you say you are again—police?"

"I'm retired."

"Retired, eh? Then you've really no authority."

"I've been retained by someone to look into the case."

"Well, you would say that even if you're poking about on your own." He squinted against the sunlight on the car's body. "I suppose it's her family who want answers." His gaze shifted to the Hughes' family home. He cracked his knuckles, then flexed his fingers. "Alan's still grieving."

McLaren took in Herb's slicked-down hair, muscular build, and combatant stand, sizing up the man in one word. Arrogant.

"They never figured out who killed her, did they?" He dried the back of his hands on his shorts, seemingly unconcerned about the wrinkles to the fabric. "The cops, I mean. That why you're talking to people?" He stared at McLaren through slightly lowered eyelids.

"It's an instance of a killer getting away without coming to justice." McLaren suddenly felt the rage of his own injustice at the hands of Harvester. Taking a deep breath, he mentally counted to ten before continuing. "I would think most anyone would feel the same."

"Oh, sure, sure." Herb pulled his shoulders backwards, as though they were stiff from washing the car. They were muscular, McLaren noted. And broad. The man did more than wash his car to stay in shape. It was hard to believe the man was nearly fifty, but Alan had said so, and he probably knew. "Didn't mean nothing by it. Just curious. You know what I mean. You talking about Marta again after this long."

"Did you see her leave that evening?"

"Naw. I don't stand at the front windows and watch people's comings and goings. Though, she's the exception I'd make if I did. Ya know?" He winked and grinned as though they shared a mutual joke.

"You found her attractive, then." This wasn't McLaren's intended line of questioning, and he found it distasteful, especially about a deceased person, but he pursued it.

"Sure! Who didn't? A good lookin' woman like that. Brunette, hazel eyes, thin. Not too thin, though. She had enough padding where it counted, if you get my drift." He patted a lock of his sun-streaked brown hair back into place.

What a jerk. First class nit. He suddenly felt very sorry for Marta if she had been subjected to this salivating nerd. He went on with great restraint. "Were you on friendly terms with the Hughes family? Did your son and the Hughes lad get on well? Hang around together, play football, perhaps?"

"We don't have a son, or any kids. If we did, I wouldn't want my son hanging out with Chad Hughes. I consider that boy a bit of a wimp."

"Why is that?"

"The kid won't join any of the neighborhood lads on anything."

"You know Chad has been invited to do things, have you?"

Herb shrugged and ran his thumb behind his ear lobe. "I don't make it a habit of spying on anybody, but I'm outside enough to see the other lads doing things. That Hughes kid is never with them."

"Doing things like what, for instance?"

"Oh, different stuff." He bent over and started coiling the hose into a neat circle.

"Playing football? Taking in a film? Going to a concert?"

Herb let the hose sag to the ground. He straightened up and frowned. "What the hell do I know? I'm a bit old to keep track of kids who aren't mine. If you're so damned interested, go next door and talk to Chad." He nodded toward the Hughes house.

"Did you see anyone around their house when it was burgled?"

Herb snorted and finished coiling up the hose. "What the hell difference does that make in finding Marta's killer?"

"Just wondering if you could add any information about it."

"Like what?"

"If you knew anyone who might have been angry with some member of the Hughes family."

"You mean, like one of the neighborhood lads mad with Chad for some reason?"

"That, yes, or someone angry with Alan or Marta."

"Man, you're round the twist. I have no idea what you're talking about. Nobody on this street would be mad enough to do that to anyone. That's kid stuff."

McLaren shrugged, looking rather disappointed. "I suppose not. It's probably just a run of the mill burglary."

"Why'd you think it could've been something else?"

"Oh, just that there could've been some kind of history with Marta."

"History?" Herb straightened up, running his hands again over his shorts. "What's that mean?"

"While the cat's away the mouse will play." McLaren flashed a grin.

"You suggesting Marta had a little something on the side and Alan didn't know what was going on?"

McLaren shrugged again. "Not so unusual any more."

"Yeah? News to me. Anyway, if something like that was going on, how's that related to the burglary?"

"If things got dicey between them, or if she refused the bloke's advances in the first place…" He let the inference build, hoping for a reaction from Herb, but the man merely picked up the coil of hose.

"Did your wife like Marta?"

Herb shouldered the hose, sighing. "She never came straight out and said, 'Gosh, I sure like Marta,' but I think she did. They didn't chat over coffee in the morning, but they talked when they met on the street. Talked about spring flowers and such. You know. Woman talk."

"Did your wife see anyone at the Hughes' house that night?"

"Nope. We were either asleep or I was in my workshop in the garage and my wife was in the back room watching a film on the telly. I can't say definitely where we were 'cause no one ever established the exact time that it happened. But this all came out in the trial. No reason to rehash it."

"And you didn't have anyone over that evening who might've seen anything?"

Herb scratched his ear lobe as he turned toward McLaren. "My mate, Danny Mercer, was over earlier. We worked on my Class Seven." He paused, his gaze wandering to the car in his garage. "Then he stayed for tea and we watched some telly afterwards. But he was gone by seven o'clock."

"You're sure of the time?"

"Sure I'm sure! What the hell is this? The trial's over, mate."

"And the break-in was later."

"Don't know when, exactly, but later that night."

"I understand Marta found the mess herself, that her husband wasn't home."

Herb tilted his head toward the house. "Pity, that, but my wife was home that evening. So I couldn't have gone over to console her anyway." Herb spread his hands, as though he were a helpless pawn in the Whims of Life.

McLaren left with a noncommittal "Thanks" on his lips and in agreement with Verity Dwyer that Herb

Millington was a jerk.

He was headed toward his car when he saw a young man working in the front garden of the Hughes house. McLaren jogged over as the boy threw a weed onto the small pile beside him. Looking at McLaren, he stood up. "Do you want something?"

"Are you Chad Hughes?" McLaren had seen Marta's photograph, and even if Marta had been a brunette and this boy was blond, there was no mistaking the same hazel colored eyes. Or the expression that stared at McLaren.

"Yeah. I'm Chad. And you are…"

McLaren introduced himself in the way that was quickly becoming a rote rendition. When he'd finished, he asked Chad how he was getting on.

"What you really mean," the boy tossed his trowel onto the stack of weeds, "is how I'm coping with Mum's death. What it's been like this past year. What am I supposed to say besides rotten? It's been hard for me, sure, but especially for my dad."

McLaren nodded, knowing that Chad and Alan were constantly reminded of Marta; she was everywhere in the house.

"And you're also wanting to know if I've got any ideas about the whole thing." He tilted his head so he could see McLaren's eyes. "You are, aren't you, or you wouldn't be chatting to me. Nice as you might be, you're a stranger, and strangers just don't pop over to talk. So you want to ask about her death, who could've done it or a motive."

"Yes, I suppose so." McLaren smiled, warming to the young man.

"Besides the obvious suspect, you mean."

McLaren glanced at the Millington house. Herb had carried the hose into his garage and was now walking back to the front door. He waved at Chad and McLaren before calling, "Good luck," and going inside.

"Slimy bastard." Chad's face flooded with color.

McLaren wanted to agree but instead asked why Chad thought that. "Do you suspect Mr. Millington of killing your mother?"

"Yeah."

Herb came back outside with a broom and began sweeping the front path, whistling.

McLaren watched Herb make his way down the flagstones. "Why do you think it's him?"

"Because it's his style."

"What, murder?"

"Not intentionally, no. But he's a hooligan."

"And you say this because…"

"I got into it with Mr. Millington shortly before my mum died."

"A fight?"

"Yeah. He'd made some indecent remarks about her and I couldn't take it any more. I went after him. A bit later, my mum was dead. I think he came after her."

Chapter Fourteen

"You don't know how I've blamed myself." Chad blotted his eyes with the side of his hand. It was a large hand, as befitted his tall, powerful build. The skin, tanned and roughened from yard work, contrasted greatly with the paler, smoother skin that played around the edges of his tee-shirt sleeves and neckline. Chad tilted his head back, looking skyward, and his voice matched his inner anguish. "God, if I'd just kept quiet. If I'd just ignored it, Mum would still be alive."

"Perhaps not." McLaren paused as Chad lowered his head and looked at him with tear-moistened eyes. "Not if someone else killed her." He spoke low, choosing his words carefully, aware of the pain deep within the teenager's eyes.

"What? Like, who?" Chad's voice was hopeful, yet challenging, as if defying McLaren to produce a more likely suspect, or to relieve him of his guilt.

"I've just begun investigating, Chad. I don't know yet."

"At least you're honest." He ran the back of his hand across his nose, then pressed it against his khaki shorts.

"I try to be."

Chad stared at McLaren, trying to make him out, then smiled. "I think you are. You wouldn't admit it if you weren't. You'd be all bluff and swagger, coming on like some of those super tough telly cops."

"I never was a Dirty Harry."

Again Chad smiled. He leaned against the corner of the house, near the front door. "Mr. Millington was always making cracks about Mum. It got to the point where I just couldn't stand it anymore so one day I punched his lights out."

"And this was over what?"

"He always did hint stuff. But this time he flat came out and said it."

"Hint stuff like what? Sexual innuendoes?"

Chad avoided McLaren's eyes, as though embarrassed by the subject. "Yeah. He always made remarks about how smashing Mum looked. Well, 'always' being several months, I guess. At least it was several months that I knew about it so I guess it went on for a while." He paused, his face reddening.

"I've found that those types of people are usually all talk, Chad. It takes two to tango."

"Sure, I realize he was probably all mouth and no trousers, just acting macho, but it hurt. My mum never did a thing to deserve it. She never flirted back, she never dressed indecently. She never went over to his house alone. She was a lady and I got sick and tired of him suggesting improper stuff."

"Like what?"

"You know. Like, sleeping together." Chad mumbled this last statement so softly that McLaren could barely hear it.

"And that's what caused the fight?"

"Yeah. Mum and I were outside and as she started to go in the house, Mr. M calls after her that he had a few minutes free, and since both of their spouses weren't home....well, you get the idea." Again he blushed, but he doubled his hand into a fist and slammed it into the door.

"That's when the fight started."

"I couldn't let that go, could I?" He searched McLaren's eyes for a sign of approval or exoneration.

"I don't think most sons, brothers or husbands would."

"He's had it coming to him for ages. This was just the last straw. He's got a dirty mind and a dirty mouth, and I had to stop his abuse of my mum."

McLaren nodded, his eyes on the Millington house. Was Millington's wife the target of Herb's verbal abuse? Worse yet, was it also physical abuse? "Did your father know about this?"

"About Millington's talk, you mean?"

"That or how she felt about it?"

"I guess he would have done. That's hard to keep quiet, isn't it? I mean, Mr. M wasn't exactly secretive about it. He'd stand in his front garden and sometimes yell stuff at Mum. I guess Dad could've heard it."

"Had your father ever said anything to Millington or to your mother? Did you ever see your father mad?"

"I think I would've heard if Dad had known. Dad's a pretty quiet guy on the whole, though he does explode if he's pushed too far. But really, nothing much rattles him. Good bank material, if you know what I mean."

"Steady in a crisis." But maybe not in his personal life.

"Yeah. I think if Dad had known about all this he would've said something to Mr. Millington 'cause he'd be madder than hell at the berk. Dad wouldn't have let it go on so that Mum was continually harassed like that."

Or let his son play the husband's part by telling Millington to leg it. "So you think that Herb Millington got back at your mother because you defended her."

"I know it probably sounds far fetched, Mr. McLaren, and I don't think he planned it. I mean, he didn't sit at the table plotting to kill her. Well, he wouldn't, would he? That's a bit over the top! But if he got mad at her, like when he's in one of his violent moods, well, that's not so out of the question."

"I've heard of his outbursts, yes."

"One night he came up to her and mentioned me and him getting into a fight, and he was mad at me because I knocked him out flat and he was mad at Mum for all the stuff that happened—"

"He shot her accidentally?"

Chad looked ill. "Yeah. Something like that. You've seen him. He's a mass of muscles, even if he's not so young. He could easily have knocked her down if he wanted." He kicked the bottom of the door. "I don't think he hid in the bushes and ambushed her. But he's got that bloody temper. He might've got into a shouting match with her and things got out of hand, like you said."

"What about his mate?"

"Danny Mercer?" He rubbed the end of his nose, as though it had an itch he couldn't reach. "That piece of trash? He could have done, sure. He's got a temper."

McLaren glanced at Herb, who was walking into his garage. "I understand Danny is quite a bit younger than Herb. How'd they become friends, do you know?"

Perhaps because the topic had shifted from Marta to Danny, Chad relaxed, sagging against the door.

"You're right, Mr. McLaren. I think Danny's about thirty. Maybe a year or two younger than that. Doesn't really matter. There's twenty years or so difference between them."

"Did they know each other when Danny was a kid? Is that why they're friends now?"

"I don't think they did. I've had the impression it's a fairly recent friendship. Well, I'm not sure how recent, but not going back thirty years, at least."

"What's he do for a living? Are he and Herb connected that way, in the same business?"

"You'd have to ask someone else, but I think Danny is a kind of odd jobs man and a messenger boy. Well, boy isn't exactly right, but you know what I mean. I heard my dad talking to Mum once about they weren't sure who influenced whom in that relationship. I heard that Danny's a bit slow mentally, but I think he plays that up. I think he's just basically lazy and looking for an easy quid. He's had a string of jobs. Mr. Millington's fairly intelligent, I think, but he doesn't leave home at regular times on the weekdays."

"He has no set working hours at an office?"

"I guess. Oh, he leaves the house most days, but sometimes not until the evening. I guess they're doing okay financially, 'cause Mrs. Millington has nice looking clothes and they both drive expensive cars. But I think Mr. Millington and Danny want the same things from life, which may have thrown them together."

"Do you think Danny does the odd jobs and messenger service for Mr. Millington? Could they have become friends through work?"

"I don't know. Mainly I just see them sitting on the front porch, smoking and laughing and drinking beer."

"Do they have any shared hobbies?"

Chad exhaled slowly, as though he sifted through his mind for some recollection. "They like to hunt. Mr. Millington's got a friend who's a farmer. They go out there every so often and shoot rabbits with shotguns. I've never seen them come back with anything, though they could drop them off some place, I guess. They also like to race cars."

"Professionally?" McLaren couldn't keep the surprise from his voice.

"No. Places like Donington Park. Mr. Millington brings his car and they race over the National Circuit. Danny's more of a motorcycle nut, but he goes along and they switch off driving their car."

"The one that's in his garage right now?"

"Are you talking about that orange and blue thing?"

"Yes."

"That's the one. It's kind of hard to miss, isn't it? Especially their racing name emblazed on the sides."

"Each to his own hobby, I suppose."

"I think they use that car at Donington. They have a Mini, but I don't see it garaged at Mr. M's, so I guess Danny must keep it at his place. But I know they like the Autograss racing." He paused and glanced at the Millington's driveway. "He must be pretty good. I know for a fact that he and Danny race in the modified saloons class."

"The so-called Supersaloons?"

"Yeah."

"That takes a bit of money, doesn't it?"

"I looked it up online one day 'cause I wondered how he could afford it if he didn't have a regular job.

The website said the guideline for that class budget is £4,000 to £20,000."

McLaren glanced at his Peugeot. It fit that class, but it lacked the bright paint and profusion of graphics, club number, and advertisements smothering the car body. "Well, it might be a good way for Mr. Millington to let off steam, if his temper is threatening to bust loose. Though it's not the best idea to drive when you're explosively angry."

"I guess it can't do any real harm. That's what they're there for, isn't it? To race around and bang into each other?"

"Sure. Well, I hope he hasn't got into altercations with other drivers."

Chad mumbled that if he did, he felt sorry for the people Herb came in contact with.

"Is he a bully?"

"If he were younger I'd say he is. But since he's an adult...I don't know. He'd probably be termed a criminal if he were ever caught in something bent. A criminal or a plain ole thug. But he's not above lying in wait for someone if the bloke is bigger than he is. That's how he works, Mr. McLaren. He slinks around, planning how to get even. But yeah, I think he could've attacked my mum if he ambushed her one night."

"So it wouldn't take much to overpower a woman as tiny as your mother if her attacker was as big and sly as Herb Millington. If he was mad enough."

"That's the gist of it."

McLaren got the gist of Alan Hughes' temper thirty minutes later. They were in Alan's office, a wood-paneled room with large windows that looked onto the bank's lobby. The Venetian blinds had been drawn up—presumably so Alan could keep an eye on the morning's activities, or the employees could see he also worked part of his weekend—and Alan was standing behind his desk, facing McLaren. Perhaps the blinds should have been down; Alan's crimson face wouldn't be visible to customer and clerk alike.

"You've got a nerve even suggesting that." Alan's fist hit the top of his desk as his anger exploded. "My wife was killed. Her body was dumped by the roadside like she was a bag of rubbish. And you ask if I knew about Herb Millington and her."

"I'm not saying they had an affair, Mr. Hughes." McLaren kept his voice low. He was all too conscious of a few looks they were getting from curious customers and employees. "I just wanted to know if you think Millington could have actually forced your wife—"

"To do what? Have the affair?"

"I was thinking more of him accosting her one afternoon or evening."

"God, this sounds like some Victorian melodrama. No, I don't think so."

"You knew about the harassment, however."

"Yes."

"Did you do anything about it?"

"Like what? Go over there with a gun and threaten him to stop it?"

"I hope not. Maybe talk to him, tell him that his advances weren't appreciated."

"Yeah, I talked to him. Once. When Marta came into the house with her face all red from crying. She didn't want to tell me what had happened but she eventually did."

"And you went outside then to confront Millington?"

"You're damned right I did. He was in his garage, working on his damned racing car, and I told him he had better stop his foul suggestions or I'd beat him to within an inch of his life."

"Is that all?"

"Is that *all*? What the hell more do you want me to do? Choke him? Punch him in the stomach? Kick him in the groin? Yes, that was all."

"And that stopped the harassment?"

Alan opened his mouth, took a breath, then blushed. He grabbed the back of his leather chair and said more quietly, "Well, no. At least, not right away."

McLaren frowned. "Oh? When did it stop, then?"

"Well, it didn't." His voice had dropped to barely more than a whisper and his face suddenly drained of color. "I-it went on right up to her death."

"How long was this? From the time of your confrontation to the night of your wife's disappearance?"

"About that long. I didn't mark if off on the calendar. But yes, maybe a month. I talked to Millington in May."

"Why didn't you say anything more to him if his attentions continued? Didn't you know what was happening? Did your wife not tell you Millington was still bothering her?"

"I— She didn't tell me. I didn't hear anything more from her after I talked to Millington, so I assumed it was a thing of the past—until I overheard one of his remarks some weeks later. The evening before she and Linnet went to the casino." He turned the swivel chair toward him and slowly sat down.

"When you heard him talking to your wife, did you confront him again, tell him to leave Marta alone?"

Alan riffled the corner pages of his appointment diary, staring at the desktop. A tea trolley rumbled past the office door and into the open reception area. "I was going to, but I didn't have time that night. Marta and I met some friends for dinner and went to see a play at the theater. *The Twisted Plot*, if you need to check up on my whereabouts. It was past midnight when we got home. I promised myself I'd talk to Millington the following day."

"But you didn't."

"No. Marta left work that next day, Friday, at noon, went to her brother-in-law's, and then met Linnet at the casino."

"Why did that stop you from talking to Millington? You were home that evening, weren't you?"

"Later I was. Chad and I went out to eat, then I helped him with his homework. By the time I thought of Millington again, it was late and I figured it would wait until Saturday morning. Then, that night, when she didn't come home, I forgot about it."

What kind of husband would forget about speaking to his wife's tormentor, McLaren wondered as he left the office. A coward? A man no longer in love? A man suspicious that his wife and neighbor actually had the affair? McLaren crossed the spacious lobby, aware of Alan's stare and the whispered conjectures of the cashiers, aware of his hard-soled shoes clacking on the terrazzo floor. Aware of the suspicions and questions shouting in his brain, reminding him that Alan had no alibi for that questionable period of time. Had there come a point when Herb Millington's innuendoes became actuality or imagined actuality, and Alan finally snapped, taking out his anger on Marta in one gunshot to her head?

The casino in Nottingham wasn't particularly busy, but it was only late Saturday morning. It would see its bulk of customers later that night. He parked away from the majority of cars clustered as near to the entrance as they could get, and walked up to the canopied main entrance. The lights declaring the casino name were blaringly bright even in the daylight, and McLaren wondered how much of their profit went to pay for the electricity bill. About as much as they spent on their landscaping maintenance, he thought, watching several gardeners weeding a perennial border. Clumps of ornamental evergreens, pruned into a smooth geometric form belying their realness, created a backdrop for terracotta pots overflowing with annuals and signs proudly proclaiming the casino's round-the-clock accessibility. No leaf littered the grass; no cigarette butt marred the pavement. The entire place was immaculate and artificial.

The interior was too. He nodded to the doorman stationed at the large glass and brass double door and walked into the gaming room. It was a blaze of red, gold, and white, with chrome furniture and recessed ceiling lighting that pinpointed specific areas: blackjack, craps, baccarat, and roulette. The slot machines, with their lights and noise, lined the perimeter of the room like pagan gods that the players placated with coins and prayers. The poker tables were isolated from the commotion, probably in that next room, he thought, giving the players quiet in which to think.

McLaren walked to the nearest roulette table. Several people were seated around it, talking and drinking and moving their chips, the columns of red, white, and black, dotting the green cloth like confetti left over from someone's win. The croupier's voice floated over the conversation at the table. "No more bets, please. No more bets." The wheel spun and he flipped the ball onto the bowl again. The ball clacked around the roulette bowl as the croupier looked at the table patrons. "Twenty-nine noir. Twenty-nine noir wins. Thank you, sir." He accepted the tip from the winning player as he pushed the chips toward the man, then started the process again, calling for bets.

McLaren strolled into the manager's office, introduced himself and asked to speak to the croupiers who were on duty when Marta was at the casino.

The man consulted last year's work schedule, compared it to who was working now, and told McLaren that of the four croupiers on duty then, two had quit, one was on holiday, and the other man was due in on the hour. "If you'd care to wait…" He indicated a leather sofa along the far wall, facing his desk.

"I'll stroll around, thanks just the same, maybe play a hand of Twenty One while I wait. What's the croupier's name whom I'll be talking to?"

The manager told him and added that he'd be coming in the employee entrance in the rear of the building. "He'll be at the first table, closest to the main door, if you miss him."

McLaren thanked him and left the office. He was halfway through his beer when he decided to try to meet the employee outside. Besides being less noisy, the outdoors afforded less temptation to hurry to his table, less nervousness at being overheard.

He paid for his drink, left by the main door, and hurried around to the back of the building. Deck chairs, garden tables, and clusters of tub plants dotted the lawn, creating restful areas for staff breaks. McLaren eased into a canvas chair, found it sturdy and comfortable, and waited. Ten minutes later his man showed up.

"I wonder if you might remember a particular customer," McLaren said after explaining who he was. The croupier eyed McLaren, perhaps wondering if this was legal. McLaren sensed the man's hesitation and tried to put him at ease. "The manager, Mr. Pollard, said you were working that night."

"Perhaps. Which customer would that be, sir? June of last year?"

"Yes. She was with another lady. Perhaps at your table."

"You expect me to remember one person out of the thousands who play at my table?"

"You'd remember her."

"Looker, was she?"

"She won big."

"How big?"

"Over £253,000."

The man smiled, as if enjoying a private joke or seeing Marta in his mind's eye. "Oh, that one. Made a bit of history, she did. She wasn't at my table that night, but I heard about it. Get with the cashier. She talked to the woman. *Still* talks about it. She's on duty now, probably. I've got to get to work, mate."

McLaren thanked him and walked back to the front

of the casino. After asking at several stations, he found her.

Yes, she'd been on duty that night. Yes, she still remembered it. How could she not? It had been a huge win, one of the casino's largest payouts for roulette.

"Do you remember anyone watching her, or following her from the casino?"

"I heard she was killed." The cashier shook her head. "Real pity, that. Excuse me."

McLaren stepped aside as a customer came up to change her chips into cash.

"Thank you, sir. Sorry about the interruption. Yes, I remember her. She was pretty and over the moon about her win. I don't mean I lack feelings for any other murder victim, but this lady seemed to be going through a hard time. Marta, her name was. She was a regular. You get to know their names, you know."

"What do you mean 'hard time'? Did she talk to you about something specific?"

"No. But I heard a bit of her conversation with her friend."

"Were they talking very loudly? Could someone have overheard them?"

"I don't think it was overly loud. At least, no one hung around them or loitered near the Women's. They'd gone in there to count their chips. I just heard a bit of their chatter when they came up to me to cash it in. They were talking about buying back something. The other woman said then Marta could sleep easier, so I guess it was a big purchase. Or maybe it was getting something out of hock."

Buying back her conscience. Or her friendship with Verity. A cheer rose from a group of people standing around a slot machine and a man jumped up, yelling excitedly. "And no one seemed overtly interested in her or followed her?"

"No, sir. I was watching because, as I said, it was a huge payoff. The two ladies talked about her bet, which was straight up on 1. Her friend laughed and said wasn't Marta glad she had switched from her corner bet of 19, 20, 22 and 23? She'd evidently been betting that combination quite a while. Anyway, as I said, I was a bit concerned about them being alone, without some man with them to protect all that money, but she had her friend with her, and they did look around the room. I guess they were making sure no one was following them."

McLaren nodded and seemed to be considering something.

"I don't think they had any trouble in the car park, if that's what you're thinking."

"Pardon?"

"You thinking someone could've gone out another exit and killed her in the car park?" She shook her head. "The police had the same idea and they took the CCTV tape. They couldn't find anybody on it. Just the two women leaving and a few people arriving. No one approached them."

"I guess they'd be able to see that."

"They've still got it."

"What? The tape?"

"Yes, sir. They've not released it yet because they haven't found her killer. I guess they still want it for evidence. You know, in case they find somebody and they need to refer to the tape."

"Was there any suspicion that the two women did

meet someone in the car park?"

"You'll have to ask the coppers, sir. But maybe the other lady took the money as a precaution. You know," she said when McLaren looked blank. "Confounding the would-be robber."

The police are confounded too, McLaren thought as he thanked the cashier and left.

McLaren didn't leave the area immediately. He walked around the building, studying the exits, the plantings of shrubbery, the location of the CCTV cameras. Was it possible that someone had slipped out of another door, waited for Marta, and kidnapped her? But the cashier had said nothing like that appeared on the security tape. He drew a notebook from out of his pocket and circled the building again, sketching it and the positions of the cameras and security guards. Was it possible that the cameras hadn't caught everything? Could someone, perhaps knowledgeable with the casino set-up, have purposely waited beyond the camera's view?

He wandered to a guard stationed at the car park and inquired.

The guard viewed McLaren as though he were planning the heist of the century. "Why do you ask?"

McLaren explained that he was investigating the Hughes murder.

"Well, the coppers have already been over this." He turned back to the CCTV screen in his small booth and talked to the monitor. "If you want to know something, ask them."

"But I'm here and I'd like to know your opinion. After all, you work with the security system. I thought you'd know if there were areas that weren't covered, if it needed improving. You do an important service to your clientele, but if the cameras miss some area, like just outside casino property—"

"Look." The guard exhaled heavily and turned again toward McLaren. He was as bulky as a slot machine, with narrow eyes that seemed to weigh everything they saw before filtering it to his mind. Which probably spun with the rapidity of the machine and came up three lemons just as often, McLaren thought. The guard leaned his arm against the hut's windowsill. "I don't install the things, pal. I just watch the monitor. There was nothing to see that night."

"Really? No one followed her outside the casino, stopped to congratulate her, even from several yards distant?"

"A few people did that, sure, but they were cleared in court. There was one bloke who spoke to her, but he kept his distance and he walked off as she got into her car. I saw her drive off."

"But no one else, no one who you or the police would term 'suspicious,' then."

"No. The cops here asked me, and I was asked again at the cop shop. The cops even looked at the tape themselves. Nothing like that showed up on the cameras. Not even walking out of camera range."

"I realize that, but I thought that if you could tell me how *far* the cameras record the scene, I could get an idea of where Mrs. Hughes' killer—"

"You hard of hearing or just obnoxious? I told you I didn't see nothing. I got nothing to do with how the cameras are set up. I didn't hear a thing that night and no one could've conked her in the car park. I would've seen that on the monitor. If someone needs aid, I get involved. If they need the RAC to fix a flat tire, I ring 'em up. But other than that—"

"Sure. Coffee and donuts till it's time to leave."

The man stood up, his eyes mere slits, his lips drawn back. "You bloody—"

"A woman was *murdered*," McLaren snapped, matching the guard's voice tone and volume. "And if you don't care about that, about helping find her killer, you're as pathetic as the scum who topped her." He stood there, feet apart, waiting for the man to charge out of his booth, ready for a fight.

Instead, the guard grabbed a pad of paper and his pen. "What's your name again?"

"McLaren. Do you need me to spell it?"

"I can spell it. B-A-S-T-A-R-D."

"Funny."

"I've got something else that'll make you die laughing, matey. You're barred from coming back here, understand?"

"You can try, but frankly, I don't think you'll succeed. Thanks for your time. You've renewed my faith in bouncers. All brawn and no brains." He walked to his car, the guard's opinion of McLaren following him all the way.

McLaren left the casino and stopped in a lay-by to put a mobile call through to Ian Shard, the police constable who had talked, however nonchalantly, to Herb Millington. As the phone rang, McLaren considered the possibility of someone waiting outside the range of casino cameras and confronting Marta. A winning that large would tempt many people. But if the police hadn't seemed concerned about that, and Marta's friend Linnet hadn't seen anyone following them…He rubbed the back of his neck. Perhaps there was another angle.

If there was, PC Shard couldn't supply it. "I didn't work that case, but I know nothing suspicious appeared on the CCTV tape. The lads were vocal in their disappointment. No other car followed her. And it was nineteen minutes later that the next car left the casino after she and Linnet Isherwood."

"Hardly what I'd call a close tail." McLaren momentarily closed his eyes, exasperated at the lack of evidence.

"Nothing's ever easy, is it, McLaren?"

"Not right now. Can you tell me exactly where Marta Hughes' body was found?" He silently berated himself; he should have brought along the computer notes.

Shard sounded surprised. "You going to look that over?"

Why would you ask that, McLaren wanted to say. Every good detective worth his salt viewed the crime scene. Charts, videos, and photos were as good as they went, but they didn't replace actually viewing the area. "I'd like to see it. It may suggest something to me."

The constable hesitated, and McLaren could practically hear Shard speculate if he'd be injuring his career if his superintendent found out. After McLaren's repeated request, the constable finally relented. "Just outside Elton. On the western end. Before the road splits for Youlgreave and Middleton."

"Where, exactly? Anything you can point me to?"

There was a grunted, "One second," the squeak of a metal file drawer opening, a rustle of papers, and a mild oath quickly following several heavy thuds. A chair squeaked. Another second or two of silence, then moments later, Shard sighed into the receiver. "Got it. Just don't let on you got it from me, understand?"

"Your name won't come up."

"See that it doesn't, mate, or I'll get the sticky end."

"Nothing will mar your perfect career, Shard."

"Well, it better not. My wife's got used to a roof over her head."

"I wouldn't dream of moving her. Let's have it."

"Like I said, it's just before the road branches. But it's on the Elton side. You know where that ruined stone barn is? It's on the western side of that. Between the edge of the barn and the road. There are weeds and brambles and such there, so look carefully. You might miss the spot."

"In that depression," McLaren said, nodding as he visualized the spot.

"Right. I don't think you'll find anything, but I hope you do."

"Thanks, Shard. That's at least two of us."

The town of Matlock lay between Nottingham and Elton, practically in a straight line on a map. The roads were nearly as accommodating, for the A6 ran into and west of it before it snaked northwest into Bakewell. From the A6 at Matlock, Marta could have cut over to Elton using the small road out of Brightgate or gone slightly north to get on the B5057. Either route would have taken her into Elton quite easily and quickly. *If* she had driven back to Matlock on the night of her disappearance. McLaren hoped he was about to find out.

He had the address of Marta's brother-in-law—provided by Alan Hughes—and decided this was the perfect time to question the relative. He followed the A6 into the town, turned left onto a major, connecting street, and wound around the western end of town until he turned down the sought-after road. The residence was at the bottom of the cul-de-sac.

Neal Clark was probably forty, McLaren judged as he sat in the front room. Of medium height, he had a superb physique. Not bulging with muscles, but his arms and thighs were well toned, in keeping with his flat abdomen. Works out, McLaren thought. Or heaves car bodies for a living.

"So you want to talk about Marta," Neal said.

"If you've no objections." McLaren eyed the man, judging if he still hurt from his sister-in-law's death. "If it's not too painful a subject."

"Not my topic of choice, but I'm okay with it. At least it's not as painful as last year. What do you want to know?"

"I'm trying to ascertain her movements that night."

"The night she died."

"We assume so, but without a witness—"

"You don't know exactly when it happened."

"Had she ever talked to you about any problems she was having, or anyone who might be bothering her?"

"At Noah's Ark?"

"There or elsewhere."

"Like, did she have any enemies?" His blue eyes, vivid and nearly mesmerizing in their gaze, seemed to hold the pain of losing Marta, registering what his face didn't betray. The thin lips were set in a straight, firm line; the eyebrows neither arched in surprise nor lowered in sadness. The face was a mask, shielding the world from his thoughts and ache.

"Something like that, yes. Had she talked to you about a particular person she was concerned about, or any troubles she had? I understand you and she saw each other that day."

"Yes, for lunch. Here. I don't mean here in my house. We met in town. We do that fairly frequently. Well, more so after my wife, her sister's, death a few years ago. Hit-and-run car accident." He said it slightly slower, the words perhaps hard to speak.

"That explains why she didn't talk to you at work."

"Pardon?"

"I was wondering why she needed to stop by your house when she saw you nearly every day at the shelter. But if you met frequently for personal reasons, like talking about your wife's death, that answers my question."

"Her sister's death isn't something we would bring up at work, no. There's enough office chatter without adding the intimate details of family. My wife's death concerns no one but me and Marta. We wished to keep it private, between ourselves, not turn it into a segment for a reality show or a topic for tea time."

"I quite understand."

"I don't work on Fridays, and it's Marta's half-day, so it's a good time to get together. The restaurants are also less crowded than on the weekends."

"As you said, a perfect time to meet up."

"Marta spent that Friday afternoon with me until she left to meet a friend in Nottingham. They were going to the casino." He picked up a chip from the side table and handed it to McLaren. The casino's logo and name were printed on it.

"Did she patronize the place frequently?" He flipped the chip across his knuckles, as many poker players do while they are waiting for their turn.

"I know she went often, but I don't know to what extent. We didn't talk about that, neither that day or any day."

"What did you talk about that day, if you don't mind telling me."

Neal sighed and slumped back in his chair. "I don't know." He ran his fingers through his short, red hair, as though kneading his brain. "Yes, I do. We talked about her neighbor and her co-worker. We also talked about Alan's birthday and would he prefer a small family gathering at their place or should we go some place for the afternoon and evening, like the racetrack or dirt car races. Or maybe biking along the Tissington Trail. I even suggested we try rock climbing at Windgather Rocks near Whaley Bridge, but I think Marta was a bit nervous about that."

"Alan's a bit of an adventurer, then."

"I don't know how adventuresome he is, but he likes sports and activities like those. Something where he can burn off his pent-up energy."

"The more physical, the better, then."

"Exactly. I always thought it odd that he wound up as a banker."

"Not the type to sit behind a desk?"

"I suppose he's had to, for the sake of his career. But he seems more suited to something more active. At least that's the impression I always had. They should've lived in a village, I thought. He's that sort of person."

"Did you or your wife grow up in a village?"

"No. In Buxton. We knew each other since school."

"So you knew Marta, too."

"Yes. There was a time when I considered marrying Marta, but Alan came along and proposed to her before I ever got my nerve up to ask her. I turned my eyes and heart toward Marta's sister and never was sorry about my choice. We were very much in love."

McLaren made no reply. There was nothing he could say.

Neal continued, his voice hazy, his eyes staring at something McLaren couldn't see. "We had summer jobs in Buxton, too. I always envied the kids who were camp counselors, but we were confined in town."

"I sometimes think that many of us never get to live where we'd be most happy. It puts a damper on our urge for kayaking, for example, if we're trapped in a town."

Neal nodded, brightening. "That's why we were thinking about doing something like this for Alan's birthday, which was 20 June."

McLaren didn't mention the significance of the date, thinking again what a tragedy Marta's death was for those who had loved her.

"We went to a studio on one of his birthdays and gave wire sculpture a try, but I don't think it had enough action for him."

"So you tried the lesson and Alan didn't wax enthusiastic."

"He didn't complain, but I think once was enough."

"Did you decide on something?"

"I believe a couple years ago Marta opted for going

to a gun club and doing some target shooting."

"Alan likes to do that?"

"He did then. I don't know if he's continued or not."

McLaren shifted in his chair and glanced at the wall clock. The day was getting on. "So you talked about the birthday that afternoon. You said you also talked about her neighbor and co-worker. Would that be Herb Millington, her neighbor, and Verity Dwyer from the animal shelter?"

"Yes." Neal sat up and leaned forward, his elbows on the tops of his thighs. He pressed the tips of his fingers together and looked at McLaren with the same pain-filled eyes, yet his voice had tightened, as though holding back anger or disgust, and his words came lower and faster, nearly clipped in his desire to finish the subject. "I told her she needed to tell Alan about that sleazebag Millington. That would stop the harassment. Or let me come over there and beat the bastard to within an inch of his life, but she didn't want me to get involved. Said she'd handle it."

"And Verity?"

"Marta's conscience was bothering her and she didn't know what to do."

"About what?"

He grabbed another poker chip from the small bowl on the table and ran his thumb over its ridged edge. "The money. I suppose you know about it."

"The money from the shelter."

"Yes." Neal's fingers closed around the chip, pressing against it until his fingers blanched. He nodded as he considered something.

McLaren didn't rush the man, but looked around

the room. It was uncomplicated, simple, straightforward in its facade, as Neal was. Furniture of simple wood or chrome frames held solid colored fabric. A brown carpet stretched into the adjoining room—the dining room—where the same hue was picked up in the large, burlap-matted watercolor above the table. Another watercolor, smaller and matted in pale blue mat board, hung over the sofa. No knickknacks other than a small silver sculpture, metal-cased clock, and a box of matches occupied the fireplace mantel. There seemed to be nothing to dust or conjure up memories.

As though sensing he was wasting McLaren's time, Neal finally spoke. "Marta hadn't hesitated in loaning the money to Verity. She always did such generous things for friends. But now she was having second thoughts about her impulsive action. After all, it was a lot of money that she was out, and she had grown afraid that Verity would never repay it."

Chapter Fifteen

The small clock chimed the hour, its tone so soft that it would have been lost if Neal had still been talking. McLaren grabbed the poker chip he'd been flipping with all the tenacity of a man holding onto the edge of a cliff. The sun seemed to sink immediately below the horizon and he strained his eyes to make out Neal's face in the haze that threatened to engulf him.

"*Marta* loaned Verity money?" He tried to speak calmly, keeping the astonishment from his voice, but his voice had cracked after uttering the first word. He covered up his shock by coughing.

Neal jerked his head up, seeing McLaren's raised eyebrow. "Why…yes. I thought you knew."

"I'd heard something about the money," he said, not untruthfully, "but not the full details."

"There's really not much to it. Verity needed several hundred quid for some bills that had piled up. She didn't want to borrow money from the bank. The interest would have added to her financial problem. She was desperate to get it taken care of. I guess her creditors were applying pressure." He slumped back in his chair and relaxed his hold on the chip in his hand. "Anyway, Marta loaned her the money. I don't know how much, but it was a sizable chunk. That's why she was headed to the casino that night. She wanted to win big so she could replace the money she'd loaned Verity before Alan found out. He's a real stickler about that sort of thing. He must have 'Don't lend money to friends or relatives' tattooed on his chest." He tossed the chip back into the bowl and crossed his legs. "Seems to me there are times to make exceptions."

McLaren stared at the watercolor above the mantel. It had been painted by Marta and depicted another probable holiday spot. Switzerland, he guessed, scrutinizing the snow-capped mountains and herder's hut. A car horn sounded on the street, bringing McLaren back from the depths of the painting. "And the casino…did she come back here after she finished that night?"

"That timeline of yours again?"

"Yes. I'd like to find out where she went and when. It could help pinpoint who was with her."

"As to that, I've no clue. She didn't come back here."

McLaren opened his mouth to say Marta had told Linnet she was stopping at Neal's on the way home. Instead, he faked another cough and merely looked at the man. "I just wondered."

"Sorry, but I can't tell you any more."

I'm sorry too, McLaren thought, walking back to his car. And just who the hell is telling the truth about the missing money?

McLaren got to the stone barn late afternoon. He had left Nottingham by the A610, continued up the A6, and stopped for lunch in the village of Cromford. Traffic was heavy, being the height of the tourist season and a Saturday, so he was later leaving than he had wanted. At Grangemill he took the B506 north before turning west for Elton. The village never failed to fascinate him, from the stone church and churchyard several steps above road level, to the pub of sporadic open hours, to the ancient stone circle on the nearby moor. I should live here, McLaren thought as he drove past the centuries-old inn now accommodating a bed-and-breakfast. It's a paradise of stone farm buildings and fields, enough to keep me in cold, hard cash for years.

He turned off the main road, poked along behind a tractor, then spotted the stone barn. It matched the image in the emailed photo. He glanced at his notes from Jamie's phone call. West of the village, a half-mile out, on the right side of the road. He smiled, hoping good luck would be with him.

The building was remarkably preserved, its walls upright and solid. The roof had lost some tiles, but it was sturdier than similar structures McLaren had seen. Near the roof's peak, a large hole permitted sunlight, rain and birds into the loft, the heavy bough of the overhanging oak still cradled in the opening. A few sunflowers poked from this void, where their seeds had taken a foothold. On to the eastern side of the barn, the years hadn't treated the lean-to as kindly, for the two adjoining walls were little more than piles of stone, moss- and lichen-covered where they wallowed in the shade. Of the two remaining walls, birds had built nests and weeds had wrapped their tendrils around the window frames.

McLaren parked on the left side of the road, half-amused at the remnants of his detective skills, and walked over to the barn.

The weeds and grass were high in the open space, higher still near the building's foundation and in the ditch bordering the road. Scraps of paper, plastic carrier bags, and a sheet of stationery were trapped within the stems where the wind had blown them, trapped for a long time, judging by the faded print and the cracked and shredded edges. The sunlight glanced off the stationery's imprinted logo and the bags, and winked to him as he jumped the ditch. He pulled the broken-off stems from his shoes and wandered to the barn.

The wooden door stood solid and grim, its exterior battered from decades of abusive weather. But the door held firm even if its paint had faded and cracked, the wood where it was exposed to the elements dull and rough. Splinters at the doorjamb, opposite the door's dead bolt, spoke of someone's attempt to enter the building—kids bent on mischief, or the farmer, who had misplaced his key? The door stood slightly ajar now, revealing a black-as-night interior. McLaren stood to one side of the door, his cop's instincts on edge as he placed his outstretched palm on the wooden panel and eased the door open. The hinges complained fiercely, squealing into the stillness with the intensity of a suspect yelling for his lawyer.

McLaren remained where he was, staring into the interior, letting his eyes adjust to the darkness. Great place for a murder.

Why had she ended up here? Had whoever picked her up at her house driven her here for a meeting? If so, did they talk inside the barn? The building had to have some significance, otherwise they could have talked outside most anywhere. McLaren looked again at the ground leading to the barn door. Maybe her body had simply been thrown here.

McLaren snapped on his torch and played its

brilliant beam around the barn's interior. The dirt floor was spotted with cigarette butts and crumpled cellophane packs, beer bottles and discarded crisps packets. A teenager's rendezvous.

He went inside, cautiously shining the light on the floor, and picked his way over the rubbish. The torchlight revealed nothing unusual, nothing that looked as though it had been there for a year. Shifting the beam from side to side, he walked around, peered into the corners, gazed up at the rafters, tipped over the old buckets and wood crates and bales of straw. Nothing.

The wooden steps leading to the loft were dust-covered and cobweb-strewn. But dust settles and cobwebs gather in a year, McLaren thought as he angled the torch along the stone wall and up to the landing, then back onto the step nearest his feet. It seemed solid enough. He pressed his right shoulder against the wall and carefully climbed the stairs.

His right hand held the torch and though it accented the backless steps and showed where to place his feet, he felt ill-at-ease. No handrail kept him safely on the staircase; it must have fallen, or been yanked off years ago. He felt for the reassuring coldness of the stones behind him. The blackness closed around him, thick and still except for his labored breathing and shuffling gait. A wooden plank groaned as he put his weight on it and birds above in the loft chattered excitedly, yet silence quickly descended and in that abrupt quiet he felt as much alone as he had ever felt in his life.

A mouse scurried across the step, its tail carving a thin trail in the dust. McLaren stopped, pushing his back against the wall. The beam of the torch threw the rodent into exaggerated relief, a monster of light tan fur startlingly bright against the darkness beyond. The mouse scuttled across the plank and jumped onto the floor before McLaren let out his breath. Dark spaces did that to him—pushed the memories into the open and unleashed the demons from their locked cages. He stood there for a moment, taking a deep breath and slowly exhaling, listening for the faint rustle of cellophane or dry leaves as the mouse jumped for cover, waiting for the rest of the pack to hightail it to safer quarters. But the only sound was the caw of a rook somewhere overhead and his heartbeat in his ear.

He slowly panned the torch's beam across the remainder of the steps, hoping he would see no other mouse. The steps were vacant except for wisps of hay, dust, and dried clumps of mud. McLaren aimed the light back at his feet and climbed, the methodical, measured thump of his footsteps thudding into the interior space. The light angled against the wall, revealing chinks where the mortar had cracked and fallen, fingerholds of moss, and a seedling wedged into a crevice and holding on with all the tenacity of its roots. He brushed off a strand of cobweb and groped along the wall with his free hand, as Braille writing slides beneath reading fingers, the stones slipping beneath him as he ascended. Step by cautious step he climbed, dislodging hay strands and dust.

Occasionally a stone's rough edge caught his shirt or dug into his flesh, and he silently berated the stonemason for his hurry or clumsiness. By the time McLaren reached the landing, his shoulder was sore and bruised from the pressure of his body rubbing against the stones. But the stability of the wall had

saved him from a fall—and had kept the memories at
bay. He shone his light around the loft.

It was brighter up here. Sunlight seeped through
the jagged hole in the roof and illuminated sections of
the enclosure. A large barrel crowded into one corner
and some old farm tools leaned lazily against the wall.
A coil of rope, its ends frayed and probably chewed by
mice, sagged over the barrel top. A dirt-covered padded
horse collar hung around the newel post on the landing.
McLaren walked into the space.

The straw was thick in places, barely covering the
wooden floor in others. It smelled of dust and mold and
there were tunnels near the far wall—probably where
animals had hollowed out nests or warrens. He kicked
apart the burrows, the old fear taking hold of his mind
and heart. The disturbed straw laced the air with dust
that turned a golden tan in the shaft of sunlight. It fell
heavily, rather than floating, to the floor. He shook his
head, holding his breath until he stepped away from the
clumps, and coughed.

A stump of candle and a box of matches lay on the
windowsill nearest the road. A chipped china saucer
bearing clumps of candle wax sat on the floor. Damned
kids. Did they want to burn down the place? He strode
to the window, picked up the candle and matches, and
shoved them into his back pocket. He took a slow look
around the area. As he turned back toward the landing,
he saw the glint.

An empty beer bottle snuggled half-in, half-out of
the straw, the sunlight glancing off the smooth, amber
glass. It seemed to wink at McLaren, the golden gleam
fading and glowing as a tree branch waved outside in
the breeze, its leaves sporadically masking the sunlight.

He watched it for several seconds, mesmerized by the trick of the light until the glint faded. More rubbish, he thought, leaving the bottle where it lay and clomping down the steps.

The ground outside the barn had grown over in the year since the cops' fingertip search. McLaren stood in a patch of sunlight, envisioning the line of constables crawling over the ground shoulder to shoulder, pulling up grass and weeds, clearing the area down to the bare earth. They would bag everything they found: cigarette ends, pull tabs from beverage cans, cellophane package wrapping, scraps of paper, broken lipsticks, broken combs, earrings, coins, keys, inkless pens, plastic straws, paperclips...Anything and everything. There was no indication at the outset of a case what way it would turn and what may prove important. So it was all bagged and preserved. Which was why, one year later, McLaren was surprised to see that the land had recovered so well, swathed in a healthy mix of grasses and flowering plants. And why he walked over to the large oak tree to the north of the barn, several yards away. He'd find nothing where the police had searched.

The grass was flat at the tree's trunk, as though it were a popular spot for picnickers. A crushed lemonade carton and a small notebook suggested someone had left in haste not too long ago. As he bent to pick them up, he noticed a large stone, approximately a foot tall and rounded, barely visible among the mass of tall weeds and ivy. A nice spot to sit and sketch. Or write. He pocketed the notebook, walked over to the stone, and yanked up the plants in a yard-wide circle. He had nearly cleared the ground when he discovered a silver charm of a downhill skier tangled in the dense stems near the roots. Probably from a bracelet, he thought. He picked it up, blew off the soil and dust, and admired its shiny surface before he slipped it into his pocket.

The remainder of the area yielded nothing unusual.

This spot, farther from the stone building, had not been subjected to the ruthless search of the previous year, for the grass grew even and thick between the gravel side of the road and the edge of the wood. Clumps of Queen Anne's lace and wood dock dotted the patch of green, waist-high and impenetrable in its exuberant growth. Several large boughs from the trees fringing the glade had crashed to earth at one time. A large tree trunk angled out from the forest's border. Bramble and creeping thistle, tall and reaching for the sun, seemed to explode from the ground around the trunk. McLaren abandoned his casual search of the low depression alongside the road and lifted the boughs. Nothing but matted grass met his eye. He poked through the growth with the broken branch, then with his fingers, feeling the wet earth beneath. Still nothing. He stood up and gazed at the trunk. Tiers of many-zoned polypore fungi enveloped one end of the trunk. The sunlight played upon the half-circled brackets, enhancing the browns, grays and tans that radiated out in wavy rings. The top of the trunk had splintered, possibly from its fall, but the mid section of the dead wood looked solid. Had it been here last year?

He waded through the stinging plants, the prickly leaves and thorns tearing at his flesh and clothing. Ignoring the angry red welts and drops of blood, he pushed aside the plants with his feet, then stepped on the stems to crack them and keep them from springing up again. After clearing the entire length of the trunk, he got on his hands and knees. The exposed earth beneath the edges of the trunk was damp. No yellowish grass or wildflowers stretched outward into the clearing. The wood had been there a while, McLaren reasoned, but had the search crew moved it? He needed to see if anything was trapped beneath it.

Thrusting his left hand under a large bough, he pulled at the branches with his right. His fingers touched something smooth. Trying to determine the object's identity, he felt along the flat surface. It tapered slightly. McLaren yanked harder at the branches but the bough did not shift. He stood, ignoring the dampness of his trousers. Tugging and kicking the trunk did not budge it from its position. He picked up a fallen branch and used it against the trunk as a lever. It snapped in two at the first hint of pressure. He turned toward the barn, exasperated, his eyes moving toward the upper story. A long-handled rake and shovel leaned against the wall in the loft. They would make acceptable levers. But to get them he would have to enter the barn again, mount the stairs, and confront the dark and the nightmares. That was not an option. Not now. One time was enough to flirt with the memories that he had shoved into the recesses of his mind. He could not face them again so soon.

He threw down the branch and strode to his car. Getting in, he told himself the car needed a wash anyway. The engine started with a purr and he eased the vehicle off the road. The depression paralleling the tarmac wasn't long, slanting upward and flattening out to meet the general lay of the land. Yet, the grass and wood dock were thick in patches, perhaps hiding holes or broken bottles. He set the parking brake, got out, picked up a dead branch, and jabbed into the vegetation. The soil was solid, yielding no surprises. He tossed away the stick and got back into his car. The hell with proper procedure.

The earth was firm, erasing the question of getting stuck. He steered around one of the large, fallen boughs and stopped in front of the trunk. It looked larger when viewed from within the car. Yet, he reminded himself, the top part was rotten and would probably break off when the trunk started rolling. With that thought to cheer him, he backed up and aimed the car's front bumper directly at the trunk's midsection. He stopped when the bumper nudged the wood. He took a deep breath as his foot pressed down slowly on the accelerator.

Nothing happened. For all the engine's groan, the downed tree remained where it was. McLaren applied more pressure and the car crept forward, the tires digging into the earth. The trunk stirred, finally inched forward hesitantly as it came against bumps of packed soil and tufts of grass. Chunks of bark slid off beneath the bumper as the dead wood rolled. When McLaren judged he had cleared the site, he braked, letting the trunk come to rest against a small birch. He backed the car, angled sharply to the right, and drove back onto the grassy verge of the road.

When he walked back to the trunk, he saw that he had shifted it a good half dozen feet from its original spot. The exposed ground stretched pale tan and brown the length of the trunk; no plants struggled toward the sunlight. McLaren smiled. Maybe the search team hadn't bothered to shift the dead wood; maybe they'd been too rushed or considered it too far from the body, which had been near the barn.

He saw the silvery object immediately. He squatted and pulled it from its imprisonment in the damp soil. Flicking off the mud, he rotated it slowly, looking at it with a growing sense of excitement. It was a heel from a woman's shoe, a high-heeled shoe. A dress shoe. The sunlight glanced off the silvery patina and he blinked. Jamie's words sounded in his mind: victim's right shoe missing.

Feeling clever, he put the heel on the grass and continued prodding the rest of the soggy earth. The area was large and his fingertips soon became sore and dirty, but he had no thought of stopping until he'd searched it thoroughly. He started his hunt at the tree's midsection, where the shoe heel had been buried, and worked steadily, slowly toward the larger end of the trunk depression. He found nothing. Returning to the midsection, he searched toward the crown. Quarter of an hour later he was rewarded for his meticulous work. His fingers closed around something hard.

He drew it from its near imprisonment and flicked off the globs of mud. It was circular—or had been before it had broken—about the size of a walnut shell and black or dark blue. He got up and walked to a dry patch of soil, where he wiped the object across the grass. Mclaren slowly rotated it, trying to make out what it was. He pulled his handkerchief from his back trousers pocket, spat repeatedly on the object, and cleaned off the major portion of mud with the linen. It still had mud wedged into the ridged rim, but he knew what it was. A poker chip. A fragment of a chip, actually. He angled it so the sun slanted across its surface. Was there printing on it, or just the usual design found on most commercial chips? Was it from Noah's Ark or a custom-printed chip from a casino? Either way, he smiled as he carried the treasures gingerly back to his car. It was prophetic. Hadn't he always been called in to clear up messes when the chips were down?

Chapter Sixteen

In other circumstances, McLaren would have hesitated about getting into his car wearing wet, muddy clothing. But the car's exterior was also wet and muddy from the trunk rolling, and—perhaps even more important—he was tired and wanted to wrap up his day.

He leaned slightly to the left as he looked at the fragment of the poker chip. His makeshift cleansing had removed most of the mud and he could now see a bit of writing on its face. Part of the paint was scratched but he could make out the first two letters: ON. Could be part of a word, like 'one,' he thought, recalling a slogan on one of the animal shelter's chips: One pet, one heart of unconditional love. Of course, it could also stand for the amount of the casino chip's worth: One hundred. He sighed heavily and looked at the rim. The edge of the chip also seemed to have a band of white on it, like the usual chips found at a casino. But the Noah's Ark chips had also had that, so he was really no closer to a solution.

He laid the chip fragment and the high heel on the car seat, yanked his mobile phone from his pocket, and called Neal Clark. He whistled tuneless as he waited for the phone to be answered. It was on the fourth ring. "When Marta met you before she went to the casino, how was she dressed?"

Several seconds passed before Neal recovered from

his surprise to answer the question. "How? You mean, evening clothes or jeans? That sort of thing?"

"Yes. Do you remember the shoes she was wearing?"

Again a lapse of silence fell between them. A rook shrieked to an unseen companion before flying to another tree. "I think she wore high heels. Yes." His voice grew stronger as her image cemented in his mind. "A blue and silver dress with silver-toned high heels. Is that what you want?"

McLaren rang off, thinking it was perfect.

Linnet Isherwood echoed the dress and shoes color also, but added that the dress had cap-sleeves and had been knee-length. "She wore a silver bangle bracelet. It was a Möbius strip design with some phrase engraved on it. And she also wore a necklace of blue beads. Does that help?"

McLaren assured Linnet it did and asked one more question. "Did she ever wear a charm of a skier, either on a bracelet or necklace?"

"No, not that I recall. Not that we were the greatest of friends, so I can't swear. But I never saw one. Sorry."

He assured her it didn't matter and thanked her before hanging up.

Asking Marta's husband, coworker Verity Dwyer, and three other friends about the silver charm produced nothing but verbal head-scratching, confusion, and strong denials that she ever owned it. Alan flatly denied Marta had such a piece. "I saw her everyday, in all situations," he said rather hesitantly, leaving Marta's state of undress to McLaren's imagination. "She didn't have anything remotely like that. She went in for finer jewelry, like silver chains and bangle bracelets, semi-precious gems. Charms were too…" He tried to find the right word. "…too cute."

"You knew every piece she had, then."

"Certainly. Her jewel box sits next to my tray where I keep my cufflinks, tie tacks, and such. I've seen the box's contents thousands of time. She never owned a charm like that, or any charm."

Which just about closed that subject.

He frowned, trying to recall if the computer reports he had printed out had mentioned clothes or jewelry. He had no recollection of it, if there had been. Maybe Jamie hadn't emailed that. He punched Jamie's phone number into his mobile.

"You find anything at the barn, then?" Jamie asked.

"You free for a drink?"

"Yeah. Always. When? Now?"

"No. I need to get home, shower and change out of these muddy clothes."

"Muddy clothes? What the hell have you been into, Mike?"

McLaren related the tree trunk adventure, giving only the broad scenario. "I'd like your opinion on this, Jamie. If you've got time tonight."

"How can I refuse? My cop's curiosity is up."

McLaren rang off, revved the car engine into life, and drove home.

It was a measure of their friendship that Jamie hadn't hesitated to meet him. McLaren toweled off after a quick shower. He had left his muddy clothes in the middle of the kitchen floor not wanting to trail the dirt through the house, and now changed into jeans and a tee-shirt. And, he admitted as he combed his hair, that Jamie didn't need to ask *where* to meet. The Split Oak, in Somerley, had become their standard meeting place. Not because the food or drink was outstanding—though both were very good—but because it was convenient to both men. McLaren lived in Somerley; Jamie lived five minutes down the road, in Castleton.

The car park at The Split Oak was full that night and McLaren had to leave his vehicle opposite the grocery shop. It had closed hours ago but a small security light shone from the shop's interior. He walked along the pavement, passing the newsagent's, a clothes shop, bakery, and combination gift shop/tearoom. The space between the bakery and gift shop housed a small park where one of the shops in the row had been demolished. It was more of a rest spot. McLaren passed the grassy rectangle that had been filled with a few small trees, some park benches, and a sundial. Nothing more than an environmental use of space. He crossed in front of the streetlight throwing a yellow glow onto the grass and pavement. His shadow, black and thick, stretched across the road, losing itself in the darkness at the foot of the buildings. He quickened his step, conscious of the guitar music filtering from the pub's open door and the rumbling in his stomach. He passed Jamie's car, parked along the curb, and entered the pub.

As many others of its era, it had been a coaching inn during the days of Elizabeth I and King James VI. A refuge from the night and storm. And from highwaymen. It had offered a slice of comfort in the wilds of Derbyshire's mountains and moors, a spot of civilization for which travelers were only too glad to pay. The slate roof sagged across the oak beam ceiling and the casement windows let in blasts of winter when the wind blew westerly across the moor, but it held history and charm and ghosts, perhaps, within its thick-set walls. And a good acoustic band on Saturday nights, McLaren mentally added as he joined Jamie at his table.

McLaren finished the last of his dinner—soused mackerel, glazed carrots, leeks with brown butter, and fruit salad. He bypassed his usual favorite: soles in coffins, and opted tonight for the lighter fare. The mackerel had been extraordinarily good and he was thinking of ordering something else, but felt content for the moment to work on his pint. The pub was noisy with the laughter of weekend fun and the competition of a darts game. Which suited McLaren fine. There was less chance of being overheard. He leaned back, balancing the glass beer mug on his knee, and watched his friend down a forkful of cider cake before he told about finding the silver charm and shoe heel. When Jamie had been duly impressed, McLaren explained why he wanted Jamie's help.

"What bothers me," McLaren said as a cheer erupted from the direction of the darts game, "is that Marta Hughes' body was dumped. Not so much the physical dumping, because you have to get rid of the body somehow, but that it would require some amount of strength to drag it out of a car."

"Unless she was killed there."

"Which might just be correct. Look, her car is sitting prettily at her house. No unexplained blood, hair or fingerprints were found. And I can't see someone waylaying her on the road, dumping her at the stone barn, going back to get her car and then leaving it at her house. Besides the question of logistics, like how the hell did he get away from Marta's house if he drove her car there, it doesn't make sense. First of all, why risk all that maneuvering? Someone might see you either as you got into her car or drove her car or parked it at her house. Second, why even bother to do that? If she was waylaid, why not leave the car where it was? And third, since the lab boys found nothing foreign in her car, I can't see some bloke cocooned in a macintosh or sweats, gloved and wearing a plastic bag over his head to keep his DNA out of the car. Even gloves and clothes will leave trace evidence. No, she was alive when she got home, Jamie, but *she* got into someone's car, was driven to the barn outside Elton, and probably killed there."

Jamie laid his fork on the plate and nodded. "But from what you've told me, Mike, for all that Herb Millington seems a somewhat likely suspect and has muscles even the Incredible Hulk would be jealous of, he might not be able to shift a dead body by himself. That's dead weight, pardon the pun."

"But his mate, Danny, is an odd jobs man."

"And being a helpful bloke and friend, he could have helped Herb with the body. Sure."

"That's what friends are for."

"Why would she get into either Danny's or the Millingtons' car? You said she had this ongoing problem with Herbie. She wouldn't go anywhere with him, especially at night. That makes no sense."

McLaren agreed. "I thought maybe I was too close to it, or had lost my edge. I've been out of the job for a year."

"If you've lost your edge, Mike, I'm the Chief Constable."

McLaren eyed his friend's physique. "You'll have to add a few stone." He lapsed into silence while Jamie tapped his foot in time to the music. Moments later, he snapped his fingers.

"What?" Jamie shifted his attention back to his friend.

"Why does it have to be Danny's or the Millingtons' car? Maybe she got into *someone else's* car." He cocked his right eyebrow and watched the astonishment grow on Jamie's face. "Well?" He smiled as he grabbed his beer.

"Certainly makes more sense if she got into Verity's, for instance." He saluted McLaren with his mug. "Speaking of driving, I've done some digging around and I came across a speeding ticket."

"Must be more remarkable than issued to A.N. Other, I take it."

"You'll be interested." Jamie took a swallow of ale.

"You sound confident."

"You *will* be interested," he repeated. "I know you."

McLaren smiled. "That's why we're here."

"You ready for this, or do you want to keep making smart comments all night?"

"I'm ready to be awed."

Jamie looked around and leaned forward a bit, as though sharing a conspiracy. The band started singing about lost love. "I don't know why I'm doing you this favor, after your last comment, but…" He rushed onward, giving McLaren no time to reply. "I did a bit of digging around for you. Limited use, I know, since I can't get into the police files on this one." He grimaced, silently apologizing, but McLaren shook his head. It would be worth Jamie's job if he were caught doing unauthorized work such as that, even on his time off. Jamie nodded at McLaren's meaning and continued. "Anyway, I *do* know that your victim, Marta Hughes, received a speeding ticket the night of her murder."

"Marta…"

"The driver tripped the speed camera, which took the photo. The registration plate number showed up nice and clear."

"Linnet Isherwood didn't mention that."

"The woman who started you back on your illustrious career." Jamie swallowed another mouthful of beer.

"Don't know how illustrious or starting me back, but she came to me, asking me to reinvestigate the case."

"Which you rushed into."

"I didn't rush into anything," McLaren said, slightly annoyed. "I gave it some thought."

"While she was talking, I expect."

"I gave it a good deal of thought, Jamie. I wasn't eager to plunge back into all this. You ought to understand that."

"Of course I do. But I know you, Mike. You love police work. You couldn't have said no to Linnet Isherwood even if it had meant your life. It's in your blood calling to you from a great distance, luring you back to the job."

"Always did like the sound of fire engine bells and cop car sirens. Nothing beats a good adrenalin rush," he half-joked, then sobered. He did love the job, he admitted to himself. Helping people, solving puzzles, righting injustices. It *was* a siren song, beckoning him to pick up those unrighted injustices, but if there would be any adverse effects from his now-amateur meddling…He stared into his beer, as though contemplating something, then asked where the ticket had been originated.

"The ticket was issued just south of Elton," Jamie said. "23:47 hrs."

"And we know she left the casino at 23:00 hours," McLaren said. "Or close enough to call it that. Heading toward Elton or from Elton?"

"Toward," Jamie said. "Heading north."

"So we know she was alive at that time."

"Or someone else was speeding, anxious to dump her body."

McLaren snorted, still convinced Marta had been killed at the barn. "If she never saw Marta alive after they left the casino, Linnet wouldn't know about the ticket, though, would she?"

"Good point. What does it prove?"

"I don't know yet. What road was this?"

"Along the A61, north side of Ripley."

"Not the A615 going into Matlock, then, or the B5057 to Elton where her body was found."

"Sounds as though she was going home after all, heading north toward Chesterfield." Jamie picked up his glass and took a drink. The singers finished their song and those people listening applauded.

"I read the reports you sent, Jamie. Thanks."

"Get any ideas from them?"

"Don't know about ideas, but it's interesting that Linnet Isherwood was briefly under suspicion."

Jamie set down his glass, his face grim. "Because

her husband left her and the kids prior to all this financial trouble of Marta's, you mean?"

"Isn't that good enough motive?"

"They ruled her out because she didn't leave the casino in Marta's car."

"Yeah. My new friend, the goon at the casino car park, admitted that Marta and Linnet left in their own cars. The casino cashier confirmed that, too, and told me that the cops had seen the two women leaving separately on the CCTV tape."

"And there is no photo of Linnet Isherwood's car, as there is of Marta's as she tripped the speed camera. You know, Mike, if Linnet had been following Marta home, about to take Marta for another ride after Marta had parked her car, *Linnet* would've been speeding, too! Linnet couldn't let Marta get out of her sight. After all, Marta might not have been going straight home, and Linnet wouldn't have known that."

"Spoiling some kidnapping plan or such." McLaren's fingers drummed against the side of his empty beer mug. "Sounds nice, but it doesn't work."

"Why not?"

"Linnet knew Marta might be stopping at her brother-in-law's after the casino outing. She wouldn't be speeding to keep up with Marta. She'd most likely drive home and not know about Marta's speeding. Good try, though."

Jamie mumbled help was not as appreciated these days as it used to be, then eyed his friend's glass. "You need another? My round, I think."

McLaren shook his head. "No. Just that, talking about cars...You got another few minutes or so?" McLaren asked without glancing at his watch.

"Sure. I'm a grass widower this weekend. Paula's at her folks'."

"I've got a couple mysteries of my own that I'd like your opinion of." He told Jamie about the beer bottles—the ones found in and on his car, the missing bag at Noah's Ark, the bottle thrown at him when he was forced off the road—and about the disappearance of Karin Pedersen. "Normally, I'd let all this go." His fingertips stroked the lip of his glass. "But I'm beginning to think I'm losing my mind. I saw Karin enter the hotel but the clerk denies she was there. I saw all those bottles on my car, bagged them to bring to you…"

"Thinking I could get them printed for you."

"But they disappeared from my car! And I *swear* they were there, Jamie. I *know* I locked my car before I went into the animal shelter. I *always* lock my car. It's a habit."

"You couldn't have forgotten just this once, Mike?"

McLaren frowned, staring at his friend. "No! It's a habit. You think that just because I'm not a copper anymore, I ignore a basic safety—"

Jamie waved away McLaren's argument. "I know it's hardly likely, but you had your mind on the case, on questioning the shelter employees."

"I wasn't thinking about the case *that* hard! Anyway, why would anyone steal a bag of empty beer bottles? It's absurd."

"Suppose the bloke didn't know it was empty bottles? Suppose he just strolls past your car, glances inside, sees a nice, big paper bag, thinks it's something expensive, something he can sell, so he reaches in and grabs the bag, only to find out later when he opens it in a nice, safe alley, that it's just rubbish."

"Because…" McLaren's tone grew bored. "Because the bag was open, so this accommodating thief could see what was in the bag before he snatched it. Because he couldn't just reach into my car since—"

"I know, I know. The car was locked."

"Plus, I don't recall there being anyplace especially close where he could stop to examine his ill-gotten gain. And, I parked so that the passenger side, where the bag sat, was parallel to the street. It's a busy thoroughfare, Jamie. Besides the cop working the traffic accident, there was a street cleaner. There were pedestrians, shopkeepers, drivers. All these people passing by that damned animal shelter. I can't see the chap taking such a risk."

"Maybe he looked the part so no one paid him any mind."

McLaren rubbed his head, excruciatingly tired. "Meaning?"

"Meaning that if he wasn't dressed as a rag and bone man, and if he strolled up to your car from a believable direction…"

"Like, he looked as though he came from the shelter, where the car was parked…"

"So no one happening to see this would question his proximity to your car, and he looked as though he were unlocking your car door with a key, except that he was reaching into your car through the open window—"

"The damned car *was locked!*"

"Could or could not be correct. But if he jimmied the car open…" His eyebrow went up as he left the inference unsaid. "Not everyone uses a sticky jam knife to open letters, Mike."

McLaren exhaled slowly as he considered the possibility. "Could do, I suppose. I hadn't considered a professional thief with proper tools. Still, it's a hell of a chance to take, breaking into a car in broad daylight."

"Murder's *also* a hell of a chance to take, but *someone* did."

The trip home wasn't long, perhaps five minutes, but McLaren slowed on approaching the sharp bend where he'd had the near collision with the bottle-throwing driver. The headlights threw brilliantly bright patches of light onto the road and into the canopy of leaves. Tree boughs jumped out of the darkness in the headlights' glare, seeming bigger and more threatening than in daylight. McLaren passed the rock cliff, a sheet of light grayness, and then the great oak that marked the road to his house. He turned off. Immediately the crunch of gravel replaced the lullabying hum of car tires on tarmac, and he slowed as the tires sought more traction in the loose base.

A perfume of honeysuckle announced his arrival at the widened spot in his drive, and he steered the car to the place where he always parked. He turned off the engine but sat for a half minute, letting the scents and sounds of the June night wash over him. Roses, early blooming lilies, and hesperus cast their intoxicating aromas with the abandonment of a woman; a nightjar and barn owl called out to some unseen mate. Downwind, a fox yapped, then the land fell quiet.

Last time he'd sat in the car on a June night, he thought, inhaling deeply of the scene of honeysuckle, was last year with Dena. He bent his head, leaning it against the steering wheel, recalling the kisses and conversation, the plans for their shared future. Then he had left the job and all that had ended. His happiness had also ended and Dena's departure created a wound in his soul that he thought would never heal.

McLaren eased out of his car, suddenly tired from the day's pursuits and acrobatics. He slammed the door, making certain it was closed, and turned the key in the lock. Despite his belief that it was a regular habit, he paused and turned back toward the car as he clicked the remote lock device. The yellow parking lights blinked on and off and the horn beeped into the quiet of the night. He tried the door latch, making sure the automatic locking system was working. The car was secure. He turned and made for the kitchen door.

Trying to recall it later, he couldn't decide if he'd heard anything prior to the event or if it'd just not registered. Like sounds or sights too common to be memorable. But in a rush of power and near silence, an arm shot out of the darkness as he unlocked the back door. Fingers gripped his throat and a hand grabbed his upper arm and twisted him around. A knee slammed into his stomach and something solid and heavy smashed into his head. His hand groped at the air, at anything solid, to keep himself from falling. Laughter...or the owl's hoot...bounced in his ears. A blinding pain caused his stomach to tighten...echoes of crunching gravel...then darkness and oblivion.

Chapter Seventeen

Jamie Kydd did more than think about it, as he had phrased it to McLaren before going home that night from the pub. He rose uncharacteristically early Sunday morning. Uncharacteristic because when his wife was out of town, Jamie usually slept until eight or so. But McLaren's stories of the disappearing hiker and the reappearing beer bottles had invaded Jamie's dreams. So he disregarded his regular grass widower routine and was showered, shaved, dressed, and out of the house as the first slants of sunlight hit the chimney pot.

For all his kidding last night, Jamie believed McLaren's statement. Habit aside, no cop would walk away from his unlocked vehicle. So what was the answer? That the car had been broken into was obvious. And by a professional, for they had found no chipped paint or torn weather stripping around the door when they examined the window last night. But would a professional risk breaking into a car, in daylight, for a bag of empty bottles?

Jamie turned the question over in his mind as he drove to The Hanoverian Hotel in Hathersage. The bottles episode seemed to have begun with McLaren's rescue of the injured hiker. But again, why? Jamie glanced at his watch, determined to find out the answer to that and to Karin Pedersen's disappearance before he was much older.

The hotel was stirring by the time Jamie left his car in the hotel car park. The village bakery was doing a brisk business, as was the newsagent. Already cars were parked along the main road. And probably winding up the hill to Little John's grave, Jamie thought as he glanced at the church tower just peeking out of the blanket of trees. He watched a couple—obviously tourists—stop on the pavement and consult a map before he entered the hotel.

The aromas of fried eggs and ham, grilled tomatoes, and brewing coffee hit his nose as he closed the front door. It also reminded him of the inadequacy of his own breakfast, a day-old scone and a hurriedly consumed cup of tea. He pretended the smells weren't there and walked into the reception area.

Even at this early hour, a clerk was on duty, freshly scrubbed and dressed immaculately. He looked up, smiled, and wished Jamie good morning.

"Good morning to you." Jamie flashed his brightest smile. He didn't feel particularly cheery, having slept only a few hours, but he put on a good show. His police training was good for more things than handing out speeding tickets.

"May I help you, sir?" The clerk set down a stack of letters, simultaneously looking hopeful and bored. "Do you wish a room?"

"Actually, I was hoping you could help me in another capacity."

The clerk's smile remained plastered to his face, but a doubtful look had crept into his eye. "Certainly. If I can, sir."

"I'm trying to find a friend of mine. Karin Pedersen. I'm concerned about her whereabouts because she was supposed to have phoned last night and I haven't heard from her. She'd mentioned that she was staying here, so I'm hoping that you might know something about her. She's a small woman, in her twenties, with red curly hair—"

"The woman is known to me."

"Wonderful! Is she staying—"

"But not in the capacity you believe."

"Oh, yes? She's changed her plans, then?"

"I know nothing of her plans." The clerk mutely dismissed the inquiry by picking up the letters. "Nor do I know anything of her."

"But you just said—"

"I know *of* her, that is all. I do not *know* her. She is not a guest of The Hanoverian."

"If she's not a guest, how do you know of her?"

"Because," he said, already exasperated, "yours is not the first inquiry about this woman. There was another gentleman Friday. He was quite insistent that this person was lodged here. I had a rather difficult time persuading him she was not. In fact," he squared up the stack by tapping the envelope edges on the desktop, "I really do not believe I convinced him. He left muttering. I fully expect him to return. And when he does…" He nudged the phone a bit closer to his right hand.

"But this is extraordinary! Karin distinctly told me she was spending the night here. I can't believe it!" Jamie turned slightly so he could see the side door that led to the car park. "I hope nothing happened to her. Though I expect she would have rung me up if she'd been delayed. She's hiking." He turned back to the clerk. "You don't think she could have fallen, do you?

Have you heard anything on the news?"

"I heard nothing on the news or from any other source. In fact, the other man mentioned something about her having a scraped knee, I believe it was. I seriously doubt had your friend suffered from such an injury, it would have detained her. Now, if you don't have anything further, I have a lot of work to do." He placed the letters in the Out tray on the desk and walked to the postal card display rack.

Jamie headed toward the door. From the depths of the hotel he heard a vacuum cleaner being run. Across the hall, behind the closed doors, the softer sounds of conversations and the rattle of china plates. He turned toward the clerk, who was inserting new cards into the stand. "There couldn't be a mistake, could there?"

The man looked up, a card in his hand. "A mistake?"

"My friend couldn't have registered with someone else, while you were at tea, perhaps?"

"There is no such person registered at this hotel. If you do not believe me, perhaps you will believe our reservation cards." He strode to the desk and produced the same stack of cards that he had shown to McLaren. Jamie glanced at each card as the clerk flipped through them, nodding at the obvious conclusion. When the clerk had returned them to the box, he said, "I trust you are satisfied that your friend is not here, has not been here, and has no reservation to stay here. Now, if you don't mind, as I said, I have work to do. Good day, sir." The clerk returned to the card stand as Jamie walked from the room.

He paused by the front door, his mind trying to make sense of the situation. McLaren had jested that he was going insane, and now Jamie nearly believed him. But if he had seen Karin enter the hotel, Jamie wasn't going to doubt him. Something had the stench of week old fish.

He half-turned, bent on questioning a staff member, and had taken a step toward the rear of the building, when he abandoned the idea. If something odd was going on at the hotel, surely the staff had been instructed not to say anything. And, even if a maid had seen someone fitting Karin Pedersen's description, it didn't prove it was Karin. There could be another red haired guest. He decided to catch one of the staff on a cigarette break, outside the hotel, and walked across the road to the bakery.

A woman was placing croissants in the large, glass display case but looked up when Jamie entered the shop. He nodded at her and glanced around the main room as he approached. The shop's age was immediately apparent in its blackened oak timbers, white plaster walls, and sloping ceiling. But certainly not in its fare. The scents of warm bread, pastries, and tarts beckoned. He felt the same response from his stomach that he had at the hotel, but this time he didn't ignore it. He bought a cinnamon scone and a pot of tea and sat at one of the small tables overlooking the street.

The village was fully awake now, tourists snapping photos, traffic building on the main road, shops open and their daily sales or specials declared in bold signs. Several people were hurrying toward the church as the peal of bells called through the warm air. Jamie stared at the street, trying to imagine Karin Pedersen's destination once she left the hotel. It was the only such accommodation in the village, so her reason for pretending to have a reservation at The Hanoverian—if that was the correct word—was still a mystery, but Jamie was convinced she had been there.

Finished with his meal, Jamie approached the shop assistant, who was ringing up a sale. She waited until the customer had collected her purchase before asking if Jamie wished something further.

"A French loaf, please." He eyed the long, crusty loaves standing in a wicker basket behind the counter. He could always use a loaf of bread. Plus, it never hurt to pay for potential information—and good relations. "Ta." He paid for the bread, then asked, "I don't suppose you remember seeing a friend of mine Friday. Or perhaps yesterday."

The woman shrugged. "Can't say, can I? What's your friend look like? Why are you asking? If she has a complaint about something she bought here…"

"No, no, nothing like that." He spoke hastily, wanting to squelch any animosity. "I was supposed to meet her in Hathersage Friday and she didn't show. I was wondering about her, that's all."

"If you think she's gone missing, why not ask the police?"

"Oh, I don't think it's anything like that. She's hiking down from Howden Moor. Probably delayed for a day or two."

"Blimey. Bloody awful long way, that. Why not ring her up and ask when she'll be coming?"

"I'm afraid it's not that simple. She has no mobile."

The clerk blinked. "No phone? Why not?"

"She broke it in a fall." Jamie said the first thing that occurred to him. "She rang me up on a mobile she borrowed from another hiker she met. She wanted me to know she'd be out of touch for a bit. So I have no idea if she's still walking or I missed her."

The shop assistant waved to a customer leaving the shop. "That's too bad. I still think it's a job for the police, but what's your friend look like?"

"She's small and thin, with curly red hair. Early twenties. Her name's Karin. Karin Pedersen."

"No, 'fraid not. No one like that's been in Friday. Or Saturday. No red haired hikers. I'd have remembered. My sis has red hair and I'm always looking at other redheads to compare hair color." She returned to wiping down the countertop.

"Perhaps someone else was on duty Friday and saw my friend." A suggestion of authority underlined the hopeful suggestion.

The woman paused in her cleaning and considered the idea. Outside the shop, a woman comforted a crying child with a hug and an elderly man instructed his Labrador dog to 'stay' while he went into a neighboring shop. Shaking her head, the assistant returned to her cleaning. "We're open only from seven in the morning till five in the afternoon. I was on all day. Like I'm on today." She attacked a smear of sticky fingerprints with a renewed application of spray cleaner and more muscle.

"Perhaps when you went on break, or stopped for your tea…"

Without looking up from her cleaning, she replied. "I worked straight through. I always do. If your friend shows up today, I can let her know you're looking for her. Where shall I tell her you'll be?"

"Thanks, but I'll just hang around The Hanoverian.

That's where we're supposed to meet." He grabbed the bread and left the shop.

Thinking Karin might have been hungry and needed to eat before she left Hathersage, Jamie tried three more businesses—a teashop, a small restaurant, and a smaller grocery. His account was the same and the responses were the same: no woman of Karin's description had been in the establishment on the day in question. Or recently. They were sorry, but perhaps his friend had eaten in the hotel restaurant. Or stayed at one of the bed-and-breakfasts in the village. Which just might explain everything, Jamie thought, if Karin had decided to bed down elsewhere if the hotel's price was too high for her budget. He thanked them and returned to the hotel.

A couple, probably in their early twenties, was packing up their car. Three suitcases waited on the ground as the man unlocked the boot. The woman cooed to an infant and rearranged the blanket enveloping the child. Jamie picked up the baby bottle that had dropped onto the ground, handed it to the woman, and headed toward the back of the hotel. A maid and waiter stood near the door, taking a smoking break. He walked up to them and rattled off the now-familiar lines.

The maid shook her head and said she'd seen no such guest. "I've done up most of the rooms already this morning, sir, and seen most of the occupants. Not a red haired woman in the group."

"She couldn't be still here, perhaps sleeping late… Someone you haven't seen…"

"Could be, of course. But I know who's registered in each room."

"Oh?"

"Yes, sir. I don't snoop! Heavens, I don't mean that! But I know by the hotel registration. I need to know when I go to each room if I'm serving a single occupant in a double room, or a family."

"Of course. Helps you with the towels and sheets," he said, not unkindly.

"Yes, sir. So I don't believe your friend is staying with us. Not that I'm one hundred percent certain, but I don't think so." She chewed her bottom lip and frowned slightly. "Unless…"

"Yes?"

"There is one lady that could be her, I guess. All depends on your definition of 'red hair,' though."

"Hers is very red. Almost a fiery red."

The maid shook her head. "No. Can't be her, then. This woman's hair is more carroty. And she's old. You said your friend's in her twenties?" Her eyebrow went up, as though silently commenting on the ten or twelve years' difference in his and Karin's ages.

"Yes. Perhaps her hair looks duller because she's indoors." He mentally crossed his fingers.

"Can't be her. Sorry. Our guest is a lot older than that. Probably fifty. Walks with a cane, too. Can't see your friend hobbling all this way on a cane."

"Not her, then. Thanks anyway."

The maid crossed her arms over her chest, her cigarette dangling from her fingers. "You seen her, Robbie?"

The waiter took a last puff on his cigarette, then crushed it in the sand-filled stand near the back entrance. He was short, dark and muscular, and had the appearance of always being ready for a fight. But he was courteous to Jamie, perhaps unsure if Jamie were a guest. He barely glanced at the maid before looking at Jamie. "No. Doesn't sound familiar."

Jamie said, "If she had dinner somewhere else Friday night and was out all day yesterday, and hasn't come down yet for breakfast, you mightn't have seen her yet."

"Could be, sure. But I've not seen her in the hotel at all. Usually a guest will call down for tea or coffee of an afternoon or evening, or even ask one of us about something in the area. Tourist stuff, you know?"

"And no one like Karin has done that."

"Not to my knowledge. 'Course, I wasn't on Friday night. I work mornings and afternoons mostly. So I wouldn't know about any room service requests that night. But I haven't seen her this morning." He stopped, his mouth open, then snapped his fingers. "'Course, she could be in the dining room right now. Want to see?"

The waiter led Jamie and the maid down the hall and opened the double doors of the dining room. They lingered in the doorway, eyeing everyone in the room. After several seconds, the waiter lowered his voice. "She there?"

Jamie shook his head and turned to the two people peering over his shoulder. "She could still be in her room, but it's pointless to wait. Or waste any more of your time."

They walked back outside and the waiter consulted his watch. He drew another cigarette from the pack in his pocket while the maid replied. "If we see her, we can ring you up, if you like." She smiled, the sunlight on her brunette hair lightening its dark shade.

"Thank you. If it wouldn't be too much trouble."

"Not at all, sir. You're worried about your friend. If she shows up I'll let you know. And I'll ask the waiter who was on duty last night. Perhaps he's seen her, or taken her tea in her room. Ta." She put the piece of paper with Jamie's phone number into the pocket of her work trousers and left him with "Hope you find her."

So do I, Jamie thought, but not for the reason you think. He strolled back to the hotel car park and stopped opposite the side door. There was no mistaking that it was a side entrance for the convenience of guests arriving by car. The hotel name was sprawled over the doorway in large, well-lit lettering. There also were no container plants or shrubs that she could have ducked behind, giving McLaren the impression that Karin had entered the building but had actually afforded her cover. No, if McLaren saw her walk inside, she went inside. But that didn't explain the clerk's unwavering statement that no Karin Pedersen was a guest at the hotel.

Jamie repocketed his car key, grabbed the side entrance door handle, and slowly opened the door. It was heavy, probably steel, but swung open easily. He eased it shut, nervous for some inexplicable reason that the desk clerk would hear him and investigate, and stood with his back to the door.

The entry area was small, holding the odors of tobacco smoke and fried foods. Yet it hadn't the claustrophobic feel Jamie associated with minute spaces, for it was painted in white and apple green. A helpful sign declaring Guests' Rooms and Reception pointed to the two destinations, its background whiteness tainted red from the glow cast by the EXIT sign over the door. To Jamie's left a narrow hallway, brightly lit by a row of recessed canister lights, stretched toward the back of the building; ahead was another door with a glass insert. Beyond that he could see the reception area and part of the clerk's desk. He turned to his left and walked down the hallway.

A flight of thickly carpeted stairs extended to the next floor and Jamie climbed the steps two at a time. The passage smelled of carpet cleaner and lilacs and the walls were papered in a muted floral print. The polished wooden handrail slid beneath his hand as he sprinted up the steps, his heavy, gold wedding band making faint rubbing sounds along the rail's slick surface. At the landing, to his right, the hall stretched toward the front of the hotel. Guest rooms lay along the length as far as he could see. He ran lightly down the hall, looking at each door as he passed. Nothing seemed irregular. The main staircase opened up to the ground floor at the end of the corridor. A large potted palm squatting on the landing nodded in the draft from the air conditioning unit wedged into the front window. Jamie jogged back down the hall, then ascended to the top floor.

It was identical to the floor he'd just left, housing only rooms and a maid's closet. A small boy stood beside the partially open window at the front of the building, offering breadcrumbs to the pigeons cooing and crowded together on the narrow outside ledge. Noises from the street rushed in through the window—conversations, laughter, dogs barking, a police car siren. The boy seemed oblivious to the world beyond the pigeons. He tore up the bread and placed each piece in a specific spot, covering the ledge in systematic order, like a row of checkers. As fast as he put down a piece of bread, a bird would grab it. Other birds not yet fed or wanting more pecked at his hand and fingers. The boy shook them off, scolding them for their gluttony and impatience. When he had finished, he dusted his hands over the ledge, knocking off any remains crumbs, and turned. It was then that he saw Jamie. A grin broke. "We're going to see Little John's grave now. Do you know about him?"

"He's Robin Hood's trusted friend."

"One of his Merry Men. They lived in Sherwood Forest, but they're not real. I have to be going now. Mum doesn't like it when I'm late." He ran a few feet down the hall, stopped, then turned back toward Jamie. "I made a poem for Little John. I'm going to put it and a flower on his grave so he can read it. I want to be like Robin when I grow up." He ran to his room and banged the door closed.

So much for fame, Jamie thought. He went to the window and glanced outside as he closed it. From this height he could see the bakery, teashop, and post office across the street, their roof tiles glistening from the morning's heavy dew. He turned as the door to the main stairway opened and an older couple stepped into the hallway. Nodding to Jamie, they continued with their conversation and entered their room. Jamie waited until their door was closed before he scampered back the way he had come, taking the steps downstairs and returning to the side entryway.

He stood near the side entrance, wondering what his reconnoitering trip had proven. At least he could report to McLaren that he'd found nothing sinister in the hotel, no remnants of a fight with enemy agents. Though if there were anything sinister going on, he reasoned, it was probably on Karin Pedersen's part and not the hotel's. Still, he needed to check as thoroughly as he could; he wouldn't be able to sleep if he didn't. He eased up to the inner door and peeked through the small glass inset. The clerk wasn't in sight. Jamie angled his head so he could see the entire desk. Still no clerk. He said a quiet, silent prayer, slipped through the open door and tiptoed into the reception area.

No one was at the desk or small table that held pamphlets and flyers of area attractions. Jamie paused for several seconds, thinking perhaps the opening door had triggered a beep in the clerk's retreat behind the front desk. No one appeared. He repeated his prayer and slipped behind the desk.

The wooden box that held the registration cards sat where he'd seen it earlier, beside the phone. He leafed through the cards but found no Pedersen. He scanned the hotel guest book for the previous two days but again found no Karin Pedersen signed in. He was reaching for the large calendar on which reservations were noted when he heard the sound of footsteps. A masculine voice called to someone either in the main hallway or dining area. Jamie rushed into the back corridor as the front door slowly opened. He crouched and pressed lightly against the door to keep it from swinging. No footsteps followed him to the back hallway. He let out his breath as the phone rang and the clerk's voice answered with a formal "The Hanoverian. How may I assist you?" Then, still hunched over, Jamie crept outside.

## Chapter Eighteen

Jamie's other hunch—that Karin had changed her overnight plans and was safely ensconced in a local bed-and-breakfast, oblivious to the hunt for her and innocent of devious activity—proved to be as much of a dead end as everything else he had tried that morning. The area's handful of B&Bs and the medieval hall-turned-guest-house had no guest of Karin's ilk. Nor had a Karin Pedersen registered in any of them in the past week, the day of McLaren's misadventure, or for the upcoming week. Karin Pedersen, evidently, was a hallucination of Michael McLaren's mind.

At noon, Jamie paused for lunch. He returned to the tearoom, not because he was enamored with such places, but because it was one of the few places he could sit over an inexpensive meal. He made out a list of people McLaren had talked to, then a list of the odd occurrences happening since he had taken the case. Jamie stared at the two lists for many minutes. Besides the broken poker chip, which could signify Noah's Ark or the casino Marta had patronized, he could determine nothing linking people from Marta's life to McLaren's trouble. Jamie stuck the sheet of paper into his jeans pocket, paid his bill, and left.

He sat in his car, the windows down, and rang up McLaren. He leaned back, the car seat upholstery smelling faintly of fast food meals, cigarette smoke, and perfume. Funny how this defines my life, he thought. Fast food and cigarettes characterizing the hectic schedule of his job, the perfume a lingering remembrance of his wife, his private life. He shook his head. He kept them separate, fiercely protective of the time with Paula and his off hours, making it a point not to bring home work, even the emotional dregs, that would infringe upon their time together. Yet the two worlds were here, tied together like some eternal knot.

Jamie shook himself from his reverie and realized the phone had been ringing for quite a while. He hung up, then punched in McLaren's mobile phone number and stared again at the lists as he waited for McLaren to answer.

After thirty seconds, Jamie rang off. Must be struggling with another log, he thought, half smiling. Or left the phone in his car. He pocketed his mobile and drove to the local doctor's house.

A sound—urgent, harsh, and relentless—broke through the dark morass of nebulous images. McLaren moved his head slowly as he tried to open his eyes. A beer bottle hurled at him. He ducked. The movement brought instant pain and more confusion as he cracked his eyes open and saw linoleum floor, a base unit, and a splash of shiny whiteness. Wooden spindles near his right hand seemed non-threatening and supportive of his weight. He grabbed the closest one just above a horizontal piece of wood and pulled himself over on his right side. His universe tilted and spun, a turmoil of black, silver, and red, the colors deepening in hue as the whirlpool enlarged and swirled faster. Yet, the unceasing sound called to him, adding to the buzzing in his head. He tried to sit up, pulling himself mentally from the spiral that churned at his feet. A bottle bobbed in the spinning mass and a poker chip rushed at him. He reached for it as the wave of sound rang louder, but the chip spun away to sink into the center of the whirlpool. Again he sought the firmness of the polished wood, somehow knowing it would rescue him from the madness. His fingers closed tightly around the slender wood and he pulled himself upright. Opening his eyes, he saw a flat piece of wood attached horizontally to the spindle, and an even larger and longer slab of wooden slightly above that one that seemed to support a length of dark blue fabric. Was it his police uniform? Was the unending sound the siren of his patrol car? Was he calling himself to work? He grabbed the edge of the fabric and pulled. The cloth and several hard items flew at him. His head seemed to explode from the pain, and he fell back onto the floor, surrendering to the whirlpool.

Jamie's afternoon matched his morning as far as gathering useful information was concerned. The local doctor was adamant that he had treated no one of Karin Pedersen's description, nor had his receptionist received a call from such a person. However, to appease what he diagnosed as Jamie's anxiety, he consulted his appointment diary. No, he informed Jamie, sitting back in his desk chair, he had not seen anyone with a cut on that day. Or the day prior or afterwards, he added, flipping the pages. Was Jamie certain he had the correct village? He blinked behind his round spectacles. Perhaps his friend was in Hatton. Perhaps Jamie had misunderstood.

Jamie assured the man that he had not misunderstood and stood up.

"If the wound was only superficial," the doctor continued as Jamie was about to thank him for his time, "perhaps she merely cleansed it herself. Nothing wrong with soap and water."

"That's a possibility, I'm sure." Jamie didn't believe it, but he agreed to continue the conversation. "But I think the cut required something more extensive. It bled rather profusely."

"Of course, there are the hospitals, if the wound required stitching up. Have you inquired at Buxton or Chesterfield?"

"No, sir. I thought I'd ask around this area first."

"And there's always the chemist's."

Jamie drew back his hand and blinked. "Pardon?"

"Here in the village. Just down the street. You've not inquired in there, I assume."

"No, sir. Frankly, I hadn't thought that far."

"Could be your friend purchased an antibiotic ointment and some sort of first aid dressing. You know, sterile gauze, adhesive plaster or those pre-medicated cloths. If her knee needed attention but she didn't want to have it properly attended to, she might have looked after it herself." He smiled as Jamie thanked him and hurried from the office.

The chemist's shop was on the edge of the business district, up the road from the establishments Jamie had called at that morning. It was a small building, squeezed between a mountain bike/camping centre and the pub, its façade the same gray stone that comprised every building in the village. Health and beauty products sprawled across the interior, extended ledge. The placard above the door proclaimed 'Hathersage Chemist Shop' in white lettering against a black background. Jamie said a mental prayer, took a deep breath, and walked inside.

Head-tall sales shelves and the white-and-black checkered ceramic floor disclosed the shop's orderliness. Jamie pushed the triangular gate on the waist-high railing that separated the shop proper from the entry, and passed the tower of stacked plastic carrier baskets. He turned down the bath and body products aisle, heavy with the scents of perfume, soap and hand lotions, and sought out the shop assistant.

He had finished his recital and was preparing to be disappointed again when the clerk said, "Yes, your friend was in here."

"You're sure?" He replied more slowly than usual, forcing the excitement from his voice, hoping he sounded mildly interested. "Friday?"

"Oh, yes." She removed her glasses and wiped the lenses before putting them on again. "I recall her quite well. A cute girl, though rather thin, with a mass of curly hair. Red as fire. You couldn't help but notice her, even without the wound to her knee. I thought it should be seen to properly. You know, by our doctor. But she insisted it looked worse than it was. I suppose she knew what was best for her."

The buzzer above the door alerted the clerk to a woman entering the shop.

Jamie let the clerk answer the woman's question about the location of the cough medicine and move on before he continued. "And she bought items for her cut knee, then?"

The woman looked at Jamie as though it were obvious. "Certainly! Some astringent, a large sterile gauze, and some adhesive plaster. She had a few scrapes on her palms. Probably from bracing herself when she fell. But they were minor. She also bought some energy bars and a bottle of fruit juice. I guess she was going to continue with her hiking."

"She *said* that?"

"Well, no. But she had her rucksack and she was dressed for hiking. You know, shorts and cotton top and hiking boots. I just assumed that she would do, seeing as how she bought what a lot of hikers buy. Food, I mean."

Jamie nodded slowly, running an index finger across his chin. Mike would be glad to know he wasn't going insane. But what's this hide-and-seek game really mean? He considered his earlier question, that Karin had changed her accommodation plans purely as an economic measure, then tossed it out. If she had, why hadn't the bed-and-breakfasts in the area any record of her stay?

"I shouldn't be alarmed, sir. She suffered a cut knee. It wasn't life threatening."

As though not hearing, he said, "What time was she in here? Do you remember?" That would answer his question. If it was soon after McLaren had delivered her to The Hanoverian's door, she could have continued her trek, perhaps stopping the night at Bamford or Nether Padley. But they were a good several hours' walk from Hathersage, never mind that they were the village's closest neighbors. And if she were headed for another village, why not ask McLaren to drop her there? Unless she had changed her mind after he had left, having seen the hotel's price list. But what would it mean if she had left hours later…

The clerk smiled, as though giving assurance and

proclaiming it was the easiest answer in the world. "That I do recollect. It was nearly five o'clock."

"You're certain?"

McLaren had dropped Karin at the hotel just after noon.

"Yes, sir. I remember because we close at five on Fridays. Pardon me." She checked out the woman with the cough syrup, paperback novel, shampoo and box of facial tissues.

Jamie waited impatiently—his arms folded across his chest—and read the weekly specials posted on the display board near the stack of carrier baskets.

The clerk thanked the woman for her patronage as Jamie turned back to her. The buzzer sounded once more, this time announcing the customer's departure. The clerk moved a stack of advertisements to the side of the counter, took a deep breath and patted her graying hair into place. "Now, then. About your friend...I thought, when she came in, that she'd probably be the last sale of the day."

"Was she limping?"

"Pardon?"

"Like she had sprained her ankle. Or did she seem fit, other than her cut knee?" Jamie was afraid of the answer but needed to know Karin's physical state. McLaren had mentioned her injured ankle. If it had really been hurt, Karin wouldn't have hiked any farther that day. She should still be here in Hathersage.

"No, sir. At least, not that I recall. I think I should have noticed, though. And if the ankle had really bothered her, wouldn't she have bought an elastic bandage or small splint or something to bind her ankle? She only bought the items for her knee."

Jamie agreed that made sense. Still, the entire episode seemed bizarre. "And this was at five o'clock." He spoke woodenly, trying to understand the timing.

"This is important, isn't it?" The woman angled her head, as if studying Jamie's expression. He was frowning, but it was through puzzlement, not fear.

"Yes, it is." He took a deep breath, mentally flipped a coin before he responded. "She's missing. I'm trying to find her."

"In that case…" She snapped her fingers and beckoned Jamie to follow her. "Just back here. Won't take us more than a few minutes. Oh, Chris," she called to a young man stocking the shelf with plastic combs and hair coloring dye. "Watch the register for a few minutes, will you? Ta. There's a dear."

"Where are we going?" He followed the woman to a small room that jutted out into the main floor area. One side of the room had a wall-to-wall window, the glass of which was dark. Probably one-way viewing, Jamie thought as the woman unlocked the door and flipped on the interior light.

"We may look 1800s on the outside," she said as Jamie entered the office, "but we're 21st Century in here." She indicated the small console that held a wood-encased panel of buttons, small lights and a toggle switch. Above the panel a half dozen small TV monitors, each one displaying a different image, showed bright against the wall on which they were mounted. A telephone receiver was affixed to the wall, affording instant communication.

Jamie glanced at the monitors showing the store's aisles and customers, then eyed the screen revealing the pavement outside the front door. A man stopped to light a cigarette before crossing the road. A cyclist came into view then rapidly shot out of the frame as he pedaled down the street. "Impressive." Jamie shifted his eyes from the monitor to the clerk's face. "Have a lot of trouble with shoplifting?"

"Not now. I know many of the bigger stores, as well as most town centers, have a security guard monitoring the cameras. We do during the busy times. But when we don't, there's always the videotape for the court trial." Smiling, she patted the small counter top on which the control console sat. "It's paid for its cost many times over."

"I don't doubt it." Besides recording shoplifters in the act, these closed-circuit television cameras also were powerful tools as preventive surveillance such as sports events and in locating missing persons. If Karin had passed enough of these CCTV cameras, he'd have a nice record of her journey.

The shop clerk pulled out Friday's tape recording and slipped the cassette into a recorder. As she rewound it, she said, "Not only do I know your friend was in here at five o'clock, the date and time are displayed on the tape. Now, then." She stopped the tape and she and Jamie watched the next few minutes of footage in silence.

Karin's bright red hair was immediately identifiable as she entered the shop. The clerk was correct in her memory of Karin's purchases, but it was after she had left the shop that Karin proved most interesting. He leaned closer to the monitor. The clerk, sensing that Jamie needed to see something, enlarged the image showing the exterior scene.

Karin stood outside the shop, to the right of the

door, still in the CCTR camera's range. She lodged the bag of purchases under her left arm and withdrew a mobile phone from her rucksack. After punching in a number, she waited for several seconds, then talked into the phone. The call lasted only ten seconds or so before Karin rang off and slipped her phone back into her sack.

His eyes still on the tape recording, Jamie asked if that was it. "Does she leave now?"

"No. She was still there when I closed down. I don't know when she left. I lock up and leave by the back door." She nodded toward the screen but Jamie didn't notice, his attention on Karin.

Pedestrians and cars passed Karin, shadows on the pavement and on the storefronts across the street shifted positions slightly, and still Karin remained in front of the chemist's. Jamie was beginning to wonder if she had stood there all night when a car slowed, angled into the open space along the curb, and waited while Karin walked up to the passenger door. An indistinguishable form leaned across the front seat and opened the door. Karin dumped her rucksack and purchases from the chemist's into the backseat before getting into the car. Seconds later, the car drove off.

Jamie stood up, hardly believing what he'd seen. If Karin had a friend with a car, why hadn't the friend been summoned to drop her in Hathersage? And if McLaren had deposited her on the hotel's doorstep just after twelve o'clock, what had Karin been doing for four, five hours before this friend arrived? Where was she now?

The clerk was taking the tape out of the recorder as Jamie turned and leaned against the counter. She shoved the cassette back into its box. "Was that any help?"

Jamie assured her it was, thanked her, and left the store, more optimistic than he had been in hours. But what really made him whistle was that he had the mysterious car's make and model—a gray Mercedes CLC coupé. And he had a registration number that began YV59.

Chapter Nineteen

Late afternoon slanted through the western windows of McLaren's house when he finally regained consciousness. The kitchen floor was hard and cold, an alien bed for him, but he hadn't been aware of any surroundings other than the strange blackness that had engulfed him, and the cacophony of sirens and screeching car tires. He lay as he was, staring at the white ceiling, trying to understand where he was and why every one of his bones and muscles raged with pain. He carefully lifted his right arm and held it so he could see it without moving his neck. It was fresh agony to move it, to hold it steady so that he could focus on it. His muscles screamed to be free of their burden, but he forced himself to keep it there. He shifted his head downward, bringing his chin closer to his chest so that he could better see this arm. He winced. His bare flesh and shirtsleeve were caked in smears of dried blood. Same with his left arm. He dropped his arm, laying still, his eyes closed, forcing himself to remember what had happened. He had returned home late Saturday night. He and Jamie had met at the pub, he had driven home, got out of his car...

A wave of pain coursed through his right arm and shoulder as he turned over, pressing his palm against the linoleum. His elbow buckled in his agony and his side hit the floor. He remained how he had fallen, amazed at the intensity of the pain, closing his eyes and losing track of time.

The shadows had begun their slow creep into the kitchen when McLaren finally managed to sit up. He had grabbed onto a table leg and hauled himself to his feet. Now, sagging against the leg, he could see the wall clock. 7:17. In the evening? He turned his head, making sure the sun wasn't playing tricks. It hovered above the western line of horse chestnuts, poplars and oaks claiming the crest of the hill. The top of the near stone wall glowed in the heavy, golden light and already cast a purple shadow that sought the eastern rim of the field. No, McLaren conceded, the sun wasn't crazy. He was. What had happened to the morning? What day was it?

The annoying sound, faintly remembered from his nightmare, abruptly returned, jarring him fully awake. He glanced outside again, nearly expecting to see a police car parked outside on the patio. It wasn't until the third or fourth ring that he realized the sound was the ringing of his home phone.

He tried leaning forward and getting onto his knee in an attempt to stand, but surges of nausea engulfed him. He fell back to his sitting position and slumped to his stomach. The light rocked wildly between piercing brightness and smothering blackness as McLaren pulled himself toward the phone, bracing his elbows and knees against the floor and scooting ahead inches at a time. The worktop looked to be a mile above his head as he stopped at the counter's base; he knew he could never stand in time to answer the insistent ringing. He reached above his head, fumbled for the long, coiled cord, and pulled. The phone crashed to the floor. He righted the phone base and grabbed the receiver in a none-too-steady hand. "Hello? Yes?"

"So, you're finally home." Jamie's voice poured over the phone like a lifejacket flung to a drowning man.

McLaren nodded. His jaw, he discovered, hurt like hell and was difficult to move.

"You there?" Jamie's concern replaced his jest.

"Yeah. Barely."

"Why? Where've you been? I've been ringing all day. You been busy?"

"Not in the way you mean."

"You take a day off from the Marta Hughes case? What'd you do, spend the day with Dena or do some urgent stone wall work?"

"I'd feel better if I had, but no. I've been right here, evidently."

"Evidently? What's the matter, Mike? Someone there? Can't you talk? Say something about the weather if someone's there and you're in trouble."

"Now you sound like a bloody spy movie, Jamie."

"Well, at least you're all right."

"No, but I'll let that pass right now. You doing anything tonight?"

"Why? Want to meet at the pub again?"

"I'd rather you come here. Bring something for dinner, if you can. Chinese take-away or fish and chips. I've got stuff to drink." He winced at the thought of beer.

"Sure, Mike. Only, you sound strange. You ill? I still don't believe you're not being held hostage or something. Say something about Dena if you need me to call the cops."

"Just bring the bloody food, if you would. Hurry

up." He replaced the receiver on the phone, pushed it aside, then sat there for a moment, breathing deeply. His neck hurt like hell, hurt more than merely sleeping on it wrong would produce. Or straining the muscle when he'd tried getting up. The area throbbed and burned, a deep pain that came from the muscle. He got to his knees, then pulled himself to his feet and, holding onto furniture as though he were walking on a storm-tossed boat deck, stumbled into the bathroom.

He pulled off his shirt, torn and blood-streaked below the site of the throbbing flesh, and dropped it onto the floor. He flipped on the fluorescent light fixture and stared into the mirror above the sink. A patch of broken, red skin stared back. He winced as he leaned closer to the mirror. The edges of the wound were jagged, as though the skin had been jabbed and the weapon then twisted. It had bled profusely, McLaren thought, for not only was his shirt bloodstained but the wound was also a mass of dried blood and raw flesh. It wasn't as deep as a knife wound, but it was deep enough, situated at the side of his neck just behind the jugular blood vein.

He stood upright, exhaling slowly, his eyes still on the wound. God, if he'd been hit an inch more toward his throat…He closed his eyes, sickened by the thought of bleeding to death, of the narrow escape. Staring again into the mirror, he could easily and vividly see the lesser wounds to his arms and hands. Dried blood probably makes it look worse than it is, he told himself. Still, he'd evidently fought hard, judging by the numerous smaller cuts and scrapes covering his arms and hands, and the bruises that were changing colors from deep violet to green.

After washing and drying the wound, he pulled a bottle of astringent, a sterile gauze and some adhesive plaster from the bathroom cabinet. He swore as the liquid touched his raw flesh, but vigorously dabbed the wound with another dose. He then covered the wound with the gauze, sticking it to his neck with long strips of the adhesive. When he had finished with his neck, he washed his arms and hands, and rubbed more of the antiseptic over the cuts.

He shed the rest of his clothes in the bathroom, leaving them on the floor, and walked into his bedroom where he slowly dressed in shorts and an oversized tee-shirt. Then he walked barefoot into the front room, switched on a table lamp, unlocked the front door, and eased down onto the couch.

While he waited for Jamie, he tried to remember the fight, tried to recall anything about his attacker. He sank into the cushions, letting his head rest against the back of the couch, and stared at the wall, seeing only the short walk from his car to the kitchen door.

It had been dark, with no light coming from the house except the table lamp in the front room and a smaller lamp on the kitchen table. But even the kitchen light had not illuminated his attacker, who must have hidden behind the large shrub rose near the door. There was no other place, he thought. He'd transplanted or uprooted the boxwoods and peonies shortly after moving into the house, thinking he was one up on crime prevention, eliminating favorite ambush spots. He had left the rose because it had been a small bush. And because he could not fathom any burglar willingly lurking behind such a jumble of thorns.

Despite the pain of his jaw, McLaren smiled,

thinking that his attacker was tending to his own scratched skin. He had to have been marked. The rose had grown nearly to the roof's gutters, a dense shrub leaving little space between it and the house wall. Hopefully the bastard would have scratches on him.

But what had he used for a weapon?

McLaren closed his eyes, focusing his mind on the appearance of his wound. As a copper, he'd seen drunken fights with broken beer bottles, seen the injuries those weapons had inflicted. His wound looked like those.

His throat and stomach muscles tightened and he stared at his shaky hands. What was happening? Was he imagining all these beer bottle episodes, or did they have a meaning?

The house was uncomfortably warm in the early evening, having trapped the heat of the day. But McLaren was too tired and hurt too much to get up and open windows. So he lounged on the couch, listening to the caw of the rooks in the oak tree near his front door and tried to think.

Beer had to be the link, the clue to his attacks and the police stop and the theft of the bottles in his car. If it were just bottle-related, any types of bottles would have been used. Yet every one of these episodes had included beer bottles. What was the significance?

The rooks took flight in a squawking, dark mass as McLaren thought through every confrontation, every fight he had ever had. Most of the episodes had been while he was in the job, and the majority of those had been drunken brawls in countless pubs. No one fight stood out from the hundreds he'd been involved in. And even then, he'd been included merely as an outsider, as a copper doing his job. He'd lectured no one; he'd taken no one's side. He didn't even remember the parties' names or faces and he'd received no threats before or after seeing them into jail cells. No, these beer bottle incidents were personal, as though he should know a name or recall a major incident.

His eyes strayed to a tiny photo on the wall. It hung between the bookcase and a large, antique map of Derbyshire. It was a photo of Dena, encased in an oval, wooden frame. Funny he hadn't seen it when he'd removed the other traces of his life before he left the job. Maybe the light from the table lamp brought it out of the shadowy recess. He hardly ever sat here...He muttered something beneath his breath as he stared at the oval shape. The photograph was too small to make out facial features at this distance but he knew her expression, knew the tint of her eyes and the way his camera had caught on the light on her cheek and the wind-blown hair. He cursed his forgetfulness from his house cleaning. When he felt better he would box it up with the rest of the remnants from that life. He had no desire to remember last spring.

Last spring. Last May. There was something else about that time. He struggled into a sitting position, his heart pounding in his chest. A name and scene flashed across his mind's eye. He slowly leaned forward, his forearms on his thighs, his breathing coming faster as the face of Charles Harvester danced before him. Charlie Harvester; the colleague who had tried to arrest McLaren's friend Nigel for attacking the burglar invading his pub. The burglar had lunged at Nigel with a broken beer bottle before Nigel had fought back with a fireplace poker. Defended himself and his wife,

McLaren remembered, the anger he thought he'd buried now filling his heart. Was the burglar out of prison? Was this some nasty taunt to tell McLaren that he was free and about to seek revenge? Perhaps he'd enlisted the aid of one of his toe rag mates to harass McLaren.

If someone overheard him and Jamie talking in the pub last night maybe Marta Hughes' killer was hinting, not too subtly, to back off the case. But had beer anything to do with her murder? As McLaren reasoned again, sinking back against the couch cushions, a beer bottle had to mean something to McLaren, had to be associated with his recent attacker or with someone he had wronged in the past.

Neither Linnet nor the cashier at the casino had mentioned that alcohol had been a concern the night of Marta's win. Had there been an altercation at the casino, possibly between a drunken roulette player and Marta, and this was the man's revenge for McLaren taking the case? But that suggested that the casino customer knew McLaren was working on the case. And knew where McLaren lived.

He exhaled slowly, the back of his hand massaging his forehead. There were several possibilities, but which was the correct one? He got to his feet and, again using the furniture as handrails, lumbered into the kitchen. Standing at the end of the worktop, he stared at the fridge. How badly did he want a drink?

The ringing doorbell interrupted his mental debate. Yelling that the door was unlocked and for Jamie to come in, McLaren trudged back into the front room.

"Come and get it while it's hot." Jamie set the bags of fish and chips on a magazine laying on the coffee table. "No mushy peas. They were out of them. I know you won't mind. Hey, you here? You really should lock your door, Mike. Any hooligan could barge in. You could be— God! What the bloody hell happened to you?" He stared open-mouthed at McLaren as he walked up to the table.

"*Now* you give me advice about that hooligan. Some friend."

One of the bags of food fell onto its side but Jamie didn't notice. "You want a doctor? You okay? God, you look like hell. Those bruises…*What happened?*"

McLaren turned toward the kitchen. "You want a beer?"

"Sit down. I'll get it. You look like you shouldn't even be walking." He stayed until McLaren was seated in a straight-back chair, then darted into the kitchen. Minutes later, he returned with a tray loaded with plates, utensils, beer, and glasses. When he'd poured out the beer and handed the glass and a plate of fish and chips to McLaren, he sat on the couch. "Now." He swallowed a few chips before settling down to business. "Let's have it. What the hell happened?"

McLaren rested the glass on his thigh. "You won't believe it. Even I can barely believe it."

"I won't know if I believe it or not until I hear it. Give."

"There's not much to tell, actually. It happened too fast."

"You sound like a ruddy victim in a police report."

"I feel like one."

"Fine. I sympathize, Mike. What happened?"

"When I left you at the pub and drove home I parked the car in my usual spot."

"Where it is now?"

"Yeah. I got out, locked it, and walked up to the kitchen door. I don't recall being aware of anything unusual. I had no sixth sense that something wasn't right. I got my key out to unlock the door and that's it."

"What does that mean?"

"All I remember is walking up to the door and then waking up on the kitchen floor." He flexed his jaw. "I'm a mess, aren't I?"

"You must have unlocked the door before you were jumped." Jamie ignored the question. "Right. You crawled inside sometime later. I can't see your assailant graciously carrying you in. From the looks of you, he wanted to kill you."

"Bloody nice thought. Thanks." He chewed on a chip as Jamie rambled on. "You probably blacked out from the exertion of getting to the kitchen. When did you regain consciousness?"

"Not long ago. When you rang."

"What time? I've called a few times today. Wanted to astound you with my sleuthing."

"I don't know what time. Yeah, I do. Seven something. The last time you called, then. When I asked you to come over with dinner."

"Little after seven, then. So you were out nearly twenty-four hours. God, I'd hate to see the bloke you tangled with."

"I probably got the worst of it, Jamie. He wasn't lying on the ground outside, was he?"

"I came in the front door."

"Right."

"But I'll ease our minds." Jamie jogged to the back door, opened it, looked around, then closed it and returned to the front room. "No one outside."

"I didn't think so, but thanks for checking."

They sat, eating their dinner, each trying to make sense of McLaren's attack. As McLaren took a swallow of beer, Jamie said, "Do you know what he hit you with? Had to have been more than his fists. You're cut." He nodded at McLaren's arms.

"I've my theory, but give me your opinion, *if* you've the stomach for it. Or perhaps it's bad timing." His fingers touched his bandaging as he waited for Jamie's answer.

Jamie put his plate and glass on the table and came over to McLaren as he pulled off the gauze. He angled his head slightly to get a better look at the wound. "Beer bottle. Or something round and that size. But I'd say beer bottle. Nice jagged rim to gouge you with." He sat back down and picked up the beer glass. "Do we agree?"

"Yeah, but there's no prize for guessing correctly."

"Don't need one, Mike. Just having you still in the Land of the Living is my prize."

McLaren avoided his friend's eyes, suddenly embarrassed. He flashed Jamie a quick smile before relaying his theory.

"Do you know if Tyrone Wade Antony is still in the nick?" Jamie asked on hearing McLaren's idea of the pub burglar.

"Haven't had time to check. This only occurred to me a half hour or so ago."

"I can find out. Did you look outside to see if this yobo left anything? You know, torn off button, house key, wallet, blood spotting."

"My blood's probably the only thing out there, but have a look if you want to play detective. I'm not up to crawling around. Especially not in the rosebush. I think that's where he hid."

"Right. Just give me half a tick." He jogged into the kitchen, grabbed the torch that was recharging an electrical socket, and trotted outside.

McLaren had finished his fish and was downing the last of his beer when the kitchen door banged shut. A few stamps on the floor told him Jamie was knocking bits of grass, rose leaves, and twigs off his shoes. There was a dull click as he evidently plugged the torch back into the outlet, and a metallic clatter as his latchkey fell onto the tabletop.

"Bloody rose." Jamie dabbed his fingertip on his tongue and then applied his saliva to the scratches on his arm. "I should send you the bill for a new shirt."

"Find anything?"

"Besides discovering how low my tolerance of pain is? Sorry, old man. Neither hide nor hair."

"I'd have liked you to unearth something a bit more concrete, like a driving license, but I'll pretend I'm content."

"Written documents are rather nice, aren't they? *Now* what's the matter? What did I say?"

McLaren snapped his fingers and held up his hand. "God, what a complete berk I am. I forgot about the notebook."

"What *are* you on about?"

"Yesterday when I was poking around the site where they found Marta's body, I found a notebook. It was at this little picnic area, near that rundown barn."

"Yeah, I know the spot."

"I grabbed it, intending to leaf through it to see if it had any bearing on her case, and I forgot about it. You don't think *that's* what my attacker was after?"

"Could be, I suppose, but that would imply that he was there and saw you take it, Mike. You didn't see anyone there, did you? Any happy picnickers or birders tramping through the wood?"

"No. I'd swear I was the only one there, and I'd been inside the barn and across the road at that clearing." He caught his breath as he envisioned the scene. "He could have been *in* the wood."

"Like several yards in, so he was hidden yet could see you in the clearing?"

"Yeah."

"How far is that clearing from where you found the notebook?"

McLaren stared at the ceiling, trying to estimate the distance. "Probably too far away. Maybe several hundred yards."

"Did you have the notebook in your hand when you placed it in your car, or had you stuck it in your trousers pocket?"

"Uh, I had it in my pocket."

"You don't sound like you could swear to that in court, Mike."

"Yeah, I put it in my pocket. I saw it on the ground, picked it up, pocketed it, and did a fingertip search of the area. I took it out and laid it on the car seat when I got back into the car after looking at the tree trunk site."

"So the notebook should be in your car now."

"Would you mind?"

"Why not? The night's young. Be right back." Jamie left the room, grabbed the torch and door key and ran out to McLaren's car. Seconds later he had locked up and strode into the front room. "This what you're worried about?" He dangled the small notebook before McLaren's eyes before dropping it on his lap.

"At least I didn't dream that." He opened the cover. "Thanks." He flipped through the pages, making noncommittal sounds . When he got to the last page, he closed the book and tossed it onto the coffee table.

"No good?"

"Nothing pertinent in it. Somebody's nature journal."

"Waxing lyrical over fungi and bird's eggs and first crocus of the spring, no doubt."

"It could have been something. Ow! Damn." He grabbed his upper arm and pressed his fingertips into his aching flesh.

Jamie picked up his beer and relocated to the couch. "You know, Mike, when you first took on this case, I didn't give it much thought. I mean, it seemed straight forward enough. But now..."

"I've tried to figure out what Marta's case has to do with beer, but unless there's something in her past that I don't know, I can't see it."

"You know what I think?" Jamie sat forward. "I think it's connected to your disappearing friend, Karin Pedersen. Didn't this all start with the beer bottle in your car, when the cop stopped you?"

McLaren nodded and picked up his glass. He held it up to the light, as though he were going to salute someone with it. "I didn't know the bottle was there until the officer found it."

"And all that was minutes after you left Karin at the hotel."

"Quarter hour, maybe. I don't know precisely. I just know I was startled to see the cop pulling me over."

"You know, whoever made the call to the police about you driving drunk, had to know your car."

McLaren's fingers encircled his glass, holding on for dear life.

"He had to know the make and the model."

"You're saying it's Karin?"

"Not necessarily. I don't know how or if she's mixed up in any of this. But she had a good look at your car when you stopped to give her a lift. She could have phoned from any shop in Hathersage. Or on her mobile. Could be someone else, too. Someone who knows you."

"Like Dena?"

Jamie shrugged, reluctant to confirm McLaren's suspicion with words.

"That's daft!" He set the glass on the beer mat. "Why would she phone in a false report? How would she know I was in Hathersage?"

"You don't know, Mike. She could have been following you."

McLaren rolled his fingers into a fist and slammed it against the arm's chair. "Watch your mouth! Why the hell would she do that?"

"I don't know. I'm just saying that *someone* who knows you, who knows your car, rang up the local cop shop and reported your erratic driving. You don't have any suspicions?"

McLaren shook his head and slowly straightened his fingers. "It's absurd! This whole thing. And it all started with Karin Pedersen and that damned beer bottle the cop found in my car."

"I don't suppose *he* could have planted it, could he?"

## Chapter Twenty

McLaren stared at his friend. "*Planted* it?"

"Don't tell me you've never heard of a bad copper, Mike. There are always payoffs if you look for them, rewards for doing a favor for someone. Drugs seized during a raid, money from some bloke wanting to avoid jail time, money or gifts for your blind eye. You know what goes on."

"Sure, but I've never been a party to any of it."

"I didn't say you were. I just suggested this copper might be. You've also heard stories of 'evidence' planted by the police to get a conviction. Maybe somebody has it in for you and paid this copper to slip the bottle into your car. Did he seem suspicious?"

"No. And I don't think he could have had it secreted on his person." McLaren reached for his glass, saw it was empty, and sank back into his chair again. "Besides, I was watching him. He didn't get that close to the passenger seat to slip it in without me seeing him. A pack of weed, sure. He could have palmed it. But a bottle? They're rather large and cumbersome. You ever try slipping one out of your jacket in a hurry?"

"So we're back to your wounded hiker. You're sure you don't know her?"

"I wouldn't swear to it in court but no, I don't think so. You're saying that someone paid her to incriminate me?"

"Or she did it on her own. Maybe you jailed her brother or boyfriend. I don't know. Just watch out, Mike."

"I always do." But last night's attack proved that diligence didn't always work.

"Well, try harder. You're scaring me to death."

"*You're* scared? *I* was the one beaten." But he knew what Jamie meant, and he *was* scared. Scared of the unknown assailant and scared of the door that seemed to be opening before him, beckoning him to walk into the past.

"Not for long, though." Jamie opened another beer and poured it into his glass. He took a sip. "Not beaten in this case."

"Why? What are you on about?"

"I spent the better part of the day nosing about in Hathersage."

"You must have learned something."

"Not as monumental as Copernicus' discovery…"

"I'll tell you where it ranks."

"…but you'll be impressed." Jamie related what he had learned that morning, including the CCTV video surveillance. "The car was headed east. There are only four shops farther on, and I looked at their CCTV tapes. The car didn't stop and I couldn't make out anything I hadn't seen in the chemist's tape. But the car matches the description of the one that ran you off the road. We got a partial on the car registration number."

"This is outstanding, Jamie!" McLaren leaned forward, beaming. The darkness seemed to be receding. "We've got a car make and model, its color…"

"But only a partial plate number. And I'm afraid I can't follow that up and find out whose it is. It would

252

mean my job if I was caught out."

"Sure. I wouldn't ask you to, Jamie. Of course, it's too dangerous." He paused as he caught Jamie's eye. They both recalled a similar event when a police officer had looked up a number on his off-duty time, only to be found out and fired. McLaren got to his feet. "But you got more of the number than I did. Excellent! I can keep my eye out for the vehicle when I talk to the main players in this case. I'll be careful. Don't worry about me, Jamie."

"I'm more than worried about you right now." Jamie stood up. "What do you want? Can I get it? Your bruises are deepening in color. Are you sure you don't want to see a doctor? Need something attended to, stitched up?"

"I'm fine. Just stiff and sore. No, I don't want anything in particular. Just couldn't sit any more." He stretched slowly, testing his back and arm muscles. "I feel a bit better, so why do I still feel bad about this case?"

"Yeah, well, you still look unsteady on your legs. Sit down before you fall down."

McLaren snapped his fingers, and he turned toward Jamie, the moment of triumph gone from his eyes. "Fall down. That's it!"

"I told you to sit—"

"No! That's not what I mean. This whole thing is tied to my downfall. Somebody wants my undoing. Either my career or else physically." He gingerly massaged his bruised jaw.

"But you're not in the job any longer. That doesn't make sense."

"So it's my death, then." The words were barely

above a whisper as the realization sank in.

"Maybe not your death, Mike. That's awful drastic. But a lesson learned, perhaps."

"Which points to someone just released from prison."

"Unless Dena's just getting around to giving you her opinion about your broken engagement."

McLaren snorted and sat down. "Wouldn't take her a year to do that. Besides, a man attacked me. I can tell the difference, even in the dark."

"So she hired someone."

"You have no career as a comedian. This isn't funny."

"Because you still have feelings for her or because you respect women in general?"

"Just drop it, Jamie. I'm in no mood for this. My body hurts."

Jamie downed a mouthful of beer, then cradled the glass in hand. "Have you given any thought to your other body, Marta Hughes?"

"In what aspect?"

"The recovery site. Why there? She didn't live in Elton. Did she know someone there?"

"That's been nagging me, too. And I aim to find out before too much longer."

After breakfast the following day, McLaren searched for some clue to his attacker. It wasn't that he had no confidence in Jamie's exploration, but a night hunt via torch wasn't McLaren's idea of thorough. After all, most crime scenes were sealed off and reconnoitered by daylight. There was no reason he couldn't do the same. So, with the sunlight slanting through the trees, he poked among the bushes, perennials and grass. He found it some yards from the kitchen door, as though the wind had played with it before tiring of the game and dropped it, or it had slipped unnoticed from a pocket. A scrap of paper barely larger than his index finger. Ordinarily, he would have wadded it up and dumped it into the rubbish bin, but he turned it over. In bold, jagged script, his house address scrawled across the paper. He set it on his kitchen table before driving back to Elton.

Elton's residents gave McLaren no new leads that Monday morning even though he asked at the pub, the bed-and-breakfast and the vicarage. No one recognized Marta's photo when he showed it, other than from last year's splash across the newspapers. So the killer with Marta dead or alive in his car had deliberately headed here. But why? Because he knew the area and felt safe here?

Which would signify that Marta's killer had either lived in or been employed in Elton.

McLaren noted the time as he drove to the Hughes home. It was nearly eight thirty, an odd hour for his errand. Alan may have left for the bank, but he hoped to catch him at breakfast, where they could talk in less intimidating surroundings and without the interruption of the banker's job. He exhaled slowly on seeing the family car in the driveway, and jogged up to the front door.

When asked again about family, friends, and coworkers, Alan and Chad still couldn't explain why Marta had been at Elton. They had no family there, nor did Marta have friends in the area. "Though," Alan suggested somewhat as an after thought as he shrugged into his suit jacket, "one of her colleagues from the Ark may live there. I really don't know. I never met them. I just knew their names."

McLaren eyed the man's hands. They held no signs of a fight. He opened his notebook. "Would you mind giving them to me? I can ask around."

"It's been a while, of course. Let me think." He picked up his briefcase, set it by the opened front door, and stared at something above McLaren's head. A police siren screamed several streets away, underscoring the faint tick of the clock on the mantel. Alan nodded, evidently content with his mental list. "Right. Verity Dwyer, the coworker Marta knew best. She's in jail, I think. Over that trouble with the funds."

"Not in jail. Doing community service."

"I knew it was some sort of sentence. Anyway, then there's Emlyn Gregg. He's the vet. At least, I suppose he's still there. I believe there's another assistant or two, but I don't know their names. Marta hardly worked with them. I heard only snippets about them. And of course, the boss, Neal Clark. Have I forgotten anyone, Chad?" He turned to his son, who was sitting in the chair next to the front window.

"Other than Linnet Isherwood, that's the lot." The reply came flatly.

"I'll see if some of them live in Elton." McLaren pocketed his notebook and pen. "Verity lives in Youlgreave, but that's close enough for my purpose. Thanks, Chad."

"Personally, I think you're on the wrong track, Mr. McLaren."

"Oh, yes? In what way?"

"I still think Herb Millington was involved in

Mum's death."

"Because his advances were refused?"

"Yeah."

"Millington would be that angry to kill your mother?"

Chad shrugged, as though comprehending another person's temperament was nearly impossible. "Like we talked about, maybe not deliberately kill her. But stuff happens. You know."

"And you think Herb got into an argument and perhaps went home and got a gun and shot her."

"Yeah. Something like that. And he got scared and—" He swallowed, the words hard to say.

"And hid her body," McLaren finished.

Chad nodded. "It's not so daft, is it? I've heard of stuff like that happening. People panic."

"Well, motive's a bit weak, in my opinion, but deaths have happened from arguments that got out of control. I'll look into it."

"It's not that weak, Mr. McLaren." McLaren paused in the open doorway, noting the boy's unscathed hands, and let Chad continue. "Not if you know him.." Chad reiterated what they'd discussed a couple of days ago.

"Danny influences Herb, does he?"

"I don't know how much and I don't know in what ways. We know Mr. Millington's temper is out of control, but I've seen Danny egg him on, laughing and teasing him, which makes Mr. M even madder. It's like Danny's playing a game. He laughs like a hyena when Mr. M breaks something."

"Does Danny goad Mr. Millington on purpose, or do you think it's just a reflex action since he's not very intelligent?"

"You'd have to ask a psychologist, Mr. McLaren. I don't know about mentality and ingrained behavior, but Danny's never shied away from a fight or from provoking Mr. M." Chad pressed his lips together, suddenly ill as he recalled past events.

Alan muttered that both men should be under a psychiatrist's care. "It's a shame, really. Herb may have a temper but the outbursts are usually confined to his house. Danny explodes wherever and whenever anything ticks him off, even in public places. I've seen it."

McLaren asked if Danny had ever been jailed for violence.

"I have no idea. Do you, Chad?"

"No. And I don't want to get that involved with him to know."

McLaren mumbled his agreement, then frowned. "What's his wife think of all this? I assume he's married…"

"I'm not acquainted and I've never heard him discuss her. Not that I hang around Mr. M's to hear them chat, but I've heard enough comments about Mrs. Millington to know those two gits do talk about their wives."

"You wouldn't know where Danny lives, do you?"

Chad muttered that he thought it was Bakewell, but he wouldn't swear to it.

McLaren sighed, disappointed on hearing the village name. Bakewell was about six miles from Elton, as the crow flew.

He tried another approach. "Would you know any of their haunts? Other than the race tracks. Do Danny or

Herb hang out in the old barn outside of Elton?" The mental images of cigarette ends, empty beer bottles, discarded fast food wrappers, and the half-burned candle shone in his mind.

"I don't know," Chad said slowly. "I'm trying to remember anything they said… No, I don't think so. Do you know, Dad?"

Alan shook his head and picked up his briefcase. "Because Marta's body was there, you mean?"

McLaren nodded. When neither Alan nor Chad said anything more, McLaren said, "Well, I'll check into this. I appreciate your help."

"Uh, McLaren…" Alan followed McLaren outside and paused on the front walk. "I know Chad wants to help, but I wouldn't put much weight on what he said about Danny Mercer's temper. We've never had anything to do with him. He comes to visit Herb and stays over there. So there's nothing that warrants Danny and my wife getting into an argument."

"I'm still going to talk to Danny, but thanks."

"Then you're in luck. That's him next door now." He nodded toward the neighboring house. McLaren turned around.

"Thanks for saving me the trip. I'm sorry to make you late for work."

"Quite all right. I'm not that important."

"Well, thanks again." He nodded to Alan and walked to the Millingtons' house.

Danny Mercer, a compact bundle of barely-contained energy and muscle, was ringing the front door bell as McLaren came up the front walk. He turned on hearing McLaren's approach and made no pretense of hiding his curiosity at seeing such an equally tall and muscular man appear seemingly from nowhere. Danny exhaled loudly and jammed his hand into his pocket, saying that the family didn't appear to be at home.

"Could be at work," McLaren suggested.

Danny snorted and flipped his ponytail over his shoulder.

"Actually," McLaren stood with his feet slightly apart, "I wanted to speak to you, if you have a minute."

"Me? Why? You selling something?"

"I'm not selling anything. If you're Danny Mercer. Alan Hughes pointed you out."

Danny glanced at the Hughes house, as if expecting Alan still to be pointing. He leaned against the white porch column. It nearly matched the color of his hair. "Oh, yeah? Why'd you need to know? Who are you?" His voice had risen slightly, betraying his agitation, but his eyes darted back and forth, as if trying to discern McLaren's character and reason for apparently hunting him down.

"Mike McLaren, but I doubt my name means anything to you. I'm investigating Marta Hughes' death. It happened last June, you may recall. You knew Marta, I'm told."

"Yeah? Who told you?"

"Does it make any difference?"

"Yeah. You a copper?" His eyes narrowed, betraying his suspicions.

"No, I'm not." McLaren reasoned that it wasn't a lie, though he could have added information to his statement. But Danny didn't seem the type to snuggle up to anyone in that profession, no matter how flimsy the prior association. He watched the man's arm muscle flex, giving life to the open mouth of the cobra tattooed just above his right wrist. No scratches, as might result from a close encounter with a rose bush, dotted his flesh.

"You're just trying to help Chad and his dad, then."

"Yes."

"You must have some experience in this sort of thing, then."

"What do you mean?"

"Sniffing about, asking questions. That kind of thing."

"I'm not a cop."

"You said that."

"Do you want to help the family or not, Mr. Mercer?"

Danny scrolled through images on his smartphone as he strolled to the edge of the porch. He stopped, his attention on the screen.

The man's eyes shifted as they evidently read the sought-after bit of information. He gave Danny several seconds, then repeated his question. When silence replied, McLaren coughed. Danny typed a phone number into the keyboard and held the phone to his ear. McLaren pushed Danny's arm to his side and grabbed a handful of his tee-shirt, pulling Danny toward him.

"What the hell you doing that for?" Danny tried to step back, but McLaren held him firmly.

"I asked you a question. Twice. I'd like an answer."

"You got it." He tried to raise the phone but McLaren clamped his free hand onto Danny's arm.

"You're not being very civil, Danny. And you're wasting my time."

"Hard cheese."

McLaren rolled his fist, pulling the shirt fabric more tightly across Danny's chest. "You seem unconcerned about a woman's death. Even if you didn't know her, I'd have thought common decency would dictate you'd want to see her murderer brought to justice." The words slipped out before he was aware of it. He swallowed quickly, hoping he'd shown no chink in his façade. "Now, I'll ask you nicely again. And it'll be the last time, so I suggest you reply." He eliminated what little distance there was between them, smiling as they stood chest to chest.

Danny nodded rapidly, his breathing shallow. "Sure. Fine. What do you want to know?"

"Thank you. That's better. I'd like your knowledge. Chad Hughes says you're around here a lot, seeing Herb Millington. I just wondered if you had seen anything or anyone the night of Mrs. Hughes' death."

"*Seen* anything? Like what? The bloke sneaking into her house?"

"That would be helpful." McLaren smiled, easing the tone of his voice and the tension on the shirt material. "But I thought that since you're here so much you might have heard something. Like someone going by on the street."

"I'm just mates with Herb. I don't know what goes on around here. You'd best ask a neighbor."

"I will. But I was hoping you might also have something to tell me."

"That sounds like you want a confession."

"You guilty of anything?"

Danny shook his head, his gaze on McLaren's fist as he released the shirt.

"So what about that? Did you have a fight with Marta Hughes, maybe become so mad at her that you went back later and shot her?"

"Man, you're daft. Why would I even talk to her? I wouldn't know her from Adam." He returned his mobile to his pocket. "I didn't do anything to her."

McLaren patted Danny's chest and smoothed away the fabric wrinkles. "If you do hear anything and want to talk, tell Alan or Chad Hughes. They know how to reach me. Thanks for your help." McLaren walked back to his car, aware that Danny was watching his every step.

The next stop on McLaren's itinerary was Noah's Ark. Hopefully he could speak to a different employee this morning.

Chesterfield bustled with Monday morning traffic and he had to wait nearly a quarter of an hour for an accident to be cleared from a road, but he breezed the rest of the way to the animal shelter. There were no other cars out front, so he parked near the front door. Anything to save a bit of pain.

The bell at the front door announced his visit and set off a cacophony of barking from the back pen area. The young woman arranging a display of pamphlets and a sign of a book at the front desk looked up and asked McLaren if she could help him. She was a different employee than the receptionist he had talked to previously, and he was glad to get someone else's information. After he had introduced himself, she said it was time that the police found Marta Hughes' killer.

McLaren agreed but refrained from pointing out that if anyone found the killer it would be he, not the police, and instead asked if she had any idea why Marta would be in Elton on the night of her death. "Sometimes you overhear a casual remark." He paused, tacitly giving the woman permission to gossip. "If she was going to meet a friend near there, or if she had a family member living there, that would explain it." He smiled encouragingly and picked up a pamphlet.

"I'm afraid not. I didn't know a thing about her after work life. And especially not that day." She shrugged, signifying she wasn't included in Marta's social affairs.

"So you don't know why Marta would be in Elton. You don't know if she knew anyone in the area, or if she met anyone there for some reason. Girls' night out at the pub…"

"No. Of course I'd like to help." She leaned against the edge of the counter, frowning. She was short, which forced her to look up to meet McLaren's gaze. She appeared to be in her early fifties, a graying brunette with large, brown eyes that blinked at McLaren from behind tortoise shell spectacles. The pamphlet she held sagged between her fingers as she thought back to last year. "Of course, the whole thing was a tragedy. Not just Marta's terrible death."

"What else happened?"

"Why, the scandal with Verity Dwyer." Her tone implied that McLaren should know about it. "It was dreadful. When the money went missing, the boss had no alternative but to let her go. He obviously hated to do it, but his hands were tied. The Board, you know." She grimaced and looked slightly green, as though reliving the event or hearing the board members' angry voices.

"Since the money disappeared during her shift, yes.

It must have been difficult for Mr. Clark to do, letting her go."

"Especially since they were kin. Well, by marriage."

"Mr. Clark is Marta's brother-in-law, I believe."

"Yes. Quite right. He said he felt bad about having to terminate her position." She laid the pamphlet on the counter and pushed the glasses farther up on her nose. "I still keep in touch with her. Still ring her up occasionally, see how she's doing, if she wants anything."

Besides her job back.

McLaren picked up the pamphlet the woman had just put down. It was a tri-panel brochure, full color, on slick paper. The shelter's logo shone predominantly on the cover. "Nice job," McLaren said, meaning it. He read a sentence aloud, admiring the wording. "'Shelter from Life's storms comes in many forms. Noah's Ark. Here for you when it floods.' Nice."

She beamed. "Yes, isn't it? What's nicer is that the shelter didn't have to pay for it. Not the graphic layout or the copywriting."

"Really?" McLaren opened the brochure and glanced at it before refolding it. "One of the staff do it, then? This looks professional quality."

"No one here could do that. We're quite lucky in that a friend of the shelter is a writer."

"A friend...like a volunteer?"

"No, he doesn't put in any hours here. But he helps out like this. He's a friend of Linnet Isherwood. Do you know Linnet? Perhaps you might, since you're working on Marta's case. Linnet and Marta were friends."

"Yes, I know Ms. Isherwood. Nice that she has a

friend who can do this."

"Yes, indeed. It's saved the shelter a lot of money, which of course pleases the Board."

"I can imagine."

"And with a non-profit organization such as the Ark, such free services don't go unrewarded." She added the last part quickly. "Mr. Clark isn't greedy. He shows his gratitude at the annual banquet that honors the volunteers and staff." She smiled broadly and picked up the brochure. "And in Mr. FitzSimmons' particular case, Mr. Clark's showing his appreciation in a more practical way than a plaque or certificate."

"Oh, yes? What might that be?"

She scooted the cardboard-backed sign toward McLaren and waited for him to read it. The sign was made of the same glossy white paper as the pamphlet but a large graphic of a book cover occupied half of the paper. A date, name, and small book blurb constituted the rest of the space.

"*A Dog's Calling*." McLaren read the title aloud. "Sean FitzSimmons not only captures the heart of the working dog trained to help in tragic situations but also does it with love and great understanding.' Sounds like an interesting book." He angled the sign squarely on the countertop. "This is the writer, I take it, who wrote your new pamphlet."

"The very one. A remarkable chap. Quite talented. As you can see, we're holding a book signing this coming weekend for his new book. I believe it came out this past week."

"How nice of you."

"It's just a little thank you to him. I expect he'll sell a lot of books. Such an interesting subject, these specially trained dogs."

"Specially trained…like dogs who sniff out bombs?"

The woman laughed, shaking her head. "I don't believe Sean has had experience in that field. Of course, I'm not sure, but this book seems to be about dogs that help disabled people. Fetching things and opening doors and waking up the owner if their medical problem worsens. Did you know dogs can detect changes in breathing?"

"It does sound a fascinating subject."

"Yes. I'm looking forward to the signing. It's too bad Verity can't come."

"She fond of dogs, then?"

"Oh, yes! But she's especially interested in the subject. She always said she'd like to have a business where she and her dog would help in disaster or emergency aid, going to earthquake zones and finding people trapped beneath the rubble, or working with dogs that could detect cadavers. I think she reads every book or watches every television program on that subject."

"So she can't come to the signing? That's a shame."

"Yes, it is." She lifted her glasses and rubbed the bridge of her nose. "Of course, if it were up to me, I'd have her here in a heartbeat."

"But the Board wouldn't like it," McLaren guessed.

"No." She sighed and replaced her glasses. "They are immovable as far as that topic is concerned. I've asked. They said 'no' most emphatically."

"Perhaps you can give an autographed book to her.

Not quite the same, I know, but if she likes the subject…"

"Yes. That will have to do. It's nearly like being here, I suppose."

"She'll appreciate your thoughtfulness, I know."

"I don't know about that, but it will ease some hurt. Maybe I could suggest she attend anyway. Perhaps she won't be noticed in the crush of people. But it might do more harm than good if she were spotted. You never know about these parties. We've got a caterer coming in, so it should be a nice event."

"The author no doubt will be very happy with whatever arrangements are made."

"I suppose so. They're not temperamental, are they? Authors, I mean. Not temperamental like operatic singers or rock musicians?"

"Doesn't that depend on the individual person?"

"Could do, I guess. It's just that I'd never known a writer before I met Sean. He doesn't look like I imagined. The stereotypical look or preconceived notion that an author is all tweed suit and a pipe smoker."

"Sounds rather 1940s."

"I suppose it does. Sean is rather unconventional, so I don't know why I expected that attire. He practically lives in a leather WWII bombardier's jacket and jeans."

"A bombardier's jacket?"

"At least that's what he wears in his publicity photo." She walked behind the counter, pulled out a book, and handed it to McLaren. "Do you know him?"

McLaren shook his head, oddly relieved that he didn't know Sean FitzSimmons. He stared at the brown eyes looking seriously from the back of the book jacket photo, feeling his body tense up. The pub burglar who had threatened McLaren's elderly friend and caused his own altercation with Charlie Harvester had worn a leather bombardier's jacket. For one second, he thought…

"Nice photo, isn't it?" The woman went on. "I suppose he went to a professional to have it done."

"Yes." McLaren's gaze was still on the jacket as he handed the book back to her.

"Will you be at the signing this weekend?"

"I'm not sure, but thank you for the invitation." He left with an idea taking shape in his mind.

Chapter Twenty-One

McLaren didn't leave the animal shelter car park immediately. He sat in his car and phoned Jamie to find out about Danny and Sean FitzSimmons' police records. As he put it to Jamie, "I know FitzSimmons isn't the scum who attacked Nigel, but he still made the hairs on the back of my neck stand up. I can't place where I've seen him, but find out about him and ring me back."

After a quick lunch grabbed at a Chinese restaurant, McLaren drove back to Elton. Killers usually dumped bodies at spots they knew, where they felt they wouldn't be seen. They knew the area, wanting a quick-in-quick-out location.

According to Neal and Alan, Marta had grown up in town, had worked during the summer in town. But had Marta's killer lived in Elton as a child? Had he worked here, as an adult or after school?

Nothing seems different, McLaren thought as he wandered into the barn. Early afternoon sunlight angled through the gaping windows and the hole in the roof, underscoring the forgotten, dusty farm implements and the discarded tin cans from recent trespassers' meals. He made the rounds of the barn, ground, and loft, but found nothing new from his original search. Though what he expected to find, he couldn't have said. Still, he felt the pull of the place, as though something whispered beneath the straw or behind the shed door. He walked outside, inexplicably glad to be free of the darkness and the closeting walls, and made for the makeshift campfire ring.

He picked up a castoff branch and poked through the fire ashes. Nothing presented itself in the black residue. Nothing hid beneath the large stones placed in a circle forming the pit. Other than a piece of crumpled aluminum foil left from cooking. He picked up the foil and flattened it out. Parts were blackened from the fire, but sunlight glanced off the clean, silvery sections. Shiny. Like the little charm he had found here.

He pulled the charm from his pocket. He wore a clean pair of jeans and a lightweight denim shirt. The charm, too, caught the light and it threw back, brighter and mesmerizing. Was it just some lost trinket from a girl's bracelet after all? Alan Hughes had been adamant that Marta had never owned such a charm.

He shoved it into his pocket as he walked back to his car.

Shoppers crowded the bookstore in Bakewell that afternoon. A large, colorful poster on the wall above the cash register proclaimed Sean FitzSimmons' forthcoming book signing, but McLaren bought the book anyway and was soon seated in his car at the car park along the river. The sun beat down on him; he leaned against the car seat, letting his aching body soak in the warmth. The throbbing in his shoulder had lessened slightly and he closed his eyes, taking in long, deep breaths of new-mown grass, the river, and the wet shore. His left hand lay in his lap but he flexed the fingers of his right hand. They were still stiff, having delivered the majority of his blows. The knuckles and back of his hand still held the small cuts and scrapes from the fight, but the swelling had resided. Soon the bruises on his face would fade and the scar on his neck would be the only lingering physical reminder of the attack.

A child ran past his car and McLaren opened his eyes. The parents hurried after her, calling her name as they reached her. McLaren sat up, rubbed his eyes, and grabbed the book. Its jacket was identical to the display graphic in Noah's Ark, showing a golden Labrador dog with a mobile phone in its mouth. Skipping the glowing endorsements on the cover, McLaren opened the book and leafed through the front matter. Publisher, publication date, ISBN were duly noted without sending up flares. He turned over the page.

The dedication leaped from the paper and seized his throat. He re-read the words before their implication sank in. 'To my Songbird, my love and support. It's downhill from now on.' Downhill. The skier charm from the area outside the barn. And songbird. There were dozens of songbirds—larks, thrushes, warblers, pipits, chats. And a dozen varieties of finches. He stared at the dedication again, his palm suddenly clammy. Finches. The linnet was a finch.

He stared out the open car window, across the River Wye, his mind superimposing the silver skier charm over Linnet Isherwood's figure. Was she the songbird and skier? Was the charm hers? If so, why was it at the site where Marta's body had been found?

Turning back to the first page of the book, McLaren read the list of 'Other Works by Sean FitzSimmons.' Though this current book was the only non-fiction work listed, Sean had been busy. A series of thrillers, judging from the titles. Slowly closing the book, he silently cursed himself. Linnet had mentioned that she had an author friend; he had even spoken to the man on his mobile when he'd met Linnet at Castleton. He hurled the book at the passenger door and sank against the seat back.

What had he got into? What did it all mean?

A group of ducks quacked noisily near the stone bridge as they fought for the bit of bread and dandelion leaves thrown down to them. Bits of bread, he thought. Pieces of the whole. Is that what he had now, pieces of the murder case?

His copper's sixth sense nagged him until he retrieved the book from where it lodged between the door's interior and the side of the seat. Propping the book against the windscreen, he maneuvered it so the sunlight fell on it, pulled his mobile phone from his pocket and snapped a photo of the book jacket back. A minute later, he emailed some questions and the photo of Sean Fitzsimons' smiling face to Jamie.

On the drive back home, Sean's charming grin seemed to dance ahead of McLaren on the road. Both the animal shelter's flyer and the bookstore's poster had touted the man's 'current' book. McLaren slammed the heel of his palm into the steering wheel. He was an idiot, no better than a probationary copper, losing his edge, taking the phrase to mean another *nonfiction* book. He hadn't remembered the novelist Sean.

The tea things were washed and drying in the dish drainer when Jamie phoned that evening. McLaren glanced at the caller ID display, not in the mood to talk to his sister, and was relieved to see Jamie's number. He answered with a hopeful "I'm all ears, lad," and grabbed a pen and a pad of paper before sinking back against the sofa cushions.

"You didn't mention payment in that little email you sent," Jamie said.

"Same as usual. Unless it's the knock-your-socks-off variety information you're about to give me."

"Don't know about that, but I'm looking forward to the beer."

"You found out something, then."

"Don't I always?"

"You're a bloomin' marvel, Jamie. Now, what is it?"

"In answer to your questions, in no particular order, number one: Danny Mercer has no convictions. Not for drug possession, distribution, use."

McLaren exhaled, shaking his head. "So he wasn't lying when he said he was clean."

"Refreshing to have someone tell the truth for once."

"What about G.B.H. or theft or something?"

"He's the type who would assault someone, you think?"

"From what I've seen and heard, I do. Both he and his pal Herb Millington seem top-heavy with muscles and anger."

"Don't ask me about Millington, Mike. I didn't know I had to look for a record for him. But nothing on Danny Mercer."

"He's either been incredibly lucky with his punches or he hasn't done anything."

Jamie said he wouldn't know, and continued. "Number two: your prince charming author, Sean FitzSimmons, has previous convictions for burglary."

"Hell."

"Ditto. He served his time in and was released from HM Prison Wealstun in West Yorkshire."

McLaren opened his mouth to respond but stopped short. Wealstun. Verity Dwyer's brother was currently in Wealstun. Was it important? He shoved aside the question for the moment. "Right. Wealstun. Category C prisoner."

"Then to HM Prison Sudbury—"

"God, what a joke Release On Temporary License is, doing community work."

"Do you want to hear this or just make editorial comments?"

"Go on." He exhaled loudly.

"But FitzSimmons wasn't without female company this whole time."

"Hell."

"You said that, Mike. He had visits from Linnet Isherwood."

"Damn."

"She brought him all sorts of lovely things a month before his release. So he'd feel right at home when he sniffed the fresh air of Freedom."

"Goodies such as…"

"A leather jacket."

"Many people wear leather jackets, Jamie. I've got one. You've got one."

"Bombardier style? Shades of World War Two?"

"I know that's what buddy Sean's wearing on that book jacket photo that I emailed you, but…"

"It's a dead ringer for the jacket the lovely Linnet brought him in his last throes of prison life."

"How do you know?"

"I rang up one of the guards there when I got your questions and the photo. Of course, I can't swear it's the same jacket, Mike, but it's a hell of a coincidence, isn't it?"

"I'd hate to take odds. Did you find anything on the other question?"

"The one about Tyrone Wade Antony's restful stay compliments of Her Majesty's prison service?"

"Yeah." McLaren grimaced hearing the name of the pub burglar and forced Charlie Harvester's grinning face from his mind. "Where is he? He still in?"

"He's still a guest, occupying a cell in Strangeways."

"Manchester. Category B convicted prisoner. Good. Close, but not the same country club, then."

"Still trying to work out where you saw Mr. FitzSimmons?"

"Maybe he was a model prisoner, learned the errors of his way, and kept to the straight and narrow on his release. The name doesn't ring a bell with me."

"Don't let the name fool you, Mike. I knew a killer whose last name was Pope."

"I usually don't forget faces, but he has me stumped all around."

"Maybe it was a particularly nasty case and you've forgot it."

"Well, it'll probably wake me up some night."

"And about your bosom pal Alan Hughes being at the theater…"

"I can tell from your voice. He was."

"At least the four theater tickets were used, Mike. Unless his wife went with someone else, but that still doesn't give him an alibi for her murder. That was

Thursday evening and she disappeared on Friday."

"I figured it was a stupid question."

"But the urge to track down every lead is still strong. I know." Jamie let McLaren sigh heavily before adding, "I checked on this other theater-going couple for you."

"Jamie, you're—"

"I know. Flattery is always welcome, ta."

"You're also full of—"

"Intelligence and thoughtfulness. Thanks. I know how you cherish a thorough job. Anyway, this is a tradition stretching back several years. Both couples have occupied these seats for as long as they've been going to this theater. The Hughes and the Russells. It's a small building and the staff knows them by sight."

"So there's no question they weren't there."

"Not unless they have identical twins or were swathed in actor's makeup, no."

"Which, as I said, is not really proving anything since the dates don't match. And I can't believe in a convoluted mess like Hughes hired someone to kill Marta. That doesn't make sense either. Well, thanks for the help, Jamie."

"You can thank me with a beer Friday night. Stay healthy." He rang off and McLaren laid the phone beside him on the couch and leaned back.

The house was quiet, wrapped in the sounds of early evening. Gold-hued sunlight streamed through the west-facing windows, gilding the top of the leather chair and the book spines lined up on the shelves. Leather and books. A man's room. Warm, yet solitary. Would another human presence make it more comfortable?

It had been filled with others' presence years ago, he recalled. As his childhood home, growing up here, sharing everyday life with his parents and sister. Celebrating the large milestones of Christmas and birthdays, sharing the enthusiasm of smaller triumphs—a first solo bicycle ride, an outstanding school report, a first job and the first car it brought. He stared into the hallway, expecting to hear the sound of his father's whistling, his mother's laughter at a joke his sister told. He shifted his gaze to the window and the front garden. He hadn't changed it when he'd bought it. He hadn't the courage. The rope swing, grayed and smaller than he remembered, still hung from the elm in the back garden. His mother's birdbath still stood under the willow. His sister had told him he was making a mistake when he bought the house. She'd warned him that the memories would be too real and painful for him to find peace there. But he purchased the house anyway, moving in last July on quitting the job and Staffordshire. Gwen was wrong. The memories were soothing. He was content to live with the ghosts and the voices that echoed down the hallway.

His eyes traveled to Dena's photo and he thought of Linnet and her comforting visits to Sean. Prison was a place to be endured, to mark time until you were free. Had Sean appreciated Linnet's friendship, supporting him even when he had made a bad choice? Perhaps the book's dedication was his repayment for her time and concern.

Dena seemed to stare at him as the dusk thickened, turning the air gray and the furniture into dark, textureless shapes. A copper's life wasn't much different than a prisoner's, in some aspects, he mused.

Cops needed love and support if they were to emotionally and mentally survive their jobs. It was hard enough dealing with an abusive public who were drunk and called you four-letter names, hard working with demanding superiors and coworkers who tried to sabotage your work or who simply hated you, were jealous of you. Hard to work through cases, make arrests, clean up crime, lower statistics to please the higher-ups, get reports written and submitted on time. And to do all this without someone at home who loved you, sympathized with the pressures, understood your moods…Well, that was asking for a mental or physical breakdown. Cops needed to come home to warmth, where they could relax and be human beings and not have to fight those job-related problems. He stared back at Dena, discerning her smile in the fading light. Was she smiling, holding out her hand? Had he made a mistake one year ago? Was it too late to bring her into his life if she still wanted him?

He wriggled into the depths of the cushion and propped his shoeless feet on the edge of the coffee table. What had he missed that he could never regain? Was there any love left in her? In him?

He shifted position, rolling over on his hip. Something hard dug into his flesh. Leaning back into the couch, he straightened his leg and thrust his hand into his jeans pocket. He pulled out the silver charm and the scrap of paper.

The charm clattered onto the tabletop, startlingly loud in the quiet. He unfolded the paper. He didn't need to see the handwriting; he knew what it said. But the dark, spiky scrawl held his gaze as though he could still see it in the half-light. For, the obvious was clearly visible to McLaren now. His attacker had been sent deliberately to his address.

Chapter Twenty-Two

McLaren stared at the paper, oblivious to the mantel clock striking the hour and the fox yapping somewhere on a neighboring ridge. Who hated him so much that he would be targeted like this? Who had he hurt in his career? He wasn't even a cop anymore.

His fingers slowly relaxed, the flesh returning to its normal hue, as he thought about the criminals he had arrested. Many had uttered threats at him—that was almost expected from both sides of the law. Most he had forgotten on leaving the courtroom; many he had talked about with Jamie or colleagues; very few produced insomnia.

Still, this scrap of paper was different. It spoke of some great hatred, perhaps long standing, and the need for revenge.

Pain shot through his upper arm as he reached for the charm. He grabbed his shoulder and winced, settling back into the cushions. The bookstore clerk had averted her eyes when he bought the book today. Perhaps she was afraid he was a gang member and would bring the violence that obviously was a part of his life into her store. Conversely, Marta Hughes' co-worker at the animal shelter hadn't seemed to notice his bruises. Maybe he was more in tune with animals and their needs. McLaren gingerly touched his jaw and drew his fingers across the mottled flesh. At least the swelling had begun receding.

He took a deep breath and sat up. Grimacing, he grabbed his tea. The liquid had cooled and tasted of sugar and milk. He set the cup on the table and paced the room. The only criminal in his life right now, albeit indirectly, was Sean FitzSimmons. Were he and Tyrone Wade Antony, the pub burglar, mates? Had Sean decided to carry out some sort of punishment on behalf of his friend? McLaren shook his head. It seemed far fetched for so short a prison sentence as burglary, no matter if Antony was a persistent offender. There had to be another connection. He paused beside the coffee table, looked again at the charm, and opened his hand. The paper scrap fluttered onto the table, coming to rest on top of the skier. McLaren swore, turned out the light, and went to bed.

Tuesday morning dawned with a clear blue sky and a fresh breeze from the west but McLaren didn't notice. He rang up PC Ian Shard and asked if there had been other burglaries in Chesterfield on or close to the Hughes' break-in. "Was that an isolated incident, or was it part of a string, either before or since?"

"You trying to get info on the Hughes murder, then?" Shard's voice took on a cautious tone.

"I'm simply asking about their break-in, if there were other homes broken into at the time."

"Yeah, with an eye for the big prize. Look, McLaren, I've heard about you. I know you're an ex-cop. Staffordshire's not that far away that news doesn't travel. Your Big Man Status there doesn't give you any authority around here. So my advice is to leave well enough alone."

"Sounds like some sort of threat, Shard."

"You've got an overactive imagination, mate. I'm handing you some advice, that's all. Thought you could use it."

"The information about the Hughes case is public record."

"Really? Tell that to the Super. I gave you what you asked for last week. Now, trot along and repair a wall."

The click cut off McLaren's next remark.

He sat for several seconds, the noise of the disconnected phone line falling on his unhearing ears. Where was he with the case? In which direction should he proceed? He hung up the receiver, finished his coffee, and drove into Castleton.

The sun had not yet peeked above the mountain ridge when he parked opposite Linnet Isherwood's house. It would be nearly noon before sunlight slanted directly onto the road and rooftops. McLaren consulted his notebook, making certain of her address, and scanned the house nameplates. That was it—the two-story with the bright green door and trellis of morning glories. "Morning Glory," he read, thinking the house name appropriate. As he started out of his car, Linnet rush out of her front door. He was about to call to her, but something in her determined expression made him stop. He sank back, wanting to melt into the shadowy car interior. She jogged up to a car and unlocked its door. McLaren's hand froze on the interior door handle. The car was a gray Mercedes CLC coupé, registration plate number YV59.

McLaren sat frozen to the spot, trying to sort through the confusion and meanings of the mental images crowding his mind. Why was Linnet driving the car that had picked up Karin Pedersen in Hathersage? Was Linnet linked with his traffic stop or the beer bottle? Were she and Karin merely friends?

A phone call to Jamie silenced some of the questions. Yes, the car was registered in her name. He tossed his phone onto the car seat, jammed the car key into the ignition, and followed Linnet's flight, vowing he'd tail her until she met up with Karin.

The A6 into Buxton was heavy with Tuesday morning traffic, for which McLaren thanked his guardian angel. He could keep Linnet's car in sight without running the risk of being seen. She seemed to be headed into town, for which he was thankful; tailing her to a lonely moor, for example, would have blown his whole operation. It would be hard to remain hidden behind some heather.

In Buxton, Linnet drove up Terrace Road and turned right into the car park opposite the town hall. Three cars separated them as McLaren noted her slow drive through the lot. He paused to let a mother pushing a pram cross the entrance, then parked several rows from the Mercedes. He bought a pay-and-park ticket, displayed it on his car's center console, then, despite his complaining muscles, dashed off to follow Linnet.

The town hall clock showed 11:20 as McLaren approached the building, a dark two-story Victorian edifice showing the years of coal smoke and car exhaust fumes. He passed to the east of the hall, heading back the way he'd come, jogging down the sharp incline of The Slopes, a grassy area overlooking the rest of the town. McLaren stayed behind a crowd of tourists and office workers, glad of the near-noontime rush and the sunny day. Sunglasses and baseball cap helped with his anonymity.

At a bench near St. Ann's Well, a short, dark-haired man smiled as Linnet came up to him. He tossed his newspaper into the rubbish bin before giving her an ardent kiss. More than friends, McLaren thought as he pretended to tie his shoe. And more interesting every day. The man was Sean FitzSimmons.

McLaren didn't need the author's book jacket photo to identify him. He'd stared at the face hard enough to burn it into his mind. As he slowly straightened up and watched Sean slip his arm around Linnet's waist, McLaren recalled Jamie's information about the leather jacket. How involved was Linnet with Sean? How long had she known him before he'd entered prison? Judging from the kiss she returned his past didn't seem to bother her.

The couple walked back up the hill and crossed High Street. He followed at a slower pace, not wishing to catch them up. They strolled past several shops before ducking into The Old Sun Inn. Probably having lunch, he thought as he hung back from the pub's entrance. He lingered by the doorway, giving the impression he was studying the menu displayed in the front window and letting several more customers find tables, before entering.

The pub smelled of hot meat pies, warm breads, and brewed coffee. He walked partway into the front room, scanned the area as though looking for a lunch date, then spotted Linnet and Sean near the back corner of the adjacent dining area. A snug, actually, he thought, turning his back on the smaller, intimate room. He took a table closer to the front in the main room, putting distance and a dozen tables between them. He also cozied up to an ancient grandfather's clock that leaned against the wall. Perfect. The broad front and far side of the clock's wooden case afforded cover as good as a boulder. He could lean forward casually and have a straight view of them, then lean back against the wall and sink from sight. Besides the cap, he also wore a large bandana around his neck. He pulled it up higher, so its folded edge came up to his jaw, and angled his chair slightly so he could rest his right shoulder against the wall. Then he ordered lunch and watched the show.

They had chosen an atmospheric setting for whatever they were about to do, McLaren thought, glancing at the pub's interior. It had been a coaching inn, catering to travelers and horses. The past still clung to the building, a whitewashed exterior and antique-filled interior. A cheering fire would fill the stony heart in the winter, with the leaded casement windows tattooed with frost. But now the June sun angled through the open windows, filling the room with the warmth and scents of summer.

He leaned forward, glancing at Linnet and Sean. Even if he had been seated at the next table, McLaren doubted he could have heard their conversation, for the couple seemed to keep their heads bent and only inches apart. He also doubted their apparent need of secrecy, for the room was noisy with the clatter of china and cutlery and the drone of other customers. Canned music filled any brief voids when the droning stopped. McLaren picked up his coffee mug from the low, knee-high table and held it casually in front of his face. He took slow, periodic sips, as though he were content to linger over lunch, having nothing else to do the rest of the day.

He was halfway into his ham and tomato sandwich when Linnet and Sean paid their bill and left the pub.

McLaren left the uneaten half of his sandwich on the plate, grabbed the bill, and thrust it and more than enough money at the cashier before sprinting out the door. Linnet and Sean were waiting for the pelican crossing lights to change on the High Street. McLaren jogged toward them. He stopped short, turned to look in a store window and wished for a horde of tourists to swamp the pavement. When the light changed they crossed the road, turned right and walked toward the car park. McLaren slowed to a leisurely stroll, always keeping several people between them. Sean walked Linnet to her car and waited while she opened the door before giving her a goodbye kiss. McLaren paused at the corner of the town hall building, pulled his cap low on his forehead, and pretended to consult his watch. But he saw Sean smile, pat the pocket that bulged from a bulky envelope, and accept something from Linnet. As she got into her car and drove off, Sean turned and crossed the car park, heading back toward the Slopes and Terrace Road. McLaren hesitated only for a split second before he dashed toward Sean and knocked against his right shoulder, throwing him off balance. As Sean stumbled and tried to keep from falling, McLaren grabbed his right arm and hand, steadying him.

"Frightfully sorry." McLaren brushed off Sean's back and shook his hand. "I do most sincerely apologize. I hope I haven't hurt you." He placed his hands on Sean's shoulders and turned him around as though inspecting for broken bones or torn clothing.

Sean shrugged off McLaren's hands and straightened his shirt. "I'd think you could be a bit more careful about where you're going. It's crowded, if you haven't noticed." He brushed his hands together.

"I know. I'm so sorry. I'm late back to my car. The ticket's about to expire. You're all right, then?" He said it more as a statement than as a question, but he frowned as he looked at Sean, all concern.

"Yes, yes, I'm fine. Only, be more careful. There are mothers and children about."

"I know. I apologize. Sorry."

"You said that," Sean mumbled through his gritted teeth. "You're either a flaming berk or you're squiffy."

"Right, guv'ner. I confess. I've had a couple. You know…" He grabbed Sean's shirtsleeve and leaned toward him, as though whispering something secret. "Boss' birthday lunch. Couldn't not go and then keep my job, could I? Had to have a couple with the boss to show him respect and good wishes of the day and all that. All the good wishes I could think of, the old bastard." He turned slightly, as though looking for the restaurant that held his employer.

"Well, you overdid it, mate. And you're tiresome, to boot. Now, hop it!"

"Certainly, sir. Right you are, sir. Immediately." He saluted Sean and nodded. "Now, where's the car?"

"How should I know? If you weren't sloshed, you'd know, you berk."

McLaren pulled himself up to his full height, blinked, and replied seriously. "If I weren't drunk, I'd take offense at being called a berk, but between you and me…" He smiled and patted Sean on the shoulder. "That's okay."

"And if you keep this up, I'm calling a copper. Now, lay off!"

"Yes, sir. Sorry, sir." He swayed slightly, holding on to Sean's upper arm as though it were a lifeline. "Well, if you're sure you're not hurt…"

"I'm fine." He turned, obviously wanting to be rid of McLaren's clinging hands, and walked briskly down the hill.

"I'm fine, too, mate," McLaren said as he jogged to his car. He waited until he was back on the A6 before he uncurled the fingers of his right hand. In his palm lay a silver charm of a downhill skier.

Telephone Information was very accommodating; it gave McLaren the home address of Sean FitzSimmons. McLaren scribbled it on his notebook, closed his mobile phone, turned the car around, and followed the A6 southeast toward Bakewell.

He entered the town from the north, the A6 becoming Matlock Street. The Catholic church and Bath Street slipped past before he came to the small roundabout at the junction of four streets. He paused before he could ease into the traffic flow around the circle, the town busy with Tuesday business and tourists. Once clear of the intersection, he turned right onto King Street, lined with shops, passed the huge building on the corner, and turned onto Butts Road. He parked cattycorner from the address he'd been given and looked around. It was a quiet street, several blocks from the busy town center and lined with trees. If the bulky envelope in Sean's back pocket was money from Marta's casino win—not farfetched, since the money had never been found—Sean could afford some nice items for his home. Or a lengthy holiday somewhere exotic. Wasn't that how people usually spent their money? McLaren took off his bandana and cap, and drove to Lloyd Farmer's house.

The retired police sergeant welcomed McLaren with a grin and an offering of a cuppa, but McLaren declined, stating what he needed. "I thought you could introduce me to a friend of Sean FitzSimmons." McLaren twirled his car key on his index finger. "Or a neighbor."

"Someone who knows the lad. Sure." Lloyd nodded as he grinned. "Nothing like a bit of info straight from the horse's mouth."

"I know you'll have kept up with everything going on in town."

"Retirement or not, eh?"

"You're a walking encyclopedia, Lloyd. And don't give me that 'retirement' bit. Thirty-five years in the job was just the preface. You're still as interested in Bakewell goings on as you were when you were in uniform."

"So that's why you dropped by. I should have known it wasn't for my scintillating conversation." He grabbed his latchkey and laughed. "Come on, then. I've just the chap you need to talk to if you want news about Mr. FitzSimmons."

During the short drive, McLaren told Lloyd how he had become involved in Marta's murder case. Lloyd kept quiet throughout the narrative but when McLaren had finished, he said, "So now you're shifting stones to find a murderer hiding under one of 'em."

"That's about it, yes."

"Well, I'll pray for your success. I remember that case. Nasty, it was. You need to catch who killed her."

"With your help, I hope to. This it, then?" He parked in the same spot he had a quarter of an hour ago near FitzSimmons' place and glanced at Lloyd.

"That's also the chap you need to talk to." He motioned to a man about sixty years old. "Shall we?" He got out of the car and walked briskly up to the man, forcing McLaren to hurry.

Sam Browder was weeding his perennial border but looked up when Lloyd and McLaren came up to him. He shaded his eyes from the sun, his glove soiled with damp earth and bits of grass. Lloyd introduced McLaren, assured Sam it was completely unofficial and that nothing would be noted down, then walked back to the car.

McLaren nodded to Sam and wished him good day. The older man leaned against his spade, got to his feet, and asked how he could help. "I recall that incident. Last June, it happened. Shocking. All I could think about for days after watching the news on TV. That poor lady gone missing. And then when they found her body later, in the wood…" His voice trailed off as he looked into the distance.

"I realize it's been a year, a long time to recollect anything, but I wonder if you remember if your neighbor Sean FitzSimmons was home all that evening, presuming he lived here then."

"That evening? When? All night? I went to bed around midnight. And yes, he was here last year. Has lived here, in fact, for years. Well, lived here except for those times when he was in prison. He'd been in twice before, I believe, before this last time. Small offenses, I understand. Well, depends on how you categorize small. But things like burglary and breaking into cars. Which always surprised me, because he's a quiet neighbor. Not rowdy or prone to late night drinking parties. Keeps his place nice, too. Polite, pleasant man. I understand he's written some books, too. Maybe he just got onto the wrong path for a bit but has settled down."

"Seen the light."

"Changed his way, yes. Whatever...he lets his place to a mate when he's serving time so it would still be lived in. I guess he didn't want trouble with burglars or vandalism. You know, if his place looked deserted." He snorted, shaking his head. "Sounds daft. Him in the nick and worried about others of his sort. Life's strange."

"About him being here that night..." McLaren verbally nudged the man.

"Oh, right."

"Do you know if he was in, perhaps due to his car being in the shop, or if he came home when you happened to look outside? Anything like that?"

"I know exactly what happened. I remember it crystal clear because it stuck in my mind for days, it was so odd."

"Yes, sir." McLaren waited, nearly holding his breath. If the man's memory was good...

"I retired last year, so I was staying up a bit later than during my working days. He'd just got out of prison a while before, perhaps a month or so, I can't recall. Anyroad, Sean had been out earlier that day— probably either at his girlfriend's or trying to find a job. I guess his writing income wasn't that regular or that much so he had to find something like office or construction work."

"His girl friend...do you happen to know her name?"

"Certainly. She's over here often enough. Was before and after his stretches in the nick. Linnet Isherwood."

McLaren took the information straight-faced but felt his heart jump. It made sense. If Linnet had taken Sean's favorite jacket to him prior to his release from prison, they had to have been more than acquaintances. He nodded. They hadn't foreseen anyone getting that jacket information when they thought up Marta's murder. The jacket definitely linked the two.

"I didn't actually see him leave or come home," the man continued. "But I knew he'd gone some place rather unusual. His car had been clean that morning. I know, because I saw him washing it."

"And it was different later in the day?"

"The next morning—I get up early to do a bit of gardening before it gets too hot—there was the car muddy as hell. Like he'd driven across a newly plowed field."

Or off-road in a forest, McLaren thought, recalling the spot where Marta's body had been found.

"I wondered where he'd been but never asked. Wasn't my business, was it?"

McLaren replied that it wasn't but silently cursed that the man wasn't nosy.

"I learned years ago not to poke my nose into other people's lives." The man added it as though defending himself against McLaren's unspoken condemnation. "So I was kind of surprised when Sean volunteered a bit of his private life to me."

"Oh? What was that?"

"He wore a silver charm around his neck. On a necklace. I saw it on numerous occasions, so I was quite familiar with it."

"Must be unique for you to remember it."

"It seemed so to me. Most pendants or such that I've seen men wear are coins or medallions or religious symbols. This was suited more for a woman, I thought. Belonged on a charm bracelet, but he wore it on that necklace."

"And it was…"

"A skier. Very lovely but odd. He was in a talkative mood, quite happy. He'd won several thousand pounds at the races. I guess that was why he wanted to talk. He must have given a bit to his girl friend Linnet, 'cause she's been dressing fancier these days." He picked up his spade.

"When was this? That he's had the charm, I mean."

"Oh, about a year ago, I guess. I think around the time his publisher accepted his first non-fiction book."

McLaren thanked the man and returned to his car. Lloyd grinned as McLaren started the motor. "That was profitable, then."

"As if you didn't know. Thanks, Lloyd."

"If you need anything else…" He left unsaid that McLaren could phone him any hour of the day or night. "Thanks for the lift." He got out at his house.

"Any time. I'll come back for that cuppa, shall I?"

Lloyd waved over his shoulder as he walked toward his house.

McLaren couldn't remember later which route he took out of town. His mind played and replayed the snippets of information and the problems they produced. If Sean hadn't yet found work, how did he afford to live? Could be it was off his savings, or the money from Marta's casino win…If the latter, what did

Linnet give him at the pub? And why give him money a year after Marta's death? The questions multiplied, persistent and mocking, as he drove to Verity's home.

He stopped for a quick snack, hungry since he'd had only part of his lunch at the pub in Buxton, then got to Youlgreave and Verity's house mid-afternoon. Verity was unloading groceries from her car. Helping her was her former boss, Neal Clark.

McLaren remained in his car, alternately hiding behind an open newspaper and watching Neal. He and Verity weren't on bad terms as McLaren had imagined, for Verity spoke readily enough to him. She even laughed in response to something he said and nodded toward the house. Neal picked up the last bag and followed her inside.

It was too good to pass up, as the saying goes. McLaren tossed the newspaper onto the car seat, and jogged up to the house. He paused slightly, judging where the kitchen might be, then walked around to the back. A small flagstone patio led off the kitchen door and held several wicker chairs, matching table, and a cluster of ornamental shrubs in large porcelain pots. He stood behind the tallest cypress and listened at the open window.

The conversation seemed to be nearly over. The thud of tins hitting the table and the squeak of cupboard doors opening and closing intruded into the speech but McLaren made out several sentences. He leaned closer, wanting desperately to see what was happening, but reluctantly refrained from peering over the windowsill.

"Don't worry, Verity." Neal said, soothing and reassuring. A cupboard door banged shut. "I've got it figured out."

"I'd like to believe you, Neal." Verity sounded tired, as though she'd been living on hope too long. "But I don't see how."

"Leave that up to me. What's £20,000? The way I look at it is we owe it to you."

Another door closed, drowning her reply, if there was one. A chair scraped across the floor and a cat mewed before Neal said, "Think it over. It can't miss."

His voice faded and McLaren ran back to his car, just getting in and closing the door before Neal and Verity appeared at her front door. She waved to Neal, calling her thanks to him as he drove off.

She remained there for a moment, standing in the open doorway like a bronze statue, perhaps looking after Neal's departing Lexus. Her hand left the doorknob and crept to the doorjamb, supporting her weight as she leaned forward slightly. She plucked a spent rose from the bush nearest the door, then seemed to remember something and returned to her car.

The conversation bothered McLaren. If Marta had stopped at Neal's on the way home that night to give him the money she'd won, had he taken it from her, killed her and transported her to the barn? There was no evidence he had. No unexplained deposits in his bank account, no sudden accumulation of luxury items. The police had checked that during their investigation. Of course, Neal may have the money, sitting on it until he felt safe using some of it. But nothing pointed to him. He was a non-starter as far as the police and McLaren were concerned.

McLaren let the scenario fade and called to Verity as he came up the walkway.

She peered into the late afternoon sun, unsure at

first who was coming toward her. She had grabbed a small paper bag from the car and now shifted it to one arm as she shaded her eyes against the glaring light. When she recognized McLaren, she relaxed. She paused as McLaren grabbed the remaining paper bag and slammed her car door, then preceded him into her house.

"Just set it down anywhere," she said as she walked into the kitchen. "Vegetables from the green grocer's and some frozen items."

McLaren followed her and put the bag on the table. He stood there, unsure if he should offer to help put things away, if he should talk while she worked, or if he should wait until she was finished.

Verity solved the dilemma by telling him to sit down and offering a cup of tea. "I won't be a minute, if you can wait while I get the cold things into the fridge." She opened the freezer compartment and shoved a carton of ice cream into its interior. "I almost forgot about them."

No wonder, with your unexpected company… "No hurry," McLaren said, enjoying the feel of the room. It was smaller than his own kitchen but boasted the lighter color scheme of apple green, pink, and white. Appliances seemed to be new or nearly so, their exteriors free of smudges. The floor was hardwood and shone with a just-waxed brightness. He waited until she reappeared from the depths of the pantry before asking if she'd heard about Marta's casino winning. "I don't mean if you heard that she won," he clarified as Verity folded one of the grocery carrier bags. "If you heard what had happened *to* it."

"You didn't?" She picked up the second bag and

flattened it on the worktop. "No, of course not. You weren't involved." She stuck the second bag inside the first bag and hung it on the pantry doorknob. "And you think I, as an interested party, would have heard. Or at least kept tabs on the case."

"Something like that, yes." He looked at her, hoping she hadn't taken offense, then grinned as she smiled.

"It's become my main hobby. I used to knit and embroider, but not since—" She broke off, pressing her lips together.

"If it's too painful…" he said when Verity shook her head, and said, "You think it's too painful to talk about or think about? God! That's all I do think about! It's an obsession with me. Not like stalking, but close." She leaned against the refrigerator door and again asked if he wanted a cup of tea.

"No, thank you. I just popped in to ask a question."

"Well, pop away. Anything to help, as the saying goes."

"About the money…"

"Oh, right. What happened to the money?"

"If it was ever found." He knew but wanted to hear her answer, to see if she could be trusted as truthful.

"I know it wasn't with her when the police found her body. Well, it wouldn't be, would it, if someone found her first, or if her killer took it? But I never heard if they found it later. I kept up with the story through newspaper articles and the telly. But I never heard that anyone had found the money and turned it in. I was always hoping someone would find it. It would have meant a lot, you know."

"Kind of make up for the money missing from the

animal shelter," McLaren supplied.

"Yeah. Something like that, although it still wouldn't have cleared me of stealing that money. Still, anything found in connection with Marta would have been nice to hear." She exhaled loudly, puffing out her cheeks, and rubbed her forehead. "God, that seems a million years ago."

McLaren glanced at the Noah's Ark calendar hanging on the back of the kitchen door and took a chance. "Marta's husband wasn't implicated in her death, I know. Do you know anything about Linnet's husband?"

"I know he left her right around the time of Marta's death. I don't know when exactly. I can ring up a friend if you need to know."

"That's not necessary right now, thank you. Do you know why he walked out? I think I heard that Linnet and her children were in financial trouble because of it though."

"I don't know the reason. Linnet and I weren't that close for her to confide in me. But I do know that she was having a rough go of it for quite a while, nearly a year, I think. Well, you would do, when your husband takes off like that, and him bringing in more than half of the household income. Linnet's back on her feet, but only just. It's been hard on her and on her kids. She had to do without things and get a second job, working some weekends. The only saving grace is that her kids are older. Late teens and early twenties, I believe. Three of them. So even though the demand for school uniforms and such isn't there, and the oldest one lives away from home, she's still got to put food on the table and pay the utility bills. The younger one is eighteen, I believe. He helps out with an after school job, but it's not easy."

"Sounds as though she could use a bit of financial help."

"If you're hinting that she stole Marta's money because they were at the casino together, you're wrong. And I doubt if they stopped somewhere on the road. That wouldn't make any sense. The police were thinking like that at the beginning, but ruled it out."

"And there's no speed camera photo of Linnet's car racing along after Marta," McLaren finished.

"That ought to prove something. Don't those speed cameras give a time when they're tripped like that?"

McLaren nodded, thinking it a solid alibi. "But it didn't capture the driver's face. It was too dark."

Verity continued as though he hadn't spoken. "I think they finally divorced. I think it was toward the early part of this year. End of January or first part of February. She must have got a decent settlement out of him 'cause the few times I've seen her, she's been dressed nicely. Unless she frequents the charity shops."

"Nothing wrong with that. A friend pointed me in the direction of one last Christmas. I've been thankful to him ever since."

"Nothing like a true friend to help smooth out life's bumps. Linnet was lost without her husband, but she's got a good friend in Sean. Do you know Sean FitzSimmons? He writes. He's having a book signing at the shelter soon, I heard."

"I think that's correct, yes."

"Linnet probably thanks her lucky stars daily that she met Sean. He takes good care of her."

"I'm sure she does. How did she meet him?" Don't

tell me it was through a prisoner welfare program. She didn't seem like the philanthropic sort.

"One of those odd twists some lives take. She met Sean through a mutual friend."

"That does happen sometimes."

"Yes. Purely by chance, though. Linnet was at a pub and just happened to come upon her friend, who was drinking with Sean. The friend introduced them and—" Verity snapped her fingers.

"Instant attraction, I take it. Who's the obliging, timely friend?"

"You might know him, I don't know. He's a cop. His name's Charlie Harvester."

Chapter Twenty-Three

McLaren had a lot to think about on the drive home. Was Harvester somehow tied to Sean FitzSimmons, a convicted criminal, and to Linnet? It seemed bordering on the fantastic, but given Sean's criminal history and the fact that they were acquaintances, if not drinking buddies…

McLaren turned onto the B6061 and stopped momentarily in a lay-by, ringing up Jamie on his mobile phone. "I need a favor, Jamie," McLaren said, his mind torn between what he'd heard about Harvester and Linnet's statement about her financial situation.

"Sure. What do you need?"

"It's a bit shady," he said slowly, as though giving Jamie a chance to back out.

"Lovely. I need a bit of excitement."

"Right." He relayed the information about Harvester and Sean being acquainted, but refrained from saying how he knew this. "I need Harvester's work schedule."

"What? You mean during Marta's death?"

"No. Now. Currently when he's working. If it's tonight, that would be the best news I've had all day. Can you find out?"

"What's going on, Mike? Are you going to ambush him?"

"Is he still with Derbyshire Constabulary?" It was

all he could do to talk about the man, let alone think of Harvester now working in a constabulary in McLaren's home county. "He-he hasn't transferred back to his old job in Staffordshire, or somewhere else?"

"Far as I know he's still here, in B Division. Look, Mike, what's going on? Are you going to do something dangerous?"

"Not rushing into a burning house, if that's what you mean."

"I don't like the sound of this."

"Nothing for you to worry about."

"Now I know it's dangerous. Or at least illegal. No, on second thought, if it is illegal, don't tell me."

"You're turning into your mother, Jamie."

"I'll take that to mean personality-wise and not physically."

"Ring up the station and ask a daft question. Shouldn't be too hard to think of something."

"Thanks for the compliment, Mike. And just what am I supposed to ask?"

"Anything that sounds important, that gives the impression you need information that only Harvester would have from a case he's working on."

"Oh, fine. How do I know what he's working on? He's not exactly sitting at the next desk."

"Fake it. Make it sound ambiguous. Top secret. There's enough stuff going on these days that nobody wants to stick their necks out and get involved in another officer's case."

"So what do I do when I find out when he's working?"

"Ring me back on my mobile. I should be home in about twenty minutes."

"Where are you?"

"On my way home."

"Fine. Keep your little secret. I'll expect some sort of payment for all this trouble."

"Two beers, then."

"Throw in a steak dinner and it's a deal."

"You like it medium rare, if I remember right."

"I'll call you back shortly."

McLaren rang off, feeling as though he was about to get one up on Detective-Inspector Charlie Harvester.

Jamie rang back in fifteen minutes, just as McLaren was walking into his house. McLaren tossed his keys onto the kitchen worktop and grinned at Jamie's news. "I don't know what gods you pray to, Mike…"

"Whoever will get my job done."

"Well, your prayers are answered. Harvester is working tonight. He's still with Derbyshire B Division, but B Division loaned him to D Division. Some sort of big case, evidently. D Division has a runner murder on. They've been at it for weeks and aren't making much headway."

Those prolonged investigations into undetected murders were always McLaren's bane, but tonight… He grinned. "So Harvester is loaned out to help the lads. Wonder if it's help as much as it is B Division wanting to get rid of him, even if it's for just a week or so."

"He's working out of Derby station. He should be there until two a.m. or so."

Lovely. All the way down in Derby. A nice, long drive back home to Buxton. "Did you talk to him?"

"No. He was out. But the bloke I chatted to says

Harvester told his underlings he'd be back in the office in Derby for about two hours. I guess he wants everyone to know how late and hard he's working."

Nothing like scoring points with the Superintendent. "I hope he doesn't decide to go home early."

"The constable thought I could catch him until that time, so it seems he'll be out of your hair for a bit." He paused and swallowed. "Do you want some help, Mike? I don't know what you're about to do, but if you need help—"

"You just go home, Jamie. Prop your feet up and watch 'New Tricks' on the telly, and leave me to do my work."

"'New Tricks' isn't on tonight."

"A figure of speech. I'll be fine."

"Sure. You sound fine. This whole thing sounds fine. Only, it stinks like three-day-old fish."

"Thanks, mate. We'll have our dinner this weekend if it goes well tonight."

"If not, I'll order you a takeaway delivered to your jail cell."

"They'll never catch me."

McLaren hung up on Jamie's reply. He made himself a cup of tea, heated some leftover peas and Brimstone Chicken he'd made several days previously, threw together a simple green salad, and sat at the kitchen table. Over supper, he wondered if he was about to land in jail, as Jamie had joked. He tried to remember back to when he and Harvester had worked together, tried to recall the man's method of working. He sat back in his chair, holding his mug, and shut his eyes. Hadn't Harvester kept case notes at his house?

Besides the official documents at the station. There had been rumors about it, how Harvester—the eager, steamrolling detective who let nothing stand in the way of his advancement goals—filled manila folders with personal notes on suspects and victims. How he spent his nights ruminating over motive and opportunity and suspect. McLaren stared out the window, barely noticing the gray clouds rolling in from the west. With any sort of good luck, he'd find out if the rumors were true, if Harvester kept case notes—or personal notes—lovingly boxed at his home.

Harvester hadn't moved his residence since the altercation with McLaren. His house was at the end of a cul-de-sac in Buxton, a sleepy road thick with trees lying off Carlisle Road. That road, in turn, was clogged with two-story brick houses and dog-legged onto the busy A515. A straight-shot in to Ashbourne, in the southern part of Derbyshire, which housed the police station where Harvester normally worked. But the quiet cul-de-sac was nicely removed from the rush of the A515, backing up to a golf course and a woodland of conifers and deciduous trees. The wood sheltered the cul-de-sac from Buxton's noise; it also provided a great deal of privacy, for the street was dark, despite the effort of the streetlamps.

McLaren sat in his car, staring at the large two-story of red brick. It seemed a lifetime since he'd last been here. And, if he were honest, it *was* a lifetime—someone else's life. *His* life, when he had been an enthusiastic constable with no objective in life but catching bad guys. Now he was staring at the house that belonged to a bad guy—a bad guy in McLaren's book. The images of the department Christmas party welled before him briefly, then dissolved into the blackness of the road as he shifted his gaze. Breaking and entering was always risky, and it wouldn't do to be caught. Especially with his and Harvester's history. But he had checked with some of his mates at the police station, making certain Harvester had no burglar alarm. No security cameras had been installed, either. He didn't know about motion detectors on outdoor lights, but he had to chance that. So he parked several houses down from Harvester's residence and watched, noting cars and lights and escape routes, feeling rather safe. Both houses neighboring Harvester's were dark, as was most of the road. The occasional car passed on the Manchester Road to the north and on the A53 to the south, but on the cul-de-sac, nothing stirred but a prowling tomcat, the tree boughs and some black clouds.

Quarter to one. Good enough. Not many people out on a work night. He pulled on black gloves and black knit stocking cap, got out, eased the door shut, and crept to the house.

A storm blackened the night sky, for beyond the pale orange glow of the streetlamps McLaren could make out an inky mass as a fork of lightning split the air. A gust of wind, cool and laden with dust and leaves rushed down the road pushing more debris before it. A metal wind chime rattled anxiously and the cat ran for cover. Another spear of lightning streaked across the sky and a crack of thunder seemed to split open the heavens. A handful of rain pelted the road as McLaren edged toward the house.

He kept to the darker patches of the lane, where a streetlamp was burnt out or he could fade into the massive, nondescript shapes. A tree bough shivered overhead, creaking ominously as the wind hit it. McLaren slipped over the low brick wall fronting the garden and slid quietly onto the ground at the wall's base. He crouched where he landed, listening for a dog barking, waiting for a house light to flick on. He counted slowly to three hundred before he moved.

The land between the narrow strip of front garden hugging the wall and the house was a stretch of short-clipped grass. McLaren remained bent over—running as best he could, keeping to the blacker smear of boxwood hedges that separated Harvester's property from his neighbor. He bypassed the front door, needing the relative obscurity of the back entrance. The hedge jabbed and scratched his forearm as he squeezed between it and the side of the house. The cracking of small twigs boomed louder than the thunder in his ears and he hugged the house to avoid the hedge. As he rounded the back corner, the sky opened up. McLaren gained the shelter of the canopy as the rain drilled the ground.

He stood against the back door for several minutes, listening to the storm and to the house. He heard nothing but the wind in the trees, the rain as it drummed roof tiles and cars and terrace flagstones, and thunder. The house remained quiet and dark, as though it had curled up for the night to avoid a wetting. His hand rested against the door as he steadied his nerves. Planning the burglary had seemed nearly a game and he'd told himself that he needed the information to help Marta Hughes. But now that he was here, at the house of his most bitter enemy, he felt his courage dissolving. Harvester had become a hazy memory these last months, a pain that had dulled, a face that had softened as in a mist. Being at his house renewed the pain, sharpened the face into features, gave voice to his threats. Do I have the resolve to go through with this? Do I want to enter my enemy's domain and feel his presence? He closed his eyes and tried to calm his labored breathing. He had come this far; Marta needed justice.

McLaren took several deep, slow breaths and opened his eyes. The door still loomed before him, heavy, black and barred. Still there was no sound from the bowels of the house. After several minutes had passed, McLaren faced the door and flicked on his small torch. Shielding the light with his body, he opened the door with the near expertise of a professional burglar and slipped into the house. As he did, the wound split open and he felt the same terror and rage as if it were last June.

He stood in the kitchen, simultaneously fighting the impulse to run from the house and smash everything he could lay his hands on. But there was no time for personal agendas. Nor was he a vigilante. He would get even with Harvester some other way.

But his feet would not move. He remained as firmly stuck to the spot as if his shoes had been nailed to the floor. The linoleum was shiny with a recent waxing, throwing the light from a bedroom fixture into his face. Odors of coffee, fried eggs, and pipe tobacco lingered, bringing Harvester's face out of the darkness with amazing vividness. McLaren felt his heart leap; for one insane moment he could have sworn the man was standing next to him, his lit pipe in his hand, talking. McLaren stared into the shadowy corner near the

309

fridge. Nothing moved; nothing spoke. Still, the room seemed to hug him, smother him with scents and memories. He lurched forward, like a sleepwalker, leaving the ghosts hovering in the dark.

A small light had been left on in the kitchen and deep within the house. One good thing he's done, McLaren thought, snorting. He snapped off his torch and bent down as he crossed in front of the curtained windows.

The light from the front room and a bedroom streamed into the hallway, and McLaren walked slowly along the corridor, still listening for a dog or Harvester. He reached the bedroom and paused in the open doorway. If Harvester did keep personal notes of his cases, where would they be? In a wardrobe, in a filing cabinet in a spare bedroom? He entered the room as the thunder broke again and walked slowly to the dresser. Linnet's photo sat to one side, angled toward him. He flicked on the torch and stared in disbelief. Above the sprawling signature Linnet had signed 'This will have to do until I'm with you.' He clicked off the torch, dazed. Were Linnet and Harvester lovers? Had they planned this entire thing, hiring him for some reason, perhaps as some sort of revenge for last June? McLaren resisted the urge to throw the photo against the wall, and turned instead to the bed.

It was made, the top sheet taut and neat with its hospital-style corners. A lightweight quilt was folded at the bed's foot. McLaren gingerly lifted the pillows and quilt, then replaced them and lifted the edge of the mattress. He bent over, peering underneath. No manila envelope or file folder stared back at him. He pushed the mattress back into place and tried again a few feet farther on. Again nothing was revealed. He repeated the procedure until he had checked the entire mattress, then got on his hands and knees and peered beneath the bed. The only things the light from his torch revealed were a pair of slippers sitting side by side and a magazine on gardening. He snapped off his torch, stood up, and rummaged through the wardrobe and the drawer in the bedside cabinet. Nothing.

The same was true of his search of the rest of the house until he came to a room obviously used as a library and home office. He found years' worth of case notes in Harvester's filing cabinet, all neatly and accurately labeled, standing like cops lined up at attention on dress parade, the folder dates covering the whole of Harvester's detective career. McLaren opened one folder and scanned the pages. Harvester's notes were typed neatly and filed by date. Some points were cross-referenced but mainly it was a straightforward account. There were, however, a few handwritten notes on smaller pieces of paper, as though he had thought of things at his desk or while in his car and had jotted them down hurriedly so he wouldn't forget. Nothing seemed irregular. Harvester had evidently proceeded according to correct departmental policy.

Several pages were allocated to suspects. They were as uncooperative on the night of Marta's disappearance as some had been now. Several people had been home, with varying degrees of alibis. Herb Millington had been up and the lights on in house. He also had been dressed, so that could be read any way you wished. Danny Mercer's mother had been asleep but opened the door quickly enough. Danny had stumbled into the front room, his hair tousled, wearing an oversized tee-shirt and boxer shorts, and blinking at the light. Harvester concluded he had been asleep. Noah Ark's coworker Verity Dwyer had been mending hymnals at church, her presence verified by the minister and others. Same for boss Neal Clark, who had been at home when questioned. 'We therefore cannot confirm that they weren't there, as there being no neighbors or witnesses to place them elsewhere,' Harvester's handwritten note concluded.

McLaren closed the folder but kept his thumb inserted as a bookmark. That's why the case had boiled down to forensics. No witnesses to the slaying and her body found ten days later. He read the information about the bullet—a .38 caliber. He leafed through the pages to read Harvester's conclusions on who owned any weapons. There was nothing.

He moved a small lamp off the desk, set it on the floor, and pulled his small digital camera from his pocket. He switched on the lamp and positioned the pertinent pages so that the lamplight fell onto the paper. He took two photos of each page in case his hand shook. When he had finished, he shoved the camera back into his jeans pocket, returned the report to the file folder and replaced it in the filing cabinet. He turned off the lamp and set it back on the desk.

A car door slammed somewhere in the street. Flicking off his torch he ran to the front window. Cautiously, he parted the heavy brocade curtain slightly. The car's lights blinked a few times as the driver evidently clicked his remote control lock device, then the man dashed to a house across the street, dodging and leaping over the puddles that had formed in the earthen and tarmac depressions. McLaren exhaled slowly, let the curtain fall back into place, then sprinted through the house and eased outside. He closed the door quietly and slipped back the way he had come.

The drive home seemed inordinately long, the road stretching to a distant point that appeared unobtainable. Lightning streaked across the blackness as the tree branches scrambled to catch it. The windscreen wipers continued their mesmerizing sweeps in front of his eyes, pushing aside the rain that slid down the glass. His headlights caught a fox running along the side of the road, his tail sodden and mud splattered. He turned into his lane and felt the soggy earth beneath the car tires, heard the splash of water as he slowly drove through the puddles. When he finally sat in his front room with a cup of tea and the photographed pages printed out from his computer, he stretched his legs out on the sofa and reread Harvester's notes.

Nothing glared at him, new and important, on this more thorough read. But Harvester's personal life had sneaked into the pile of Police Officialdom. Scrawled on the edge of a page was a note: 'Linnet, 7:00, dinner, The Barking Dog.'

McLaren sat up, nearly spilling his tea. He set the cup on the saucer and stared at the page. The date at the top indicated that they had known each other at the beginning of the case; known each other so well that Harvester was calling Linnet for a dinner date. McLaren threw the papers at the far wall, his animosity building. Harvester had violated one of the primary rules of police investigation: do not become involved with a witness or suspect. Just how far had Harvester become involved with Linnet? Had it destroyed his case? Had he overlooked certain things she had done?

McLaren rose, picked up the spilled papers, and returned to the couch. He leafed through the pages, noticing that there were other similar notes jotted in page margins. All were suppers and all were a discreet distance from the police station in Ashbourne. After all, McLaren thought, still fuming, it wouldn't do to be caught in public with a witness or suspect.

He laid the sheets of paper on the coffee table, walked into his bedroom, and undressed. As he got into bed, he listened to the thunder rolling across the sky. It seemed to be echoing his own grumblings. Harvester had left the Staffordshire Constabulary the same time McLaren had. But, unlike McLaren, who had quit, Harvester had transferred to the Derbyshire Constabulary. And on that fateful day when Marta's body had been found, officers from B Division had been thin on the ground. Harvester, in A Division, had been called in to help. And the rest, as they say, was history. McLaren closed his eyes, cursing the past year, cursing Fate. He fell asleep to the sound of the rain against the windows, still cursing, but now it was at Harvester.

A mental nudge so quiet, yet persistent, muscled into his dream. He'd been wrestling Harvester, had him around the neck and was about to plunge with him into a river when the obstinate whisper woke him. He blinked, staring into the night, trying to determine where he was. As the room grew recognizable, he sat up, the sheet falling from his chest. He rubbed his eyes and glanced at the alarm clock on his bedside cabinet. 4:17. He groaned and sank back onto the mattress. His hands grabbed the sheet but he made no other move. Frowning, he looked at the ceiling. What was the problem? What had bothered him so much that he'd woken?

He closed his eyes, trying to remember his dream. Was it something about Harvester or Linnet? He propped himself on his left elbow and stared out his window at the night sky. He'd been fighting Harvester. They were about to plunge into a river…He rubbed the back of his neck, trying to loosen his tight muscles. But there had been something else. A voice calling to him. There had been no other people in his dream—just him and Harvester locked in a death-like grip. Where had the voice come from? A spectator on the shore?

He sat up, his body tensing as the voice sounded in his ear. It was feminine and sounded vaguely familiar. Dena? No. He concentrated. The woman was short and thin and seemed to know him. Her voice was soft, barely audible, yet persisted, calling his name.

He stared at the clouds as they skidded across the sky. It was like that, he thought. She was obliterated by a mist on the shoreline. He strained to see her but the darkness thickened.

As he sank back onto the bed, the moon broke from an imprisoning cloud. The mist in his dream evaporated in a sudden gust of wind and the voice grew louder. McLaren sat up. The woman was Verity Dwyer.

Exhaling slowly, he wiped his forehead with the edge of the sheet. Why was she calling to him? Because maybe she was mixed up in Marta's death after all. Because maybe she had stolen the casino winnings to finance her disaster dog business. He lay down and hadn't realized that he'd fallen asleep until the early morning rain rattled against the gutters, prodding him awake.

Jo A. Hiestand

Two hours later he was in Castleton. He had showered, shaved and dressed hurriedly, as though he had to meet a deadline, but he had taken a few minutes to fill his travel mug with hot coffee. Breakfast was a cold slice of pizza, left over from dinner several nights ago. He ate it while he drove.

He wasn't in such a hurry, however, that he was careless. He drove slowly the length of the wet road on which Linnet lived, looking for her vehicle. It wasn't there. He parked several cars from her house, in case she returned before he left, grabbed the photo of Harvester, and walked up to one of her neighbors.

"'Morning." He smiled hopefully.

The man, in his early thirties and dressed in a suit, had just locked his front door and was shifting his briefcase to his other hand. He paused, looked at McLaren, and asked what he wanted.

"Just a bit of help. It'll take only a minute."

"If you're lost…"

"No. I wonder if you'd take a look at this photo and tell me if you've seen this man around here." He held out Harvester's photo and the man stepped closer.

"Why? What's he done? You a copper?"

McLaren explained who he was and that the man in the photo might be involved in an old murder case.

"That right? Let me have a look." The man took the photograph, looked at it for perhaps several seconds, then nodded. "Yeah. I've seen him. Used to be around here quite regular. Haven't seen him for a while. He the dead bloke?"

"When did you see him? Do you remember?"

"What…like a specific date?"

"An approximation will do. Last winter, this

spring…"

"No. It was longer ago. Last spring. Yeah. That's it. Last spring. Last year. He was here for a couple months. He was seeing Linnet, my next-door neighbor. They were dating for a while, probably until the end of May or so. I've not seen him since."

"When you say you saw him a lot, what does that mean? Did he pick up Miss Isherwood for dates? Mow her lawn? Fix things around her house?"

"He was around her house, all right, but I think it was more like a sort of live-in boyfriend. He'd come in the evenings and he'd still be here the next morning when I left for work. You figure out what that means." He glanced at his watch and started toward his car.

"Sorry. One more question, please, sir."

"Sure. I thought you had finished. What else?"

"Was he here regularly, like every night, or every other weekend?"

"It was every weekend, or just about. This went on until the end of May. Must've been real sudden."

"Why do you think that?" McLaren took a step closer, not wanting to miss what the man said.

"Well, Linnet must have been crazy in love with him. I've never seen her smile so much or even sing when she was pottering about in her garden. Her husband had left her, I guess you know, and I thought she'd never get over that. Then along comes this chap, the one in your photo, and it was like instant love. She was over the moon. Then I don't see his car or him any more and she's back in her depression again. She cried for weeks. Literally. Sobbing. I didn't think she'd ever get over him."

"It does take some people a long time to recover

from a broken heart."

The man nodded, consulting his watch again. "Probably a bit more than just a boyfriend-girlfriend breakup, if you ask me, 'cause she took to wearing a ring around her neck."

"Sounds like an engagement ring."

"Could be for all I know. But he must've made it up to her."

McLaren looked interested. "Oh, yes? Are they back together, then?"

"No. At least, I haven't seen him around. Maybe she goes to *his* place. I don't know. But someone sent her that fancy car of hers. Last August, I think."

"Why do you say that? She couldn't have bought it?"

"With her husband gone and her working those piddling jobs? I don't think so. This came from someone with a lot of cash to spare. Sorry, mate, I've got to hop it. Hope that helps." He was down his walk and out his front gate before McLaren could thank him.

McLaren sat in his car, turning over the new information in his mind. End of May last year was around the time he and Harvester had left the Staffordshire Constabulary. After the pub burglary incident when he had thrown Harvester into the rose bushes. Was this the reason for the beer bottles that kept cropping up in his life? Were they a subtle reminder about the pub burglary and Harvester's absence from Linnet's life? Had she been in love with Harvester and he left her due to the pub incident?

He rubbed his forehead, trying to understand the whispers that echoed in his mind. Linnet wore a ring on a chain. He'd seen it the first time he had met her. Was it Harvester's ring or her engagement ring? And now she had evidently taken up with Sean FitzSimmons. What did that mean? Was it nothing more than looking for a meal ticket, or was it something more?

He pictured her again as he sorted through the questions. Her husband had left her; Harvester had left her. She had been financially strapped. So how does a woman desperate for money get expensive clothing? And a Mercedes a mere two months after Marta Hughes is killed?

Chapter Twenty-Four

He glanced again at Linnet's house, the questions whispering to him. When her husband had left, she'd been nearly desperate for money. Whether intentionally latching on to Harvester or not, she had reasoned she would soon be financially safe. The diamond ring—most probably an engagement ring—that she wore spoke mutely of that brief episode. But when Harvester left Staffordshire, Linnet tried to get money from Marta when she won at the casino. McLaren felt sure of that. Be a good idea to find out if Linnet had access to a gun.

But it didn't make sense. If Linnet was mixed up in Marta's murder, as he now thought, why had she hired him to find Marta's killer? Then the photograph in Harvester's bedroom stood out with alarming clarity. If she still had feelings for him, as the ring implied, and Harvester had broken the engagement—perhaps due to his Staffordshire disgrace and his uncertain future—then maybe all this had been set up for McLaren's failure.

He nodded, sitting back in the car seat. Linnet had known he wasn't in the job anymore—that he had never worked as a private detective. Yet she had come to him when she could have hired an experienced investigator. She probably was assuming he would fail and then she and Harvester would get a huge laugh over it, with

Harvester spreading the news around the office. McLaren sat up. Sure. And the beer bottles were just a little touch to remind him of his tangle with Harvester during the pub burglary, to rub it in and hint that he wasn't clear of him yet.

McLaren swore softly and grabbed the ignition key. But was Harvester involved in this? McLaren couldn't see how he would be, if he were busy with the runner murder in D Division. No. Harvester was just a personal sideline with Linnet. She needed someone else to help her. Probably someone used to being a thug and in constant need of money. And who better to fit both criteria than her ex-con friend Sean FitzSimmons. Or ruffian Danny Mercer.

McLaren turned in his car seat, considering his next move. He had spoken to everyone associated with the case and gleaned all that he could get, he was sure. So how could he catch the killer? And quickly, too, if the suspect was nervous and considered doing a bunk.

An empty plastic bag tumbled down the road, pushed by the wind. McLaren stared at it, as if he had never seen trash blown about. A smile crept across his lips and he turned the key in the car's ignition switch. He was back at the stone barn in fifteen minutes.

He had whispered prayers during the drive to Elton, hoping against all common sense that the sheet of paper he had seen last week was still there.

He braked his car opposite the barn, and ran to the tufts of tall weeds defining the edge of the road. The trash still lay imprisoned among the thick stems. He pushed a few stems aside. Thankfully, the grass and weed stalks held it firmly.

He withdrew it by its corner and angled it in the

light. An edge had cracked off and the printing had faded somewhat but the logo and membership name were still plain enough. He placed the paper on top of his wallet, wanting to protect it against further breakage, and walked back to his car, where he looked more closely at it.

It was a membership to the racing club near Chesterfield. The autograss association logo took up the header on the paper; Danny's name and racing number were printed on the Club's member information line.

McLaren typed the name of the club into his smartphone and then punched in the phone number. He whistled a snatch of "The Poor Murdered Woman" under his breath, suddenly feeling overwhelmed by the injustice of Marta's death, Verity's sentence, and the killer's year of freedom. He broke off when a voice on the other end of the line asked how she could help.

McLaren went through his usual introduction, though merely stated he was investigating an incident. "I wonder if you can tell me of any events Danny Mercer may have attended in June last year."

The woman said she'd be pleased to help in whatever manner she could. Yes, Danny Mercer had participated in a number of races, particularly in June. In fact, he had raced every weekend. She gave the dates and asked if she could be of further assistance.

McLaren said that was all he wanted, thanked her, and rang off.

Two race dates danced off the page: they flanked the date of Marta's trip to the casino. He exhaled deeply and muttered, "Idiot."

He was already heading back to Bakewell as he closed his phone.

The Mercer house was a small dwelling on an equally small street. The houses echoed each other in color and structure, showing no imagination. Perhaps they echoed their owners' lives, McLaren thought as he parked and got out of his car. Or testified to the financial struggle of those dwelling within.

Danny's wife responded to the ringing doorbell by yanking the door open. She looked to be ten years younger than Danny, just past her teenaged years, but already there were circles beneath her eyes and a slight twitch to her left eye. Was it a result of life with Danny, or nerves due to her job? She eyed McLaren, perhaps wondering why he was there so early on a Tuesday morning, and shifted the mug of coffee to her left hand. It was gray, the same color as the bakery uniform she wore. She kept her free hand on the edge of the door, as though barring McLaren's entry into her home or guarding some secret. Her reaction on hearing McLaren's introduction and the reason for his visit was to take a sip of coffee and frown.

"You say Linnet just found Dan's racin' membership card?"

"Linnet Isherwood. She and he have a mutual friend, Herb Millington." He paused, waiting for the wife to recall the names.

"Why's she not handin' it over to Dan instead of you, if you said she has it?"

McLaren smiled, looking sheepish, and scratched the side of his head. "It would be better, but she broke her leg last evening and with the cast on, well, she can't get around too well, so I'm acting as delivery boy."

"She could've posted it, save you a trip."

"True, yes. And she was going to do that this

morning, but she fell last night." McLaren shrugged, holding out his hands as if to say he merely followed orders. "This way, Linnet will know Danny has it. It'll ease her mind."

The woman nodded, indicating it seemed to make sense. "This Linnet. It could be Lin. He's talked about a Lin at times. I'm not clear on her last name. I thought it was Esterwad, but I wouldn't swear to it. But Lin, now…"

"So your husband does know Lin, then."

"He knows a Lin. I suppose it could be the same woman you're talkin' about. But if it isn't, I'm not certain you're at the right place, Mr…What's your name again?"

"Ellison." He grabbed his former fiancée's surname and spoke in an even voice. "Mike Ellison. They're more acquaintances rather than friends. They know each other from the racing club. They belong to the same one."

"I can't recollect her, but maybe we met at one of the meets." She kept her voice low, holding the conversation between them. "Does she race?"

"Yes, though she takes it as more of a hobby than your husband does."

"That's probably true." The woman glanced behind her, as though she could see the back of the house. "There's not many things my Dan throws hisself into, but racin' is one of 'em." She returned her gaze to McLaren and held out her hand. "I can take the paper and see that Dan gets it."

"Sure, but I'd like to talk to him as long as I'm here. It's about an upcoming event at the club. Is he home? May I speak to him?"

"He left about a half hour ago. He went to work. He'll be back in time for tea, if you want to come back then. Or I can tell him to phone you." She eyed him, not knowing what a talk between her husband and this man involved. "You want to leave the membership with me, then?"

"I may as well keep it until I see him tonight, if that's all right."

The woman glared at McLaren, seemingly miffed that he evidently didn't trust her. "Suit yourself. Just tryin' to save you a trip back."

"I appreciate that, but I live in Matlock." He chose the town due to its nearness to Bakewell and the Mercers' house, implying it wasn't putting him out to return. Also, a large town like Matlock could harbor thousands of people that Danny Mercer wouldn't know. Far better anonymity than a village. McLaren flashed a smile, as though the eight-mile drive was a stroll in the park. "I'll get back a bit before tea, then, so as not to miss him. What kind of car does he drive?" He glanced at the driveway. It was empty. "Just so I'll know he's home when I come back. I don't want to disturb you if he isn't in."

"His car don't work. Hasn't worked proper for ages. I tell him he needs to get a real car, but he won't listen." She scowled, as if to say "Men!"

McLaren commiserated with her situation.

"I hate takin' the bus." She set down her cup on the hall table and picked up her handbag. "At least he got the statue here before his car broke down."

"Statue?"

"A nice thing for my garden. We would've had to wait another week for it to be delivered if Danny couldn't pick it up then to have it all set up in time for my birthday." She smiled tentatively, as if recalling the gift. "But he got it loaded, brought it home, and worked like a Trojan to get it in place. But he's like that, my Dan is. Always helpin' whenever me or the neighbors need him. He fixed Mrs. Carthy's step walk for her, and he picked up old Murphy's groceries. And he got me my statue." She stepped outside and closed the door. "I never did get such a nice birthday gift as that statue last year."

"I'm glad your wish was filled, then."

"Oh, I never asked for it. Danny just said he thought it'd look nice in the garden and did I want one? I said yes, never dreamin' he'd buy one so quick. But now that it's there, I've grown to love it."

McLaren thanked Mrs. Mercer for talking to him and walked back to his car. He sat there, pretending he was talking on his mobile phone, but he kept an eye on the house. When Mrs. Mercer left several minutes later, McLaren remained in his car in case she returned for a forgotten item, or Danny came home. It wouldn't be the first time a husband had drawn the wool over a wife's eyes.

He leaned back against the headrest, the conversations with Alan and Chad Hughes and Mrs. Mercer echoing through his mind. Danny's wife had just painted Danny as a shining citizen. Was that the true Danny, or was the Hughes' version more fitting? Did breeding tell, or did environment mold you? Danny's grandfather held a distinguished World War II record; Danny had been reared around the relics of that record. Had the stories he'd heard steered his life's path, or had his hooligan mate negated all that?

And why this need to buy a statue, especially when his car wasn't working?

When a quarter of an hour passed without any further house activity, McLaren walked into the back garden. The sculpture rested in a small, grassy clearing surrounded by clumps of Siberian iris, hostas and rhododendrons. It seemed a perfect place for it, shady and quiet, reminiscent of fairy haunts he had imagined as a child. The statue, in fact, was a two-foot tall metal fairy. Her open wings could have lifted her in flight at any moment, but she balanced on top of an elaborate metal pedestal, one leg bent and the toes of the other leg firmly soldered to the pedestal.

He grabbed the base, picked it up and laid the ornament on its side. The ground beneath the base was bare. No yellowed, dying grass had been smothered. Meaning, McLaren thought, the ground had been disturbed for some reason. Odd for something that had required no scraping away of the lawn, no concrete platform, or inner support rod.

McLaren scanned the yard. A three-pronged cultivator sat on a garden chair near the back door. He grabbed it and quickly clawed at the soil. The digging was easy, unlike the hard packed soil that greeted him whenever he planted something in his garden. It took only seconds to scrape away the earth and reach the object buried inches below. He leaned closer and laid the cultivator beside him, using his fingers for the final few seconds' work. He maneuvered his fingers beneath the object, the cardboard giving slightly against his grasp. As he pushed the box up, he brushed the remaining soil from its top, finally lifting it and holding it in his hand.

He grinned as he set it beside the garden tool and gingerly removed the lid of the shoebox. Inside were a carton of .38 caliber bullets, a Webley Mk IV .38 caliber revolver, and a woman's silvery shoe missing its heel.

Chapter Twenty-Five

The Webley Mk IV was a relic of World War II, McLaren thought, staring at the revolver and the box of ammunition. Were these items part of the glory-day relics of Danny's grandfather? Was it the service revolver he had used in the war and retained on returning home? Many soldiers kept their side arms when the war ended, either their British pistols or German Lugers, souvenirs of their years overseas. This had to be the grandfather's revolver. And it was a .38 caliber, the same size as the bullet that had killed Marta Hughes.

It might not be evidence, but the shoe fit that definition. Especially if Danny's fingerprints were on it.

He pushed the soil back into the hole, tapped it down with his foot, then righted the sculpture and returned the garden tool. He replaced the lid on the shoebox and picked it up. Danny had hidden the revolver after using it to kill Marta, McLaren realized as he got into his car. Or Linnet had used it. Either way, the shoe and revolver linked Danny to Marta's murder just as Linnet's car and expensive clothes linked her to the stolen casino money. He set the box on his backseat, elated at the discovery.

But the feeling didn't last long. He still couldn't place Danny at the murder scene.

He slammed his palm into the steering wheel,

frustrated that he was so near to closing the case. Had he missed something? He leaned his head back and closed his eyes, snippets of conversation reverberating in his mind.

Danny's wife had mentioned their car. Had it been drivable last year or had it been out of commission? Had he borrowed the friend's car and, if so, what would that be?

McLaren opened his eyes and sat up. Someone—Chad perhaps—talked about Danny and Herb sharing the racecars and that Danny might have the second car at his home or stored in a garage. If so, Danny would have his own set of keys. Which meant his own transportation. But that still didn't connect Danny with the murder scene.

McLaren brought a map of the area up on his laptop. He had no idea from which direction Danny would have met up with Marta that night. Bakewell seemed obvious, since it was his home and the casino trip had lasted well into the evening. But if he and Linnet planned the murder, it seemed logical that Danny would be closer to the casino when he killed her.

But that meant he would also need a car. His or Herb's.

The idea of tracking down the car nearly overwhelmed him. But maybe it wouldn't become the proverbial needle in the haystack. He grabbed his mobile and rang up Jamie, telling him about the car, the gun and the missing shoe. "I know that heel I found at the stone barn will fit this shoe." The volume of his voice underlined his belief. "You'll see when you get it to the lab."

Jamie's words rushed over the phone. "Hold on,

Mike. Danny could say he found the shoe. After all, you found a heel. And as for the gun, he can always claim someone else fired it and planted it in his garden to incriminate him."

"If you'd let me finish—"

"Do you have proof he was at the murder scene?"

"No, but I'm coming to that."

"Shoot."

McLaren let the pun pass without comment. "Can you look up a car registration for me?"

"Probably. What do you want?"

"Any cars owned by Herb Millington or Danny Mercer."

"Shared ownership, or just any cars each of them own?"

"Any. Both. Just whatever you can find. Without getting caught." He added the last phrase unnecessarily. Jamie would be careful.

"You want it now, I assume."

"As close to now as you can make it. You can ring me on my mobile."

"What are you looking for, Mike?"

"A way to catch a killer."

"Meaning what?"

"A bit of time spent online. I'll sit right here and wait for it. Call me when you've got something."

Jamie muttered that everyone had their methods, and rang off.

Ten minutes later, McLaren answered his ringing mobile. "You got something for me, Jamie?"

"Don't I always?"

"I'll let that pass. What did you find out about Danny Mercer?"

"You don't want to hear about Herb Millington's vehicles?"

"Sorry. The case is warmly embracing Danny at the moment. Does he own a racecar?"

"He and the person you don't care to hear about jointly own one car that is registered for autograss racing. Danny owns another car strictly by himself."

"What's that?"

"A Mini."

McLaren glanced at the membership information. Danny was in Class 4, which sported a lot of Minis. And although that wasn't conclusive, it tightened the noose a bit more snugly around the man's neck. "Herb's name isn't on that car registration?"

"No. Just Danny. Why? Have you got something?"

"Yeah." He related what he had learned from his phone call to the racing club.

Jamie muttered that McLaren must have Irish blood in him. "I've never heard anyone with more gift of Blarney than you have."

"I can't help it if she got the impression I was a copper."

Jamie refrained from commenting. "So, is that it? Where are you with Danny?"

"Well, right now I need you to accompany me if you've got the time when you get off."

"Accompany you where? To the Mercers' house?"

"No. I need official police presence when we confront Linnet Isherwood."

"When *we* confront her? This is your case, Mike. You're doing very well without the lads in blue."

"But I'll need you to make the arrest. I'm a civilian, remember?"

"Just barely. Maybe I should loan you my warrant card."

"I'll take that as a joke and not as a serious suggestion. Bring your handcuffs and anything else you want. You can follow me in your squad car."

"Uhh, Mike…"

"Yes?" His breath caught in his throat, fearful that Jamie would suggest he contact the Chief Constable.

"You're not going to be doing anything illegal, are you? I mean, I'm not going to get a reprimand or something for helping you."

McLaren let out his breath. Jamie hadn't suggested that McLaren go it alone. "We'll review the case before we drive over to Linnet's. If you feel I'm totally round the twist, I'll bend to your opinion and call it off."

"Fair enough. Thanks."

"I'll be on the street when you get out. Find me." He rang off and headed to The Crispin Inn in Ashover, feeling he owed himself a celebratory lunch and a hand washing.

Early twilight was descending on the village of Castleton; the last vestiges of color clung to the western sky. The eastern side of Peveril Castle loomed dark and forbidding against the curtain of pale pink and yellow, gray shadows slowly consuming the land. Down in the dale where the village nestled, the sunlight had already vanished, yet still anointed the rooftops and treetops with an ochre-hued mantle. McLaren and Jamie parked halfway down the road from Linnet's house—a precaution in case she remembered the make, color and model of McLaren's car or happened to see the police car. They also checked the back garden, making certain no one was there who might be a potential problem.

When they were satisfied that they weren't walking stupidly into a trap, McLaren rang the front doorbell.

Through the open window he heard the bell ringing deep with the house. Music sounded and a wooden-legged chair was shoved back. The soft padding of shoes thudded on a hard floor, then the click of metal as the dead bolt moved in the doorframe. There was a squeak of protesting hinges and moments later Linnet Isherwood opened the front door.

"Mr. McLaren!" Her exclamation nearly caught in her throat on seeing him. She forced a smile but it quickly faded as her hand went to her throat. "I-I didn't expect to see you so soon. You've something to discuss about Marta's case?" Her eyes had drifted from McLaren's face to Jamie's, then to his uniform. She glanced back at McLaren. "You brought a police officer? You've solved the case, then? Are you going to make an arrest?" She smiled again but remained in the open doorway.

McLaren answered her questioning look by asking if they could come in.

"Why, certainly. Of course!" She stepped aside, opened the door wider, but remained there as they walked into the front room. "You'll have to excuse my attire. I-I wasn't expecting anyone. I was exercising." By way of confirmation, the music in the back room erupted into a loud tattoo of drums, brass and strings. She gave a half-hearted smile, as if unsure she should turn off the music or not.

"Would you care to join us?" McLaren motioned to the sofa. "This is Constable James Kydd. Derbyshire Constabulary." He added the distinction as if it were an afterthought.

Linnet nodded, closed the door slowly, and leaned against it. She was dressed in designer-label black leotards, halter-top, and soft-soled ballet-style shoes. A red and purple print scarf was tied around her waist and a matching hand towel lay across the back of her neck. She eyed the two men as they waited for her to sit down, then hesitantly moved to a chair near the front window. She sat but the men remained standing. Looking up at McLaren, she said, "A police officer? Then you *are* making an arrest in the case." Her voice cracked but she pulled a limp smile from a recess of her soul. "Th-that's wonderful news. Who is it? Can you tell me?"

Her gaze was fastened on McLaren, as though mutely inquiring if it would be proper police procedure, but she turned toward Jamie when he cautioned her. When he'd finished, she got to her feet, alternately staring at each man. In the stillness McLaren heard the last bars of her recorded exercise music, a selection of Handel. Or Haydn. Then abrupt silence filled the house as the CD ended.

Linnet's hand went to her throat again, as though she needed a physical touch to convince her she wasn't experiencing a nightmare. Her voice shook from fright but it was abnormally loud as she said, "*Me!* This is absurd. You've made a mistake. I went straight home after our casino outing. Anyway, why should I kill Marta? We were best friends."

"Exactly. And, being best friends, you expected Marta would bail you out of your financial difficulty when she won big."

"That's ridiculous. I was nowhere near Elton."

"Maybe not that night, but you were later."

"Oh, really? And when was that supposed to be?" Her voice had regained its strength and her anger underscored her words. "Why would I even go there?"

"You planted a silver charm. The type used for bracelets and necklaces."

"Amazing. The police never said anything about a charm."

"They didn't find it, and that's what first bothered me. Constables are quite good at fingertip searches. Nothing escapes their exploration. They wouldn't have overlooked this, not anything so shiny. They overlooked it because you hid it there after I took the case."

She glared at him but fright shone plainly. "Absurd."

"I found it, though. Just as you hoped. It hasn't been in the ground long. The metal's still shiny, not tarnished as it would be after a year. Look familiar?" He took the silver skier charm from his jeans pocket and held it so that Linnet could see it.

"No, it doesn't."

"It should. You've seen two of them. The first one you probably gave Sean FitzSimmons on the publication of his novel. There's the author photo on the dust jacket. He's wearing it on a chain around his neck. The dedication of his book even mentions it. And links you to it." He pointed to the silver skier. "It was probably some token between you two. I don't know and right now I don't care. You got it away from him and planted it at the crime scene to implicate him in the murder."

Linnet started to protest but McLaren cut her off. "The second charm you gave him in Buxton. I saw you hand it to him just before you parted after lunch." His fingers closed over the charm and he returned it to his pocket.

"What a fertile imagination you have. This doesn't prove a thing. You could have bought that charm at any jewelry store."

"I could have done, but I didn't. I got it from Sean. But if you're so sure I'm lying, ask him." He pulled out his mobile phone and held it out for her. "What's the matter? Don't you want to know if I'm lying or not?"

Linnet made no move for the offered phone, instead chewing her bottom lip. Her face had drained of color but she didn't reclaim her chair. A car backfired in the street and seemed to prod her into replying. "I-I believe he's out of town."

"Phone reaches around the world."

"No." She shook her head but her eyes held the desperation of a caged animal. "I-I don't want to disturb him."

McLaren continued, shoving the phone into his pocket. "I thought originally that Sean had killed Marta. He was a good choice, wasn't he?"

"What do you mean? Sean and I are—"

"Friends? Lovers? No. Not really. Maybe that's what *he* believes, but he's nothing to you. Not in that sense. He's a tool, isn't he? You tricked him into believing you cared for him but you used him. He's a great decoy, Miss Isherwood. I congratulate you on finding him."

Linnet shifted her weight onto her other foot and tried to look nonchalant, but the fear still shone in her eyes. "Decoy?"

"Certainly! You thought I'd zero in on him, didn't

you? Sean FitzSimmons, ex-con and perfect murder suspect. The police would find out about him and look no further. He had many skills that you needed. One was his record as a burglar and car thief. You asked him to break into my car subtly so I would begin to doubt my reason. You told him to steal anything he could find. I applaud his skill. He accomplished it in broad daylight without leaving a trace on my car. But he was probably surprised to end up with that bag of beer bottles. Did he show them to you?"

Linnet remained silent, her arms crossed on her chest.

"And to ice the cake, in case the coppers were a bit slow in suspecting him, you planted the charm near the spot where they found the body. Was it supposed to have been lost when Marta fought Sean for her life?" His last words exploded in his anger and he stepped toward Linnet.

"You're insane. You have no proof for any of this. Now, if you're quite finished, I wish you'd leave. I have other things to do than listen to fiction. I would sue you for slander if it weren't so laughable."

"Fiction is another element of it, isn't it? Sean is a fiction writer, an author of thrillers. He's good at thinking up plots. Did you get him to plan where, when, and how to kill Marta? Or had you thought of it by the time you'd met him? I'm sure you didn't talk this over with your friend Charlie Harvester."

Her eyes widened and she opened her mouth, but McLaren went on.

"I know about you two. I heard it from a very reliable source, how matey you once were. Might still be, for all I know. After all, you've still got his ring."

She'd had enough time to think and pounced on McLaren's statement. "What ring? Am I wearing any ring?" She held out her hands so the men could see her fingers. They were bare. "You're obsessed, McLaren. Was your mother frightened by a jeweler?"

"*This* ring." He strode toward her; his hand shot out and he grabbed the necklace she wore. He yanked on the chain, pulling the bottom length of it from beneath her halter-top. A diamond ring slid down the length of the twisted silver. He threw the chain at her and her hand clamped over the ring. "You must still love him, though I don't know why, after he broke off your engagement."

Jamie's hand wrapped around McLaren's upper arm, pulling him slightly away from Linnet.

"You may have killed Marta for her money."

"Ridic—"

"But you hired me for revenge."

"Revenge? For who? When?"

"Revenge for Harvester. You still love him. You found out, probably from him, about the pub incident. You thought I needed to pay for Harvester's ultimate disgrace and reprimand. So you hired me, no doubt thinking I'd fall on my face with this case and make a fool of myself. The beer bottles were a nice touch. Did Sean give me my 'lesson'?" His hand went to a bruise on his cheek. "It took me a while to realize where I'd seen him. I thought it was from my days in the job, but it was the night of my beating. I just had a glimpse of him by the lamplight from my kitchen table, but I couldn't place his face for a while."

A smile gradually claimed Linnet's face. She leaned against the fireplace mantel, her fingers toying with the ring that hung from the necklace. "At least he did *something* right. I'd written your home address down for him so he'd know where to find you. I dashed it off in a hurry, never thinking I should have typed it, that you might compare it to the check I wrote to retain your services. He told me how he ambushed you." She gave a short laugh and shook her head. "We thought you'd mess it up." Her voice grew bitter. "We thought all the fight had gone out of you and that the case had grown too cold for you to discover anything. We..." She took a deep breath before correcting herself. "I thought you'd latch on to Sean as the killer and I'd get my revenge when Charlie proved Sean's innocence in court. I didn't really want you to solve Marta's murder. You were smarter than we thought."

"Too bad you weren't a tad bit smarter."

She stepped toward him, her hand raised, but Jamie caught her wrist and forced her arm down. Shrugging, she relaxed. "You think you know it all, don't you, McLaren? But you don't. You haven't any idea what happened to Karin Pedersen or about those reappearing beer bottles. Did they upset you?"

"Your doing, I suppose."

"Of course. I knew where you were going after you left me in Castleton when we talked. I had an idea the route you'd take and let Karin know. She's a friend."

"Mobile phones are a wonder, aren't they?" He snorted.

"We weren't one hundred percent certain you'd drive that way, mind you, but it was no big deal if you didn't. Karin faked her wound and sat by the roadside. I gave her your car description. It was simple. All she had to do was wait and wave away other offers of help, if there'd been any. And, as I said, if you didn't show up, well, no harm done. It was just a bit of fun designed to annoy you."

"And the beer bottles?"

"That was Sean. We wanted to remind you of that little pub episode with Tyrone Wade Antony and your dismissal from the Force. And Charlie Harvester. Did it work?" She smiled, lowering her eyes like a 1920s vamp.

"But Harvester didn't have anything to do with the murder, did he?" McLaren said as Linnet shook off Jamie's hand. "Or with framing Sean."

"No." She said it almost as a shout of victory. "We just talked about 'wouldn't it be wonderful if one day Michael McLaren fell flat on his face?' but Charlie had nothing to do with any of this. I was the only one involved."

"Hardly you alone, Linnet. You had to have help. As you pointed out to me, you were home. But Danny Mercer wasn't." The faintest smile played at the corners of his lips as the shock registered on her face.

A faint noise, like a door latch catching in place, came from the back of the house. Linnet pushed herself away from the mantel and said rather loudly, "Danny Mercer? Whatever made you think that Danny is mixed up in Marta's death, Mr. McLaren? Is that why you brought this police constable with you?"

Another sound, louder and sharper, cracked the brief silence. The bang of a door slamming and the rattle of Venetian blinds hitting a window jabbed McLaren into action. As Jamie handcuffed Linnet, McLaren ran into the kitchen.

Chapter Twenty-Six

The blinds were swinging as McLaren yanked open the door. He paused momentarily on the threshold, looking for Danny, wary of an attack or weapon. The sound of running feet came from the direction of the road. McLaren dashed down the alley and to the front of the house.

Danny ran down the center of the road, dodging oncoming cars and glancing back, his figure bright in the headlights. He paused at a new Skia and tried to insert his key but he probably couldn't control his shaking hand. McLaren charged up to him, Danny abandoned his car and sprinted down a side road.

The daylight was rapidly failing, the parked vehicles, rubbish bins, and clipped shrubs dark shapes against a murky backdrop. McLaren paused at the mouth of the side road, trying to distinguish forms in the gloom. A movement to the left centered his attention for an instant, but it was a dog sniffing at the refuse bins. McLaren jogged slowly down the street, landing lightly on the balls of his feet, making no noise other than his ragged breathing. He kept a zigzag course, crossing and recrossing the road to peer behind bushes and cars, any place Danny might be hiding.

He turned sharply toward the sound of scraping metal, his body tensing, his heart rate increasing. A man was dumping rubbish into his refuse bin.

At the house next door, an older woman opened her front door and the light from her front room spilled onto the front pavement. McLaren dashed to the cypress standing like a sentinel at her front gate and glanced behind it. No Danny.

He had jogged to the end of the road and was about to retrace his steps when a shape emerged from the front garden ahead. He stopped abruptly, startled by the sudden movement and the realization that the massive form was two people walking close together, holding hands. As the couple moved into the faint light from the house, the young woman smiled tentatively at McLaren. The man, however, mumbled something into her ear and nuzzled her neck with his forehead. His left hand, McLaren noticed, was around the girl's shoulders. His right hand was in his jeans pocket. The girl shifted her eyes from the man to McLaren, then repeated the gesture as her lips silently formed the word 'help.' McLaren nodded and walked past them.

The older woman eyed the couple as she finished setting out her rubbish, then called her dog and went inside. As the front door closed with a dull thud, the road sank back into darkness.

McLaren turned and charged after the couple, covering the scant distance in seconds and shouting for the woman to run into the road. McLaren grabbed Danny's left arm; he angled it behind Danny, using it as leverage to simultaneously release the woman and force Danny to the ground. She scooted behind a parked car and crouched, her fingers gripping the back bumper, her head peeking above the boot as she watched the fight.

It was brief. Danny swung at McLaren with his right fist but missed. His foot lashed out at McLaren's legs and he succeeded in landing one blow with his heel before McLaren brought him to the ground. He kept his hand on Danny's arm and placed his foot on Danny's back, pressing him against the pavement as he regained his breath.

"Are you all right, miss?" He looked at the woman from his bent over position.

She got to her feet, sliding her hands to the car's boot in an effort to support herself. "Yes, thanks." Her voice quivered slightly. "I was walking up to my car and he jumped out of the shadows and grabbed me. He made me walk with him, pretend I knew him. Who is he? Do you know him?"

"He's a man who made a wrong decision, unfortunately. Get up." He grabbed Danny's shoulder and helped him to his feet. McLaren eyed the woman, uncertain if she'd escaped injury. "You're sure you're all right? He didn't hurt you?"

"No, I'm fine. Just a bit scared." She dusted her hands on her jeans. "I expect I'll laugh about this tomorrow. Or at least be the envy of my friends. You know," she said when McLaren smiled, "helping catch a burglar. Or whatever he's done." She tilted her head, trying to make out Danny's features in the darkness. "He do something like that? Are you the police?"

"I'm taking him to the police now." McLaren tightened his grip on Danny's arm. "And yes, he did something like that."

"Oh."

"I'm afraid, miss, I'll have to send a police officer to your house to ask you a few questions, since it is a police matter." His voice trailed off as he studied her face, assessing if she were emotionally stable for the interview.

"Yes, certainly. You'll need some kind of witness statement, I expect." She pointed to the last house in the row. "I live just there. Will it be tonight?"

"An officer will contact you to let you know. He'll tell you he's calling on behalf of Michael McLaren. That's me. Michael McLaren."

"I'd like to help, if I can." She glanced again at Danny, perhaps memorizing his features and clothing. "Whenever the officer comes is fine. Thank you for helping me."

"Enjoy your fifteen minutes of fame tomorrow." He left her on the pavement. It wasn't until he had turned the corner that he could no longer make out her figure in the darkness.

The rest of the story came out as McLaren walked Danny back to Linnet's house. Though sullen and angry at first, Danny finally admitted that he and Linnet had split the casino winnings when he killed Marta. He used some of the money to buy his racing car, some he still had, and some he used to buy drugs. Marta had got into his car that fateful night because he said he wanted her advice about a problem he had.

"She hesitated at first, but she was like that, trying to help people, so she never suspected a trap." Marta had broken the heel off her shoe as she tried to run from Danny at the barn. "I never could find it," he confessed after explaining that he'd kept the shoe as evidence in case he needed to blackmail Linnet at some future date. He hadn't missed the racing club membership until weeks later. By then he was too nervous to go back to the barn to look for it. "I had it on the front seat, where I left it after my previous race. I guess it fell out when I pulled her from the car."

McLaren's stomach tightened as he imagined the small, thin woman trying to run through the wood, but he said nothing. He was neither judge nor jury. Nor God, he thought, wondering briefly what would become of Danny. The man had begun his narrative by answering McLaren's questions in short, thunderous snaps, but by the end the replies had subsided into muffled whimpers.

Jamie cautioned Danny and handcuffed him as a second police car drove up. He nodded to the officer, opened the back door, and settled Danny in the rear seat.

Linnet, in Jamie's car, sat sullen and silent, and stared straight ahead. The village had grown quiet. A ribbon of ash gray clouds seemed pinned just above the horizon in the west. There were no moon or stars in the blackness that stretched above their heads. No fox barked, no owl called, no breath of wind stirred the tree branches. It was as if they were the only souls awake in the bleak landscape.

McLaren tilted back his head, taking a deep breath of cool air, looking into the vastness of the somber sky. He felt small, as he always did when standing in the throat of the Winnats. Or when walking through Dove Dale. The enormity of nature welled up around him, threatened to engulf him in its wildness and beauty. The thud of the car door slamming closed pulled him from his reverie and Jamie walked up to him.

"Hey, Mike, the Super will want you to write up a few things." Jamie closed his fist around his car key, searching for something prophetic to say. He cleared his voice and went on. "Uh, can you fit it in between your stone wall work?"

"I'll have to, won't I?" McLaren gave Jamie a half smile, suddenly very tired. "Never ends, does it? I thought I left report writing behind a year ago."

"You're either optimistic or a fool. And I don't think it's the latter." He slapped McLaren on the back. "Nice work, Mike. The Super will be in touch soon."

"Sounds like a threat. Thanks for the hand, Jamie." He waved as Jamie walked back to his car.

On the drive home, McLaren thought about the case. He would get nothing more than the retainer Linnet had already given him, but he was strangely unaffected by the loss of the rest of his fee. Perhaps he did live to see injustices righted after all. Was it a remnant of his police training, the job and what it stood for, or was it a quality deep within him?

He wondered briefly how Danny had known when to kidnap Marta, when she would arrive home. Linnet had no way of knowing Marta would win at the casino that night. Perhaps it was as simple as Linnet ringing Danny, using her mobile phone from her car in the casino car park, to tell him this was The Night. McLaren squinted at an approaching car's headlights as he imagined the short one-sentence message. Perhaps Linnet had said something months before. "I'll let you know when we go to the casino, so you be ready any time. She's bound to win big one of these nights." Danny would drive to Marta's house when he got the word and wait for her in the shadows.

McLaren exhaled loudly as his fingers curled around the steering wheel in anger. Of course he didn't have to prove that. The police could search mobile phone records in preparation for the trial. It was enough right now that he had placed Danny at the murder scene and given Jamie the probable murder weapon and the missing shoe. Danny's fingerprints would be on both. McLaren smiled, for the first time in months feeling happy about the future.

He turned the car around in the lonely stretch of The Winnats, the windswept mountain pass of the Pennines. Without thinking he headed back the way he had come, driving through Castleton and heading south toward Kirkfield. He had several miles of dark highway to cover and he settled back in the car seat, the B6061 rolling beneath the wheels and his mind rolling through the week's events. His fingers loosened their grip on the steering wheel and he turned on the stereo. The cassette tape recording started up, the strains of the guitars and viola as familiar as Dena's face, which hovered before his eyes. As his folk group's rendition of "Near Woodstock Town" began in earnest he realized it was Wednesday. Unless things had drastically changed in the past year, Dena would be at her sister's house in Hathersage. He turned the car again and headed for Hathersage as he cranked up the tape's volume and sang along.

Several songs and several miles later he entered the village. It was little more than a splash of light in the surrounding dark countryside, its restaurants and pubs open for the night crowd. McLaren passed the Hanoverian Hotel before turning onto the road housing the local police station.

It was long past regular office work hours and the road was deserted. A few streetlamps shed orange-tinted light on the landscape but outside these pools the street was dark. The familiar blue police lantern shone above the police station door. McLaren parked his car opposite it and got out. He took his time assessing the area, wanting no wayward pub-crawler or village resident to spot him. So he sauntered to the police station, pretending to window shop in the closed establishments nearby. He stopped short of the entrance to the station and picked up a beer bottle lying at the curb. The brown glass caught the light from the police lamp and seemed to wink at McLaren. The irony wasn't lost on him, and his pent-up rage and hurt broke from him in an unstoppable rush. He felt the weight of the bottle, its curve sitting snugly in his hand rather like a rock for mending stone walls. Taking a deep breath, he threw the bottle at the lamp. A satisfying shattering of glass rewarded his effort and he ran back to his car.

He slumped against the car seat, imaginary newspaper headlines flashing through his mind. 'Ex-Cop Caps Cold Case.' 'Ex-Cop Comes Thru When Chips Are Down.' 'Killer's Second Mistake: Hiring Ex-Cop.' He smiled at the reaction the story would undoubtedly cause, both in the media and throughout the Force. He'd again be the topic of conversation around police station water coolers and break rooms, but this time he wouldn't mind. The talk would be about good police work, not the titillating gossip of a ruined career.

Opening his mobile phone he punched in Dena's number. He gazed at the police lamp, at the blue glass broken on two sides where the beer bottle had caught it. The light bulb, he noticed, was shattered. The street lay dark and unpopulated. Police...beer bottles. His thought broke off as Dena's voice came to him over the phone. He grinned as he imagined her face. "Dena, sweets. I'd like for us to try again. I'm learning to release my emotions."

*COLD REVENGE* has a companion song. "Cold, Haily, Rainy Night" is available on a single-song CD recording. This bluesy folk song is arranged and performed by The Thin Dimes, and is available through the author's website:

http://www.johiestand.com/coldrevenge.html

### A word about the author...

Books, scouting, and music filled Jo A. Hiestand's childhood. She explored the joys of the outdoors through Girl Scout camping trips and summers as a canoeing instructor and camp counselor. Brought up on classical, big band, and baroque music, she was groomed as a concert pianist until forsaking the piano for the harpsichord. She plays a Martin guitar and has sung in a semi-professional folkgroup in the US and as a soloist in England.

This mixture formed the foundation for her writing. A true Anglophile, Jo wanted to create a mystery series that featured a British police detective who left the Force over an injustice and now investigates cold cases on his own. The result is the McLaren Mysteries.

Jo's insistence on accuracy—from police methods to location layouts—has driven her innumerable times to Derbyshire. These explorations and conferences with police friends provide the detail filling the books.

In 1999 Jo returned to Webster University to major in English. She graduated in 2001 with a BA degree and departmental honors.

She has combined her love of writing, board games, and music by co-inventing a mystery-solving game, P.I.R.A.T.E.S., which uses maps, graphics, song lyrics, and other clues to lead players to lost treasure.

Jo founded the Greater St. Louis Chapter of Sisters in Crime, serving as its first president. She is also a member of Mystery Writers of America. Besides her love of mysteries and music, she enjoys photography, reading, change ringing, and her backyard wildlife.

Her cat Tennyson shares her St. Louis home.
http://www.johiestand.com

Thank you for purchasing
this publication of The Wild Rose Press, Inc.

If you enjoyed the story, we would appreciate your
letting others know by leaving a review.

For other wonderful stories,
please visit our on-line bookstore at
www.thewildrosepress.com.

For questions or more information
contact us at
info@thewildrosepress.com.

The Wild Rose Press, Inc.
www.thewildrosepress.com

Stay current with The Wild Rose Press, Inc.

Like us on Facebook

https://www.facebook.com/TheWildRosePress

And Follow us on Twitter
https://twitter.com/WildRosePress

www.ingramcontent.com/pod-product-compliance
Lightning Source LLC
Chambersburg PA
CBHW071515260626
47170CB00002B/374